THE PAST NOT TAKEN

THREE NOVELLAS

Also from John D. Beatty

Crop Duster: A Novel of World War II
Sergeant's Business and Other Stories

The Stella's Game Trilogy

Stella's Game: A Story of Friendship
Tideline: Friendship Abides
The Safe Tree: Friendship Triumphs

The Liberty Bell Files: J Edgar's Demons

THE PAST NOT TAKEN

THREE NOVELLAS

JOHN D. BEATTY

• J D B • C O M M U N I C A T I O N S , • L L C •

JDB COMMUNICATIONS, LLC

WEST ALLIS, WISCONSIN

For Shannon Elizabeth,
*.who **might** have been...*

THE PAST NOT TAKEN

The Road Not Taken

A poem by Robert Frost, 1915

Two roads diverged in a yellow wood,
And sorry I could not travel both
And be one traveler, long I stood
And looked down one as far as I could
To where it bent in the undergrowth;

Then took the other, as just as fair,
And having perhaps the better claim,
Because it was grassy and wanted wear;
Though as for that the passing there
Had worn them really about the same,

And both that morning equally lay
In leaves, no step had trodden black.
Oh, I kept the first for another day!
Yet knowing how way leads on to way,
I doubted if I should ever come back.

I shall be telling this with a sigh
Somewhere ages and ages hence:
Two roads diverged in a wood, and I—
I took the one less traveled by,
And that has made all the difference.

If I <u>Had</u> Done Saturday What I Had to Do Sunday...

There are certain days, like some ad jingles and the downwind reek of an outhouse, that we remember distinctly, even late in life. On *those* days, we chose *this* road, *not* the other.[1]

Two roads diverged in a yellow wood...

The path of our lives is determined as much by *quick* decisions as by those we ponder for years.

University of Southern New Mexico, I thought that sunny Sunday morning in June while I was grading freshman/sophomore exams in my TA[2] office. *Small town, small school, small adjunct[3] position with a small, married former professor who had the hots for me when she was here. It's a sure thing. All I'd have to do is say...*

I looked down *this* road and decided *that road's a dead-end that leads to a woman I'd rather NOT lead into. Can this beggar be that choosy?* I glanced again at my response...*I accept your generous offer...*already in the envelope. *I would have sent it yesterday, but...*

Then I heard laughing and yelling outside. I looked, but I could *barely* see a boisterous gathering on the Wilson-Schuman Athletic

---

1 I'm an academic. I use footnotes. Get *used* to it.

2 Teaching Assistant. Also book-grunt, grad-hack, and scut puppy.

3 A salaried, limited contract job, and barely that, with no tenure possible and few privileges.

Fields.[1] But I *could hear* a *mass exaltation* of a *glorious* spring day after yesterday's *miserably* cold rain and wind.

And I decided *to HELL with these unoriginal scribblings! I'm going to join that Frisbee game.*

Then took the other, as just as fair...

I had no sooner reached the game than I saw Melanie Hubbard watching from the bleachers. "Hey, Meli! How've *you* been?"

"*Curtis! HI,*" she called back, sounding *relieved.* "Am I addressing *Dr.* Curtis Durand yet," she asked.

"*Wednesday,* I defend for the last time." I watched with her for a moment, pondering which of two questions to pose: *want to play,* or... "mind if I *join* you?"

"Let's *walk.*" She headed around the exuberant game and offered her hand. I took hers *lightly;* she *gripped* mine.[2] "What brought you up to State during Spring Break?" We had seen each other from across the street as I got out of the car their History Department had sent.

"Job interview." My handlers had admonished that we were running late, so there was no time for any more than a wave and a quick "hi!"

"Ah." We walked on. "Dad's still your advisor?"

"He *is.* You're *done* at State?" Starting in my freshman year, Meli played the role of my *companion*[3] for the school's mandatory social affairs, despite our *grade* difference.[4] And we often hung out when she came home. But before this past December, *that* was about *it.*

"*Yeah,*" she sighed, squeezing my hand. "I am now *armed* with a master's degree in public administration."

"You don't *sound* happy." Despite her hand, I walked with my head level—practicing my *scholarly façade*—my face like a Stoic statue.

"*Should* I be?" She strolled slowly, swinging our hands.

Odd answer. "You always *seemed* cheery." She was the youngest daughter of the eminent Doctor Albert Hubbard, Jenson Foundation Professor of American History at Crest University, *the* leading authority on early American politics. Dr. Hubbard was also the curator of the Jenson Collection of early American documents. "And it *is* what you wanted."

---

1 Named for its biggest donors/sponsors, a common university practice for both inanimate objects and academic positions.

2 We weren't *strangers,* but *this* was new.

3 This *apparently* awkward social pairing was because *I* was *special;* of which, more later.

4 I was born in May; she in late September the same year, and so was a *grade* behind me ...a different *kind* of May-September relationship.

"True, but my *cheeriness* was just a clever disguise, my friend."

"Why?"

She didn't answer but pulled me closer as we stopped to watch. More ebullient players had joined the fun, running around in shorts and briefs and bell-bottoms and swimsuits; in sandals, running shoes and bare feet; in t-shirts, bikini, tube, and tank tops; with *and* without undergarments; laughing and running, throwing and catching in the *glittering* sunshine and gentle breeze.

"*They're* having fun."

"Yeah," her voice distant.

She glanced down, then *up*, then *around* as she walked, not looking *at* anything. It *felt* like she had made some big decision. "How've *you* been?"

"Surviving." At Christmastime, I unloaded on her about Sherry, my girlfriend of over a year. Sherry had *finally* realized that I would fulfill *my* obligations to the Jenson Endowment and *not* follow her to law school in January as she *expected*. Our breakup was *ugly*; Meli kept me from drowning in self-pity. Several *non*-committal *non*-dates followed. Anything *more*, we believed, would have been awkward for Dr. Hubbard and the Endowment. *Appearances*, you know. Crest University is a *very* conservative institution, you understand.

That, and *she* had a boyfriend at State.

"You remember Adrian Cooley?" Her voice was hollow. Our pace slowed.

"Yeah." Professor Cooley, formerly of Julliard, was in the Music Department when I started at Crest. In the middle of the fall semester in my junior year, she left with no explanations offered or given.

"Know *why* she left?"

"No."

"She was unmarried, pregnant, and wanted to *keep* her baby. The Regents invoked a *morals* clause in her contract." Crest was a private school with its own governing body—the *Committee of Regents*, who co-owned Crest University—that functioned as the state board with a similar name and was known to be straight-laced.[1] "Did you ever *know* Nathan Izzard?"

"Not personally." Professor Izzard, formerly of MIT, had led the Math Department. In the middle of my senior spring semester, he left the school for unstated reasons.

"His *daughter* got pregnant, wanted to *keep* the baby."

---

1 Because we took no state *or* federal money, they could dictate the terms of everyone's employment.

"So..."

"Annie was seventeen; there was *no boy* in sight. The Regents pitched *Nathan* out like they did Adrian." We walked along in silence for a few more paces. "How long have we known each other, Curtis?"

"Since the fall of '73, so going on *nine* years," I answered; she squeezed my hand. *She IS pretty...*

"Do you *like* me?" *Easy to get along with...what's with...?*

"I *do*; a *lot*." *She's funny, and a good listen...WHAT?* I stopped; she took a step ahead, *not* letting me go. "Are you *in trouble,* Meli?"[1]

"*Yep*." She *didn't* turn. Her voice was but a whisper above the game, but I *heard* it as if it were thunder overhead.

"Does your *family* know?" She had a brother and two sisters, all of whom I'd met. Her sisters were married; her brother was in high school.

"*Not* yet. I *just* got home last night, trying to figure out *how* to tell them." We meandered a little further, turned to watch the game again. There were *two* Frisbees and at *least* fifty people—students *and* faculty—chasing around the field.

"The *father...?*"

"Steve said 'so long' when I told *him* last week." She sighed, glancing at me quickly, with a look that said *you guys are all alike*. "I'm going to *keep my* baby...."

"Want *help?*" *WHAT did I say...?*

"I *need* help, Curtis," she said quietly. "The consequences for *Dad* would be...."

"Yeah. If *this* place were any more straight-laced, we'd need diagrams to tie our shoes. You've *thought* about this...."

"The *baby*; sure. This *conversation*; a *lot*."

"How did *it* go?"

"Me: 'I *need* a guy to *say* he's the father and *wants* to be with me.' He: '*I'll* be *proud* to, Missy.'" She sighed, glanced at me again. "One version of *that* or another. It's *always* better than what *Steve* said. But, *sometimes*, in my *head*," she shook her head, "sometimes *he* says 'are you *nuts?*'" She waited a moment before she whispered, "I was hoping *you wouldn't* say that *now*."

Am I nuts for taking this seriously? "Nope, I can't see *me* saying that." *HAVE I LOST MY MIND?*

"*That* was an odd thing to say."

---

1 When dial phones still worked and dinosaurs roamed the Earth, young women *in trouble* were unmarried and pregnant.

TELL me about it. "This is an odd conversation, Meli."

"I'll *give* you that."

"But your family would *know* I wasn't...." *Maybe I've lost my heart; perhaps NOT my mind.*

"They'll *know* what I *tell* them. I'll *tell* them we *got together* at State during Spring Break."

I'd spent *most* of *my* spring break proofreading, duplicating, and binding the final draft of my dissertation for submission[1] right after Easter, and *WAITAMINUTE!* "We barely *know* each other, Meli."

"I *know* you're my *friend* who, moments ago, asked if I needed *help* with one *helluva* problem." She smiled warmly, squeezed my hand gently; her eyes twinged with uncertainty. "And my *family* knows you." We walked on, circling the game. "I *thought* I knew *Steve. They* didn't know *him* at all. Just before Spring Break, we had a *big* fight; *I* thought we could fix it *after.*" She smiled an odd little smile. "It's *not* like I haven't *thought* about you in those *tight* corduroy pants."

"You *remember* those?" *Not like I haven't thought about YOU in that bikini—and imagining you in less—often.*

"Like it was *yesterday.*" Now, everyone knows that corduroy was *the* fabric of the '70s. In my freshman year, I owned *one* pair of brown cords that were too tight that I *might* have worn *twice* around the school when I had nothing else *clean.* I'm no ladies' man; I *never understood* how to attract the attention of the opposite sex. "They got *every* girl's attention."[2]

"*My* family's never *heard* of you. This would be *very* sudden for them. And my committee may not *like....*"

"Then *defend* well and *help me, babe.*" She said *help me, babe,* with such *force* that it startled me. "*I'll* win our *families* over."

"So what's this 'Steve' *look* like? Could I...?"

"A *lot* like you. That's what attracted me to *him.*"

"Um...I...are there any *other* candidates for *this,* or am *I* the only one?" *...CRAZY enough to think about THIS life-altering decision for more than an instant?*

"*Nobody else,* babe." We walked on for a few steps. "Frankly, *you're* the only one who I *knew* I could trust *and* who *might* agree." She glanced at me with a smile, her eyes *still* uncertain. "*Your* voice is the one I hear when

---

1 I had submitted the *first* draft in December; got critiqued—not *challenged*—on it in February and March. Wednesday, I would *defend* my essay, and they would tell me how I did.
2 Damned if *I* know *how.*

I think about *this* dialogue." She sighed. "I *thought about* calling you last night and inviting myself up." She cleared her throat. "Couldn't think of an *excuse*...and it was *still* raining." Last night *was* the thunderous climax to a day of soaking, cold rain with occasional lightning.

"Would *I* go where *you* go, or *vice versa*?" *So, I'm thinking...*

"My *only* possible is *here*, working for the county. You?"

"A *couple* of promising interviews; nothing's *set*.[1] *And* there's a post-doctorate post *here* I put in for."

"Then we'll be *here*."

I thought deeply, hard, earnestly, and *quickly*. *She's my friend/ occasional fantasy, and she needs help. Did she actually ask, or did I jump up and volunteer? I can't remember. But what if I'd just asked her if she wanted to play? Would we still be having this conversation? Probably...*

Yet knowing how way leads on to way,
I doubted if I should ever come back.

God have MERCY on me... "I'll be proud to, Missy." *OK; I jumped up.*

She pulled me close. "Curtis, my *dear friend*," she whispered, her eyes suddenly bright. "We could do *this* one of *two* ways: *sham* or *real*." She smiled. "I'd *prefer real*."

"Me, too. I really *like*...." *How will I support her AND a child let alone ME?*

"We'll need to *act* like a *couple*." She looked around again as if making sure we had an audience. "Let's make *this* look like we've *done it before...please*?"

We *had* pecked lips and cheeks in the past, but this called for *more...* and she *did* say *please*. "Shouldn't we go someplace and *practice*?"

She gave me a *soft* slap on the jaw as she grabbed my face, whispering, "*Just pucker, babe*."

"I'll..." It *was* soft, tender, *just* bordering on passion. "*...Pretend* you just told me *we* were *expecting*," I sighed, her hands around my face, mine around her waist. "Then *hold* me like I *just* said I was *happy*, too." She enfolded me gently, *gratefully*. She felt comfortable in my arms—the first time in *years* I had *that* feeling.[2]

"*We* need to talk to my parents."

"*I* have *exams* to grade."

"Can the exams *wait*?"

"They'll *have* to. I *gotta* tell you, Meli, *this isn't* what I had in mind for proposing." *Not that I'd thought of that much.*

"You're *proposing*?" She seemed *surprised*...a *little*.

---

1 Neither was *especially* promising, but *this* was no time for quibbling...and New Mexico was *out*: no insurance and chicken feed for pay.

2 Sherry was OK with *sex* but not with *displaying* or *expressing affection*.

"Isn't that what I *should* be doing?"

"I guess." She suddenly looked as if the idea was a revelation. "I didn't hear *that* in my dialogues." She smiled broadly. "Think *I* didn't want the bended-knee version of my *first-ever* proposal?"

"Want me down on one *now?*"

"*Sure.*"

Out of the corner of my eye, I saw at *least* two people stop and stare at us as I knelt before her, and Meli smiled *brighter* than the *brilliant* sun at that moment.

For the *life* of me, I *cannot remember* if I *asked* her to marry me *then* or *not.*

But I remember *that* smile.

Thus ended, to date, the most *extraordinary* minutes of my life.

***

"Mom; Dad," Melanie called from just inside the front door of her family's large townhouse not far from the fields. "Anyone *here?*"

"*Hello,*" a voice answered from the kitchen. "Just getting some tea. Would you *like* some?" Melanie's mother, Helen, was a mild woman who had made me feel welcome in their home since I first entered it freshman year.

"Um, no, not *now*, thanks, Mom," Melanie said, leading me into the kitchen, her hands firmly around my right bicep. "Are *you* busy?" I couldn't decide if her death-grip on my arm was to keep *her or me* from running away.

"A *bit*. Evaluations." Helen was an assistant professor of English.[1]

"Can they *wait*," Melanie asked as we reached the kitchen. "We... where's *Dad?*"

Helen glanced back and forth at us before she set her pencil down. "Your *father's* at his office." She brushed her hair back casually. "*This* is a *we* conversation?"

"*Yeah*, Mom." Melanie sat at the kitchen table across from her mother; I was *compelled* to sit next to her.

"*Including* dead rodents?"

Did I mention that Melanie's mom *was* smart?

"*Including* dead rodents." And we *all* knew what *dead rodents* meant in those ancient days of sacrificial bunnies.

---

1 As an *assistant professor* Helen fell behind her husband in the pecking order of academics, who was a *full professor*. Unlike titles of nobility, neither had *any* juice with either *maître Ds* or hotel managers.

"I'll *call.*" It took only a few moments for the call; it would take Dr. Hubbard a few minutes to walk home. "When are you *due?*"

"January."

"Seen a *doctor?*"

"Heath center at State."

Helen glared at me as I tried to imagine what *my* part in *this* conversation should be. "*Proud* of yourself?"

"I'm *damn* proud that Melanie thinks enough of *me* to *have* me. And I *will* be proud if you and Dr. Hubbard would *accept* me."

That just came out, I *swear.* Melanie squeezed my arm like she was testing a roll of Charmin.[1]

"*Why you,*" Helen asked. "*You two* haven't spent more than a few *hours* together, and suddenly...?" She switched her gaze to Melanie, her face betraying a *hint* of disbelief. "Fill *me* in on your *secret* affair."

"We've known each other for *years*, Mom." Helen shrugged. "You *know* about Christmas." She nodded. "*That* was when Curtis and I became *close; closer* than everybody *thinks.* He came to State on Spring Break; we *got* closer still. He's *so* caring, *so* funny[2]...."

"Huh," Helen said. "*Tight corduroy pants* or *not*, you *really* don't *know*...." *That* was the *second time* in an *hour* someone remembered those *long-before*-gone-to-the-thrift-shop cords.

"*Mom*," Melanie sighed. "*We*..."

"Got drunk and slept together?"

"*No*," I declared. "It wasn't *like* that, Professor Hubbard. We talked this morning, and we *decided* to *do* this *together. My* parents were married *nine days* after they *met.*" Mom told us kids *that* story often.

Helen glared at me again. I *think* she was trying to decide if she would be angry or not. "Melanie's father and I knew each other for *sixteen* days before *we* said 'I do.' He was on furlough before he went overseas in '44." She sipped her tea. "I got the telegram that said he was killed; *still* got it in my files. They *called* a year later saying he was *alive* in China." She sighed. "Your parents *were* of a different generation, kids. But *Meli*, honey, are you *sure?* You still have *some* options...."

"*No*, Mom," Melanie said, squeezing my arm—*painfully*—again. "*We're* going to raise *our* baby together." Her emphasis on *our* felt uncomfortable—briefly. I was stunned—*later*—by how quickly I was getting *used* to this idea.

---

1 For you children who didn't see the commercials, look up "squeezably soft."
2 Intended as irony. History majors can cure insomnia, but they don't get many laughs. I was no exception.

"Well," Helen said at length, "*you two* have *known* each other longer than *we* did; *better*, too, I guess. Curtis: are *you* going to *complete*[1] this semester?"

"I *hope* I am, Professor Hubbard."

"I think *Helen's* more appropriate now, don't *you*?" She sipped her tea, frowning in thought. "You live in The Cubes?"[2]

"*My place* is so small I have to go outside to change my *mind*. They want me out at the end of July." It was barely 300 square feet, with a full bathroom smaller than many closets.[3]

"*My* room's no bigger," Melanie said, squeezing again. My hand was starting to feel like a lump of clay.

"We can move some things around *here*." Helen could *always* cut to the chase. "Any *job* prospects, young man?"

"Three: State, University of Chicago, *and* the post-doc archivist post *here*."[4] I cleared my throat. "My *family* will be here for a week starting next Friday. Can *we*, um..."

"You in *that* big a hurry?" Helen put on an enigmatic grin.

"Wouldn't the *school* pitch you *out*?" I asked.

Helen shook her head. "Not if *you're* around, no." She finished her tea, poured more from a pot. "Sure you *don't* want some?" We shook our heads. "We can *discuss* that." We heard Dr. Hubbard come in the back door. "*Bert*, in the *kitchen*." She looked at me mildly. "Just tell him what you want; that's all."

We both stood up when he entered. "Dr. Hubbard," I said with more resolve than I thought I could muster, "I want to *marry* your daughter."

When I said *that*, I believe Meli hit the bone.

"I *see*." With careful, measured deliberation, Bert placed his hat on an empty peg near the door, his sallow, hollow-eyed face blank. He glanced at Melanie. "How does *she* feel about that?"

"*We* want to raise *our baby* together, Dad."

My hand *might* have been turning blue; it *did* feel cold.

That made Bert stop and glance at Helen. "In*deed*." He turned and reached into a small cupboard by the sink with his bony hands, retrieving an old liquor bottle. "*Baby*," he said, pouring a small measure into each of four glasses and sitting down. "*That* explains your phone call, Mother." He

---

1 Defending my dissertation for the last time and being awarded my doctorate would, to an academic, *complete* my formal education.

2 The Steuben Graduate Housing Complex, called The Cubes, looked like a varicolored blockhouse designed by Picasso on acid.

3 The stall shower *was* smaller than my closet.

4 The post-doctoral position paid a *meager* stipend. I *had* been thinking about *it* a great deal. It *was* a road I'd *wanted* to take...

pushed one glass at Helen, another at me, the third at Melanie. "For each of our children and grandchildren, I've shared a dram of this expensive old liquor that was given me by my great-uncle when I *married* Helen." He sighed. "Uncle Myron passed away while I was overseas, so he never *saw* what this old booze has." He raised his glass. "To your *future*, children." He downed *his* shot—we *all* downed ours—and then he *eyeballed*[1] me. "Are you *ready* for what comes next? Married life is a good deal more *involved* than just getting a woman pregnant."

"Yessir," I answered with confidence I did *not* feel; my lower arm was *numb*; Meli's hands *had* to have hurt. "We were *talking* about...."

"Your *final defense* is Wednesday morning."

"Yessir," I answered, *instantly* shifting from *daughter's suitor* to *groveling grad student*. The latter *felt* more familiar and a *damn*-sight safer.

"*Drink* up. You've *yet* to turn in *all* your grades."

"I *just* wanted to...."

"Turn your grades in by tomorrow morning, *Mr.* Durand," Bert said. "Make time for your *faculty advisor* in *your* office tomorrow at three. Now, *I* have important matters to discuss with *my* family. *I will* see you tomorrow. Good *afternoon*."

Melanie was *so* surprised that she neglected to see me to the door... though she *did* release my arm.

And *that*, ladies and gentlemen, was my introduction to my soon-to-be in-laws who, twenty minutes earlier, had *merely* been my faculty advisor and his wife.

As I walked back to my office—the blood pulsing *painfully* back into my hand—I reflected on the last half-hour.

As yet the most surprising, *life-altering* thirty minutes of my life.

***

The first thing I saw when I got back to my office, of course, was that envelope, addressed to *Dean of Faculty, Southern New Mexico State University...*

Has that road vanished? Meli could find something, maybe, until the baby comes. Adjunct pay might go further in small-town New Mexico...

But...showing up with a bride on my arm and a baby on the way? My only faculty friend is expecting a bachelor...and she might have the power to...

Then took the other, as just as fair,
And having perhaps the better claim,

No. I take the other road, perhaps a little more fair.

---

1 You *know* when you've been eyeballed.

I burned my *eloquent* acceptance letter—that I'd spent half a day composing—over a candle that my office mate[1] and I kept for power outages.[2]

Then I could go back to grading, with my future path *much* different than it had been just a half-hour before. But, that half-a-day that I spent composing that acceptance kept coming back to me. *I hate to destroy any work that takes that long.* After all, I had drafts of papers from *high school* in my files.

Prerequisite class students— I was grading two sections of American History from 1865—passed almost by default. The *timeline* part of their exams *had* to demonstrate that they could place the Gilded Age *after* the Civil War and *before/during* the Spanish-American War, at minimum. They *also* had to match William Seward with Alaska, John J. Pershing with WWI, and Horace Greely with "go west young man" in the *matching* portion. They also had to correctly answer *most* of the questions in the multiple-choice part. Finally, the TAs read their short essays and graded them at no *less* than a *B* if they made no *major* gaffes. I plowed through a hundred-odd *dull* final exam essays on Reconstruction and the Gilded Age, the World Wars and Korea, and one thoughtful, *innovative* essay on the Cold War by a *reentrant*.[3] Finding the odd gem like that Cold War essay—revealing a *potential* scholar—made the *tedious* work worth our time.[4]

At about 6, my phone rang. "Durand and Martinez," I answered.

"*Hi*, honey," Melanie said. "You *free* tonight?"

Honey? "As it *happens*, yeah. I'll come down to *your*...."

"Let's meet you at *your* place, honey. Call when you're done?"

"*Sure*, babe." *Have I gotten THAT used to this ALREADY? THAT* revelation was...surprising and gratifying. *Maybe I CAN throw out some of those old drafts.*

It was nearly 8 before I finished the grade reports. I called Melanie and put the paperwork in Dr. Hubbard's box. Unfortunately, *that late* meant I had to grab *something* edible—if possible—from the Snack Shack in the Varian Caspar Student Union.

With my dinner in a bag, I headed back to The Cubes, where Melanie was waiting at the front entrance. "Hi, *babe*," said I, all innocent and that. "I only *have*...."

---

1 I shared the office and telephone with another TA.

2 It happened about twice a semester.

3 Our name for an older, *non-traditional* student.

4 We *noted* such essayists for observation next semester. If consistent, they would be nurtured and supported. Often, they turned out to be one-trick ponies with a flash of insight.

"*Hi*, honey." She pecked my lips. "*That's* OK; I ate." She had one of those bigger-bag-than-a-purse-tote-carry-alls[1] over her shoulder.

The elevator was quiet, despite the *constant* sound from the 2nd Floor where the music majors hung out. My 5th Floor was *pretty* quiet because history grad students—except the three *military* history majors at the end—didn't make much of a racket.

I'd done laundry and tidied the place up on Saturday, with nothing much *else* to do that I *wanted* to do. Even then, my little hovel wasn't *nearly* fit for entertaining she-who-was-to-*become* she-who-must-be-obeyed.[2] "*Excuse* the *clutter*."

"You *know* I've seen it *worse*," she sighed, slinging her bag onto my one *empty* straight chair.[3] "Did I leave a *big* leather barrette here New Year's? With a big stick through it?"

"Um," I reached in my kitchenette drawer, "*this?*" She'd stopped at my place on her way to a party at The Pit, the saloon/disco/club under the Union, and talked me into going.[4]

"*Yeah*," she grinned. "Thanks! Mom and Dad want to shuffle *us* into my *sisters'* old room. We called *them*, told my brother when *he* came home. Surprise, excitement, all the rest of the symptoms."

"Uh-huh," I replied. As I *politely* ate my fries, I realized that *this* was *a done deal,* now that others had been informed. But, I heard *no* dissent in my head. "Can I get you some water? I have orange juice I got Friday...."

"*I'll* get it, babe." She walked ten steps to my kitchenette and downed a vitamin with a slug of juice *straight* from the carton. She then decamped my (*clean*) half-full laundry basket from the old recliner (a curb rescue from a couple of years before) and sat down. "This *chair's* still comfy. Junior can't remember if he *liked* you or not." Her brother was a big guy who played football. "He doesn't *know* you. You need to fix *that*."

"Sure. I'll call *my* family...."

"Call from *our* place tomorrow when you come down for dinner."

Dinner? Huh. I nodded, ate fries, and sucked my milkshake as she scanned my shelves and stacks of paper that included *many* drafts of older papers. "I'm spending the *night*," she finally sighed, stretching her arms and legs. "*I* think they want to discuss *us* without *me* around."

---

1 As a scholar, I couldn't come up with a definition. As a male in the '80s, I didn't *dare* call it the *wrong* thing.

2 I'd understood H. Rider Haggard's reference in *She*. I never thought *that* term derogatory but, like *old man*, one of respect in context.

3 She'd been *in* my garret *several* times over the past four years.

4 She knocked on my door and said, "get *dressed. We're* having *fun* tonight."

"OK," I said *carefully*. "Do *they* think...?"

She took a deep breath. "They're *acting* like they're *buying* the story." She shook her head. "I *think* they are. Dad's *not* a good actor. Can I use your bathroom?" She nodded to the door next to the kitchenette sink.

"Sure. I *just* cleaned it yesterday."

"*Good.*" She stood and shuffled off her shoes, then shouldered her bag. "I'll *only* be a minute."

I finished my fries and gobbled my hot dog in a few seconds. I switched off the overhead light *and* the light over my kitchenette sink, leaving my bedside lamp on.

It was the strangest beginning I could imagine for a love scene...if *that's* what *this* was to be.

I was looking for something *gauzy* to cover the lampshade, *just* in case, when she emerged, still clad in the same sleeveless and *short* jean dress that she *came* in, although she *had* let down her mid-back hair. "I'm *not* going to wait around in the buff until you *invite* me to your bed," she grinned and flashed a bare hip from under her dress.[1]

Ho-boy. "Meli," I gulped, moving a stack of books out of my *other* straight chair by my table. "Let's just *talk*, OK? It's *early*..."

"And we *hardly know* each other," she sighed. She sat...I *think* gratefully. "Tell me about *your* family."

"Mom's a freelance journalist, *prodigious* knitter, and seamstress. Dad moved from carpentry to law enforcement while *really helping* Mom raise us three kids. Mom's father is in Arizona; I've seen him *twice* in my life. Mom's brother and *his* wife work at the Redstone Arsenal in Alabama. They have two girls—my cousins—but I have no *idea* what *they're* up to. Her family's not on good terms. Dad's widowed sister lives in Cicero. Sister Karen's three years older, a paralegal married to a suburb developer in Arlington Heights and has three kids, so I have two nieces and a nephew. Sister Darla's two years younger than me. She was one of the first women to graduate from the Air Force Academy and is a finance officer in Germany."

"Other than my *sisters* and *brother*," she said and proceeded to name her four sets of aunts and uncles, eleven cousins, two nieces, a nephew, and three grandparents.

By then, my dinner sat like a rock in my gut. I asked, "do you have a *middle* name?"

"Holly, after my maternal grandmother. You?" She went to my window and pulled down my window shades. Since my only window

---

1 Those things had matching shorts that she *had* been wearing.

faced north and overlooked the woods at the edge of the campus, I rarely used them.

"Harrison, after my father's oldest brother, who was killed in World War One." We stared at each other for several moments before I asked, "*Want* to...?"

"*Sure,*" she declared, reaching for the zipper on the front of her dress.[1] "*We're* either *going* to *work,* or we're *not.*" She slipped out of her dress as quickly as peeling a banana, stepped to the bed, and asked, "*which* side?"

"*Um...*" I pulled my jersey over my head, unable to process...*that.* Despite having seen her in bikinis and strapless *and* backless gowns, she was *far* more *stunning* in *nothing* than my imagination *ever* allowed for. I *not*-glanced at the *slight* swelling in her belly that I *guessed* was the baby.

"I'm going to guess *not* the wall side," she smiled, not waiting for my answer as she crawled in on the wall side while I got my pants off.

So we just laid in bed...holding hands, facing each other. "I *know* you're *not...*" she mumbled.

"I, um, *I...*" I stammered, entering unfamiliar territory. "I said *no sham,* and I *meant* it. I'll *learn* to *love both* of you. I *want* to marry you. *That* means..."

"Thanks," she whispered, suddenly *very* close to my face. "You've made me the *happiest* woman in the world."

I could feel her bare chest against mine when she inhaled. I had to scoot my hips away from her to avoid an *accident* of the *messy* kind. She *was that close,* and yes, I *was that....*[2] "I thought *that* was supposed to be *my* line."

"*You* want to be the happiest *woman* in the world?"

"You *know* what...."

"*I know.*" She smiled brightly, her eyes sparkling, caressing my forehead.

"You *know* what *we're* about to embark on?"

"*I know.*" She suddenly looked serious. "I *know* what you told my father. Want *out?*"

"*No.*" We stared at each other for what seemed to be an eternity. "*Just...checking.*"

She smiled again. "Be *sure,* babe."

"I *am.*"

"Good."

"I *need* to ask, Meli: You *knew* you were pregnant *when?*"

---

1 I *never* understood *why* those bright brass zippers were *so* oversized and had that *ring.*

2 And *you wouldn't* be, brother? Yeah, *right.*

"I *suspected* a couple of weeks ago. I *knew* Wednesday. I started taking vitamins that night. I've *been* careful."

"*Good*. You never had *any* doubt about...?"

"*Keeping* her?" She scooted *a millimeter* closer. "No. When I *thought* about giving her up for adoption, I started having *that* hoped-for *dialog* in my head. *Your voice* kept saying things like '*I can help*' and 'let's *go for it*.' So *that* idea faded."

I wasn't sure just *what should* happen next, but I *had* to slide back before she bussed me on the cheek and *softly* held my hand against her abdomen. "*Kill* the light. Let's just *sleep* tonight since I haven't *slept* in *days*. 'Night."

"Night, babe." As she released my hands after a few minutes, I realized that I was *utterly* exhausted. As I drifted off to sleep, I realized I was *deep* in *like* with Melanie Holly Hubbard.

That was a good start.

And so ended the *most surprising day* of my life...so far.

Yet knowing how way leads on to way,
I doubted if I should ever come back.

Monday Wouldn't Have Been...

With the morning light seeping around the window shade in a half-sleep, I wondered what my future looked like. The *old roads* and *new roads* had appeared and disappeared in my dreams all night. *Was yesterday just a dream? Will I wake up alone, like always?*

I opened my eyes. Her back was to me, still asleep, I *thought.* Her head lay on my *other,* practically flat pillow, her hair tangled. Then, she reached behind her and mumbled, "gimmie your *hand,* babe."

I obliged, if only to *verify.* "*You* sleep OK," I asked as she pulled my arm across her.

"Barely, but *better.* You?" I spooned behind her; she put my hand on her breast.

I had trouble breathing; *that* happened *so* fast, but I said, "this bed's too small for two grownups. *Marry* me, Melanie."

"*Yes,*" she grinned as she rolled over. "I'm bringing a *pillow* tonight."

We stared at each other for what seemed to be forever as the morning light around the shades reflected dully off the plastic book jackets on my shelf. "You're *beautiful.*"

"*You're* not bad *yourself.*" She kissed me sweetly. "Let's *not* screw this up."

"How would we do *that?*"

"By *not* caring what the other thinks, by *not* making important decisions *together.*" She pushed me on my back and reached for me under the sheets. "By not *loving* morning sex."

"Since I've never *had* it, I'd have to *try* it first."[1]

"*Really?*" She *glided* on top of me, straddling my hips and pushing the sheets off. "You need to *try* it *now.*"

"The *baby...?*" I gently rested my hands on *her* hips.

"...will be *fine.*" She put her hands on mine, pulled them over her belly. "*There* she is." She shifted her hips—and *me*—delicately, deftly. "This is *her first* time."

"*Her,*" I breathed, alarmed by the sudden *intimacy and* the *sudden...* you *know.*

"A *feeling.*" She rocked her hips gently. "Just *a feeling,* babe."

"You've *got...a* 50/50...*chance...either way.*"

She laughed brightly...and it *was* better than I had *ever* imagined it *could* have been.

***

My office mate was Doris Martinez, the only person I ever knew who *actively tried* to *look* genderless. You can imagine my surprise at seeing her in a business suit that morning, wearing a *touch* of makeup. Her short hair was not just disentangled but attractively arranged. Then I remembered... "*your* final defense this morning?"

"*Yes,*" she sighed, setting a conservatively-styled leather purse on her desk. It was a far cry from the ratty, beaded bag she'd slung around for the last two years. She looked at me with her odd smile, affecting a runway model's *brief* strut-and-turn. "What do *you* think?"

"*I'd* pass you." Crest insisted that its grad students must *look* professional at their final defense if at no other time. Candidates had been failed for violating that requirement. "At ten?"

"Yeah." She smoothed her skirt, fidgeted *discretely* with her pantyhose.[2] "I smell candle wax. Did we lose power Saturday?"

"Briefly," I guessed. "Was grading during that storm." It would have been a *perfect* time for a power outage...had I *been* there.

"Ah. You and Melanie Hubbard..." she started.

"Yeah," I said, "news travels fast."

"Saw you with her at the game yesterday *and* this morning in the cafeteria." Doris *could* recognize Melanie. Grad students had dining-in obligations at faculty homes and met their families.[3] "You *serious?*"

---

1 I rarely *slept* with Sherry. She was always in a hurry to get away from me when *she* was *done. That* should have told me something, but, like most guys, I wasn't paying *nearly* enough attention.

2 I'd never seen *her* wear them before, but I'd seen *other* women do *that.*

3 Crest billed itself as a *family*; puritanical, but a *family.*

"I asked her to marry me; she said yes."

That got a startled reaction. "*Huh.* Well, congratulations and good luck." She glanced at the clock. "I'm headed down there."

"I have a meeting *here* at three."

"OK." She picked up her purse.

"*Break* a leg, Doris," I smiled, meaning it.

"*Thanks,* Curtis." She took seven steps across the office, embraced me briefly, pecked my cheek, and whispered, "*really,* babe; *good* luck."

"*You* too."

That was the *second* time a girl had called me *babe* in twelve hours after a drought of...it seemed like forever. Two *different* ones, no less. *That* was a personal record.[1]

***

I'll tell you about my *alma mater* now because a play-by-play of the next couple of hours—me reading *my* evaluations by other grad students followed by another dry-as-dust description of me filling out *my* evaluations of *them*—would make *laundry* seem spellbinding.[2]

Alonzo Crest was a *privateer*[3] who *said* he was born in Jamaica, but reliable evidence says more *likely* Hackensack. In 1801 he and his crew captured a Spanish treasure ship worth more than the combined value of the United States at the time. In 1803, he took his sizable share and moved his large family from the Atlantic coast up the Sonoco River and started a colony he called Crest Landing—now the name of a fashionable suburb—on the river banks near where the city of Granite Ledge now stands. A skilled promoter, Captain Crest attracted settlers to the verdant hill/forest country on the river, surrounded by stony mountains. The Landing *grew* first on lumber, *thrived* on trade, then *boomed* on farming. In 1810 Crest started a teacher's school called *Crest Academy* to attract families and cash to the area.

Tiberias Weymouth Jenson arrived at Crest Landing in 1820. Jenson knew little of lumber *or* farming, but he knew *stone.* He surveyed the surrounding mountains and their *massive* nodules of mid- *and* high-grade granite. Their exploitation made Crest Landing commercially *explode*—giving cause for its name to be changed to Granite Ledge in 1835.

---

1 It's not like I was keeping *score*. It was just one more revelation, like finding out that women of all ages thought my tush in tight cords was *cute*.

2 Academic bureaucracies *thrive* on useless paper like evaluations. *Useless* because no one will say anything bad about someone who *could,* one day, be on their hiring or tenure committees.

3 Lawful pirate.

Tiberias' youngest son, Xerxes, used *his* share of the considerable family fortune to develop Crest Academy into the first college in the area in 1841. The money also allowed him to indulge in his hobby: collecting and archiving[1] early American documents. Over the decades, the archive became known as the Jenson Collection. The Collection's funding was enhanced when Xerxes married Gertrude Fortescue Crest—Captain Crest's granddaughter—in 1850. The Jenson *Endowment*—created in 1864 by both Jenson and Crest family members—took ownership of the Collection *and* the school. Crest *College* became Crest *University* in 1909.

The Jenson Scholar Grant—created in 1910—gave a full ride[2] to *one* seventeen to nineteen-year-old American history scholar every *five years* beginning in 1913. Because of its scope, the Jenson is as sought-after as a Fulbright or a Rhodes scholarship. I *won* that fierce competition in my senior year in high school, competing against applicants from all over.[3]

Crest University was an old-fashioned liberal arts school in a small city with a unique, hardscrabble but *sizable* financial base. As such, it was unaffected by the seismic shifts in higher education that promulgated "studies" programs, any of which can be likened to the close examination of a *single* tree in a *vast* forest. Thus, Crest avoided pumping out graduates whose understanding of the *real* world made them *excellent* waitstaff, fast-food workers, and "studies" professors.

The Jenson Endowment College of History had been a significant feeder of law and *other* history grad schools worldwide. Its alumni included Supreme Court justices, Rhodes scholars, and Pulitzer and Nobel Prize winners. *ALL* Crest undergraduates had to pass four semesters of history regardless of major.

The Crest School of Liberal Arts and Education still generated teachers—I had a teacher's credential from there. It was one of the last proper, dedicated liberal arts schools left in the country. In 1982, Crest *still* had Latin as a freshman/sophomore prerequisite.

The Jenson School of Surface Geological Engineering—stone quarrying and hard-rock engineering—was Crest's cash cow. Their Master of Quarry Science degree, the only one of its kind in the world,

---

1 Would that he knew *how*…more later.

2 All expenses, from freshman orientation through the doctoral dissertation, for up to ten years, were covered. No twenty-year grad students got Jenson Grants. You finished in a decade or you were out.

3 As the 1973 Jenson Scholar, I was trotted out on special occasions, paired with Melanie.

required hands-on quarrying work to graduate.[1] As an *homage* to Crest's primary income, Introduction to Geology was a prerequisite for *ALL* Crest undergrads.

***

Doris came back, flushed, but grinning from ear to ear just as I completed my last evaluation. "*Ha!*" she exclaimed, slinging her purse into our *one* upholstered chair.

"*Got* it?"

"I *did*," she sighed. She took her jacket off, draping it casually over her desk chair, with a t-shirt underneath.[2] "Gotta get out of this *corset*," she grunted as she slipped her shoes off and stepped out of her skirt. It wasn't the *first* time I'd watched her strip to her knickers—Doris called *modesty* an *archaeo-sexist affectation*. She struggled with her pantyhose for a few moments before she got them off and stuffed them into the wastebasket. "Haven't worn *those* since...can't *remember*," she declared. "Damn *conspiracy*."

"I *ain't* part of it," I said, "*despite* your protests to the contrary."

"Just *my* way to make my chops in the sisterhood. I *told* you that."

"*Every* time we made out." Since we moved into the office, we had been each other's occasional/safe/casually erotic relief make-out partners.[3] "You moving back to New Hampshire?"

"No. I found a house in Ithaca right next to the campus that I *have* to take *now*." She started pulling the pins out of her hair while standing by her desk, unisex *briefs* gracing her hips.

"I'm returning what's left of my library books." Graduate students could check books out of the Jenson Graduate Library for up to two years as long as they didn't leave campus *with* them.[4]

"I'll take *mine* too," she replied. "Just let me *finish*." She shook her hair out, then pulled a denim skirt out of a desk drawer and stepped into it. It was only the *fourth* gender-specific article of clothing I'd ever seen

---

1 Most of student athletes were *in* the quarrying program, which gave rise to the expression *rocks for jocks*.

2 Doris only grudgingly—*she* said—wore traditional women's underwear, but *never* a bra—*until* today. She *hardly* needed one, to be fair. She was no *great* beauty, but she hid what charms she *had*.

3 Sherry and I were *always* off-and-on. Doris and I had agreed that we were there to *work*. *We* were *safe* to the point of cowardice.

4 If they *did*, their records were *expunged*, as if Crest never heard of them.

her wear.[1] We hauled some twenty linear feet of books across the quad to the library between us.

Back in our office, we marveled at the emptiness as we cleared the shelves of our *own* books stacked in file boxes. "Doris," I asked, "never *asked* before, but *your...*"

"*Sexlessness,*" she sighed, plopping down in her chair.

"I *know* you're not *gay,* so *why?*"

"*Convenience,*" she sighed, "and *camouflage.* As long as the world *thinks* I'm *not* available, I can get my *work* done." She smiled craftily, arching her back. "*Now...*" she flapped her t-shirt briefly. "I'd *like* to make a play for *you,* sweet-cheeks."

"*Sweet-cheeks,*" I chuckled, "where'd *that* come from?"

"Since I *met* ya, babe."[2]

"But the *sisterhood?*"

"Oh, I still believe in much of their *cause.* Most women these days don't hold for the *crap* about a male-dominated conspiracy. Equal pay for equal work, sure, but artificial sperm so *fem*-kind can do away with men altogether? *That's* a load of crap. We *like* sex with guys."

"When was the last time *you* had any," I blurted. I *swear* that just came out.

"It's *been* a while," she smiled, hitching her skirt *way* up. "*You* volunteering *right now?*"

"*Pass,* sugar," I answered.

"*Your* loss, sweet-cheeks." she grinned, donning a denim vest before kissing my cheek—*lingeringly*—on her way to the door, her own books stacked on a hand cart. "*See you* in the funny papers, *babe.*"

***

"We'll *talk* about my daughter, Mr. Durand, but I shall leave *that* for later." Dr. Hubbard arrived *precisely* as the chapel bells completed their fourth change, and the three bells of the hour started. "You got the grades in." It was a statement, not a question.

"Yessir," I answered nervously. "Doris defended well?"

"She did *indeed.* She used French and Spanish archives we'd never *heard* of.[3] Cornell will be the better for *having* her. Tell me, does anyone in the freshman/sophomore cohort stand out?"

---

1 All in *one day...*

2 I was *relieved* she didn't mention my cords, which *she* never saw.

3 Doris was a leading authority on the politics and diplomacy behind America's Quasi-War of 1797-1801.

"A reentrant wrote a brilliant essay on the Cold War. The rest were just freshmen and sophomores."

"Doris said the same. *Her* better essay was on the War of 1812." He shifted in his chair. "I got a letter from Dr. McCord at Southern New Mexico. *She* wants to know your status, said there's an adjunct spot waiting for you." *Uh-oh.* "I *know* your *history* with her, Mr. Durand," he added evenly. "It's not *savory.*"

"Not that I *encouraged* her, sir." In fact, I did everything I could *do* to make her understand that I was NOT interested in her advances. She wasn't *physically* ugly, but I believed her *husband* would object to my accepting her propositions. She left for New Mexico in my junior year, after... "I nearly *flunked out* because of her."[1]

"That's what you *told* me at the time *and* what I told the Trustees." He shifted again. "Of course, Marylyn knew *nothing* of all that. She just left you that poor grade, never knowing *why* her contract was not renewed. *You* were only *one* reason."

"Is *not* responding an option?" I did *not* relish the idea of having to write a negative response to a sure thing—politely, of course.[2]

"Professionally I wouldn't *advise* it. Knowing your history with her, if it'll *help*, *I'll* make your excuses and say you *had* a better offer. Have you come up with *anything* for your first article *should* you be awarded your Ph.D.?"[3]

I HAVE a better offer? "I *have*, sir," I answered, hesitant to even mention what I had under my elbow and confused by...*better offer?* "An exploration of *this.*" I pulled on a cotton glove and handed Dr. Hubbard another. I carefully picked a document, yellowed with age, out from between two acid-free paper sheets. "I discovered it recently; wanted to ask *you* about it before I went any further."

Item T- 45189 was described as a letter from Thomas Jefferson to James Monroe dated July 21st, 1787, location unstated, one of several acquired from a private person by Xerxes Jenson in 1845. After the usual banalities typical of personal correspondence of the period, Jefferson wrote:

---

1 A B- in any history course is unacceptable for a Jenson Scholar.

2 The one thing *all* my evaluators said was that I was a *careful yet eloquent writer*. But, I was a *very slow* at it, going through multiple drafts of nearly every paper.

3 Freshly-minted Ph.D.'s needed to hit the ground running. The profession of history takes *publish or perish* quite literally.

...despite my misgivings in regards to this wrong-headed constitution project, you seem determined to proceed as if my views were of little moment....there is no freedom; indeed, there can <u>be</u> none, in a federal system as you describe it; only an odious tyranny...

Dr. Hubbard read the letter carefully, taking the time to examine the back, holding it up to the light. "I *see*," he mused. "You *found* one." He placed the letter carefully on the table beside him. "Have you found *others*?"

"There's *this*." Item T-7145 was also a letter from Jefferson to Monroe, dated August 1788, again from an unstated location,[1] one of several acquired from a private person by Xerxes Jenson in 1849.

...That pompous popinjay Washington as chief executive...this constitution project will go down in history as an abysmal failure with that shameful opportunist leading the country...

Again, Dr. Hubbard read closely, examining the document with great care for several minutes. "Any more?"

"Several," I said, squinting. "But what did you mean '*one*'?"

"I've seen *many* letters *like* these. What do *you* make of them as a scholar?"

"Well, sir, these two give us a different perspective of Jefferson, don't they? He didn't seem to *believe* in the Constitution that he served under for two terms?"

Although the good doctor apparently hadn't seen these *particular* items, he wasn't *surprised* by them. Did he know of letters from Founding Fathers denouncing each other *and* the Constitution? Historical scholarship was difficult, yes. Until then, it hadn't occurred to me it *could* also be a minefield. The allegations of the Hemings family were barely a blip on the horizon compared to *this*.

I owed my college education to Crest and the Jenson Endowment, both of which were *enhanced* by the reputation of Dr. Hubbard. I would have found it hard to believe that Dr. Hubbard indulged in fraud-by-omission that could ruin him, the Jenson, *and* Crest.

He shook me out of my reverie with a question. "Ever wonder why Jefferson's tombstone *doesn't* have a reference to his being president of the United States?"

"Not *deeply*; not my area." *Not my area* is a scholar's dodge; a more *learned* way of saying *I haven't studied it*. I *had* realized—too late—that my focus and that of most academic historians was too narrow to

---

1 Correspondents in the 18th and 19th centuries nearly always indicated where they were writing *from*. These items were, therefore, *peculiar* at minimum.

benefit more than a handful of other academics. There *are* ways to be a generalist in history, but I hadn't gone down *that* road. *My road* was the politics and diplomacy of the First Barbary War of 1801-1805. I examined Jefferson material *only* for his impact on that conflict. "*I* just thought it was another of his many quirks."

"While true, you *did* write about Jefferson in your dissertation. Surely *you* have a view on these letters...there *are* more, by the way."

"Where ?"

"In the Truxton Section. That's just *one* reason why they are *there.*"[1]

"*Ah.*" Xerxes acquired documents—trunks-full, and, it was said, even *bales*-full—without much thought to their provenance.[2] The Truxton Section was named after William Truxton, the 1933 Jenson Scholar. He had organized and *started* to catalog thousands of documents that lacked their creator's names, dates, *or* clear provenance. "I was looking in *there* to be thorough."[3]

"Commendable. But what do you *make* of them?"

"I *think...*" *the next few moments, words, or gestures could either destroy my career or launch it...* "...they need to be *tested*[4] for authenticity."

"Perhaps you're right," Dr. Hubbard declared. "You're not doing anything with these *soon*, are you?"

"Nosir," I answered, relieved but curious.

"*Good*; Come to *my* office tomorrow afternoon. I've something to *show* you." He took a deep breath. "Now; the *other* matter."

"Yessir," I squeaked, *sure* that I was about to be *scourged* severely about the head and shoulders with whatever was at hand for my *outrageous* conduct...in a figurative sense, anyway.

It seemed an eternity before he quietly asked, "do you *love* my daughter?"

"I will *learn* to love her. I *like* her a great deal."

"I've always thought that *like* is more important than *love* and determines how well people get along. Life *isn't* a romance novel." He hunched over in the chair, placed his elbows on his knees, his head in his hands, and gazed at the floor. "For the month I managed to avoid being captured by the Japs, I thought of Helen often. I don't *think* it was love. It was more like a *fond recollection* of her face, her smell; *yes*, her

---

1 Hence the T in their numbers.

2 Chain of possession, which points to a document's authenticity. Xerxes was a far more zealous *collector* than an assiduous or careful *archivist.*

3 Even if there was no chance I could alter my dissertation when I found them.

4 Such tests are rare for reasons that will become clear.

feel." He glanced up briefly. "We had *four days* together before I left; we spent most of it *alone.* What I *felt* for her...hard to tell *what* it was when you're that hungry, banged up and frightened."

"Banged up, sir?" I knew he never *fully* recovered from being a prisoner of the Japanese for three months, then a "guest" of the Soviets and Chinese Communists for nearly a year. I *could,* therefore, figure out the *hungry* and *frightened* myself.

"Busted my left foot and shin when I bailed out. Splinted them myself."

"Ah." *Explains his little limp.* "No rainbows or trumpets for your bride, sir?"

"Just *tremendous* fondness. Thinking of her *did* keep me going. *That's* enough for now. You are the first *historian* for whom one of my daughters has shown an abiding affection. Someday I *might* tell you about my time behind barbed wire. It *might* interest you—but *not* today." He sat up again, smiling. "Curtis, *please* call me Bert when we're alone or with family. Helen and I think Melanie's decisions have been sound. Do you *have* a ring?"

"Mom has *her* mother's ring Gramma wanted *me* to have."[1]

"*Lovely.* Melanie wants the ceremony at St. Barbara's.[2] Do you *have* any preferences in *that* regard?"

"Nosir...ah, Bert. The only time I was *there* was freshman year." Even avowed atheists and Satanists *had* to take Comparative Religion to graduate from Crest.[3]

"Very well." He stood up; I did the same. "If you two are so inclined, stay in your, ah, *room* until the spare is made habitable. Right now, there's *plaster* hanging from the ceiling...."

"I can *help* with that, sir." Finish carpentry—I learned from Dad— supplemented the meager stipend I got from the Jenson.[4]

"A generous offer, but no need. The School's *finally* doing it. But, of course, if you find *other* lodgings, we *can't* object."

"Ah, well, *financially*...." Money *was* an object for me. I *couldn't* work more than a weekend a month and get my *other* work done.[5] "I'd *like* to call *my* parents tonight if I can."

---

1 She passed when I was two; I was her *only* grandson.

2 The school's *circa* 1840 chapel was named for the patron saint of miners and others who work with explosives. St. Barbara is also associated with lightning; a *Christian Thor,* if you will.

3 Despite all the heathens who have taken classes in it, the place still stands.

4 Jenson Scholars got chump-change to *live* on plus room and board. It was enough to *survive* but *not* enough to find off-campus digs *or* party every night and weekend...even if we *had* the time, which we *didn't.*

5 I had been getting more work *this* semester, with only one section to teach and my dissertation more *done* than *not.*

"Certainly. Around *five* for dinner, then."

"Yessir...Bert."

As he was leaving, he stopped, framed in the doorway, turning his head. "Mr. Durand: *harm* my child, and I'll *ruin* you."

"Under*stood*, sir."

And if those letters ARE authentic, I could ruin YOU, sir.

***

"Didn't *realize* your father was a police *captain*," Melanie said as we walked across the campus. The Hubbard home was a mile of well-lit sidewalks from The Cubes. Since I didn't *have* a car, I walked a lot. I *had* a moped, but it was shorter to *walk* most places on campus since mopeds weren't allowed on sidewalks.

"He came home one night and said he'd got a job that wasn't so *dirty* or so much *work*."

"Cop in suburban Chicago's *not*...."

"I *think* you know *irony* when you hear it." We passed through the Freedom Arch, where bronze tablets memorialized alums, faculty, and former students who died in conflicts from the Civil War to Vietnam. "Want *me* to carry that?"

"*I'm* good." She had a suit bag[1] over her shoulder. "I'm not *that* fragile."

"Have you *found* a doctor...?"

"The family OB/GYN." We walked onto the quad just as the lights were coming up. The couples on the benches and the grass scattered like roaches in a flashlight beam.[2] "Your *mom* sounds excited."

"*Yeah*," I mused, puzzled. I'd thought she'd have been more subdued since they knew *nothing* of Melanie.[3] "They're coming to commencement next Saturday."

We walked a little farther. "Weekend after *next* for the wedding?"

"*OK*." *This* was getting...easier...*but*...

We drew closer to The Cubes. She crossed her arms, which meant she was serious *and* listening. "*What*, babe?"

"What's *what*?"

"Whatever's on your *mind*."

---

1 *That* I *could* boldly identify.

2 The quad lights came on a half-hour *after* dark in all seasons. The all-powerful, puritanical Regents didn't know *everything* that went on.

3 We weren't distant, but I hadn't *been* to Cicero in four years.

"*Aside* from the obvious?"

"Let's *talk* about *The Obvious*, my friend."

We slowed down, nearing The Cubes. "Still trying to...are you *sure* about *this*? About *me*?" *About THIS road?* That small voice of dissent in my head had dwindled to a faint whisper, but it was nagging.

She paused, drew a breath, and looked away. "My *good friend,* who I've had many *pleasant dreams* about, has volunteered to stand in for the *boy* who I *thought* I knew but who wants nothing to do with *our baby,*" she whispered, barely audible. "*You* want to *act* as the father of our child in *his* stead, to save me from embarrassment and my father from *possible* termination." She gazed at me, serious. "*That's* what's troubling you?"

"Yes." I looked away briefly. "*Any* doubts?" *There's a signpost up ahead; your next stop...*Despite my growing certainty, there *was* a *Twilight Zone* feel to my future.

She smiled slightly. "About *you*, no. About *us together?* Babies stress *any* relationship. Are *we* ready for *that,* especially since both of us will be starting new jobs?"

"That's *another* thing," I nodded. "I don't *have* anything *firm* yet. Health insurance..."

"The county's plan has *immediate* maternity benefits.[1] With *luck,* I'll hear from them tomorrow." She started to walk again. "Let's go upstairs."

I opened the lobby door, passing a couple of curious onlookers moving out of the building. We went up the elevator in silence; even the 2nd Floor was quiet. As I opened my door, she asked, "will you bail on *us*, Curtis? When it comes down to it, *will you* stick around to help raise *another* guy's child?"

I blinked at her, standing by my door, her suit bag still over her shoulder. Her face was a mixture of fear and pleading, of certainty and determination.

"*I won't bail,*" I said bravely. "I *said* I'd stand in for that *rat bastard Steve* because you *were* my friend *before* and, I hope, will *remain* my friend *always,* no matter *what happens.* And I *promise* you; I will never do *anything* to harm you *or* our friendship."

"You're not *just* doing *this* to save Dad's job?"

"*No,*" I answered, "I *care deeply* for you, Meli, but I'd *rather* we had this conversation inside," as I ushered her into my room and closed the door. "Your father...I *could* damage him *without* walking away from you."

She looked curious. "How?"

---

1 For the '80s, that was innovative. Not *all* plans did.

"I've found some letters that might change how we view some important guys. Your dad knew about them before *I* found them. It's important stuff, to do with how history's *written*."

"Ah." She opened my closet door, eyeing its humble contents as she hung up her suit bag. "What do you plan to *wear* Wednesday?"

"My *jacket's* in there...."

"*That* ratty old thing?[1] No; tomorrow we go to Chapman's, get you a *decent* suit." She walked to my kitchenette.[2]

"My *budget*..."

"Mom's *credit card*." She popped a vitamin and washed it down with water. "So, these *letters? They* a big deal?"

"Yeah. Important to history."

"Whose?" She walked back to the closet and opened her suit bag, taking out a cotton nightgown and a pillow.

"*Ours*," I said, too loud as I took my pants off. I was mildly surprised by how readily *this*—getting ready for bed with someone else—had become so *casual*.[3] "It alters our view of some Founding Fathers...."

"How?" She tossed her pillow on the bed, then undressed before dropping her nightgown over her head. Finally, she dropped *her stuff deliberately* in *my* laundry basket. And she acted like it was routine.[4]

"We have a corpus of documents that *tells us* what they were like, but these letters *change* that picture." I *politely* pulled my *clean* stuff out of the basket while she *tried* to *act* nonchalant.[5]

"Maybe it's time to reevaluate the picture." She put her hair up in front of my bathroom mirror before she slid into bed. "If you have to make too many exceptions to your theory, maybe your *theory* needs revision."

"Maybe." *I* slid into bed.

We lay quietly, listening to the night sounds in The Cubes. She grabbed my hand. "*We're* OK?"

It took a moment, but I *finally* said, "uh-*huh*...."

"Do you *owe* anyone a name?"

"Owe...*oh*. No. You?"

"Mom. Rose *couldn't* follow Mom's family MR, HR, MH, and RH tradition for naming girls. Feel *that*?" She pressed my hand into her belly.

---

1 I wondered if *that* was why State never called back.

2 Single basin sink, one drawer under a counter with a hard-wired hot plate, small refrigerator, two shelves over the sink; all of 71 linear inches.

3 With Sherry, *this* stage was always somewhat frenzied and in the dark.

4 I only mention this because I had *yet* to put away my *clean* laundry—still *in* the basket.

5 She was *betrayed* by her bright giggle.

I tried; *oh, I tried*, but... "*Maybe.*"

"Could just be my dinner. At ten weeks, it's early for her to be moving around." She stroked my hand. "Will you *love us*, Curtis?"

"I'm going to *learn* to, Meli."

"Those letters...if it *wasn't* for my *dad*...."

"Yeah." *Should that matter? He is, after all, soon to be my father-in-law and, on Wednesday morning, will hold my future in his hands.* We kissed goodnight, lingering, tender. "I *will* love you, Meli."

That was my first full day as a father/husband-to-be.

Bear with me, folks. There's STILL that signpost up ahead....

And Tuesday Wouldn't Have Been So...

I*f you have to make too many exceptions to your theory...*

Somehow, *that* phrase stuck in my head like a commercial slogan.

"Where did you *get* that," I asked that morning.

"Desmond Morris, *Dismantling the Universe.* Why?" Melanie *wasn't* bashful after her shower, leaving the bathroom door open while toweling off.[1]

"Might be something I'd want to teach. Historians get stuck in framework ruts."

"You'll be a *good* teacher," she smiled. "I've *got* the book if you want the background. What time are you seeing Dad?"

"Two. Said he wants to *show* me something."

"Any idea *what?*"

"None." I finished dressing while she put her hair up and made herself up. For the *first* time, my bathroom was graced with hairpins and makeup.[2] "Chapman's after breakfast?"

"*Doctor* first. Initial appointment."

"*Ah...O...K,*" I declared as my insides turned to mush and my sphincter squeezed tight.

---

1 A practical necessity; my bathroom *wasn't* as wide as an adult's outspread arms.

2 Sherry *never* graced *my* place. I *should* have seen our demise earlier.

"*You* don't *have* to come, babe," she sighed, smelling my fear. She was good at that.

"*Want* to, Meli," I replied bravely. "I *need* to be a full partner."

"*No,* babe,' she said quietly, stepping out of the bathroom. "I *don't* want you in the delivery room. I'll find *another* birthing partner."

"Why?" *I thought the fashion was...?* By the Age of Reagan, everyone knew that men's traditional roles in marriage were being challenged.

"Because there are a thousand things that could go *wrong.*"

"I'll leave *that* to you and the doctor," I said, probably *sounding* more relieved than I felt.

She fell silent, palpably quiet. "Curtis: if I *lose* her, we can *just....*"

"*Stay together,*" I said quickly, holding onto my nerve for dear life. "No decent interval," I said, shaking my head, "*no* hint that *we* were a sham... because we're *not.*" I looked at her, her face as serious as a half-naked woman can get. "*You* and *me....*"

"Cross *that* bridge if we *have* to, babe." She walked over and put her hands on my shoulders. "*No* sham?"

"*No.*" I didn't *have* to think about it.

She smiled and kissed me sweetly. "Me *neither.* Let me get dressed."

***

"*Not* real busy," I mused, settling into an uncomfortable waiting room chair in the doctor's office.

"No." She grabbed my hand. "*You're* more nervous than I am."

"Never *been* to this kind of doctor before." I was the *only* guy in a small room full of women, half of them *expecting.*

She handed me a pamphlet: *Pregnancy for Men.* "You *might* learn something."

I noted headlines like *Diet and Nutrition for Expectant Fathers, Intimacy During Pregnancy, Morning Sickness—A Man's Guide,* and *The Birth—Men's Roles.* A memorable paragraph read:

> *Be prepared for YOUR world to be turned upside down. She's the same woman she was before the baby, and in many ways, she'll be the same after. You'll need to meet her same emotional, romantic, and financial needs as before her pregnancy, AND those changes that she and the baby dictate after, and they are legion.*

Something—*lots* of things—momentous were happening *to* me at *great* speed. I wondered *why am I not just running away and hiding in some academic hole somewhere until this feeling of need passed?*

But last night, with our hands on the baby, we talked about *names*...

"Melanie," the nurse called. I followed them to a small examination room.

"*Mrs.* Melanie, my *dear*," Dr. Emile Georgeson declared, shaking her hand. He was a genial, portly, graying man with enormous hands and a triple chin. "I *hadn't* known *you*...."

"*Miss*, still, Doctor," Melanie corrected gently. "Still my *father's* insurance. *This* is my fiancée, Curtis Durand."

"Ah, bad *timing*, I take it," he said as he shook my hand.

"*Very*," I added. "We're getting married soon."

"Be *careful* about the insurance. So, *let's* have a look, shall we?" The doctor felt around Melanie's abdomen for a few moments. "*March*, you think?"

"*April*," Melanie answered.

"*Perhaps*." He glanced at the form Melanie filled out. "My *dear*; my *good* man, sorry, but I *need* to *look* this time. *In* the *stirrups*, dear." I looked away as he flapped her gown up; Melanie caught my eye with a resigned glance. "*Excellent! Down*, now." He reached for what *looked* like an old-fashioned ear horn, pressing it against her abdomen. "*Healthy* heart rate for twelve weeks."

"*Twelve*," Melanie asked, looking *stunned*, "not *ten*?"

"*Ten* should be a *little* more rapid, but *your math* is the *best* tool, my dear. Want a *listen*, Dad?" He looked at me expectantly; Melanie *still* looked surprised.

My response?

I stuck my ear to the horn, heard a soft *thump-thump-thump*...

I felt like I'd landed on *Mars*.[1]

Yet knowing how way leads on to way,
I doubted if I should ever come back.

Would there ever be a turning point like this? A week ago? Hell, two MORNINGS ago, I couldn't have imagined doing this...wouldn't have imagined feeling this. And what was it? Fascination, first, followed by fear, followed by...same woman she was before.

How often HAD I thought of her? As often as I thought of a world beyond Crest? No; MUCH more often than that. I was deeply in *like* with Melanie— had been, I decided, for a *long* time—and I felt a sense of obligation to her and, now, to that little *thump-thump-thump*...

I smiled at Melanie, marveling at what I heard. She smiled back with a bit of a gleam in her eye—the first traces of love, I *hoped*. Yes. *Here is*

---

1 No *air*; less *gravity*; *cold* as a well-digger's behind and surrounded by a *completely* alien landscape. Like *that*.

joy and responsibility. "I've heard about ultrasound tests," Melanie said, still smiling.

"Only County Hospital *has* one around here," the doctor said. "If I *think* you need one, I'll send you there, but it's expensive and *not* covered by *all* insurance."

My student days would soon be over. I was *acting* as a *boyfriend/father.* I would soon be a real *husband* to a *wife/mother* who not long before had been no more than a *frequent* pleasant, sometimes *erotic*, memory.

Can I pull this off?

I'd damn well better.

***

"You seem...distracted," I said, putting my new clothes in the trunk of her car.

"A little," Melanie sighed, closing the trunk. "*Twelve* weeks would put the baby *out* of spring break range; *long before* our big blow-up."

"Ah. *Then...*"

"*Then* my math is *way* wrong," she sighed as we got in. "I didn't *think* I *could* be *that* far off...."

"I, ah, *don't....*"

"*Menstrual* math, Curtis. Guys don't get *that* part of health class.[1]

If she comes in *early* January and is full size, *our* jig is *up*, buddy."

"I, ah..."

"*What am I going to DO?*" And she started to cry.[2]

"*Nobody* will do *that* math but *you*, honey," I soothed as I slid over to her, throwing my arm around her. "If they *do, we'll* take *that* heat *when* it comes; *if* it comes." She turned to put her face against mine, whimpering quietly. I stroked her hair, wondering how guys were supposed to accommodate hair clips and bobby pins with *that* gesture. "We *said you* and *me*, babe."

She sobbed for a while longer as if she didn't hear me. I was going to repeat it until she choked... "*when* and *if*, babe; *when* and *if*."

There are instants in your life when, looking back, you *knew* the road you chose was the *right* one, even if you didn't expect to be *on* that road. Melanie kissed me with *that* kind of affection, *that* kind of passion for the first time. I kissed her back, returning the sentiment. It wasn't our *first* kiss; it *was* our first that said *you're mine.*

That was when *her* baby became *ours.*

---

1 In Cicero, we didn't *get* health class at all.

2 What is it about blubbering women that both attracts and frightens men?

***

"Come *in*, Curtis, come *in*," Bert called to me from the doorway. "Punctual as ever."

"Yessir," I said, believing it to be appropriate for a command appearance. "We finished the license application; waiting for the Wasserman."[1]

"Good; good. We'll get as much of *our* family here for the wedding as we *can* on such short notice. *Please*, have a seat." Sitting in his leather lounge chair, he pointed me to his leather sofa. This seating arrangement was typical of most of our one-on-one sessions for the past near-decade, when we discussed my progress and the direction my research was taking, *and* a few personal matters but not many.

I had *discussed* my dissertation *draft*—submitted in January—with each board member one-on-one in February and March. The *final* version was submitted in April. I would be *murdered* for the final draft tomorrow if such were the case, so there would *be* no discussion of *that*.[2]

So I wondered what *this* meeting was all about.

The large room was lined with bookshelves where there weren't windows, the few bare-wall exceptions filled by diplomas, framed testimonials, and awards. It was big enough to accommodate *five* of my offices, *plus* my efficiency. "I heard the baby's heartbeat," I said quietly, staring out a window.

Bert sat back, smiling slightly. "Yet you *survived*."

"Yeah. Did *you* ever...?"

"Junior, yes. It used to be that husbands didn't even *go* to those appointments. But times change. Do you expect to be in the delivery room?"

"Meli doesn't *want* me to. Too many complications, she says."

"Word of advice, Curtis: do as she *says*. Happy *wife*, happy *life*. Here's a copy of what I wrote for Southern New Mexico." He handed me a paper:

> *Mr. Durand has had several successful interviews, and his prospects are excellent. His marriage proposal has been accepted by a fine young woman who is carrying his child. I do not believe his interest lies in a position in New Mexico without insurance.*

"I *think* Dr. McCord will get the idea." *Yeah, I think so, wife and baby and all.* "Shall I *send* it?" I just nodded. "What's *your* job status, now that *she's* out of the picture?"

---

1 It hadn't *been* a "Wasserman test" since 1980, but the name stuck.
2 At Crest, dissertation *semesters* were six months long. Candidates taught, discussed…and waited. It's the longest half-year of our lives.

"I've spent half my *life*[1] preparing to be a Ph.D. in history," I sighed. "And now that it's in reach, there are *three* applicants for *every* job. Up until I started looking around last fall, I hadn't *realized* that the market was saturated...."

"Yes, that's *so*," Bert said. "That's why we emphasized publication, to make you stand out. But, you had to work *so* much *harder* than your peers on your *exquisite* writing you didn't have the *time*. So, have you *anything* in line?"

"State has *some* interest," I answered. "So has the University of Chicago, but *they haven't* got back to me after my last interviews."

"I *want* to venture on a Founding Fathers seminar series[2] and could use *someone* to teach *some* of them. Wouldn't *pay* much because it's an *adjunct* position, but...."

"I'd *take* it," I said with certainty. "*Anything* to generate income."

"Well, we'll *see*."

"I *applied* for the archivist job *here*...."

"Ah, yes; the dean[3] rolled *that* job into *this* one," he said. *A road vanishes in the wood.* "I wanted *you* to see *this* before it is published." He handed me an ad formatted for one of several higher education newspapers that dotted every campus everywhere. "Might *you* be interested in *this* position?"

Assistant Professor of American History

"Who's *leaving*," I asked.

"Keep *reading*," he admonished.

Also Assistant Curator of the Jenson Collection. A new tenure track position. Duties include teaching two sections per semester. The successful candidate will have had a successful dissertation defense at the time of appointment. The deadline for applications is June 30th, 1982. Apply to Jenson Endowment Trustees.

"Michael says he wants to *think* about it. Tom had a *magnificent* defense this morning, but he *has* a job, and so does Doris."[4]

---

1 I first heard about the Jenson Grant when I was *fourteen* and *knew* I had to start working to win it. I was to make the final defense of my dissertation a month after my 27th birthday.

2 Seminars are short courses taken for edification or a single credit. A seminar *series* might last a semester or even two.

3 Our deans were *managers* who took our input then did what was *necessary* and *feasible* to keep the departments running.

4 Michael Barre was a Revolutionary War scholar who specialized in the financial aspects of supplying Washington's army. Tom Mecklenburg knew Andrew Jackson's State Department like the back of his hand.

ANOTHER road comes in view.... "I *would*," I *tried* to be nonchalant. "The Trustees *still* want to post it," I asked, not looking away from the ad, believing it might disappear if I did.

"State law says they *have to*."

"When...*when* did this position...?" I scanned the ad again. Our last staff meeting for the academic year had been the week *before* last. *This* didn't come up....

"Last *week*," Bert said, "after my little *incident*."

"Incident," I repeated dully.

"An attack of angina," he nodded, "that my children know *nothing* of. The Trustees want someone to slide in *just in case*."

"How did *they* know...?"

"I was *meeting* with them when it came on."

"Ah. My *father* had one of those. He gets stress tests every other year; had to quit smoking. What are *your* doctors telling *you?*"

"That I need rest; that I need *more* tests, see if I need a bypass; *get* the bypass if I need it." He rapped the table beside him with his knuckles. "The successful candidate will be installed in July."

"*Three weeks*," I said, "but the ad won't *run* before...."

"*Two and a half weeks. They* know the ad will be late; *we* know that. Defend your dissertation *well* tomorrow, Mr. Durand," Dr. Hubbard said. "For *obvious* reasons, Melanie *won't* be joining you this evening, and of course, you *can't* come to *our* home this evening. But *tomorrow...*"

It would be perfect if Michael...but they asked him first. "Tomorrow, yessir. Can I *see* Meli this afternoon? Just a kiss for good luck? But, I'm *not* to...."

"If you could refrain from telling my daughter about my condition, I *would* be grateful. But, if you want, you can hint at this job. Might cheer her up."

Your condition won't even come up.

***

We sat in her living room, holding hands, watching the sun cross the bay windows. "Tomorrow's *it*," I whispered.

"Yes," she sighed. "*You* can do it."

"I *believe* so. What was *your* defense like?"

"I took an exam that had *nothing* to do with my program—just basic math and English competency. The next day I talked with my advisor about emergency sanitary water management—my thesis topic—for an hour, and *that* was *it*."

"Doesn't sound *that* bad."

"Nothing like *yours* will be." She rested her head on my shoulder.

"No." I leaned my head on hers...quiet until, "I'm *starting* to *love* you, Meli."

That just came out.

"I'm *falling* in *love* with *you*, Curtis."

That set my heart ablaze.

"Mom's in the study upstairs." She pecked my cheek. "*Come.*"

She led me to a small bedroom off the kitchen with an old-fashioned and *sagging* high bed. I was getting to *like* making love in the daytime.

After an hour, we opened the door to find *Helen* at the kitchen table, stirring tea. "*Hi,* kids," she smiled. "Tea?" She didn't seem either surprised or angry.[1]

"Ah..." I started, *apparently* red-faced.

"*Sure,* Mom," Melanie said, sitting down. She didn't seem at *all* abashed at her mother's presence.[2]

I sat next to Melanie, trying to get over my embarrassment. "I'll...ah...."

"Earl Gray in the pot, Curtis. *Help* yourself." I did, my hands shaking a little as I passed a cup to Melanie. "It's OK, Curtis," Helen said quietly. "There's *nothing* for you to be embarrassed about."

That made me blush even more. "I'm just...."

"Not used to living so close together," Helen said. "In thin-walled homes like ours, you learn to *listen without hearing.*"

"Well, *my* neighbors can be...." I started.

"They're *not* family, babe," Melanie said. "When you..."

"Sit down to tea with them *minutes* after," Helen added mildly, "it gives you a *different* perspective." She smiled. "*I* understand; *your* love is new. With a *baby* on the way, Melanie gets more *excited*; a *lot* of women do in their first trimester."

That WAS in the pamphlet. "I don't want to take advantage of your hospitality," I croaked, despite the tea.

"My daughter's already *pregnant*, my boy, so *that* horse has already left the barn," Helen chuckled. "*But*, you're making an honest woman of her." She glanced at Melanie. "*Meli* cares for you. I'm *learning* to."

"Mom," Melanie said quietly, "can we keep *this* quiet?"

Helen winked. "*I* wished *your father* had been here when I saw that door closed." I must have done something *amusing* with my face because Helen laughed. "*Yes,* children: *your parents think of sex* in the afternoon."

---

1 I was surprised that we didn't hear her in the kitchen but we *were* preoccupied.
2 Knowing that Meli had donned *no* undergarments under her short shift *may* have made me *more* embarrassed.

I glanced at the clock—closing on 4. "I should be going." *My soon-to-be mother-in-law got horny when she became aware of...whoa!*

I went to the back door; Melanie and Helen followed. "*Good* luck, babe," Melanie smiled with a smack. "*Love* you!"

"*Break* a leg, Curtis," Helen added...and offered a cheek.

This will be a story to tell the kids once they have kids of their own.

***

Every evening of Defense Week, the liberal arts and history colleges stocked a small lounge room in the Union with snacks, soft drinks, movie tapes, and games. There, candidates scheduled to defend their dissertations or theses could do anything *but* think about *that*, if possible. After all, if you didn't know the subject matter that you'd been working on for *years* by *then*, you'd *never* know it. Attendance wasn't mandatory; a *minder* sat by the door to maintain a relaxed decorum befitting the attendees and their impending ordeals. The quasi-chaperone allowed for necking and *some* petting but no brawls or orgies.[1]

On *my* Waiting Night, three guys and two gals—four dissertations and one thesis—watched a couple of old westerns while we ate and poked fun at their lack of historical accuracy. A tall English major named Patty Hanks put at least half the dialogue in the 20th Century. When the *second* movie was over, Brian Milano—going for his Master's in military history—started playing ping-pong with Jill Francis, the first *female* military historian I ever knew.[2]

That left Michael, Patty, and I alone to face Three Stooges movies... so we opted instead for three-handed chess. It's a free-for-all game that uses an old Duplicate Chess board[3] and *three* sets of pieces on three sides instead of *four*.[4]

Patty—white—moved first and cornered me—I was green on her left—on my queen's side. It was pretty standard, but it left her open to Michael's black attack in the center, which he controlled in five moves. Then, Patty jumped-ugly down *her* queen's side, flanking Michael's center position using the empty, extra rows down that side of the board. "Michael, Dr. Hubbard offered you a position," I asked.

---

1 Or naked Twister.

2 To be clear, we *all* knew each other *somewhat*.

3 A standard 8x8 board with three *extra* rows on each side *without* filling the 3x3 corners. An early version of 4-handed chess.

4 As far as I know, it was a local invention.

"Yeah," Michael said, concentrating on his game. "Did he talk to *you* about it?"

"He *did*." I tried to avoid the melee in the center while working on Patty's block. "Looks promising."

"*Yeah*." Michael took one of Patty's rooks. "I *heard* about you and Melanie."

"Me, too," Patty mused, slicing off one of Michael's knights and ignoring *my* feeble attacks. "Sounded *serious*."

"We're pregnant," I said casually, taking her other rook and opening a gap for Michael's knight/bishop attack. "She's due in January."

Brian and Jill stopped their game and stared. "Should we *congratulate* you *both* or just *her*," Jill asked as Michael lopped off Patty's last bishop.

"I said *we*, Jill." Patty zipped her queen out to take *Michael's* last bishop; I moved *my* queen through her open front line. "Check. We're getting married the weekend after next."

"Well, *congrats*, Curtis," Patty grinned, bussing my cheek.

I shook Michael's and Brian's hands, and Jill offered a peck. "If you *want* the honeymoon suite, I'll get Dad's hotel...." Jill lived in Granite Ledge.

"*We'll* buy you a *week*," Michael offered, "the four of us here."

"I'll *ask*," I said. "Thanks."

"Unfair distraction," Patty grumbled mildly. "Where *were* we?"

"*Here*," Michael offered, taking her queen. "*Cover*-check."[1]

"You *distracted* me," Patty mock-pouted.

"Nonsense," I smiled, sipping water. "Didn't say *anything* distracting before you were doomed. Michael, you want to continue?"

As Patty got up to take Brian's place at ping-pong, he pondered the board. Brian put a Three Stooges tape in the player. "Huh," Michael grunted. "Unsafe flanks; no bishops left; all these white obstacles. Methinks *not*. Let's proclaim a joint victory."

I glanced at the clock. "Not quite eleven. I need a walk."

"I'll *join* you."

We went out onto the quad and across to Fischer Undergraduate Library. Only the lights of the cleaning crew could be seen inside.

"Waiting for the firing squad," Michael sighed, hands in his pockets. "*That* bad?"

"*Can* be, I understand."

---

1 *That* was unique to *our* game, when a player *covers another* player's check—*or* creates a block—as if it were their own, making it check*mate*. Kings can be removed from the board in Duplicate or four-handed chess, eliminating that player.

"*Then* what?"

"I've got that *one* possible job *here*, one *maybe* at Penn State. Another *maybe* at Stanford. You?"

"Possibles at State and Chicago. *Maybe* here." We walked a little farther. "Meli *may* have a job *here*; supposed to hear from them today."

"Uh-huh," Michael said noncommittally. "Piece of advice from a married man of two whole years?"

"OK."

"Balance where you're going to *live* and *work* against where you want your *family* to *grow*. Do you want to be *that* close to big cities?"

"Good point. *Her* opportunities are greater in large urban areas. *Mine* certainly would be at a bigger school."

"Yes, but your *family*...."

"True." We strolled through the Alumni Arch, where each undergrad class had a bronze plaque with the names of the graduates. *I* was there, Class of '77. So was Albert Hubbard, Class of '42. "What do you *know* of the Truxton Section?"

"I've been *in* it." We kept walking. "Some *very* odd stuff in there." We kept walking. "I've never *used* any of it. You?"

"No, me neither." We didn't stop; we *didn't* look at the statue of Tiberias Jenson at the end of the Alumni Tunnel. "I somehow feel a *need* to make some *sense* of it."

"*Cataloging* and *validating* that stuff would take a generation," Michael declared. "It's a *third* of the whole collection." Of the 85,000 items in the Jenson Collection, the Truxton Section was 28,000 or so.

"*Why* do we *never* talk about it?"

We walked on; Michael set a faster pace. "We're talking about it *now*." We went on, now at a near jogging pace. "We never *use* it in our work., Even though there are aspects of our trade we just don't talk about, like Special Agent Number Seven[1] or Number Five,[2] frankly, *that* stuff is just...freakish. According to some stuff in there, *John Jay* tried to make a backchannel deal with Britain during the peace negotiations in Paris that would have made an *Englishman* a co-leader of the US. He *also* suggested, in *one* document in there, that Ben Franklin made *advances* to him."

---

1 As Alexander Hamilton was known to Britain's Secret Department when he was reporting on Washington's cabinet meetings. Yes, Hamilton *was* a spy for Britain after the Revolution.

2 Aaron Burr's *nom de guerre* to the French.

"Huh." I wasn't quite sure *what* to say to that. We knew Franklin, Jay, John Adams, and Jefferson were in Europe while the Constitution was being hammered out, but their *personal* relations...never went into it much. "Maybe all the *more* reason to...."

"Whoever would take *that* on would be risking not just their careers but their *sanity.*" Michael stopped. "*So* much of our history would *have* to be reassessed if *some* of those documents were authenticated."

"Dr. Hubbard knows of *some* materials in there."

"He's the curator; he *should* know *something* about them." He cleared his throat. "Do you *know* of anything there that *could* be important?"

Important in this sense meant history-*altering.* If, for example, Washington could be shown to have been in British pay throughout the Revolution, *that* might alter our history. If he could be shown as liking to lounge around in Martha's dresses, *that* would *not*. The latter revelation wouldn't *change* what Washington *did* any more than the Heming's claims changed what Jefferson *did*, only how *some* people *perceived* him.[1] "Yes; so does *he.*"

We knew about possible academic fraud by someone who could ruin us. This was dangerous territory for budding academics with integrity.

He sighed heavily. "There *might* be a career *option* for *you*...."

We *discussed* that option, ambling back to The Waiting Room. Jill and Brian had *taken each other's edges off*, judging by their *slightly* disordered clothes and mascara on Brian's face. Patty must have joined in, for she, too, looked like *she'd* enjoyed a love-mugging.[2]

After toasting each other's *hopeful* success on the morrow with Dixie cups of champagne as St. Barb's bells struck midnight, we went our separate ways.

Michael and I had discussed *another* road that diverged in a yellow wood, this one paved with brittle, old, yellowing paper and smelly parchment, perhaps to beckon yet *another* road.

---

1 The historical profession has *many* open secrets that it *doesn't* write into the textbooks. Like the Hemings allegations, an *impartial* judge would rule these more *prejudicial* than *probative* and unnecessary for the story of the past.
2 The Twister game was still on the shelf.

Wednesday Was My Date
With Destiny...

I was awakened by my telephone. "Hullo?"

"*Hi*, babe," Melanie said. "Just calling to wish you the *best* of luck."

I glanced at the clock: nearly 6. "Thanks, but luck has *very* little to do with it by now, honey. I forgot to ask if you heard from the county yesterday?"

"I *did*! I'm *in*! I can *start* in July."

"*Fab*, Meli." I waited a pace. "I'm not sure *I've* got...."

"*We'll* figure it out. *Love* you, babe."

"Love *you* too."

That was getting more *natural* with each repetition.

***

"Good *morning*, Mr. Durand," Dr. Hubbard nodded, shaking my hand as I entered The Long Room. "Professors Gilchrest and Zane, you *know*, of *course*."

"Certainly," I smiled, I *hoped* winningly, shaking *their* hands. "Professor; Professor." Amy Gilchrest was the Florian Mills Professor of American History, whose grasp of Madisonian America was legendary. Anthony Zane was *the* leading authority on the history of industrial development in early America with an impressive publication record.

"Be *seated*, please," Dr. Hubbard gestured behind me. "We can get started." The dark-paneled, poorly-lit Long Room was a foreboding place, so-called because it was five times longer than it was wide. It was tailor-made for an Inquisition movie set without the iron maiden.

The old and worn high-backed, carpet-padded armchair I was offered was reasonably comfortable. Since it was identical to a row of chairs along one wall, I wondered whether, before each interview, they changed chairs to save the next candidate from the discomfort of sitting in the nervous sweat—and possibly other bodily fluids—of its previous occupant.

"*Before* we get started, Dr. Hubbard," Professor Gilchrest said, "I'd like some *clarification* if *you* don't mind."

"*Certainly*," Dr. Hubbard smiled. My inquisitor's table was six feet in front of me, lit by three old-fashioned glass-shaded desk lamps.

"*Mr.* Durand," Dr. Gilchrest asked, eyebrows knitted, "you've been *seen* around campus in company with Dr. Hubbard's youngest daughter, Melanie. *What*, may I ask, *is* the *nature...?*"

"*We're* pregnant," I interrupted. "We applied for our marriage license yesterday. We plan on the ceremony Saturday after next."[1] Academia is rife with *perceptions* of bias, on facts *not* in evidence as (false) proof of prejudice.

"I *see*," Dr. Gilchrest said, nodding *slightly*. "Dr. *Hubbard*, I'd like *your*...."[2] The *perception* that a board member is predisposed one way or another *could* tank a final defense as readily and as fatally as a faulty footnote in the dissertation revealed during the final defense.

"My family only found out about Melanie's *condition* and *their plans* Sunday," Dr. Hubbard replied coolly. "We were *surprised* by this but not *displeased*." He looked at me. "My written submission on Mr. Durand's essay was sent to this body Wednesday last; *this matter* had *no* bearing on these proceedings. Mr. Durand has been *entirely* upfront about the matter, and it is *closed* as far as *this* board is concerned." He glared at his colleagues mildly.

"Very *well*, Dr. Hubbard," Dr. Gilchrest nodded. "We can pro*ceed*...."

"Congratulations, Mr. Durand; Dr. Hubbard," Professor Zane interrupted with a broad smile. Tony Zane had a *glittering* personality, rare in historians. His work was a *joy* to read, and his classes well-attended. That aside, he was a *serious* scholar and educator. For example, one of his classes on 20th Century Europe was conducted

---

1 I figured *full disclosure* would put the matter to rest quickly.
2 I figured *wrong*.

while he wore a gypsy costume and banged a tambourine for emphasis. *Everyone remembered* that over five million *non*-Jews—including Gypsies, Catholics, Anabaptists, communists, and homosexuals—were *also* murdered by the Nazis.[1]

"*Thank* you, sir," I sighed.

"*If* we can proc*eed*," Dr. Gilchrest said loudly. In contrast, Amy Gilchrest was a pedagogical throwback to the pre-TV era. Unlike Dr. Zane, Dr. Gilchrest did *not* think *her* methods *needed* to grab and hold her student's attention; they would simply retain the material because they were *told* to. "*I'd* like first to examine your approach to what you called the 'delicate dance with the dandies of France and England,' a *brilliant* phrase, by the way...."

This is how the final defense works at Crest. We all *knew* what I wrote; we all *knew* the sources. What the *board* wanted to know was how well I could *teach* the subject matter to a roomful of young adults. In that way, the final defense is like a small classroom, where one professor asks a question; the candidate answers; *another* professor asks *another*; answer and question and on and on. That said, the stakes were so high it's like I'd imagine juggling chainsaws would be: one slip and you *lose* something.

"*You* conclude that the distraction of Napoleon's wars was instrumental in America's success on the Barbary Coast?" Dr. Hubbard, with amusement on his thin face, seemed skeptical. This came perhaps five questions later.

"The Louisiana Purchase," I explained, "was a *bigger* distraction. That the Americans could come up with the credit *privately* blind-sided both France *and* England, not to mention the Barbary sultans." You don't get many opportunities to show your superiors anything *new*, but your final defense at Crest is one of them. Crest encouraged original thinking more than most schools, even challenging the work of their professors...respectfully, of course.

"Your explanation of the American handling of the French in Italy," Dr. Zane asked three questions later, "seems a *little* thin. Care to *expand* on it?"

"As much as I *can*, sir," I said bravely, venturing onto *that* thin ice. No dissertation is rock-solid, and *this* part of mine was pretty weak. "It was *Swedish* cash that the Americans could offer Naples and Sicily. It was handled by the *same* bankers who handled the Purchase...." Part of the

---

1 *Good* professors of history *can* teach practically *any* area to undergrads. The Tony Zane's of our profession make it *come alive* and easy to retain.

defense is so the profession can assess the candidate's ability to think on the fly. This often has more to do with the candidate's *future* than their *dissertation* did.

While fielding their questions, Michael's idea from the night before was still ringing in my head, and it was starting to make sense. *That road is academic; it fulfills a need; it is unique; it is a road I hadn't even thought of before. I am still defending...*

"I'm *interested* in your views of the *Moroccan* alliance, Mr. Durand," Dr. Gilchrest said after two more questions. "They *were* the first to recognize the United States diplomatically. Any insight on *that?*"

"Some," I said with trepidation. This *was* afield of my dissertation, but she *did ask.* "Morocco *was* invested in the slave trade, but *not* in the *European* slaves that Tripoli was dealing in." And I went from there, feeling my way, guided in part by the board's facial expressions. "So the Sultanate of Morocco, not wanting to be gobbled up by the Ottomans' uncontrollable castoffs to their east, sought an alliance with, I *believe* they thought, a new country with the determination to make a go of it."

"Uncontrollable castoffs," Dr. Zane chuckled, "*good* one."

Suddenly, everyone was staring at me, silent. These silent sentinels were the gatekeepers to a profession, *not* just the reviewers of your dissertation. The final defense is the *last* hurdle, the *last* gate to pass through before a candidate can be a part of the inner workings of the history profession....

I had no *idea* how long we'd been at it. *Awkward....*[1]

I think the Long Room was chosen for these ordeals because the path of the sun couldn't be seen through its high, small windows, precluding a candidate's distraction by the passage of time....

Now, I started to sweat. My new pants were getting soaked; my new jacket felt heavy; my new tie was strangling me....

Failed final defenses end with "*thank* you, Mr./Ms. So-and-so, for your submission, *but...*" followed by a *detailed* castigation for wasting their better's *time....*

I don't know if there was a prearranged *signal* or a *mind-message* or *what* before Dr. Hubbard *mildly* intoned, "*thank* you, Mr. Durand, for your submission...."

I held my breath....

"Dr. *Gilchrest*; anything *else?*"

---

1 Think of a final dissertation defense as a *really* long interview for a *profession* rather than a specific *job*, based on an *incredibly* dense and dull *book*-length resume with *scores* of footnotes and a bibliography *almost* as long as the text.

"Mr. Durand has done a *fine* job of scholarship," she announced. "He has *done* the Jenson Endowment *proud.*"

"Dr. *Zane?*" Dr. Hubbard glanced at him.

"As good a *final defense* as a *dissertation,* Mr. Durand. I'll be *proud* to see *your work* in *print.* Your *very* hard work has paid off."[1]

Dr. Hubbard regarded me with a blank face. "I *agree,*" he grinned before he stood up, shot out his hand, and declared, "*congratulations, Doctor* Durand." Then, Drs. Gilchrest and Zane came out from behind the table to do the same....

I had achieved the goal to which I had dedicated *nearly* half my life. I was a Doctor of American History.

Sadly, I was also privy to the *possibility* that a noted leader of my field—my mentor, advisor, and future father-in-law—*might* be perpetuating an academic fraud. And I was committing an *actual,* less harmful fraud by asserting that his youngest daughter's unborn child *was* biologically mine.

Even if, by then, biology *just didn't matter.*

***

"I *knew* you would do it," Melanie whispered into my ear. "I *knew* it." She had wanted to see me as soon as possible but didn't want to wait around Jenson Hall, so I gave her my key. I'd heard the St. Barb's bells chime eleven times on my walk across campus.

"Uh-huh," I grunted, hugging her gratefully. "As easy as falling off a log suspended in mid-air three stories up." I yanked off my tie and kicked my shoes into my closet.

"*That* tough?" She kicked *her* shoes next to mine.

"There's no way to *study* for something like that." In anticipation of my success, she'd chilled a bottle of wine. "Wine," I asked. "*You* shouldn't...." The bulge in her abdomen was only apparent *if* you *looked...* which I *did* when she stripped off one of those new sports bra/tops.

"She's *still* there, babe," she smiled. "We can *celebrate,* can't we? I won't drink more than *one small* glass of wine a day," she declared as she stepped out of her running shorts and underwear.

"We *can* and *shall,*" I declared, taking off my jacket and shirt.

She donned a sheer blue halter gown. "Which *reminds* me," she picked up the phone. "Mom? Yeah: *celebration,* not a wake."

"I *meant* to ask: morning sickness?" I sat to take my pants off.

------

1 Incredibly, many dissertations get published.

"I was nauseated when I smelled pineapple the other day, but *that's* been *it*. Mom couldn't *stand* the smell of eggs when she was carrying Junior." She poured wine into my two glasses. "You *sleep* last night?"

"*Maybe* three hours."

"I *ran* a good part of the night." She handed me a glass. "We'd better *nap*. Mom expects *us* by five."

"Ah." I *wondered* about her mom. The closest Helen and I had come to *personal* was Tuesday afternoon. "Your *mom*, Meli: has she *really* accepted me?"

"She *will*; at least she *knows you*. She didn't raise a stink when Rose said she was getting married at seventeen to a guy she *hadn't* brought home yet; not as much as *Dad* did, anyway." Melanie's second oldest sister was an electrician married to a contractor. "*Mom's* been dropping hints about marriage around *me* since I finished my BA. *I* think she just wants to be *alone* with *Dad* for the first time in thirty years." She downed her wine and stepped to the bed, yawning demonstrably. "*C'mon*, babe; drink up so we can get *some* rest."

We watched the shadows of the big maples outside my window, thinking of our future at hand, and dozing off after a few *intimate-barely-chaste* minutes.

***

"Congratulations, *Doctor* Curtis," Helen beamed as I came into her house. "Never a doubt in *my* mind."

"Thanks, ah, Helen," I mumbled, trying to get my head around *that* title. "*Still* trying to get used to the idea."

"It *gets* easier," Bert called from the kitchen. "What are you drinking? You're a *beer* man still?"

"Yessir," I answered, following Melanie into the kitchen. "Take mine *cold* if I can."

"Curtis," Melanie's brother, Albert Junior, nodded solemnly and offered his hand. "*Congratulations* on your engagement to my sister *and* your degree."

"Thanks," I smiled. "You're a senior at Granite Ledge next year," I asked, trying to reconcile this 6'4" 260 lb. teenager being the son of the relatively diminutive Bert Hubbard.

"Yeah," he released my hand mercifully. I had no illusions about what this guy could do with my arm if he chose. He cocked his head towards the back door. "Want to *ask* you about something."

O...K...

I followed him out to the small patio being set up for an intimate gathering of Melanie's family...and, now, *me*. I hadn't *met* Junior more than a few times, but...*where have I seen him before? It must have been around campus, somewhere.*[1]

That question would bug me for a while.

Melanie and Helen were hauling dishes and bowls out of the kitchen to the table on the patio, shooting us an occasional glance. "What can I *do* for...."

"Know anything about football?" Junior stopped at the edge of the concrete pad.

"The basics," I said, curious. "I *watch* games...." I *tried* to swig my beer casually.

"Yeah, *me* too. Know how I got to *be* a Junior All-American offensive linebacker? The guy on the list ahead of me put his foot wrong during his last game and destroyed his knee. *His* career's over, and *he* ain't 17 yet." He sounded *concerned*.

"Ah." *He's a thinker, not just a mover.* "So..."

"As much as I love the *sport*, the *game's* become too *iffy* for my tastes."

"I'd always thought that athletes have *confidence* in themselves...."

"So *much* confidence that the urinals get clogged with hypodermics, yeah." He shook his head. "And *that's* another part of the *problem*: keeping up with the chemicals. My question to *you* is: how do I tell the college scouts that I ain't interested in *playing for money*, which *is* what the scholarships are all about? How would *you* turn down a full ride to the best schools if you don't *want* to be *obliged* to risk a *concussion* or *worse* every Saturday afternoon? I wanna stay in the *sport*, but *not* the *game*."

I'd never been *in* his situation. I only *had* one goal—the Jenson— in high school.[2] Nor had I *ever* been solicited for career advice from anyone, though I *got* some last night that still rolled around in my head. *How to couch a rejection of largesse?* "How are your grades?"

"Honor roll: 3.75 average. My folks push me pretty hard."

"If *I* were *you*, I'd develop a plan that would make sense to the *scouts*, so they *know* you're *not* just blowing them off. From what you're *saying*, you *may* end up working for their *employers* one day."

He smiled a little. "If *you* were *me, Mom* would have cut my *nuts* off when Meli got pregnant, and *Dad* would have *fed* 'em to me. I *have* a plan, sort of. Ever hear of Bill James?"

---

1 Faculty and staff *families* could use the campus amenities, such as the pool, field house, and libraries, so it was *possible*.

2 Of *course*, I *applied* elsewhere *and* for other scholarships. That's called *playing it safe/common sense*.

"*Maybe.*"

"You *might* if you were into baseball stats," Junior smiled. "He's showing baseball something *interesting.*"

Baseball stats…those almanacs…yeah, OK. I knew enough about sports in *general* not to be *wholly* rejected by other guys, but *not* enough to talk intelligently about the infield-fly rule, football free-agency, or hockey blue-line rules. Nor did I know who was the only batter to hit four homers in a doubleheader,[1] or what team made the most turnovers in a single Super Bowl,[2] or even *what* a hat-trick is.[3] So, it wasn't a stretch for me to ask, "*how so?*"

"Everyone's doing baseball *wrong.* The stats are showing that the teams that generate the most *base-on-balls* win, *not* those with the best pitchers or home-run hitters or shortstops who can catch anything within three feet of 'em." He looked wistful. "I just wonder if we're not doing *football* wrong."

I sure as *hell* couldn't tell *him* anything about what football might be doing wrong other than players suffering too many concussions.[4] "*I couldn't say*, Junior…."

"Call me *Al*; I *can't* get the *rest* of my family to call me *anything* but 'Junior,' and I'm *starting* to *hate* it."

"*OK*, Al. It sounds like *you* need to get into mathematics and…um… sports *business* if *that's* a field; or try for *management.*"

"Sports business *and* sports management *are* majors," Junior/Al said with some conviction. "*State* has a sports *business management* program. There's an increasing number of people in team management who *didn't* play. Would math and *that* be a double major?"

"Got *me.* You might take your plan up with Coach Freeman." Adelle Freeman was the Crest Athletic Director.[5] She also taught swimming, lifesaving, first aid,[6] and physiology while she tried *hard* to attract enough interest for a *swim* team—she'd won bronze in the '72 Olympics.

"*There's* a thought," Al nodded, glancing at his sister. "*Thanks* for the advice. I *might* ask again."

---

1 Roger Maris, on July 25th, 1961.

2 Baltimore Colts, Super Bowl V, 1971.

3 Any three consecutive goals or successes, especially in hockey. Ask a historian a question, and you'll be *bored* by the answers.

4 *Anyone* could see *that* even before it became a *thing* decades later.

5 Crest fielded football, basketball, and baseball teams. *Good* years, the Quarry-men finished in the *middle* of the state non-conference league standings for any of them. *Most* years, they didn't do *that* well.

6 One-credit undergrad prerequisites. All Crest grads *had* to know how to swim.

"*Any*time, Al. You *know* where I am."

As I shook his hand, Melanie joined us, hooking an arm around each of us. "*Nice* chat?"

"Sure," Al pecked her cheek. "*Just* what I wanted to know."

"Tell me that *wasn't* for my benefit," I smiled as Al went for a soda.

"*No*," she grinned as we went back into the house. "He's been *trying* to figure out what he *wants* to do in college. The folks just say 'as your heart leads you,' like they *always* do." She handed me a basket of buns. "I told him *you* might have an un*biased* view. *He* took it from there. C'mon."

We made a trip between kitchen and patio before I had the *unbrilliant* thought that handing stuff out the kitchen window overlooking the patio *might* be faster. For a few brief moments, I was *the* party-planning wizard.[1]

Rose[2] and her husband Ed Fuller arrived soon after we finished setting up. Mary, Melanie's oldest sister, arrived at the same time. I felt it was my duty to say, "hi! Remember *me*?"

"*Yeah*," "Sure, Curtis," they answered in turn, glancing at each other.

"Well, I'm *glad* you...."

"What would you *expect*, man," Ed deadpanned. "Can't *not* meet the guy who...."

"Eddie, *don't*," Rose admonished. "I *told* him *not* to say 'knocked Melanie up.' It isn't *polite*."

"Ah," I stammered, not sure if it was a *joke* or...

Then Rose cracked into a wide grin. "*C'mere*, Curtis," she spread her arms. "If *Meli* loves you, that's *all* that matters." I got a *sisterly* hug from her—a little shorter than Melanie—and another from Mary—a little taller than Meli—who also pecked my chin. "I understand you got your Ph.D. today," Rose said. "*I'm* going for my master *electrician's* license, so I can own my *own* shop."

And chat I did with Rose and her husband. And with Mary the ad executive, her daughters, and her husband Ron Valencia—a cardiologist—who arrived just before we sat down to dinner. A pleasant, athletic friend of Al's, Barb Rizzo, joined us shortly after.[3]

The young kids—the oldest was eight—weren't sure *what* to do about me. Barb *did* know about Melanie's *condition* from the campus gossip. That she *also* knew the family was to be expected. All was just

---

1 Smart people often mistake practicality for genius.

2 *Madeline* Rose, but she *hated* her first name.

3 Her father, Dr. Max Rizzo, was a professor of geology.

small talk and banter while we ate, grinning over small coincidences and snippets of campus life, until....

"Well, folks: Ed and I have an announcement." Rose cleared her throat surreptitiously. "*We're* expecting."

"*Oh*," Helen grinned. "*When...?*"

"December. *We* found out this morning," Ed nodded as he shook my hand. "Didn't think we *could* after...."

"Let's *hope* for the *best*, Ed," Bert interjected as the others shared *their* best wishes. I glanced at Melanie opposite me at the table; she mouthed *later*.

"*I* do, *too*," Barb announced. The table got a *great deal* quieter; Al went *pale*. "I've been offered an *instructor's* job at cheer camp this summer!"

"*OH*," seemed to be in order. Al started breathing again as congratulations were offered for her *less* momentous (but still *important* to a high school senior) announcement.

Jenny, Barb's 12-year-old sister, started playing with Rose's girls out on the playground across the way. Watching the younger kids, I wondered if anyone but me noticed Al's initial reaction. I could only guess why he seemed *so* concerned. Either Barb was his *that-kind-of-*friend or his *other-kind-*of-friend. Part of me wanted Al to be the *latter*; seventeen was *too* young to have to step into *that* breach.

Hell, *twenty-seven* wasn't old enough to stand in for another guy, but *I* was doing it.

***

"So what's with Rose," I asked as we crawled into bed.

"She had an abruption with Casey. Spent two months in bed."

"Ah." I snapped the light off. "Think *they* can live with me?"

"You'd *know* if they *didn't* like you." She curled into my side. "*They* like you fine."

We listened to the *silence* of The Cubes. I was the only one left on the 5th Floor; the rest had either left or moved out for the summer.[1] The other floors were *nearly* empty. "Has Barb *been* Al's girlfriend?"

"*Friend-who-is-a-girl* since preschool. I don't *think* they've *been* intimate." She sighed. "I *don't know*."

"Maybe he's just worried about his friend."

Quiet. "*He'd* step up like *you* did. He's got *your* kind of courage."

"*That* what it is?"

---

1 The school offered a dorm room to grad students who stuck around.

"You don't think so?"

"If *love* is courage, my dear, then, yes, I suppose it *is*."

We listened some more. "Love *takes* courage," she whispered.

"Love takes *optimism*." *So does this.* "Meli, I've had an idea for if I *don't* get hired anywhere. It means we'd have to rely on *your* income for a while."

"Let's *hear* it."

"Now, I want to kick it around with some colleagues at the party tomorrow, so it isn't *fully* formed...."

"So, let's *hear* it already."

And I laid out the plan for my early career *sans* actual full-time employment *with* benefits. I figured it was my—our—best shot, even if it risked her father's career by exposing *possible* frauds.

But I *had* to support my new family, whatever the cost.

Thursday Would NOT Have Been The Same...

Somehow I'd expected to *feel* more intelligent when I woke up as a Ph.D. But no. I detected *no* magical addition to my gray-cell count; I had no brilliant flashes of insight. The *ah-HAH* phenomenon would have to wait. This was *just* another day.

I looked over at Melanie, drowsy and facing me on my lumpy bed. I wondered vaguely at how my life had changed *so* radically *so* fast, watching her and thinking of the new life she carried. *How could...?*

"Just worked *out* that way, babe," she mumbled, stretching as she rolled on her back.

"You *know* what I'm...."

"I *know* your quizzical look *and* what you were looking *at*." She reached for my hand, placing it on her belly. "We've known *each other* long enough."

"But *before...?*"

"I flashed on *you* when we *conceived* her."

No way! "Do you often think of *other guys* when you're making love?"

"*Just* you; *just* the once." She smiled, her enigmatic grin. "Like we were *fated*."

"How many *other* guys...?"

"*You* are the *third* I've *ever* made love with; the *second* I've actually *slept* with as in *woke-up-together*." She swung up to straddle me. "How about *you?*"

"You want *me* to talk about *other* women while we *oh!*" Her hands were deft, swift, and *oh* so...and...

"Uh-huh."

"*You're MY...*"

"*Oh, WOW!*" She gasped for breath.

"*That* was *you?*"

"*Oh,* yeah," she breathed, still across my hips, eyes closed, a beatific smile on her face. She had an *angelic glow* about her...and it *wasn't* sunlight through the window. She leaned forward slowly, languorously, shoving her legs behind her as she shifted on top of me—she was *oh*-so limber. Our lips met delicately, sweetly, before she rolled onto her side, breathing deeply. "Where *were* we before *you* interrupted my train of thought? Oh, yeah; *your* prior girls?"

I'd barely caught my breath. "As I *tried* to say, you're my third *serious* girlfriend...."

"Did the *other* two think you had a cute butt in those corduroy pants?"

"The *first* was before I *had* them. I only *had* the *one* pair, and I...."

"They'd have *thought* it if they had a pulse," she sighed. "*I* like Monica Helen for a girl's name."

"How about Maria Helen, for *my* grandmother and *your* mom." Somehow, having two *Connie's* in my life felt...weird.

"Hm...yeah! How about Curtis Junior for a boy?"

"*No* Juniors. How about *Charles Curtis?*"

"Mm...Charles *Albert?* Your dad and mine."

"Sure." We held hands lightly, watching the shadows of the trees in the window. "We getting up?"

"What *for?*"

"Food? Avoid bedsores?"

"Let's *rest* for a while, make love *once* more, *then* go get some breakfast."

"You really *that...?*"

"I *am,* babe. I just *think* of those *tight cords,* and I...am...*ready.*"

***

"*Morning,* Curtis," Bert grinned when I arrived at his office just after noon. "*You're* looking a little *ragged.*"

My father-in-law notices that his daughter has worn me out in the morning...great. "Morning, sir...Bert. All the *excitement...*"

"Of *course.* Got *this* this morning." Bert handed me a letter from the State University History Department, written to *him:*

*...we had a very successful final interview with Mr. Durand and think
he will make a fine instructor, but we're not confident that he is a
good fit for our department at this time. Perhaps after a few articles...*

"Jack Peck is an old friend," Bert said, "and he's letting *me* know...
well. He knows *nothing* of you and Melanie, though it wouldn't make
any difference." He looked *slightly* embarrassed, as though he'd just
admitted to pulling a fast one. "You *should* have gotten *your* letter from
him before *now*."

"I *see*," I sighed. "No, I haven't received mine." *A road disappears.* "It's
the *insurance*, Bert. Meli *needs* insurance. So I guess we're down to *hoping
Chicago* comes through. But I'm having second thoughts about *them*."
I tried not to look as bleak as I felt. "I didn't get a *good* feeling about
them." *There's your cue, Bert...*

"I *understand*, Curtis," Bert nodded sagely. He rapped his knuckles
on the side table. "Have a gander at *this*." He passed me a typewritten
sheet with wide margins. "Wrote it *twenty* years ago; never showed it
to *anyone*."

*The documents in toto present a very different picture of
Jefferson, Madison, Washington, and others, which radically
changes our impressions of them as private men. That said, with no
corroborating documents anywhere else, one has to wonder about
their authenticity...*

"You *don't* think those letters are authentic," I said, blinking. *Twenty
years ago...?*

"I don't *know* if the specific items we looked at *are* or *not*, but enough
forgers have made a living selling their wares to cast some *serious* doubt.
Read on."

*...If Jefferson thought his fellow Virginian, Washington, was a "lout"
and a "bumpkin," we <u>should</u> have some indication of these sentiments
elsewhere. Yet, only <u>these</u> documents of unclear provenance in the
Truxton section make that claim. This sparsity alone should give the
scholar considerable and serious pause.*

"We should perform the necessary tests on the documents, see if
they *might* be authentic," I said confidently. *What else are you showing
me, Bert?*

"Perhaps," Bert agreed, handing me another sheet. "*From the top*."

*Even with the tools available to us, document authentication nearly
two centuries on is nearly impossible to achieve with better than*

"perhaps yes," or "no" results—the latter only if the forgers make an error. Fake documents—even their possibility—should unsettle the academic world, but few scholars seem that concerned. Authentic paper and parchments can be had or made; old inks and hand-cut quills are not impossible to recreate. Ultimately, historians have to determine if the content of suspicious documents is authentic.

"Testing is *more* certain today," I said, sure of myself.

"Not *that* much more," Bert said. "Those items you showed me could just as easily be *1797* forgeries as they could be *1897* or *1957.*"

Part of me felt like Bert just showed me that his gold mine was full of painted rocks. "Are we still *adding* to the Jenson...?"

"Not *often*. I've overseen new acquisitions since I got *this* job in '66. But, *that* doesn't mean everything acquired *before* then is authentic. Let's explore the ramifications of testing. Say a lab concludes those two letters are forgeries. We write a paper denouncing them, and that's that. But, what if the tests are *inconclusive*, as they often are? We say the content, context, or provenance are *unclear*, and we declare them *probably* inauthentic. But *what if* the labs say that they *may not* be forgeries? Then what?"

"There's a *lot* to be said for just stating the *contents*. Our duty to history includes *accuracy* and *preservation*. History *depends* on documents." I repeated the mantra drilled into us since the beginning of our training. "No *documents*, no *history*."

"That's what we *teach*. But *documents alone* are a dubious way to tell the story of the past. When the historians broke with the archaeologists, it was because archaeology couldn't give us what we so desperately *needed: accurate dates* for their finds. We insisted that *that* was the only way to assure provenance and accuracy.

"Then, we started to realize that some of *these*," he gestured to his own pile of documents, "might *not* be what they *said* they were—more accurately, what *we* said *they* said they were. We started to see that the market for forgeries is *older* than the Republic. So we rely on archives.

"The provenance of *most* of history's documents that have been in the archives since their creation or soon thereafter is *unquestionably* straightforward. These *known*-authentic papers are our *only* guides for determining *any* authenticity of anything *else*. But what of the *bales* of *unofficial* letters between public and private persons that have been *acquired* since? Or the *copies* or the early *drafts* of official correspondence stuffed into drawers and forgotten until some furniture dealer finds them?[1] What about the angry missives hastily penned—but set aside until cooler heads could prevail—their contents never intended to be revealed, only to be discovered years, decades, even *centuries* later, and subsequently misconstrued, perhaps maliciously?[2]

"Letters are becoming *so* popular with scholars these days because the *archives, many* believe, have been fully mined. Those two you showed me, I suspect, are *not* unique in their apparent revelation. There may be others that similarly call into question history's view of other notables of the period. They *all* need to be studied thoroughly before we upend our view of Jefferson. *What if* Jefferson privately ridiculed and disliked Washington and felt the Constitution was a bad job? We've always taught that Jefferson was a staunch patriot who believed in the letter of the Constitution, even though we *know* that he *also* believed that a strong central government was a mistake."

"And his headstone says *nothing* about his being president."

"Exactly. Jefferson was *proud* to serve and did so willingly, but he was *more* proud of his contributions to our independence, religious freedom, and education. He left *specific* instructions that his tombstone should reflect those *alone.* He omitted his presidency as a major achievement, *perhaps* because he believed his presidency didn't *achieve* anything *like* the Declaration of Independence. History combines what we *know,* what we *think* we know, what we can *prove,* and what we *cannot.* There's a *great deal* of the last. Part of the *business* of our trade is filtering all we know through a lens called *utility*: is our surmise—our conclusion based on *all* of this—*useful* to the consumers?"

"You *said* that when we were planning our dissertations."

"*Yes*, and we should have given it *more* emphasis. We perpetuate many myths, but we *must* if *we* are to be regarded as *useful* largely because of our shared traditions. Washington was the father of our country, inspired leader of the army. In the primary grades, we overlook the fact that he *lost* more battles than he *won* and billed Congress for more in expenses than he *would* have drawn in the salary that he refused. Hamilton may have been a financial genius, but he was also a personally unlikable *knave* who believed in an imperial presidency. *We* just say he was our first Secretary of the Treasury who was killed in a duel and leave it at that."

---

1 Maybe *my* early drafts should find their way to an incinerator?

2 Pre-19th century writers didn't wad up their unsatisfactory work and throw it into the fire—the material was too dear. Parchments—animal skins—were scraped and reused. Some writing paper could be scraped, before mass production made it so thin as to make such reuse impractical.

And we never talk about his spying for the British. "When the legend becomes fact, print the legend," I sighed, quoting a line from a movie.

"And the story behind *that* film[1] and book[2] should be required *study* for *anyone* calling themselves *historians*. It's why we make seniors in the history program *watch* it or *read* it and *report* on what they learned. The story has lessons for us *all.* Sure, the lawyer/pilgrim went out and faced the gunman—and that alone *should* have been enough—but he would have *just* been *dead* if he'd faced him *alone.* If the man who *did* shoot that gunman had told everyone '*I did the deed,*' then that good lawyer would have remained obscure and would never have been able to serve his *country* as he did in the story."

"History is made by the *silent* as much as by those who make speeches," I declared. "A *skeptic's* view of history," I knitted my brows in thought. "If you have to keep making exceptions to your theory, maybe your theory is wrong."

Bert looked startled. "Why, yes; *that* makes sense. Where did *that* come from?"

"Melanie." I suddenly had a minor epiphany. "The Lesson of Homer."

"*That's* why we make you read the classics."

"*Yes.*" Homer's *Iliad* and *Odyssey,* their famous depictions of the Trojan War, had been dismissed for centuries as legends, as had other descriptions of that conflict. Homer and scores of other poets and chroniclers who, in the ensuing millennia, wrote about that prolonged bloodletting and spoke of the intervention of gods in battles and of a giant wooden horse. In the 19th century, when the *profession* of history[3] began to take shape, scholars dismissed the very *idea* of *that* war as pure myth. Then, an amateur German archaeologist dug up what *might* have been Troy right around where Homer *said* it had been, and the controversy started anew. *There* in the *dirt* was at least *some* substantiation. "Never think *any* legend to be *completely* false," I said finally.

"Indeed not," Bert agreed. "All legends have a core of truth. *Finding* that core is an integral part of the academic historian's job."[4] He gathered

---

1 *The Man Who Shot Liberty Valence,* John Ford, 1962.
2 *The Man Who Shot Liberty Valence,* Dorothy M. Johnson. New York, Ballantine Books, 1954.
3 Before the 1800s, there were generally two kinds of history: royal and ecclesiastical, because kings and popes had the money to *pay* for the research. With the rise of nation-states and widespread literacy, there was an acknowledged need for more than the simple praise-singing of the early historians' wealthy patrons.
4 A six-week *History Business* class every summer covered just *what* a history scholar's job *was.* All Crest doctoral students *had* to take it to complete.

his papers together again, shuffling them into a neat pile. "Let's you and I publish *this* paper together, Curtis."

This is what Michael and I talked about. "I..." I spoke *before* the ramifications of the offer registered. Bert was one of the most respected American history scholars anywhere; I was a freshly-minted Ph.D.[1] with nearly *nothing* in my name.[2] "Dr...Bert, I'm *flattered*...."

"Then it's settled," Bert declared. "Take *my* old essay with you, read it, mark it up, make notes, think on it. We'll talk *later.*"

This was an academic home run—hell, a *World Series in a single inning*—but I had *no job* to support a family while I indulged myself with *this* bit of speculation which could take *years* to see print. "I'll have to talk it over with Meli. An article or even a book next year *won't* pay *today's* bills."

"Certainly, *I* understand."

"Sir," I began as we stood up, "about my appearance..."

"My boy, you needn't explain," Bert interrupted. "When *Helen* was expecting, for *some* reason..."

"*Yessir,*" I sighed, *hoping* he wouldn't go *any* further.

"*Must* be a *hormone* thing. Give *her* and *the other* time, Curtis. At thirteen weeks, Helen became *disinterested* until after she delivered all *four* of our children."

I came away with fifty-odd typewritten sheets and a promise to write my first professional paper in concert with one of the leading scholars in my field...and...

Give The Other WHAT time?

***

"OK, you guys; you *know* what I'm up against," I started. "If I *don't* hear from Chicago, we're gonna be *here.*" We had gathered in the lobby of the Crestview Hotel and Convention Center, where the History Department's end-of-year salute/party to the matriculating grad students was regularly held. In theory, it was a dinner party for fifty invitees and their dates; usually, only about thirty showed up. "I'm suggesting I mine the Truxton Section, analyze the contents, and publish as an independent scholar." But, as I verbalized the plan, I again wondered, *give The Other WHAT time?*

---

1 In *fact,* my *degree* wouldn't be *conferred* for another couple of weeks.

2 I wrote a 2,000-word piece that was published in a magazine strictly for the money...and not *much* of *that.*

"What we talked about Tuesday night," Michael nodded. I'd met his wife before, a pretty woman with a gentle manner. She and the other non-scholars were kibitzing by the bar, *doubtless* tapping their feet, *waiting* for *us...patiently....*[1]

"Yeah. Only *now*," I placed the title page of Bert's draft article on the table between us. "*Now*, I have a collaborator." I briefly outlined the conversation that led to Bert's offer. "With *him* behind it, it *might* work."

"Huh," Tom shrugged. "*Anything* to do with Melanie?" We were surprised Tom came; he *had* a job at George Mason University that he had to report to by Monday. He'd brought his long-term girlfriend with the peculiar laugh and a trust fund.

"Maybe *yes*, maybe *no*. I think it has more to do with his *finally* wanting to deal with the Truxton."

"You're *probably* right, Curtis," Jill said, sipping a drink. "I've had my doubts about *that* stash since I started working in the Jenson." She'd brought a local guy who she'd grown up with.

"It's sketchy, all right," Brian agreed. "But is it *worth* risking a new career over?" Brian was enrolled in the University of Oklahoma's military history doctorate program and was leaving for Oklahoma City the next day. *He* came alone.

"Look at it *this* way," I said. "*Someone* needs to assess all that material. *Someone* needs to make sense of it. Just being able to *date* it..."

"Much of it is *completely* without provenance," Tom intoned. "I *have* to suggest the whole thing be torched to save space."

"*What* would we lose doing that," Jill asked, shrugging. "No one knows *anything* about *most* of that material. Out of *sight*, out of *mind*."

"*One* thing we'd lose," I said. "Same thing we'd *gain*: experience with *quite* possibly the *biggest* collection of *forged* historical documents known."

Everyone stopped and stared in sudden realization. "Holy *shit*, Curtis," Jill giggled. "You *might* be *right*."

"*Damn*," Tom shook his head slowly. "Didn't *think* of that."

"We always *assume* our archives are authentic," Michael smiled. "*This* one we *may* assume is *not*."

"We may be *half*-right, though," Brian said. "There may *be* authentic documents in there."

"They're in the Truxton because their *provenance* is *unclear*," I said, "*not* because we *know* they are *false*."

---

1 The social life of historians is often restricted to *other* historians. Few others can manage to stay *awake*.

"How many documents have been lost over the centuries," Michael asked. "How much have we lost simply to aging?"

"Or because it was *purposefully* destroyed," Tom agreed.

"*How many* lost documents, *how much* lost evidence has pointed to a past we have *not* written about; a road *not* taken," I asked.

Once again, my colleagues stared at me in surprise. "'Two roads diverged in a yellow wood,'" Jill said, shaking her head. "Does Frost's poem make *more* sense now?"

"It certainly fits this context," I replied.

"'And I took the one *less* traveled by,'" Michael quoted, "'and that has made all the difference.' Most readers assume that Frost describes a path of exploration, the road *less* traveled. Historians take the path *more* traveled because we need documents to back up our journey and be *relevant* to the users."[1]

"The one he *didn't* take is the one Frost was *talking* about," I said.

"That's what the *English* majors say," Michael agreed.

"You want to take *this* road, Curtis," Tom asked quietly.

"I may not have much *choice*," I answered. "Dr. Hubbard wants to back the work. With *his* prestige behind me, I just *might* make enough of a splash to get noticed...."

"As an *iconoclast*," Brian said. "As someone who *questions* the orthodoxy."

"If you have to make too many corrections to your picture of the past, maybe your picture needs repainting."

Brian grinned; Jill smiled; Michael stared; Tom looked stunned. "Do you *really* want to describe a history we know *nothing* of, my friend?" Tom, I'm reasonably sure, was quite sincere.

"Didn't *Moses* do that, Tom? Didn't *Homer*? How about Thucydides or Julius Caesar? How about, oh, I don't know, *Winston Churchill? They* wrote histories that we use as source documents now. Can we test *them* for authenticity? What's *their* provenance?"

"Churchill's been called into question," Jill said—and we knew it was so. But, he was right more often than not, even if he was a shameless self-promoter who took more credit than he *should* have.[2] Still, his chronologies were correct; his broad strokes of his own and the actions of others he knew of during two world wars were more accurate than not. That made his the *past taken*. I was potentially going to write about a past *not taken* that no one knew *anything* about.

---

1 Or, according to some, "history repeats itself; historians repeat each other."

2 So, indeed, are most chroniclers of the past. That makes memoirs and autobiographies—and yes, *letters*—problematic as sources.

Like no one *really* knew that Meli and I...except, of course, the two of *us*.

"Keep us informed of *that* past, Curtis," Tom finally smiled as he shook my hand. "*Our* consensus is that it's worth pursuing."

"*I'll* buy the book," Jill said as she pecked my cheek.

"I will, too," Michael agreed, "but I *won't* kiss *you* for *money*."

"Good luck, Curtis," Brian said, extending his hand. "You *may* need it."

We were toasted to great applause before we sat down to eat. First, one of the adjuncts gave a long-winded, *semi*-sober toast to our future success. Next, Tony Zane gave a tiny concert on the zither, which he'd just started to learn. Finally, the entire party raised a glass, bottle, can, or cup to Melanie and the baby.

All evening, the assistant professors avoided me. They weren't privy to my *immediate* future, so I had to wonder...*why?*

Friday Would Have Been Completely Different...

We had breakfast quietly that morning, knowing we had to go to city hall and get our license. It was that more-or-less irrevocable step that stuck in our heads, I think, because not just the baby but our marriage would make everything different. "The insurance," I said.

"I *know*," she said, forking another piece of sausage. "The county uses the *state employees'* health insurance program...." She set her fork down. "I'll take *it*."

"Your father *might* have a job for me here," I blurted. "Michael hasn't turned it *down* yet; *he* was offered first."

She blinked, surprised. "Really?"

"Yeah. But, there's U of C, *maybe*...or even an *adjunct* here."

"Adjunct for *what*," she asked.

"A seminar series," I said. "Then, maybe, whatever specialized programs we have, I guess. It doesn't *matter* much, really."

"What *can* you teach?"

"Just about anything. The Crest syllabus isn't as restricted as some schools." The Crest undergrad syllabus was the same for all students for the first two years of undergrad work, specializing only in the last four semesters. Same for the MA and Ph.D. programs: *mostly* general, *partly* specialized. Crest provides a background in *all* areas of history, however narrow a student's field of interest might be.

"Huh," she shrugged. "When *is* your family due in?"

"Mom and Dad land at Holman Field[1] this afternoon at 3:15. *We* need to get to city hall."

And our uncertainty continued.

***

"Yes, well," Bert said sagely. "I *spoke* with Chicago yesterday. I'm *afraid....*" After surveying what the school was doing to fix the plaster in the bigger, vacant upstairs bedroom that shared a bathroom with Al/Junior, we met in the Hubbard's kitchen. The work would be done by the middle of the following week....

"Yeah," I sighed. *Three down, no more to go.* "*Now,* what do I do? *Hope* I can land *something somewhere next* year?" Generally, interviews were conducted in September for the *following* academic year. Vacancies advertised in June were rare and were usually for *non*-tenured positions unless someone died. Those professional dead-ends are better than waiting tables or finish carpentry, even if the latter *paid* better. My state teaching credential *might* find something. But, public schools look at Ph.Ds. and think *over-qualified.* Similarly, private schools consider Ph.Ds. much the same way, thinking they'll bolt at the first opportunity. And as often as not, *both* prove correct.

"*That's* an option," Bert said benignly. He offered me a beer; I accepted, though I didn't *feel* like it was a celebration. "Don't *panic* yet."

Why...not?

***

"Mom, Dad, *this* is Melanie Hubbard." That evening, as I introduced Meli to my parents in the hotel bar, my sense of trepidation was greater than that moment nine years before—almost to the *day*—as I opened the long-awaited letter from the Jenson Foundation that read, *the Regents are pleased to offer you...Acceptance or...?*

I doubt that many young men ever *plan* how they'll introduce their family and future wife to each other.

"Mrs. and Mr. Durand," Melanie smiled winningly, "so pleased to meet you at last. Curtis has *told* me *so much* about you." On the other

---

1 Holman Field/Granite Ledge Regional Airport was named for Simon Holman, a native of Granite Ledge killed in action over Germany in 1944, whose bravery was cited in his posthumously awarded Medal of Honor, the only Granite Ledge resident so honored.

hand, I sometimes think that young women just *know* that *both* their families will act as if they've *always* known each other.

"He didn't say *anything* about *you* until *Monday*, Melanie," Dad said in his winningly-direct-blunt way. You don't make captain in the Cicero Police by being diplomatic. "But *here* we all *are*...."

"*Hello*, my dear," Mom interjected, taking Melanie by the elbow. "Just call me *Connie*; we'll get along *famously*. We have *so much* to talk about. I brought *all* my albums of Curtis growing up; I'm *sure* you'll enjoy them. Tell me about what *you're planning* for next Saturday. Do you have a *dress*?" I think Mom had been waiting for this moment her entire life.[1]

"*Dad*," I *tried* to continue, "*this* is Dr. Albert Hubbard, my...."

"*Glad* to meet you, Captain Durand," Bert smiled, thrusting out his hand. "Your son is a *brilliant* scholar and a *fine* young man."

"Just *Charlie*, Dr. Durand. I've *always* known he...."

"Call me *Bert*, Charlie. Did you have a *pleasant* flight?"

"Was *fine*. At least the *weather*...."

"*Has* been clear, *hasn't* it? I'm *Helen*, Charlie," Helen smiled before taking off after Mom and Melanie. Soon, they were involved in whichever aspect of *our* wedding *they* were talking about.[2]

After twenty minutes or so milling around, Mom gave me her mother's ring, whereupon *I* had a duty to perform. "Melanie Holly Hubbard," I said, down on one knee in front of her, holding out the ring, "*will* you consent to marry me?"

Everything in the bar went so *quiet...just* like in the movies....

She laughed and held out her hand; the ring only fit on her little finger. "Of *course*, Curtis. Now get up and kiss me; you're blocking *traffic*."

There followed a bar-wide outburst of laughter, a *great deal* of applause, hugs, kisses, handshakes, and congratulations from our family *and* people we didn't know...*and* a round on the bartender.

That's what happens when you put a ring on a girl's finger in a public place: *strangers* buy you drinks.

As the evening went on, I was amazed at how readily my parents simply accepted my new situation, one they'd only just heard of that Monday. "Melanie," Mom told her after dinner, "I have my *mother's* veil that I've cleaned up and repaired. Curtis's *sister* used it. If you'd *like* to see it...."

---

1 I've come to suspect that *all* sons' mothers are the same way.

2 The groom's role in wedding planning consists of approving the bride's choices and paying for the license. It was early training for "yes, dear," which will be the *only* thing he *ever* needs to say after "I do."

"Connie, I'll be *proud* to *wear* it," Meli answered. Meli was right: she *had* won them over easily, though I *don't* think Mom was *that* hard a sell.

"You can *fix* lace, Connie," Helen asked. "*Oh*, I always *wanted that* kind of skill. You'll *have* to show me...."

"Did your bit in the *Navy*, Charlie," Bert said, nodding at Dad's forearm tattoo.

"Yeah. Built airfields in the Marianas."

"Yeah? I was *based* on Saipan."

"I *built* Isley Field."

"I *launched* from there in April '45 on my last mission."

"Nine months after I *landed*."

When Melanie and I retreated not long after that, Mom and Dad were in *serious* wedding-planning territory with Helen and Bert. The ladies discussed flowers and entrees; the gentlemen discussed the financial and logistical arrangements.[1]

"So," I sighed, snuggling with Melanie in our room, "I believe our parents hit it off."

"Yeah. Mom has a *closet* full of projects she doesn't know *how* to finish."

"*Mom* can show her how. Not much she *can't* do with her hands and some material. Never *knew* that about Dad."

"Me neither. He just said his last mission took over a year to complete. Our getting together brings out the secrets of our parents."

"Less *secrets* than just stuff they don't *talk* about. I *knew* about Dad's tattoo, but he always just said, 'got it during the war.' I never pressed it."

She reached for me under the sheets. "I *love* you."

"I love *you*, babe." We made love in a *comfortable* bed for the first time. It was...luxurious.

---

1 The *bride's* role may also be limited, especially if the parents are paying for the affair. She may *want* Dom Perignon, caviar and toast points, but may have to *settle* for Mogen David, egg salad and Ritz crackers.

And Saturday Would <u>Not</u> Have Taken Me To The Past Not Taken.

'The 1973 Jenson Scholar, Curtis...Harrison...Durand, *Philosophiae Doctor, America Historia, Diploma Magna Cum Laude, Phi Alpha Theta.*[1]

The Chancellor's bland Latin description of my honors—I was *second* in my class behind Tom—aroused *great* applause in my little cheering section. My sister Karen and her husband had arrived during the night; Melanie and Helen joined them and my parents in their applause. Bert smiled broadly when he handed me my diploma[2] on the stage and shook my hand.

There were 39 graduates present—most, including Doris, opted *not* to stick around for the cap-and-gown. There were *five* of us in history; *twelve* in English; *five* in music; and *seventeen* Masters of Quarry Science.

As we filed out to the strains of "Pomp and Circumstance," I marched next to Gerry DiMona, a new Doctor of Music Education who I *sort of* knew. "*Last* dance," he said. "Hear *you're* getting married."

"Yeah," I said, "this time next week."

"Well, good luck," he sighed. "Maybe *I* can reconnect with *my* girlfriend."

"She *here?*"

---

1 Translation: Doctor of philosophy in American history with *highest* honors and an honors fraternity for history majors. This impresses *maître D's* not one *whit*.

2 It was a lovely folder containing a blank piece of paper. My *actual* diploma would come after all the paperwork was completed.

"No; Madison, Wisconsin, where I'm from. I talked to her last night, says she's looking forward to my being back." He shook his head; his tassel did an odd bob. "*Almost* sounds like she wants me there to dump me in person."

"Give her a *little* credit," I said as we reached the end of the procession. "She *could* have dumped you before."

I don't know that he heard me, stopping by who I *guessed* were his parents and falling out of the column. *Eh, who am I to give relationship advice? It was probably bad advice, anyway.*

Wilson-Schuman Athletic Fields, where commencement was held when good weather was predicted, was crowded with far more spectators than graduates. I got handshakes and hugs from my parents, sister, and brother-in-law. A surprise embrace from Helen followed Melanie's hug. We started to make our way to the reception in the Quad, but I needed to drop my regalia somewhere. "Meli, can I deposit this *getup* at your place?"

"*I'll* take you," Helen offered. As we strolled up the sidewalk to their house, I got a distinct impression that Helen wanted to *say* something. "Curtis, I know this week has been a *lot* to take in, but Bert and I are grateful for what you're doing for Meli."

"Well, Helen, I'm just *happy* that...."

"That's all we *ask* for, Curtis: that she is *happy*."

Once in the house, I stepped out of my gown and hung it on an offered hangar along with my master's hood, Phi Alpha Theta cord, and sash. "There's a service in town that takes care of these things," Helen said as she carefully placed my velvet tam on a closet shelf. "*That's* where we keep ours. But there's *time* for that."[1]

She closed the closet and, *not* turning around, said, "Curtis, I'll say this once and *only* once: Bert can ruin you professionally but will do so only if *I want* him to." She turned slowly. "He thinks a great deal of you, boy. Don't screw this up and *make* me...."

"I'll endeavor *not* to Helen," I interrupted. "I'll do *everything* in my power to...."

"You have done a great deal *more* in your power than I think any mere friend would *ever* do, my *dear* boy," she smiled, her voice even.

She knows. "I'm doing what a true friend is *supposed* to do, Helen."

"After meeting your family, yes, I can *see* that." Then, surprisingly, she embraced me again. "You'll do *fine*, dear. Let's join the reception."

---

1 BA and MA cap-and-gown are *cheap,* disposable, and provided by the school. The doctoral equivalents are *not.*

***

"Just a *suggested* title...." Before our late supper at the Hubbard home, Bert asked me to join him in his den upstairs. The freshly-typed sheet he handed me said:

The Past Not Taken: An Exploration Into the Nature of Selected Archival Materials in the Jenson Collection at Crest University

I was *stunned* by the byline:

Curtis H. Durand, Jenson Endowment Assistant Professor of History, Crest University; Albert D. Hubbard, Jenson Endowment Professor of History, Crest University.

"Michael *got* a better offer," Bert said breezily. "I have a friend at Stanford who needs *him* more than *we* do."

"Ah." After thirty years in the profession, Bert Hubbard could probably call in more favors than I had socks. *My name first makes me the principal researcher...more credit than Bert.* "Jenson Endowment Assistant Professor" *makes that position immune to school budgets. Ho-boy.* "I need to ask if the health insurance...?"[1]

"Covers Melanie *and* the baby from the day you sign your contract. You can get housing in Lambert." Lambert Estates was a townhouse complex with *not*-bad semi-furnished places that *started* at about four *times* the square footage of my place in The Cubes. They also had a waiting list; some applicants waited *years* in more expensive or less comfortable accommodations in the area.

"*Another* favor," I thought out loud, instantly regretting it.

"Of a *sort*," he said. "*Expecting* applicants jump to the head of the line." *This. Is. The. Road.* "Very *well*, sir."

Bert shot out his hand. "Welcome aboard, *Professor* Durand. Your contract will be ready in a week or so."

That startled me. I went from grad student with a few, uncertain or unsavory job prospects and no girlfriend, to having a fiancée with a baby on the way, then to freshly-minted Ph.D., and finally to assistant professor and assistant curator of the Jenson Collection...all within *precisely* seven days.

I was frozen in time and space. I *felt* like I was in the same limbo-zombie-land as when I heard the baby's heartbeat....

---

1 Crest University health insurance was *employer-paid*.

I could hear my *own* heart in my head....
"*Curtis*," Helen called upstairs, "come *down* here *now!*"
That was *not* a call to supper.

***

It hadn't occurred to me how much *work* it would *be* to be an expecting father, even *after* reading that pamphlet.

I will *never* forget Melanie's brave smile, squeezing my hand as the obstetrics resident spoke *ever*-so-gently about what happened, about why Helen yelled upstairs. "We'll keep you overnight *just* to be safe."

Dr. Georgeson came a little later, looked at the charts, spoke to her like the old friend he was. He left; she began to cry; I held her on her bed, cannula rubbing my cheek. After a while, she relaxed as the sedative took hold.

I never *quite* got over how *long* that walk felt, leaving Melanie's room, shuffling down the corridors to the lobby....

It seemed a *lot* longer than it was.

"OK," I began when I saw all those expectant faces. "Meli's *fine*; resting."

"The *baby's*...." Helen began.

"*Fine*," I nodded. "She had a *panic* attack when she saw that much blood and had those cramps. *Just spotting*, the doctors said. Sometimes babies hit bladders, can cause cramps."

"*I* spotted some," Rose said. "Right around twelve or fourteen weeks. It's pretty common, Dr. G. said. Didn't *have* cramps like *that*, though."

"*I* had some spotting *earlier*," Karen said. "*Both* kids, but I'm an athlete, so they told *me*...."

"She's not *that* far along, though," Bert said.

"She's..." I stopped, not sure *which* truth to say...*REAL truth* put me out of the running for paternity. *OUR truth* would make the baby *early* when it comes...only it *won't* be *early*..."...*fine*. The doctors don't seem concerned, so *we* shouldn't be. So you guys go on home. I'll be *here* tonight; she'll be released tomorrow if nothing *else* happens."

When the legend becomes fact, print the legend.

***

And that ended *the* most *extra*-ordinary week of my life.

As I stretched out in the big chair in Meli's room that night, I tried to reflect on how the course of my life changed *entirely* in just seven days.

What if I *hadn't* vegged out in my room Saturday, *requiring* that I grade Sunday?

And the game...and Melanie just *happened* to be there. What were *her* roads if I *hadn't* been there? Would she have sought me out, to hear her imagined, *hoped*-for dialogue with me spoken aloud? Perhaps. Likely.

But will this contemplation offer any insight on how to go on with our lives? Nope. Coulda, shoulda, woulda *ain't* buying the groceries.

But....

Bert was another matter, entirely. What if I *hadn't* spoken to him about those letters? I might have published and either made a name for myself or ruined *my* reputation with possible forgeries. Or if they *are* authentic—and we *still* don't know—our images of the Founding Fathers would have suffered from it to no useful purpose, and Bert's reputation *could* have been tarnished.

> *I shall be telling this with a sigh*
> *Somewhere ages and ages hence:*
> *Two roads diverged in a wood, and I—*
> *I took the one less traveled by...*
> *And that has made all the difference.*

So many pasts *not* taken, *not* talked about.

The past not taken—by *choice*—shaped the paths of our future, giving form to our lives. It's who and what we *were* that made those choices. It has been ever thus and, ultimately, will define our story.

Our daughter, Maria Helen Durand, was born on January 10th, 1983, seven pounds five ounces.

The first of four articles that launched my career—the first published in the March 1983 issue of *The Historian*—spoke of those spurious documents in the Truxton Section as just that: spurious documents that could be so *many* different things, pointing in so *many* different directions. We didn't say they *were* authentic; we didn't say they *weren't* either. We left that to other scholars to discover, to judge the contents on their merits.

We also speculated about documents found elsewhere in other collections...*their* provenance wasn't always certain, either. The popular response stimulated *The Historian* to offer me a feature on archival science. I still produce two articles a year for them.

Our book, *On Dubious Sources*, was published in 1985 and was a modest success. I signed copies for Jill and Michael—and a few score others—at a convention that year.

Perhaps future scientists could develop tests that *could* prove the authenticity of all documents of questionable provenance.

But *until* then, they constitute still *more* Pasts Not Taken.

DAUGHTER BY CHOICE

Saturday Morning, She Knocked On Our Door

T here it was *again*, an *instant* when my life pivoted on choosing *this* path over that, one course of action over the one I foresaw only *moments* before.

Two roads diverged in a yellow wood...

I was at a State University symposium concerning increasing the number of women and minorities entering specific fields. It was a waste of *my* time, but *I* drew the short straw.[1] I saw the light on my motel room phone, where I'd stopped at about four that afternoon. So, *innocently*, I listened to *that* message Melanie left: "Curtis: there's a young woman here, Connie Emmerich...."

Connie? Mom's name. Emmerich? Joan Emmerich had been my girl-next-door in Cicero. Her father—who she'd never met—was serving a life plus ninety-nine-year sentence for his role in a bank robbery during which multiple murders were committed. When Joan's mom was struck with cancer in '63, the state of Illinois put her into foster care. But she *aged too fast*[2] in her first foster home. We met when she got to her *second* foster family in '65.

---

1 The school sent me to join several of our *educrats*. *I* think it was to warn me off going into administration.
2 She *matured* before the other kids in the home. Some thought *that* made for family instability.

But the message continued: "She knocked on the door late this morning and asked for *you*. She *says* she's *Joan's* daughter. She...." But of *course*, the system cut the rest off.

So I called home. "Yes, that's *right*," Melanie said, adding, "she *says* Joan passed away last week, babe. Sorry."[1]

"*Oh*," I said, *suddenly* feeling a *profound* agony. I hadn't *thought* of Joan in ages, *but*.... "Is this girl there *now*?"

"Hold on. *Connie: here* he is."

"Hello?" The voice was young but strangely familiar.

"*This* is Curtis Durand. *What* can I...?"

"*Mama* had a message so you'd know I *was* the real deal."

"OK...."

"No matter *what* you do, you *can* be both *right* and *wrong*."

Ho-boy. That *was* our phrase, Joan's and mine. She was the first girl I knew who shared my passion for history...and the first who had any desire for *me*. In the summer of '69, I was *all about* becoming a Jenson Scholar *and* about Joan and *that* stuff. We came up with '*no matter what you do*' when analyzing historical mistakes, not knowing we'd stumbled onto ethical relativism and Kantian deontology.[2] The day after Thanksgiving in '69, Joan abruptly disappeared...no explanations, no nothing. Her foster family decamped *just* as suddenly the day after Christmas.

"Can I talk to Melanie, please? Privately?" *Joan's been out of my life since '69, so why am I feeling SO...?*

"Hey."

"Hey. She's *Joan's* daughter, all right. How *old* is she?"

"She *says* seventeen. She's got *stuff* to *show* you."

Born in '70? HO-boy...Joan and I didn't REALLY connect, not COMPLETELY, though I was REALLY close THAT time...HO-boy! That summer was Dad's first year as a sergeant/watch commander in the Cicero Police, and Mom had her hands full between my sisters and me *and* a crime wave in Chicago. "She *could* be *mine*, honey."[3]

She snickered. "At *fourteen* you were...?"

"*Playing around; kid's* stuff. *Not* quite full..." *But, some SAY it COULD happen THAT way.*

"I *get* it."

"Does she have a place to stay?"

---

1 Meli knew *about* Joan.

2 The study of the nature of duty and obligation. I'm an academic; it's how we *think*.

3 OK, I was a *little* wild that summer.

"I *kinda* doubt it. She's toting a full duffel bag, *and* a backpack, *and* a purse. She seems lost and *very* tired. She ate a *big* lunch, was just napping. She *says* she's been on the road for four days. *When* are you coming back?"

"My *last* session is tomorrow morning, but I can *skip* the closing. Maybe mid-afternoon?"

"OK. *Drive* safe. She can use Maria's extra bed."

"OK, honey." I did a lightning-fast assessment of the remaining itinerary. *Restaurant food with educrats, exchange answerless banalities like 'how can we encourage women to become engineers' and 'why don't more Hispanics want to get into the liberal arts' and 'what happened to the Yankees this season?' Listen to MORE educrats droning about opportunities for disadvantaged communities, or...ugh!* "*Changed* my mind: I'll be *home* tonight."

She COULD be my REAL daughter...

***

"Hi," I smiled, I *hoped* genially when I shook Connie's hand about fifty minutes later.[1] "*Pleased* to meet you."

"*Hi*, Mr., um, *Doctor* Durand." Connie was a fair-skinned, hazel-eyed girl, an inch taller than Meli but half an inch shorter than me, with fair hair that reminded me of Joan's silky blonde locks. "Mama told me *all* about *you*."

"She *did?* Really?"

"Yeah. She clipped *every* article[2] she could *find* about you, *and* everything you published. I've got your *book and* all your articles. That's how she knew where I could *find* you."

"Huh. Am *I your...?*"

"No, you're *not,*" she said flatly, pulling an envelope with my name on it out of her purse. "*This* will explain." I sat on the sofa and read:

June 13th, '87

Curtis;

I'm at the end of my strength, my love. Connie's <u>not</u> yours, but she's named <u>for</u> your mother. Your mom gave me good advice that I acted on. Tell her 'thanks' for me.

---

1 I *may* have broken some laws during the nominal *one-hour* drive back to our townhouse.

2 From the time I won the Jenson, Mom submitted my major life events to all the papers in Chicagoland. Because of *Dad's* position, *most* of them were published. It's Chicagoland; it's how it's *done.*

*I'm dying of the same cancer as my mom. Connie's grandfather—
my father—died in prison years ago, so don't worry about him. <u>Don't</u>
think about Connie's father, either.*

*She <u>has</u> to leave Texas when I'm gone. No one here but Connie
and my attorney knows about you. My attorney will contact you
soon.*

*You're the only one I can trust outside Texas who could and
would take care of her. My legacy will help. Of all the lovers I <u>ever</u>
had, <u>you,</u> my <u>first</u> love, were my favorite. Some of my last thoughts
will be of you.*

*Connie's a smart girl who will help me in my last days. Keep her
and my grandchild safe.*
All my love,
Joanie

Huh. Grandchild? "*When* are you due?" I struggled to hold back my tears.
"February 10th," Connie said quietly.
Melanie nodded. *Of course, you already knew.* I passed her the letter.
Connie pulled a stack of envelopes out of her backpack. "*One* for
everything," she sighed. "*Here.*" The first envelope she handed over was
labeled *Curtis and Me.* It contained my school picture from 6th Grade
and the composite class picture from Mr. Black's 6th Grade class, with
the two of us in different corners. *Mom has <u>that</u> one.* Another snapshot
was of Joan and me at an amusement park, dated July '69. I had *more*
pictures taken that *same* day by my then-seventeen-year-old sister
Karen. *I remember when we split that batch of pictures up, the day they
landed on the Moon.*

And looked down one as far as I could
To where it bent in the undergrowth...

Connie handed me another envelope—*My Family.* There were several
pictures of little-girl Connie and grown-up Joan together, and one with
an emaciated Joan I could barely recognize, dated July '87. There was also
a portrait photo of a man in a uniform. *Connie's uncle,* the label read.
"Then there's *other* stuff." Envelopes labeled *Connie Personal, Connie
School and CV, Connie Medical;* a *big* envelope from a San Antonio
hospital read *Joan Medical.* "And...*this.*" A large envelope with two
signatures across the flap, labeled *To be Opened Only by Curtis Durand.*
It contained $15,000 in cash and cashier's checks written to me,
amounting to $40,000.
"The child's *father,* I take it, is *not* in the picture." I watched Meli

finish Joanie's letter and saw her smiling slightly.

"*He's* the reason I *couldn't* stay in Texas."

"Because?"

"The McCulloch's will *fight* for custody *if* they find out about it. I *can't* have my baby in Texas, and I *damn sure won't* give it up to *them*."

"Would *that* be *that* bad?"

"*Clan McCulloch* makes the *Borgia's* look like the Walton's. Know *anything* about Texas politics and the *assholes—pardon* my *French—*who dominate it?"

"No."

"Imagine the Byzantines *multiplied* by the Corleone's." I made an appropriate face. "*Yeah*, you get the picture. Mama couldn't help but be involved due to the nature of her businesses and her charity work."

"What did your mother *do*?"

"She owned and operated restaurants and nightclubs. She also ran a foster care transition charity since the *state* didn't seem interested."

"I see. Do you have a *plan* for *your* baby?"

"There's a couple in Michigan that wants to adopt *if* I can keep the father's family *away. Then...*" she sighed, seemed to gather herself. "I want to *try* for a Jenson."

I couldn't decide which was more *shocking*: the fact that Connie *could* have been mine, *or* that she was pregnant, *or* aspiring to win one of the most prestigious academic scholarships in the world.

Or that Joanie was gone. Not as *shocking* as *painful*.

I pulled the *Connie School and CV* envelope out of the pile. I *had* to retreat to the safety of academia if only to have time to think. *Most* high school CVs don't require much study. *This* one, though... "You were *published* in *Texas History Quarterly*?"[1]

"One article was on Susanna Dickinson;[2] a second was on Juana Navarro Alsbury."

"I know *of* the first, but...."

"Juana was Bowie's sister-in-law, got caught in the fort with the rest. After the siege, she got better treatment because her father had been a Spanish official."

"Ah." I continued to read. She had numerous feature articles

---

1 An important peer-reviewed publication. For a budding university scholar, publishing there would be a coup. For a high school kid, it bordered on miraculous.

2 The wife of Almaron Dickinson, a captain in the Texian Army killed at the Alamo. Susanna and her infant daughter famously survived the battle.

published in Texas papers and magazines, and... "*The Smithsonian?*"[1]

"I wrote about life in the mining camps of Texas in the 1850s. They said they liked my *style*."

"Uh-huh." I couldn't decide if I was jealous or *not*, but I *was*..."Hungry?"

"*These* days...*always*."

"*Come* on," Melanie grinned. We filed into our kitchen, sitting around the table while Meli pulled out Thursday's lasagna and a salad. She stuck the pasta in the oven and plopped the salad on the table. "*Dinner.* You want *more*; *there's* the 'fridge. *Help* yourself."

We scooped salad as I tried to figure out *what* to ask *first*. "*You* were born ...?" *Let's see if your answers add up.*

"July '70, in San Antonio."

OK. "Why *Texas?*"

"*That's* where Mama ran *to*. Her uncle—her *only* living relative who *wasn't* in stir then—is a Texas Ranger. He could *get* her a good foster family but *couldn't* take her *or* me himself."

Makes sense. "Ah. Joan was...*how* old?"

"*Barely* fifteen when I was born. Our birthdays are nine days apart."

Right so far; we celebrated her 14th birthday with ice cream and our first extended necking. "So *you*..."

"I was in foster care until Mama got me out when I was six. By then, she was *managing* her *first* restaurant. *Her* foster family had her working at *their* restaurant from the time she *arrived* with them." She shifted uncomfortably. "My sperm-donor/*father* was in Chicago for a convention in the fall of '69. Mama's *foster* father brought *my* father *home* one night, and *I* happened." *I should ask Dad if he knew anything about that.* "Mama had *some* man-friends over the years," she went on. "None of them *tried* anything with me. Mama would have *shot any* of 'em, seeing how *I* happened." She forked in some salad. "The boy who... let's just say it was my own *stupid* mistake that got me in *this* situation, but being conceived was *not* the baby's fault."

Connie was *not* a typical teenage girl. Quite the contrary: she was a *very* bright young woman who had a *better*-than-average head on her shoulders.

And she *seemed* as tough as a Texas mustang.[2]

The lasagna came out of the oven. We left Connie to finish a square of pasta and eat the last of her salad and glanced at the high chair in the corner. "You have a child?"

---

1 A coup for *any* non-professional writer.

2 So I'm led to believe: I'm just guessing, never having *seen* such a creature.

"Maria's with her grandparents tonight," Melanie sighed. "Thought I'd have the place to my*self* for once."

"I'm *imposing*, then?"

Melanie shook her head and said, "no, you're more a *surprise*."

"I hadn't *heard* from your mother since she *left*," I said. "Just a *little*...."

"Unsettling," Melanie soothed. "We just didn't *expect*...."

"Uh-huh." Followed by silence.

As we were cleaning up, Melanie asked, "by the way, how did you *get* here, Connie?"

"Bus to New Orleans early Tuesday morning, then a train to St. Louis *Wednesday* afternoon, then a plane to Pittsburgh *Thursday* morning, then *another* to New York; train from Grand Central *Friday afternoon*. I got into Granite City at nine this morning. I looked up your address in the phone book and took a cab from the train station to *here*." She sighed. "Look: I'll *go* if I'm in the way. I *have some* money of my *own*...."

Too many right answers. "No; *hell* no," I interrupted. *I'm NOT going to kick Joan's kid out.* "*This* is a *lot* to take in. We'll work this out, OK?" I glanced at Melanie, who nodded slightly. "You're *more* than welcome to stay until *we* figure out *our* next step. Tomorrow you can meet Meli's family. Monday...*Monday*, we'll take *stock* when we're better rested."

"Sure, Connie," Melanie said. "We'll figure *this* out together. We'll talk more about all this after you've had a good night's sleep in a *real* bed."

Connie gazed at us from the end of the table for a *long* time before she reached into the purse she kept slung over her shoulder, pulling out an envelope that had been folded *too* many times. "*This* is for *you*." It was a notarized copy of a handwritten document, in the same shaky handwriting as the letter:

I, Joan Beverly Emmerich, still being of sound mind and in complete control of my faculties, and having been informed by three physicians that I am within 90 days of my demise, do hereby grant and bestow full parental custody and guardianship of my minor child, Constance Anita Emmerich, to Dr. Curtis Harrison Durand, residing at Crest University, to take effect immediately upon my death.

Prepared by my hand and signed this 12th *day of June 1987 in the city of San Antonio, in the County of Bexar, Texas.*
Joan B. Emmerich
Acknowledged and Accepted by Constance Anita Emmerich
Witnessed by...
Notarized by...

*Prepared in accordance with the Texas Dying Bequest Statute of 1904.
Registered in Bexar County, Texas, 15 June 87*

"It's legal under Texas law," Connie sighed. "Mama's lawyer, Schuyler,[1] told us how to word it since *Mama* had to write it out longhand. Schuyler's the *first* witness." She looked away and wiped a tear. "*That* was one of her *last* lucid days. She was in *so* much pain *all* the time. She *knew* she couldn't keep it together much longer."

Now I have a teenage daughter...HO-boy. "OK, Connie," I said, then added, "call *me* Curtis." I passed the document to Meli. *Do I HAVE a choice? Legally, morally...personally?* "OK, but *we* have to..." I glanced at Meli, who seemed to go pale as she read. *Can I foist this on Meli, too? Does SHE have a choice?* "I accept *responsibility*, but *custody* is complicated."

> *Then took the other, as just as fair,*
> *And having perhaps the better claim,*

Connie seemed to accept my true-but-incomplete statement. The *truth* was that we could neither let her stay with us for *very* long—because of Crest University *policy*—nor compel her to leave without alternate lodgings—because we couldn't do *that and* sleep nights.

I owed Joanie *that* much.

***

"What *now*," Meli murmured as we lay in bed. After dinner, Connie took a long bath and emerged more relaxed and *far* less road-worn. Meli loaned her a cotton nightgown, and she bedded down in Maria's room. Marketing forces had compelled us to buy *twin* beds when Maria outgrew her youth bed.[2]

"I don't *know*," I admitted. "No *idea* what the Regents are going to make of *this*. They *could* fire me, but *this*? No one could have foreseen *this* in *any* morals clause. Push comes to shove; we *could* move if they want us off-campus."

"More expensive," Meli said, "though it *might* be more convenient than the half-hour drive that I've got every weekday back and forth to work, *and* we *could* be closer to the daycare."

"And *less* convenient for me," I agreed. "She *could* get an apartment...."

---

1 Pronounced "*Sky*-ler," not "*Shoe*-y-ler."

2 *Youth bed* is a marketing *con job* if I ever *saw* one. It's just a small bed with rails; rails I *could* put on a twin. But, maybe the marketers knew more than *we* did of what the future held.

"Not *legally*, not until she's eighteen."

"True." Silence. "I've been given *custody* and *guardianship* of her."

"By extension, so have *I*." She took my hand. "You OK, babe? I *saw* you were..."

"I'm *fine*, honey."

"No, you're *not*." She brushed my cheek with a hand. "Go *ahead*, babe," she whispered in my ear as she pushed her shoulder under my head.

So I wept, my tears making her nightie wet.

"Sorry," I murmured after a few minutes.

"It's OK, babe." She stripped her *diaphanous* gown[1] off and cuddled next to me.[2]

"Wonder what *Mom* will say when I tell her." I stroked her hand.

"Wonder what *my* mom will say." She stroked my belly.

"*Yours* didn't know Joanie; didn't give her advice. And *now*, I wonder *what* that advice was?" She pulled the drawstring on my shorts, slid them down.

"*Mine* will wonder about you being worried that a teenager might be biologically *yours*." I stroked the nape of her neck.

"Jealous?" She reached for me under the sheets, swung herself onto my hips.

"Do I *look* jealous?" I reached for her waist.

Guess not.

---

1 It *had* no bottom; it *barely* covered her behind and with a split up the middle it hid *nothing*, so *why bother? Marketing* again?

2 Whatever it *was*, Meli looked good in it. Maybe *that* was the point.

On Sunday, She Met Our Family

'Think we should *talk* about going to chapel?" Most Sunday mornings,[1] we debated whether or not to go to St. Barbara's *non-denominational* "faith" service at 9.[2] Neither Melanie nor I were avid church-goers before we got married, but when Maria was born, we felt it important that she get at least *partially* acclimated to the ritual *and* to the idea of *some* power greater than herself.

"Dunno. Heard *her* yet?"

"I *heard* her throwing up in the bathroom a couple of times during the night."

After donning my robe, I opened the bedroom door and saw Maria's door was slightly ajar. Connie was still in Meli's nightgown, *doing something* in her duffel. I cleared my throat loudly and walked the few steps down the hall to the stairs. "Morning," Connie called as I passed.

"Morning," I answered. "Coffee will be ready shortly."

"I'll be down."

I started the coffee and looked out the window at the clouds in front of the sun, promising humidity. I fetched the paper from the front stoop and found Connie at the kitchen table, an old field jacket

---

1 *If* we got up before 7, which was about half the time.

2 There was also Mass at 8, a Lutheran service at 10, and a *boisterous y'all-*come-ta-*meet*in' evangelical service at 11. *Other* faiths used St. Barb's, including Jews, Muslims, Buddhists, Zoroastrians, and Wiccans.

over her shoulders, still in Meli's nightgown. "Hi," she sighed. "*Thanks for taking me in.*"

"Welcome," I answered as Melanie joined us. "*Our* pleasure, Connie."

"Not *that*," Connie sighed. "The *Other.*"

"Oh." *The Other...yeah.* "We have to do some checking, see if that document's *legal* here. If *not...*"

I took the one less traveled by,
And that has made all the difference.

"...we'll *do* what *needs* to be done," Melanie said. The coffeepot beeped. "Coffee?"

"Not *supposed* to with the baby, but *I* need it."

"Just not *much*," Melanie said. "I was on two cups a day with Maria. Morning sickness?"

"I guess, but I *feel* OK now." Connie glanced at Melanie. "Can *you* help me find a doctor?"

"I have an appointment with *my* OB/GYN tomorrow, as it happens." Meli sipped her coffee. "Connie, now that you've met *us*, I *hope* you'll let *me* fill in for your mom, at least with *some* things."

"Mrs. Durand, I'm..."

"*Melanie*, please."

"Melanie." Connie sighed heavily. "Mama passed ten days ago, but I still *feel* her. I *buried* her *eight* days ago, but I still *see* her. I'm having a baby that I *didn't* plan for, in a place I've *never* been before, and I'm going to give that child *away* to people I've never met because I know I *can't* do what Mama did." She looked over at me. "I'm in the *legal* custody of someone I'd *heard* about but *never* met, in a place I have *wanted* to go to since I was little, that I've been *preparing* for since middle school."

She took a deep breath and smiled slightly. "I know your offer is heartfelt, and I *thank* you for it. *Please* don't think less of me if I don't *leap* into your arms. I *hope* I don't come off cold and impersonal, but *don't* think of me as a *daughter* you just met yesterday. I'd rather you thought of me as the *daughter* of a *friend* who will greatly appreciate some help for a while because I recognize my limitations." She paused and continued, "I *also* appreciate that my presence here might be disruptive. I'll *move on* if I must, but after *meeting* you, I pray I won't *have* to."

A *lot* more lucid than *I* could have been at 7:18 on a Sunday morning... at *any* age.

And Meli started to giggle; I joined her. Soon, so did Connie.

Then, she and I wept for Joanie, holding hands.

Meli loaned Connie a skirt and blouse that *didn't* look like they'd been shot with a wrinkle-gun, and we went to say a prayer for Joanie at St. Barb's.

*****

"Mom, Dad," Melanie said, "*this* is Connie Emmerich. Connie, *my* parents."

I'd called the Hubbards before we arrived and gave a *cursory* explanation over the phone; *more* would have to wait. For now, they *would* know that Connie was neither a *child* nor a *stranger.*

"Connie," Helen smiled, holding out her hand. "I'm Helen. *Please* come *have* a seat." She gestured to the living room.

"Yes, *please*, Connie," Bert grinned. "I'm Bert. Now, *anything* I can get you? Anything at all?"

"No, *thanks*, sir," Connie sighed wearily. "I'd just like to *set* for a spell."

Then Al came down the stairs. He was a head taller and a hundred-odd pounds heavier than his sallow, emaciated father. "Junior,"[1] Bert said, "meet *Connie*, a friend of Curtis. Connie: my *son*, Albert."

"*Hi*," Al smiled, nodding.

"*Hi*," Connie perked up and smiled brightly.

I could *not* figure out *why* their greeting *bothered* me just then. Al was a good-looking, muscular guy. Connie was a pretty, athletically substantial, well-proportioned gal. *Why shouldn't they be pleasant?*

But THAT seems more than "pleasant."

Maria held Al's hand. My four-year-old daughter had her mother's bright smile and personality. "This is *Connie*, Maria," Melanie said. "Come say 'hi.'"

Maria stared at Connie, unsure in a Big Kid way. Connie smiled... then winked broadly. Maria yanked her hand free, dashed across the room, stood in front of Connie, and announced, "I'm *four*, and *I* can *write* my *name*. Can *you* write *your* name?"

"I *can*," Connie said. "I'd like to *see* you write *your* name."

"OK," Maria said, extending her hand. "Come *on*." And she headed back *up* the stairs with Connie in tow.

"So much for *set a spell*," I said, watching them.

"I *guess*," Helen said. "Pretty girl, *isn't* she, Al?"

"Yeah," Al answered absently, staring where the bare legs had been climbing the stairs.

---

1 Bert had *yet* to *completely* accede to the *Al* message.

"Junior," Bert prompted, "*breathe* now."

"*Huh?* Oh," Al said, shaken from his reverie. "I *just...*"

"Like *legs*," Melanie winked at Helen, "and Connie's got some *nice* ones, doesn't she?"

"Oh," Al grunted, embarrassed. "I *guess.*"

"No *guesswork* about it," Helen grinned. "She *is* a *pretty* girl. A *hint* of the southwest in her voice?"

"Texas," I said, inhaling deeply. "Her mother passed away about a week ago. She made *me* Connie's custodian."

"You..." Bert started, blinked, then shook his head.

"Custodian, as in *guardian*," Helen breathed.

"*That's* what *this says*," I nodded, handing the document to Helen. A peal of giggles emanated from upstairs.

"You *knew* about this," Bert asked, still disbelieving.

"Not a *thing* before last night," Melanie answered. "She laid it all on us..."

"She *carries* well. How far along *is* she," Helen asked, glancing from the document to upstairs.

"She *says* twelve weeks," Melanie said. "I have an appointment with Dr. Georgeson tomorrow; see if he can squeeze *her* in."

"She's *expecting*," Al asked, surprised.

"Uh-huh," Helen said as she handed Bert the document. "You can see it in a woman's *face*; a kind of glow and a *little* puffiness."

"Huh," Al said, crossing his arms. "*You're* her..."

"*Hard* to say," Helen declared. "You *could* have a teenage ward, Curtis."

"I've had *worse* things." *But not scarier ones.* There was more laughter from upstairs. "She's made a friend."

"*Sounds* like," Bert said, examining the back of the document. "Would you *recognize* your friend's handwriting?"

"No, but she knows too many *details*; has too many *pictures* and documents. Besides, what's to be *gained* by conning *us*? She wants to be a Jenson Scholar, says she's been preparing for it."

"What grade is she in," Bert asked.

"She'll be starting her senior year next month."

"Have a look tomorrow, see if she's done the paperwork." Proper Jenson Grant applicants must state their intentions by December of their junior year of high school. Late applications are *accepted*, but they go to the bottom of the heap.[1]

---

1 The Jenson Grant for American History Scholars was worth about $100,000 in tuition, fees, books, room and board, and stipends. Applicants have to *want* it— *badly*—*very* early, and they have to maintain a 3.8 GPA to *keep* it.

"She's in *high school*," Al said, disbelieving.

"She turned *seventeen* last month," I answered. "*You're...*"

"Twenty-*two*," Al said quietly.

"Then there's the *Regents*," Helen sighed. "*They'll* have *their* say, too."

"They will *indeed*," I agreed, "but they could *not* have anticipated a situation like *this*. I *can't* just turn the girl away."

"They've fired tenured professors for morals clause violations," Bert mused, "but *that* wasn't *this*. She has *no* other family?"

"She says she *couldn't* stay in Texas," Melanie said. "To do with the *father*."

"*Yeesh*," Helen shook her head as if she'd tasted something bitter. She glanced up. "What do you hear from *Barb* these days, Al?"

"Um," Al said, "she's *here*; *ask* her yourself. Why?"

"*Just* checking. Heard anything from *Rita* lately?"

Al regarded his mother briefly. "*No*, Ma, and I'm *fine* with that." Rita was Al's *one true love* for two years until she stopped answering his calls six months before. "Why?"

"She wants to *know*, Al," I said. "She's *interested*."

"She's *nosy*," Melanie grinned at Helen, who chuckled.

"She wants to know if there's anyone *special* in her son's life," Bert deadpanned. "A *perfectly* legitimate line of inquiry on a Sunday afternoon."

"Yeah," Al grunted, getting up. "Anyone *needs* to *know* anything *else* about me *before* I go?"

"No," Helen said. "Dinner's at four; we'll start by a quarter after even if you're *not* here."

"Fine." Al made to leave through the front door just as four legs came down the stairs...and he stopped. "Hi," he smiled. "Did Maria show you her *horses*?"

"She *did*," Connie grinned back. "*All* those pretty horses. *I* said *I* can *saddle* a *real* horse; she thinks *that's cool*."

"*Yeah*," Maria added. "Connie will show *me* how."

"*Yeah*," Al exclaimed. "Well, let's *see* how you *ride* the *swings!*"

"*Yay*," Maria shouted, pulling on Connie's hand. "*Swings! Swings!*"

"Fine, OK," Connie sighed as she was pulled out the back door. Al followed, *not* looking back.

"Now *that*..." I began.

"Is a *boy* with a *pulse*," Helen said. "You *can't* tell me you *don't* find your ward attractive, Curtis."

"Not *that* way," I said. "She's young enough to be *my*..."

"And you *thought* she *might be* yours," Melanie teased.

"In*deed*," Bert said. "*This* I have to hear."

"*Do* tell," Helen chuckled lightly.

"Dimly *possible*," I confessed, "*Once* that summer..."

"But you weren't *sure*," Bert nodded. "There was a *possibility*..."

"Un*likely*, but...*hey!*" I stopped as both Helen and Bert started laughing. "OK; *enough*. We came *close*, but..."

"Close as we've come to a *true confession*, Curtis," Helen chuckled. "We find out more about our sons-in-law that way."

"Hang *on*, hang *on*," I said after a few eye rolls, "Connie *said* I'm *not*; Joan *said* I'm *not* and *she* put it in writing."

"Huh," Helen snorted. "But seriously, if she's expecting in February, that puts a dent in high school."

"She *wants* to *have* the baby," I said. "I *can't* say no."

"As her guardian, you *probably* could," Helen said. "I never *practiced* law, but I *did* study it. Guardianship can be *quite* absolute."

"OK," I snapped, "I *won't* stop her if you want to put it *that* way." I glared at Helen, closing the subject altogether. "Besides, we don't even know how *binding* that document *is* here."

"Especially if you didn't sign it yourself," Helen nodded. "I can find *out* if you like."

"I'd *appreciate* that, Helen. Now, if you'll *excuse* me, I'd like to call my folks. Can I use your den, Bert?"

"Certainly," Bert declared, glancing out the back window. I did the same, watching Maria swinging in the little park behind the row of townhouses exclusively for senior faculty. I saw other kids running around and Connie shaking hands with Barb.

She's OK; they're fine.

***

"*Hi*, Mom," I said into the phone. I glanced up at the wall, spotting one of our wedding pictures. *Voice is different...*

"*Hi*, Curtis," the voice said. "*Not* Mom; *Darla*."

"*Oh*," I said, surprised. "You home on leave?" My younger sister was in California last *I* knew.

"Yeah. Three *weeks* before I go to Italy."

"They need finance officers in Italy?"

"Wherever the Air Force *is*, Curtis, they have to pay *bills*. How've *you* been? How *are* my sister-in-law and my niece, who I've never *met*?" I hadn't *seen* her in about a decade.

"Maria's fine; growing like a weed. Melanie's good. Why don't you come over, meet *this* part of the family?"

"Karen[1] was *talking* about a road trip while I'm here. Oh, *here's* Mom. *Bye!*"

"*Hi*, Curtis," Mom said. "How's it by you?"

"*Good*, Mom. Um...remember Joan Emmerich, our neighbor? She disappeared..."

"Sure, *I* remember."

"She passed away in Texas the week before last."

"Oh? Didn't know you were in touch."

"I *wasn't*. Her *daughter* knocked on our door yesterday morning. Her name's Constance."

"*Oh, my.*" Silence.

I cleared my throat. "Joan wrote me a letter, said I should *thank* you for the advice you gave her. 'She gave me good advice that I acted on,' she said." I *had* to wait a moment. "Any *thoughts* on that, Mom?"

Mom cleared *her* throat, theatrically. "*I* took Joan to the doctor; she was *terrified* of her foster mom. She *said* her baby was *not* yours before I could even *ask*. You might well *imagine* what advice I *gave* her after *that*, in *that* situation." I didn't answer. "She ran to *Texas?*"

"Yes. Apparently, she did *quite* well there. I've got a document that makes Connie my, um, *ward.*"

"*Wow.* I'd give the *same* advice if I had it to do over."

"Just *curious*: *how* would a fourteen-year-old foster kid who didn't have two *nickels* to rub together be able to get from Cicero, Illinois to *Texas* on her own in the winter of 1969? Just *what* did your *advice* encompass, Mom?"

I was surprised when her answer came so *fast*. "A *ride* to Union Station and enough cash to go wherever she *needed* to go. She *said* she had an uncle, but not *where.*" Silence. "It was better that I *didn't* know. Your father knows I *advised* her, but not with *what* or *how*. Better *he* didn't know, either. Doing *that* much *was* illegal."

"Uh-huh. *And Connie's* three months pregnant."

"My, *my*, Curtis, your life *is* getting *complicated.*"

"So it seems. Joan named her daughter to honor *you*, Mom."

"I *am* honored...and somewhat flabbergasted. This girl's with *you* now?"

"Yes. She wants to give *her* baby up for adoption." Connie had appeared in the doorway; I mouthed *my mom*. "Your namesake's *here*. Wanna talk to her?"

---

1 My *older* sister, remember?

"Sure."

I handed the phone over. "*Hi*, Mrs. Durand; I *should* call you 'Gramma' ...OK, Connie. Mama told me about you...I *know*, but *I* wanted to thank you. If it wasn't for *you*, I might never have known Mama, who was a wonderful woman. I *wish* you'd have known her as an adult...She owned clubs and restaurants...Cancer...*Thank* you...Well, I try *not* to put anyone out, but your son and his wife have put up with me so far, and the Hubbards are *delightful*...Yes, we *have* to make a point of staying in touch... Want *your son* back?" I shook my head. "*He* doesn't, either. OK, *Bye!*"

"*Gramma*," I mock-frowned. "Sailing a *little* close to the wind, aren't you?"

"The way Mama talked about *her*, no." She sat in the overstuffed chair opposite the desk, which *I* had occupied *many* times. "But for a couple of *months* and *inches*, Mama said, *you might* have *been* my *father.*"

"She *said* that?"

"She *did.*" She sighed and smoothed her skirt. "Funny how *that* sort of thing works out."

"More *ironic.*" *That skirt and blouse fits HER better than it does Meli.*

"I *don't* want to put you out...."

"*Stop* saying that, please," I said quietly. "Mom took care of you *before* you were *born.* I'll just keep on keepin' on, to paraphrase Bob Dylan, with the family tradition of caring for *you.*"

"Mm," she mumbled, distracted. "Calling *you* 'Curtis' feels *formal...*" She sighed, a sad sound. "I've never called *anyone* 'Dad' or anything *like* that. Mama never *had* a man *that* close."

"Not sure I'm ready to be the *father* of a teenager, Connie." *Let me get used to just being the guardian of one...and a GRANDFATHER!* "At *this* stage, it *might* sound weird." *I see that signpost up ahead again, hearing that weird music...*

"Maria's going to want to know about the baby."

"You and Melanie should *talk* about that."

"*Yep.*" She stood up, smiled, "hold still," and planted a kiss on my head. "I'm to tell you the bar's open downstairs, but *I* want to go back to Maria and *her* friends."

"And your *new* friends," I added, getting up myself. "*Al's* a nice guy."

"A *sweet* guy." She smiled, a winning look. "I *think* he *likes* me."

"*I* think he does, too. You have a certain *charm.*"

"Mama always said, 'if you *have* to be *anything*, be *pleasant.*' C'mon, *Dad*-who-*ain't*," she grinned, hoisting me up and linking my arm. "Just between *us*, Dad?"

"*Just* between *us*, Connie." I clumped down the stairs with her on my arm, feeling quite close to Joan *and* Mom.

***

"So, Connie," Helen ventured, "what do you think of *our* clan so far?"

After dinner, we cleaned up; Melanie and Connie wiped the kitchen down while Helen put the leftover food away. Bert and I were doing the dishes at the sink; Al kept Maria amused. It was pretty typical for Sunday dinner at the Hubbard's...

Like *Hell* it was. Sunday dinners with the folks were either Chinese takeout or leftovers unless it was a holiday or someone's birthday. It was the same by our place, except I preferred takeout chicken. Once in a *great* while, someone would get ambitious and organized enough to go out for pizza. But today, Meli and her family conspired to put on a spread for Connie's benefit. *Perfectly* harmless...

"I *wish* you hadn't gone to all this *trouble*," Connie smiled. "*I'm* not *that* special."

Busted.

"You *are*, Connie," I said, drying another plate. "You're the daughter of my *oldest* friend."

"*Oh, shit*," Connie cried, holding her rag to her face. "I *swore* I *wasn't* going to..."

"It's all *right*, dear," Helen said, holding Connie's shoulders. "At *this* stage in your pregnancy, you're subject to ups and downs."

"I *know*," Connie mewed, "but I *never* expected *this* reception. I just thought..."

"Thought you'd meet standoffish, suspicious strangers," Melanie said, stroking Connie's hair. "You're *not* a stranger; you know too many details of Curtis' life."

"*The first* rule of the true historian, Connie," Bert added, handing me the last plate. "The *truth* is in the *details*. You *know* too much; have too much *evidence*, Curtis says, to be anyone but who you *say* you are. Because of *that*, our family embraces you."

Connie cried on Helen's shoulder for a few moments while the rest of us finished cleaning up.

The evening shadows drew long when we went out on the back patio to enjoy the temperate if *wet* dusk. "If I *might*, Connie," I offered, "I'll check on the status of your application tomorrow."

"The *second* was accepted," Connie said absently, watching Maria, who had brought one of her many jigsaw puzzles out to work on the picnic table. She not only *loved* them, but she was also *brilliant* at them. Some she'd worked and dismantled so many times the pieces were loose. "I *have* the *letters...*"

"Second," I asked, glancing at Bert.

"I *kinda* jumped the gun," Connie sighed, "submitted an application in my *sophomore* year but couldn't get a faculty endorsement." She glanced up at Maria's grinning satisfaction at completing *another* horse puzzle—again. "*Good* girl," she smiled, to Maria's delight. "Got *another* one?"

"*Yeah*," Maria declared, dashing for the door.

"She's got a *million* of 'em," Al said. "She'll bring down at *least* two more."

"Take *this one* up," Connie began, but Al stopped her.

"*She'll* want to do it," Al said.

"But they'll get mixed up," Connie protested.

"Look in *this* box," Al pointed to the box Maria had already brought down. In *it* were pieces from several *other* puzzles. "I'm surprised that *this* one was complete."

"When she gets on my *last nerve*," Helen sighed, "I tell her to clean up her puzzles. She dumps 'em *all* out, does 'em *all* at once. *That* usually takes half a day, and she's ready for her nap *or* bed."

"I've *watched* her," Bert said. "She does *just* enough to...*here* she is." Maria came out the screen door with three boxes. She started on the top box, right on top of the first puzzle, frowning in concentration.

It was just then that Jenny Rizzo and Jerry Hoffmeier, clad in shorts and sandals, came strolling down the alley. "*Hey*, guys," Al waved, "come and meet Connie."

Jenny was Barb's younger sister; Jerry was the son of Harold Hoffmeier, professor of chemistry. They were inseparable friends who had been next-door neighbors all their lives. This was what I *knew* at the beginning of their staccato exchange. In *thirty seconds*, I learned that both were Connie's age and grade; Jerry attended Granite Ledge Academy; Jenny was a cheerleader at Granite Ledge High, *and* Connie had been a cheerleader too. *And* they all *loved* ice cream but *not* the Beatles, preferring the Stones or The Who for *vintage* rock bands.[1]

"We *gotta* be *going*," Jenny grinned at the end. "See ya *around*, Connie."

"Be *seein'* ya," Connie drawled as Jenny and Jerry ambled down the alley like wraiths.[2] "What's your *major*, Al," she asked, watching her two new friends depart with a distinct grin on her face.

---

1 There was a great deal *more* that they discussed, but *that's* what I *caught. This*, I believe, was when I *started* to *feel old.*

2 Together, they *couldn't* have weighed more than 150 pounds.

"It *was* sports business management with a minor in statistics. They *hired* me *here* as football coach and head of athletics marketing."[1] He related his journey from All American offensive linebacker to *this* field, finishing with "...so I think that *some* people have the right idea: limit the total *player* weight of the teams on the field to protect everyone, *including* the line. We're trying it out *here*, just to see how it affects the game."

"I've known enough guys who got their *bells* rung," Connie said, "had *this* broken or *that* torn, and they were never the *same* again. Something's *gotta* give. *Some* conferences in Texas want to try to restrict the size of the *line*." I'd watched Connie listen to Al and watch Maria simultaneously. She *looked* as if she were engaged with *both*—a rare skill.

"You *know* football," Al asked, surprised.

"*Honey*, for *Texans*, *football* is a *religion*," Connie drawled, *laying* it on a *bit* thicker than she *had*, with a *bit of* a smile and a *tiny, soft* wink at me.[2] "A Texas *gal* cain't hardly *talk* to a Texas *guy without knowin'* somethin' about *football*."

"Yeah?" Al was *fascinated*. "The Quarrymen have a scrimmage game Friday. If you're *free*, the faculty brats come and watch—kind of a party. Hitch a ride with *somebody* from here."

"*Ah'd* be de*light*ed, *suh*," Connie drawled again, *this* time with a big grin. She glanced at me with a wink. "*May* I, *Dad*?"[3]

Melanie suppressed a grin; Helen smiled; Bert shook his head; Al started. "Not too *late*, young lady," I said, resigned.

Just don't lay it on TOO thick, darlin'.

***

"Your *dad*," Melanie shrugged, holding the phone out. We'd just got in the house after walking across campus in the cool evening, watching Maria run around as she tried to keep from yawning.

"*Hi*, Dad. I *just* talked to Mom and Darla...." I watched Connie take Maria up to bed, chatting about horses.

"Yeah. Your mother asked me to *fill* you *in*."

"On...?"

"The reason the Alterman's[4] left so suddenly back in '69." There was a pause. "I've kept *that* file *here*. *They* ran away because we were *about*

---

1 It was *said* that Adelle offered Al *her body* if he would take over as football coach. Al and Adelle *always* denied it; so did Adelle's husband.
2 Connie could *encode* winks. *This* one said, "be *cool*, Dad."
3 *That* wink said, "just *family*, Dad."
4 Joan's foster family.

to arrest Coolidge Alterman for pandering. His *family* didn't get any further than Springfield; we nabbed *him* in Skokie."

"Joan...?"

"We got a tip from a Sergeant Willard Gerard of the Texas Rangers, based on his *niece* Joan Emmerich's affidavit. She *had* to tell the Texas authorities the circumstances of her pregnancy to get placed in a foster home *there.*"

"So, does anyone *know* about Connie's father?"

"We have a *name*; we know he *was* from Virginia. I can look into it. Joan's *father's* still around..."

"*Joan* wrote that he was dead."

"He had a heart attack, *nearly* died. The state sent out a notification that he *had* died—I don't *know* why. The only reason *we* know is because he was arrested in Cicero. He's in a federal nursing home in Tennessee. I can *get* the details."

"Joan never knew *him.* For my *own* peace of mind, see what you can find out about Connie's father, please?"

"I'll let *you* know." Silence. "Joan *told* your *mother* that this girl's *not* yours? It was *possible?*"

"Um...*Some* of the stuff we *did* that summer *might* have..."

"You *knew* how *it works?*"

I want to have this conversation with my father? "I *did*, Dad, but there was *no*...ah...I *wasn't...*"

"But *you...?*"

DAD! "*Yeah. Once* I was *close*, but *not....*"

"I suppose we *were* too busy that summer to supervise you *that* closely, but *you* were, what, *twelve* and having...?"

WAKE UP, DAD! "I turned *fourteen* that *May.* I knew *all about* both birds *and* bees; enough to know what *not* to...*you* know."

"From *who? We* never had *The Talk.*"

Of course, he HAD to have gotten it from HIS father. "From Karen *and* the neighborhood."

"Your *sister* Karen? Didn't know she *liked* you that much."

"I think *Mom* put her up to it."

"*Sheesh.* I'll have to *talk* to Connie about *that.* Never expected *this* conversation with my *son.*"

"Think your *son* expected it?"

"*Probably* not." I heard his tight giggle. "I'll get *back* to you on the *other*, Curtis. 'Night."

"*Thanks*, Dad. 'Night."

Bizarre...

***

"*That's* quite a story," Melanie said in bed later. I'd just told her what Mom did for Joan eighteen years ago. "Not every neighbor would do that."

"Mom *isn't* every neighbor," I said. "During the war, she volunteered for the Red Cross, made her way to California, and was ready to go to Hawaii when the war ended." I waited, listening to Maria's clockwork musical carousel that she *couldn't* get to sleep without hearing. "*That's* how she met Dad; in a demobilization camp."

"Huh. Maria's taken to Connie."

"Connie's had some *practice*. Babysitting? Or maybe she's just good with kids." Silence. "If that document *isn't* legal here, do we *want* to seek legal custody? She *needs* a place to go."

"At the risk of your *job*?"

"We'll *see* about that. Attitudes about morals clauses in labor contracts have been *changing*."

"But the Regents *could* fire you *first, then* wait out the lawsuit."

"I still have my teaching credential."

"Teach in public school? *Quite* the pay cut."

"There's Granite Ledge Academy."

"How well do *they* pay?"

"*Better* than public schools, but *not* as much as *here*." Silence. "*We'll* see." She snuggled next to me. "We'll *do* it."

"Thanks, babe." I kissed her head.

"There *might* be an alternative."

"Yeah?"

"Al."

I stopped breathing for a moment. "*Ho-boy*."

"He *might* think about it. All he'd have to *do* is..."

"Fib convincingly about the baby's conception, as *I* did. *Connie* would have to be convincing, too. So would your *folks*. And they're *how* many years apart?"

"Yeah; *five*. Dad *isn't* that good a fibber." She sighed. "I don't *think* he believes you're Maria's father. She's *too* different from you."

"He hasn't *said*..."

"He *won't*. He's satisfied that you're treating Maria as if she *were* yours. That's all *he* cares about."

We were quiet again, listening to Maria's carousel wind down. "You have an appointment with *your* doctor[1] tomorrow?"

---

1 We had a "family" doctor through the HMO, "Her" doctor was her "female" doctor, or OB/GYN. Such were the conventions of the time.

"Just routine."

"You *sure?*"

"What if I *wasn't* sure?"

"*Could* you be...?"

"I *am* late."

"*That* late?"

"*Yup.*"

"Then we'd *have* to find a bigger place, wouldn't we?"

"With a garage and a big yard."

"And a white picket fence."

"Yeah. What did your *dad* want?"

I told her about Joan's foster family and Connie's father, *not* about her grandfather and our *unconventional* exchange. "If he turns anything up, I'll ask Connie if she *wants* to know."

"Probably for the best. God *knows* how many *more* young women he raped."

"True. For all we know, he got *caught* already."

"*Hope* so."

***

"*Mama*, Connie's spitting up," Maria called from the hallway. This was about midnight.

"*Where*, honey?"

"In the potty."

"Ask her if she's OK, honey."

We heard..."You OK, Connie?" "I'm *fine*, baby. Just something I *ate.*"

A few moments later..."*Connie* says..."

"We *heard*, honey. Tell her there are crackers in the kitchen."

"I know *where*, Mama."

"Fine, honey. *Show* her." We heard them clump downstairs.

"Thirteen *years* between their ages."

"Thirteen years and a million *miles.*"

"Closer than *that*, I think. They're *pals*. She'll make a *good* mother one day." I listened as Melanie fell asleep again. I waited half-asleep until Connie and Maria came back upstairs. I heard Connie softly singing, "Twinkle, Twinkle, Little Star" as she re-wound Maria's carousel about a minute later.

Then, other than the carousel, all was quiet again.

We definitely need a bigger place.

Monday Morning We Had
To Go To Work

'**M**orning, everyone," I announced, coming into the already busy kitchen at 6:30.

"*Morning, Dad;*" "*Hi,* Daddy;" "*Good morning* dear," were the responses I got.

I'll let the reader figure out *who* said *what.*

"Connie, *you* OK this morning?" I was a little surprised to see her in shorts and a tank top, *slightly* glistening with sweat.

"I *was* OK after Maria showed me where the saltines are. Whoever *heard* of *that* happening at night?"

"*Mom* was sick in the afternoon with Al," Melanie said, watching Maria. "I didn't *get* sick with *her,* but the smell of *pineapple* made me ill."

"*My* mom was sick at night, she said," I added, suddenly aware that Maria didn't *know....* "Different women, different effects."

"I suppose," Connie handed Maria a sippy cup. More than our casual conversation about morning sickness, Maria was intent on her cereal and her newfound eating-not-splashing-with-her-spoon skills. "So, *what* time's your appointment, Melanie?"

"10:30, but Maria needs to get to school[1] by 8, and *I* need to get to work." Melanie turned to me. "Can *you* bring Connie...?"

---

1 We called Maria's daycare "school" to get her accustomed to the idea.

"*I* can go with *you*," Connie interrupted. "I want to walk around, see the sights. Just gimmie an address for the doctor, and I'll *find* it. Need to find a *shoe* store since my running shoes are *about* shot."

"You *run* in the morning," I asked as Connie frowned at her shoes.

"When I *can*, yeah," she answered, putting *another* bowl of cereal in front of Maria. "At night if I've got the energy. Know a mile marker around here?"

"From here to my parent's place is a little *short* of a mile," Melanie answered, intent on making *her* breakfast. "The *north* entrance is three-quarters of a mile away by the roads; *south* entrance is just *under half* a mile; *east* entrance *is* a mile. I run *any* of 'em maybe three nights a week."

"I'll *join* you *next* time. I went from here to Jenson Hall on the sidewalks this morning," Connie said, pouring a glass of milk. "It *feels* like maybe half a mile, *half* of it uphill. Hope you don't *mind* my *helping* with my *pal* here," she said while stroking Maria's head. "I *need* to be *useful*. For my peace of mind, I *can't* be just takin' up space."

"Hey, *help* all you *want*," Meli answered, sitting down to toast and eggs. "Getting the *three* of us going..."

"*Ain't* easy," Connie said, reaching for a banana. "Can *I* make dinner tonight? Nothing *much*: broiled pork chops, steamed cauliflower, stewed tomatoes, and boiled potatoes. We've *got* the stuff, and I *promise* I won't *break* anything."

"Um, sure," Melanie said, grinning widely. "Just don't think you *have* to..."

"I took care of Mama for her last *two years*," Connie said, peeling her banana. "Before *that*, I did *most* of my own cooking because she was *so* busy." She sat down next to Maria. "I'd rather *work* than *watch*."

"Fine," I nodded, dropping my toaster pastries into the toaster and turning the knob down. "Just don't feel *obliged*..."

"We want you to feel at *home*, Connie," Melanie added. "*Not* like a servant."

"Then I'll be doin' *my* share." Connie smiled at Maria and took a bite of banana. "Good kid."

"I *like* Connie, Mama," Maria added with a mouthful of cereal.

"*We* like her, too, baby," Melanie said.

"*Speaking* of home," Connie smiled at Maria, stroked her forehead, ate the banana. "I have a *duffel bag* with..."

"Maria's closet," Melanie said. "She doesn't *fill* it."

"I *also* have a *laundry bag* that needs..."

"Washer and dryer are in the basement under the stairs," I said. "I'm guessing you can figure *them* out."

"Just so's I don't *have* to go to a *laundromat*," Connie sighed, tossing her banana peel into the trash, glancing at the clock. "You'll want to *leave* by...?"

"No later than 7:40," Melanie answered.

"*Plenty* of time," Connie sighed. "Coffee; couple *eggs*; shower; get *Maria* dressed; start a load of laundry..."

"*I* can handle Maria," I offered. "You've got other stuff this morning. Get your *laundry* started; get *you* started. How do you want your eggs?"

We were out of the house by 7:35, almost like we'd *practiced* it.

I could get used to this...

***

"*All* right," Bert said. "Document T-4916: John Jay[1] to John Rutledge,[2] date *and* place unknown, source unknown. What can you tell us about *it*, Lew?"

"The *ink* is iron gall, as expected, but *remarkably* acid-free," Lew Carmody said. A physics professor whose *hobby* was history, he'd volunteered his lab's services.[3] "The logwood dyestuff was *not* well prepared: there are large particles in the ink. For someone of John Jay's stature, one would *expect* a better ink."

"Uh-huh," I nodded. "Go on."

"*Beyond* the ink, the *instrument* was a little surprising. Jay wrote *most* of his correspondence with a quill pen. But *this* document was written with a metal nib pen, *probably* bronze and *not* well worn, so it could have been steel or iron. *Steel* nibs weren't *mass*-produced until 1822, though they were first *made* around 1770. Jay *died* in 1828, so it's *possible*." Lew shrugged. "It's *not* commercial paper; it's hand-made with *spring* water. Forgers would use *distilled* water paper to avoid ink deterioration, extending its salable life."

"And the *seal*," Nina Hirschfeld asked. She was an assistant professor of American history who'd joined our little band of explorers *investigating* the documents in the Truxton Section.

"Simple blue sealing wax, common for the period," Bert said. "A *partial* signet impression consistent with Jay's Treaty of Paris seal."

---

1 Among other things, the first Chief Justice of the Supreme Court.

2 One of the first Associate Justices of the Supreme Court, best known for having had the *shortest* term as *Chief* Justice—138 days.

3 At *cost*. Still, material testing wasn't cheap.

"OK, the material's authentic," Nina said. "The justices were riding *circuits* then; didn't *hear* a case as a *court* until 1793, *after* Rutledge left.[1] Say Jay's on the road, Some local may have lent his *best* pen to his guest, but the *rest* was just what was on hand."

"A *reasonable* surmise," Lew said. "*Especially* when we consider how it was folded. It wasn't sanded[2] properly, or *long* enough, because there's a *crease* of ink transfer on the right-hand side."

"Very well," Bert said. "Context?"

"The *year* would be 1790, *probably* late in the year," Nina said. "Jay's writing regarding Hamilton's request for the Court to endorse *his* idea for Congress to assume state debts." She knitted her brows, nodding. "*Could be* he *may* not have even known *where* he *was*. Even *so*, he *would* have written his location as 'On the Circuit.'"

We stared at the document that had truly *no* provenance until now. Just knowing the *content* wasn't enough; even a date wouldn't help, *especially* if the contents were inconsistent with the historical record. "Un*less*," Nina went on, "it's a *draft* letter..."

"Perhaps," Bert nodded his head. "Say he got *lost* while riding circuit and had a *thought*. He *borrowed* pen, ink, and paper at the next opportunity. He *neglected* the date—if he *knew* it—was in a *hurry* and *folded* it too fast, intending to finish it another time. Later, he decided it was good enough, sealed it up, and posted it."

"And *left* it to bedevil *us*," I sighed. "Category *B*, then. I'll expand the original catalog entry."[3] We'd created three categories for the Jenson Collection's documents:

- A—provenance *clear*; document authentic;
- B—provenance *likely*; document *probably* authentic;
- C—provenance *unknown*.

We had examined and tested nearly a thousand documents in three years, placing each in Category B or C. *None at all* had moved to Category A.

We spent the rest of the meeting going over four *more* documents. *Three,* we moved to Category B. The *fourth*—T-6592—was a polemic

---

1 He left the Court but was appointed again by Washington in 1795 after Jay was elected governor of New York. No one *said* history was all that exciting.
2 In those days, a writer spread fine sand, shredded cotton waste, or wool waste on a finished document to dry the ink.
3 We added what our investigations found.

against the 1791 whiskey tax, written with a vegetable-based ink with a duck-quill (narrow-line) on scraped (re-used) parchment. But the science couldn't tell *who* wrote it or *when*—though it was *likely* before 1794.

Thus, T-6592 *stayed* in Category C.

And so, there now remained a mere 27,045 Truxton documents waiting to be examined.[1]

***

"Is Dr. Hardin in," I asked the secretary. I'd only been in the Jenson Endowment Executive Building twice before: when I'd first got to Crest and was lauded as the 1973 Jenson Scholar, and again when I signed my contract as an assistant professor. Said domain of the Regents and the Jenson Foundation was *not* for us mere mortals.

"He *is*," the older woman answered. "*Who* shall I say is *asking* and concerning *what*, exactly?"

"Dr. Durand, American history; about a contract matter."

"Wait *here*, please." She got up and left through a pair of massive oak doors behind her. Dr. Morse Hardin—doctor of education (EdD) and great-great-grandson of Xerxes Jenson—was the Chairman of the Committee of Regents and the public face of the Committee. Between them and the Jenson Foundation, the seven Committee members—descendants of Captain Crest and Weymouth Jenson—owned the entire facility.[2]

"Dr. Hardin will *see* you, Dr. Durand," the secretary announced when she returned a few minutes later. She led me, silently gliding on thick carpets, through a small lobby into Dr. Hardin's well-appointed office. Dr. Hardin was a small man who looked like he *should* have been jovial but, in my limited experience when I signed my contract and a few *other* encounters, was short and abrupt, bordering on abject rudeness.

"Dr. Durand," Dr. Hardin said, standing up as we entered. The secretary discretely took sat in a small chair along the paneled wall. "*Pleased* to see you again. Please be seated."

"Doctor," I said, shaking his hand and sitting down. "*You're* looking well."

"As are *you*, Doctor. Now, please; *what* can I do for you?"

"A private matter," I began, cocking my head at the secretary.

"Policy as soon as you said 'contract,' I'm afraid; need a record of the meeting. Mrs. Stevens is discrete."

---

1 *My* cross to bear; it *was* my idea to clean out that Augean stable.

2 The division of ownership between them was unclear to all but themselves and the gods. As long as the paychecks kept coming and the budgets kept expanding with need, no one outside their little circle of multi-millionaires *needed* to know.

"Very well, sir." I laid out the situation with Connie, my relationship with Joan, and Connie's condition. I finished with, "we *can't* in good conscience just tell her to hit the road, sir."

"Indeed *not*, Doctor. And it's *admirable* that you've taken in a stranger in need of help. Tell me, does it *seem* like Crest and the Endowment might *profit* from *her* being a Jenson Scholar?"[1]

"Her CV is quite impressive, though I haven't yet done my due diligence on it. I just wanted to get out in front of any controversy before campus gossip reached *your* ears."

"Ah, *yes*, of *course*." He cleared his throat loudly. "Put your pen down, Aggie." He drummed his fingers on his desk briefly. "Glad you came here *first*, Curtis—may I *call* you Curtis if you call me Moe?"

"If you wish, Moe."

"A *delicate* matter, unfortunately. When we were first made aware of your *situation* with Melanie Hubbard, we were assured that *your* intentions were honorable, and you carried through. You're still together, yes?"

"We are; *very* happy, too."

"Splendid. So *many* marriages that start under such conditions end in disaster. The morals clause in the employment contracts does *not* define third parties like your ward, nor could they have *anticipated* such a situation. I *believe* they date from *before* the *last* century. You're looking into that custody document?"

"Yessir. Helen Hubbard said she'd check into it."

"Ah. I was in school *with* Helen while Albert was overseas. *Brilliant* mind."

"Yessir." I was *surprised*, not *stunned*, to learn that Moe *knew* Helen. "If it's not legal *here*, Melanie and I want to do what it takes to *become* her guardians."

"Good; *splendid*." Moe looked over at Mrs. Stevens. "Start again, Mrs. Stevens."

"Before she *does*," I interrupted, "I assume that our familiarity is limited to *private* conversations. I will not abuse the privilege—no shouts of '*Hey*, Moe, what's *happening?*' across the quad."

Moe smiled; Aggie giggled, pen poised. "You *assume* correctly, Dr. Durand." Moe nodded for Aggie to continue. "*Now*, as President of the Committee of Regents, I endorse your actions in assuming responsibility for your ward, Dr. Durand. If legal steps are necessary

---

1 This was the *second*-most important consideration: whether the selected scholar would make the *school* and the *program* look good. The *first* was whether or not they would likely *complete*.

for *this* state, so be it. *Her* child is to be adopted? *Splendid* decision on her part. I see *no* bars to your actions, Dr. Durand. I shall have to take this matter before the Committee, of course, but I foresee *no* difficulty."

I left, surprised. Given the horror stories we'd heard about the morals clause in our contracts, I felt sure that I'd be in for an uphill battle. Instead...support.

Huh.

***

As I crossed the campus to the Sterling Admissions Building, I thought about what was *expected* of a Jenson Scholar...what a Jenson Scholar *is.*

The Jenson Grant for American History is awarded every five years to a 17-to-19-year-old history *scholar* who, with their 200-word entrance essays, exhibited distinct traits before they were even considered:

- An ability to think in historical terms;
- The capacity to be an all-around scholar, maintaining a GPA no lower than 3.8 on a well-rounded curriculum;
- A capacity to learn how to think about, research, publish and teach the intricacies of the American experience;
- Willingness to forego all behaviors attendant to the typical young adult college experience.

Jenson Scholars are expected to work *hard*, eking out an existence in dormitories in a *very* conservative, small university in a city of fewer than 30,000 people best known for cut stone, stone *cutters*, and historians.

The *profession* of history—what Crest history majors are trained for—is treated like a priesthood, where *many* are called, but *damn* few are chosen.[1] Jenson Scholars are thus hardies who can withstand the pain of spending up to a decade of their lives *working* to keep their grades up. While their classmates go on Spring Break to drink, carouse, and otherwise do what *normal* young adults do in college, Jenson Scholars have to *study.* As daunting as *that* is, there are still a *hundred* or so teenagers from all over the world who apply every five years.[2]

"I need to know an applicant's status, Polly." I'd reached Sterling in just a few minutes despite the humid heat.

---

1 History *buffs can't* cut it; the emphasis on *facts*, not *lore*, is too intense.
2 As of 1980, about *half* of the Jenson Scholars completed.

"Over *there*, Curtis," Polly Winfield pointed to a collection of file folders standing on the edge between bookends. "*This* cycle's crop."

"Do you have them on your *terminal?*" Polly was an American-Sinologist, noted for her work on Asia's earliest immigrants to America. She had been the 1968 Jenson Scholar and worked in the admissions department for the summer and fall terms of '87.[1]

She turned to her keyboard, a big, imposing, and *loud* thing connected to the school's mainframe computer; a big deal, then. "Name?"

"Emmerich, Constance." Each department had a PC/terminal; *ours* was in Bert's office, waiting to be set up and connected to the network. All professors and assistant professors were *supposed* to get their own before the January term.[2]

Polly typed in the name; the screen flickered. "Constance A. Emmerich, Alamo de Bexar Memorial High School, San Antonio. Application *received* September 13th, '86; the *first* to get in. Application review *complete* September 29th; *acceptance* letter sent October 1st. *Huh*; says that she applied in '85, no faculty endorsements *and* too early." Polly looked up. "We *probably* sent a *nicer* rejection than usual."

"So she's *good*, then?"

"Yep; she's *good*." She looked askance. "What's this *about*, pal?" Polly had been my mentor. *My* mentee, the 1978 scholar, flunked out of the program in her sophomore year, unable to pass Latin a second time *despite* tutoring. The 1983 scholar was doing well, I understood.

"She's the daughter of a friend who just passed away. Her mother gave *me* custody. She knocked on my *door* Saturday afternoon."

"Oh, WOW," Polly giggled briefly. "When we start reviewing these next month, with *her* CV, she'd be on the top of *my* list. Of course, *your* participation..."

"Yeah, I know," I sighed. "I recuse myself if *she's* in a batch." To choose future Jenson Scholars, the *other* Crest History Departments[3] culled the best *twenty* applicants. The American History Department then chose the *top five* applicants. If *we* couldn't cull five out of the *first* batch, we'd get a look at the *next* twenty, and so on. From *our* selections, the Jenson Committee—a group of *earlier* Jenson Scholars[4]—pick the *one*

---

1 She was *also* eight months pregnant that August. Timing is everything.
2 We were *not* holding our breath for *any* of these events to occur since the Science, Geology, and the Math departments were ahead of us in the queue.
3 African, Latin American, and Eurasian.
4 Of necessity, there was *some* overlap.

they believe has the best chance of success and who would bring the most *credit* to the school and the program.[1]

I left Admissions at close to three that afternoon, planning a stop at Jenson Graduate Library to see if my books had come in—new books for the January semester, *maybe*. I had *not* expected to see Connie, in shorts and a t-shirt, toweling her face as she left Hermann Fieldhouse. "Connie," I called, "over here!"

She waved and smiled, diverting in my direction. "Hey," she said, wrapping her hair in one towel while another hung around her neck. "Just did some laps in the pool. I met Adelle Freeman; I never *met* an Olympic medalist before."

"Well, OK," I answered. "Did Meli's doctor..."

"He *did*. He confirmed it, *again*. I'm twelve weeks; *big* surprise."

I glanced at her abdomen reflexively—she wasn't *showing* unless you looked hard. "You *carry* it well."

"Thanks. Athletes *do*, they say."

"You *run*; you *swim*. What *else* do you do?"

"I *was* a cheerleader; *that's* over." She shrugged, resigned. "I *walk*," she added. "I had a *bike* that I rode a lot. I *can* drive, but I just *felt* better about walking or biking when I could."

"South Texas can get pretty *hot*, I understand."

"*Tell* me about it. I spent most of my *time wet* one way or another. But it keeps the pounds off; Mama had *her* issues with weight, and *I* inherited them." She smiled, her arms folded across her chest. "I can *throw* or *punt* a football, played shortstop in a slow-pitch parks league. I did some barrel racing in middle school, but I was *never* a competitor. But, I *can* saddle a horse. I do all *that* to compensate for what I do when I'm *not* doing *all that*, which is *reading, writing,* and being *useful. Please stop* me if I'm intruding or trying *too* hard. I know I *tend* to do that."

"Well, you *do* seem as if you're making a *lot* more effort than you *need* to."

"I *just* want to fit in."

"We've *all* taken to you. Do your own *laundry*, and you'll be fine. I *just* checked on your Jenson Scholar status, and you're in the running. I'd have to recuse myself if *your* name comes in. I informed the Regents of *our* situation. The Chairman doesn't see a problem."

"Problem," she asked.

"*Don't* panic when I say this: there's a *morals clause* in our contracts that precludes unmarried pregnant women from the campus. It's

---

1 The Regents had *little* to do with it other than a welcome letter, because the Jenson Foundation that *paid* the Grant was a separate entity. Some, not all, Regents were also Foundation members.

gotten professors fired in the past. But that *won't* be a problem for *us*. Our contracts did *not* foresee our unique situation. As such, I've been assured *we* needn't worry."

"Only thing *I've* got to worry about is the McCulloch's finding out about the baby," she said quietly. "But if I'm putting *your* job in danger, I'll find *other* accommodations."

"*Once* and for *all*, *stop it*," I snapped, *probably* too fast. "You're *here*, with *us*. You're part of *our* family now. Meli and I *talked* about it. If we *have* to, we'll pursue *all* the legal options." I *had* to stop.

She turned and looked at me; shed a little tear. "*Including...?*"

"Would you *want* to be adopted?" *That* just came out, I *swear*.

She didn't *really* answer but reached out her hand with a fragile grin; I took it. "Let's go *home*, Dad," she whispered. "Talk about *that* later."

Her mother's barely in the ground, and I'm offering her a new family...what am I thinking?

***

"We'll have to find something *off*-campus," I sighed, settling into the living room after dinner. "This place is soon to be *too* small." Though Connie didn't *act* any different, she *smiled* a lot that evening.

Meli told me *she* was due in December as soon as she got home from work. The news of our second child was *far* more *welcome* and less *scary* than that of our first. But it made our *space* problem worse.

Our townhouse was a bath-and-a-half/two-bedroom with a den.[1] The basement was *just* large enough for the physical plant and washer/dryer. We had two parking slots outside and ready access to the children's park, with swings and slides and all the rest. For a Big Kid and two adults, it was plenty. It was not *nearly* enough for an infant, a Big Kid, a pregnant teenager, and two adults. There *were* bigger places in the Estates, but the waiting list was *longer* than a year.

"Sorry," Connie mumbled at length, "didn't *want* to..."

"*Stop* right there," Melanie said, "we've *always* said that our *next* baby would make us move. We talked about this *long* before you showed up."

When DID we TALK about this? Oh, yeah...take the HINT, bright boy. "That's *right*, Connie. Can't take a chance that the next wouldn't be a boy, or twins, even." I shrugged. "Winters can be hard on cars in these mountains,[2] anyway, so we've *wanted* a garage."

---

1 A 10x12 room that Meli used, with a built-in desk and shelves and barely enough room for two chairs. Faculty had their *own* offices, of course; why would we need *more*?

2 Granite City is flanked by mountains, some surpassing 6,000 feet.

"Yeah," Melanie agreed. "I've seen some *nice*-looking places on my way to work."

"I saw one right off the campus," I said. "Saw a 'for sale' sign on it last time I passed it. Shouldn't be *that* much." That ranch house was *way* out of our price range, and I knew it, but I was committed.

And the phone rang; Melanie got up to answer the phone by the stairs, expecting her parents or a sister to call to congratulate us on the new baby. "Hello...Yes, this *is* Mrs. Durand...Yes...Yes, she *is*...She's *seventeen*...What...*What* are you *saying*...What...I don't *understand*...But I...He's *here*." She held the receiver out, looking worried.

"Curtis Durand," I answered sharply, thinking it was either a lawyer *representing* the McCulloch's *or* a genuine McCulloch calling with demands. *Upset my wife, will you? I'll give you a piece of....*

"*Doctor* Durand, *this* is Alan X. Jenson."

"*Yessir*," I answered, somewhat relieved despite the stern tone of his voice. Alan Jenson was Xerxes Jenson's great-great-grandson, member of the Regents, multi-*multi*-millionaire, and the majority owner of Jenson Stone.[1] I knew him only well enough to pick him out of a crowd. "*How* can I...?"

"You can *start* by explaining yourself to *me*, Doctor. You are *fully* aware that the young woman you are sheltering violates not just the morals clause in your contract but also the laws of *God*, are you *not*?"

"I'm aware that some people *might* think in those terms, sir, yes. But I'm *also* aware that the good Christian cannot drive the needy away. This young woman needs shelter, respite. 'Suffer the little children,' the Bible says in Matthew, does it *not*?"[2]

"*Hardly* appropriate, Doctor. The Lord was talking about 'come unto me, for such is the kingdom of God,' meaning let all those who *wish* to believe in Him. He did *not* mean...."

"He wanted *Mary* not to suffer, either."

"*That's* inappropriate, Doctor. Mary was the mother of God. Are you suggesting that your *houseguest* is..."

"Of *course* not, sir, and she's *far* more than a *houseguest*." Connie looked startled; Meli embraced her. "I *am* arguing that the Lord hates the *sin*, *not* the sinner, and *Connie*..."

"That's *not* biblical, even if it *is* godly."[3] There was a pause. "Doctor, that's *precisely* the kind of thinking—and *debating*—you should use when

---

1 Which handled the stone the school quarried, thus representing a large fraction of the school's income.

2 Matthew 19: 14.

3 There's *nothing* in the Bible about hating sins and loving sinners.

you address the Regents Thursday morning." He chuckled lightly. "It's high time we did *something* about those morals clauses in the contracts, and *yours* is the *best* case to argue their obsolescence. You have *my* vote, son, Moe's, and one *other,* but you'll need to win over at least *one* more. There will be *five* of us at the meeting, *including* Moe and me. Is that custody assignment we hear about *legal* here?"

HOW did...? "I can't *say*, sir," I answered. "If it *isn't*, Meli and I will do whatever it *takes* to make *sure* she's protected." *Never mind how...*

"Admirable, Doctor. Why didn't your friend try to contact you with such a weighty matter *before* she passed?"

How...? "Connie believes that the father's family would want custody, and that would *not* be good, according to her. If Joan *had* called or written, there *are* means that a ruthless man such as their patriarch could use to find *me* and harass *her.* I haven't done a *great* deal of research on the matter yet, sir, but Connie *has* been truthful."

"I understand, Doctor. Now, may I *speak* with your ward briefly?"

I handed the phone over to Connie, who seemed to gather herself up as Melanie got Maria up to bed. *"This* is Constance Emmerich...Twelve weeks, sir. I'm grateful that Curtis and Melanie have taken me in...sir? There's a family in Michigan...Yes, I can...*Thank* you, sir...*She's* taken Maria up to *bed*...Yessir...Thursday at nine, then, sir." She handed me the phone and went upstairs.

"While we wait for your *lovely* wife, who I ambushed," Alan said, "I'll apologize to *you.* But you *have* to be aware, Doctor, that the Committee members you'll need to convert to your side are *not* predisposed to listen to your *complete* arguments. They will become even *more* recalcitrant if you make gaffes *then* like you made *just now.* Make your arguments *legal*, make them *moral*, make them *logical*, but stay off the theology if you don't know it. Most of my fellow Committee members—cousins, in-laws, and *other* hangers-on that they *are*—*think* they *know it*, but *argue* as if they *do."*

"I *understand*, sir," I said, watching Melanie come down the stairs, listening to Connie singing to Maria as she wound her carousel. "What *time?"*

"Be in the committee room lobby *at* nine," Alan said. "Five minutes late, and you've lost already. Make sure the young woman is presentable. They'll make *some* allowances, but not many. No flashy jewelry, *little* makeup, hair out of her face. She's a *pretty* girl, I'm told."

"She *is*, sir. Is she to plead her *own* case?"

"Perhaps. There's been a *lot* of arguing this afternoon, Doctor. I believe much of it is based on the *expense* of having to redo all the contracts *if* the Committee sides with *you*. Some want to lay eyes on your *pseudo*-Jezebel if only to verify that she's *not* a painted harlot."

"Yessir. *Meli's* here, sir."

"Until *Thursday*, Doctor."

"Yessir." I handed the phone to Meli. She spoke pleasantly, said "I understand" often, and hung up. "She needs clothes."

"Yes," I said, watching her go back upstairs before the phone rang again.

"Curtis; Helen. A *preliminary* read on your document is that it's enforceable here. Murray's[1] *sure* of it. And *congrats*, Curtis. You must be *thrilled!*"

"I *am*, Helen, thanks. We're *probably moving* before the baby comes." We chatted for a while; I didn't feel it necessary to talk about the Committee meeting because the whole *school* would know about it soon enough. Meli came down again and spoke to her mother; Connie came down after putting Maria to sleep.

"Busy day *again* tomorrow," I sighed.

"I need to call Michigan," Connie sighed. "Just a *few* minutes." She dialed, reading the number out of a small notebook. "Mr. Templeton; Connie Emmerich. I'm just calling to let you know I'm *at* Crest University, in the home of my guardian...Mama passed the week before last...*Thank* you, sir...*Yessir*; today...I'm twelve weeks; the 10th of February...I gave them *your* information for the billing...I'll be enrolling at Granite City High for my senior year...Curtis and Melanie Durand; Dr. Durand is my guardian...The number *here* is...The *address* here is...*He's* a professor of history...If you hear from *anyone* in Texas except Mama's attorney or my Uncle Will, please let *one of them* know. Yessir...My *best* to your wife... Good *night*, sir...Yessir, he *is*." She handed the phone to *me*, surprised.

Um... "Curtis Durand," I said, not sure what *else* to say.

"Dr. Durand; *Attorney* Fred Templeton here. Forgive the interruption of your evening, but *I'd* like some answers. Was Constance known to you *before* she got there?"

"I grew up with her mother," I answered...true as far as it *went*, as long as *it* didn't *go* very *far*. "We *were* good friends."

"I see. Her *custody* isn't an *issue*, then?"

"Nosir," I answered. "She's *already* pals with my daughter."

---

1 Murray Walking Elk was a practicing attorney and a county auxiliary judge who led our Pre-Law faculty. He was also a full-blooded Cherokee who practiced at the tribal court nearby.

"OK, then. I've never *met* the young woman, but an attorney I engaged in Texas *has;* said everything she's told us is true. Are you financially *able* to *support...*"

"She has a legacy," I said. "Not substantial, but *enough.*"

"My wife wants to *meet* Constance before the birth. Will *that* be possible?"

"I don't see why not. Granite City has a train and bus station, and there's Holman Field, a regional airport with commercial service."

"We can fly in, then. My Texas attorney says that the boy's family has become aware that Constance is expecting." *Uh-oh.* "They *seem* to be on the *fence* about what to *do* about it. Dr. Durand, we'll contact you again soon."

Connie sat on the stairs next to me, looking tired. "It's *all* happening," she whispered, hooking her arm around mine. "And I *just* summed up my life in *one* phone call."

"A *handy* capacity, honey."

Melanie sat behind us and put her hands on Connie's shoulder. "Connie, honey, the Regents are going to want to know *what happened.*"

"They have the resources to find out on their *own,*" I said softly. "But they *might* want *your* version of *how...*"

"Yeah." Connie looked over at me. "It *wasn't* my idea."

"You mean...?"

"*That's* what I mean. Wanna *hear* what happened?"

I froze. "*Not here.*" We *were* about fifteen feet from Maria's bed.

We moved to the kitchen. Connie sat at the end, Meli and I on each side. "Pretty *simple,* really," Connie said, her voice even, staring into space. "At the end of basketball season, the cheerleaders elected the squad *leader* for the next year. I *won. Quite* an honor."

"Sure," Meli said.

"Yeah. Jasper McCulloch said the quarterback had to *try me out* before the football team would *accept* the election. He *was* a quarterback where such boys are worshiped like *gods.* Nobody'd *heard* of *that* before, so nobody paid *attention.* My pal Leona threw a swim party at her place to celebrate the end of the cheerleading season. I got my invite the same day Mama said she had *no* chance of seeing me *graduate.*" She looked at us. "I *should* have known *then.*" She looked away. "She told me I had to live *my* life and just go and have *fun.* So I *went.*

"It was *OK. Somebody* snuck booze and beer and weed in. *Somebody* got pushed into the pool. *Some* gal had her *top* pulled off by *another* gal's guy—typical swim party *bull*shit. Then *Jasper* and *his* outfit showed up.

They *weren't* invited, but what the *hell*, we all *knew* each other. They crashed a party. So *what?*

"Well, for about an hour, it was just more of the same with more *guys*. Then, I went to the bathroom, and when I came out, three of Jasper's guys grabbed me and dragged me to the gazebo—right in the *middle* of the party. Jasper and *his* guys are all *big* guys. *We* were *mostly* gals 'cause *guy* cheerleaders are rare in those parts, and only a handful of us *had* boyfriends who'd *come* to those. Kids *yelled*, but....

"Jasper's guys hauled me belly-down over the gazebo rail. I said *NO* as *loud* and as *often* as I *could*, *wrestled* and *fought* as much as I could, but *they* didn't *care* and there were *four* of 'em.

"Well, Jasper pushed my *bottom* off, and...*he* was *done* pretty fast. The next thing *I* knew, Leona gave Jasper two twelve-gauge *vocabulary lessons* with her daddy's garden gun[1] while his shorts were around his ankles. His gang turned *me* loose; Jasper was on the *floor* of the gazebo, bleeding; Katie Morrison wrapped a towel around me. The *cops* show up, and..." she looked at us again. "You can *guess* the *rest*. There were a dozen or so uninvolved *witnesses* to both Jasper's assault *and* Leona's *lesson*."

We waited, watching a single tear roll down her cheek, listening to the kitchen clock *tick-tick-tick*.

"You OK, honey," I asked at last.

"I've *been* OK since Leona *shot* that bastard," she sighed. "No: I've *been* OK since I told Mama I was *pregnant*. She said *that* was the *best* birthday present she'd *ever* got." She looked at me; smiled. "Except for that *kiss* you gave her on her *fourteenth*, Dad. 'My first *real boy-kiss*,' she called it."

"*Tongue* and *everything*," Melanie kneed me.

Tongue and more. "Uh-huh."

Connie smiled again and looked at Meli. "Maria *isn't* Curtis's."

Melanie shook her head. "We *needn't*...."

"No. That's a *family* matter. Do *you* care if I call Curtis *Dad?*"

"*No...*" Meli started. "*Might* take some getting used to, a teenager calling my husband 'Dad.' It might *confuse* Maria, though. Just...keep it to a minimum, in *private*, between *us. Not* in public. *Gossip* around campus...."

"But it's an *honor*, Connie," I said, meaning it. "When you have kids of your own with someone you *care* for, they'll call you *Mom* or *Mama*, and you'll *know*."

---

1 A shotgun loaded with dust shot—lead pellets so small a hundred or more can be packed in a 12-gage shotgun shell—and rock salt. Commonly used on vermin at close range.

"Yeah." Connie sighed, stood up, and stretched, wiping her face with her hand. "I need to *run*." She pecked both our cheeks. "'*Night*, Dad; Mom."

'*Night, honey.*

Tuesday Was When We Got More Information

'**C**an you *find* a *dress...*?" Melanie asked Connie that morning, setting cereal in front of Maria.

"Chapman's has some *nice* stuff," Connie said, drying her face and arms. "I got shoes at the sporting goods store across the street from there yesterday. I *also* need to do *something* about my *hair.*"

"Carol's Cut and Curl down the block from Chapman's," Melanie said, yanking her toast out of the slots. "Use *my* name—I've been going there for*ever*—tell Bea it's an emergency *and* that you're pregnant."

"You got *cash*," I asked, perusing the cereal shelf.

"About $50 and change. What's a half-decent dress *cost* around here?"

"Give her $250, Curtis," Melanie said, buttering her toast. "You'll need dress *shoes*, stockings, a *slip...*"

"I haven't *worn* a slip since..." Connie moaned, slipping out of her shoes.

"Thursday, you *should* wear one," Melanie declared, sitting down with her breakfast.

"*Yes*, Mom," Connie sighed, rolling her eyes.

"How do you plan to *get there* and *back*," Melanie asked, not missing a beat...but with *her* look that said, *huh?*

"Al said *he'd* take me," Connie said, reaching for the fruit bowl. "I *called* him after my run last night. I'll buy him *lunch.*"

"Oh," Melanie said with a smile. "Should I *warn* my brother about *you* or *vice versa*?"

"Your brother can find out about *me* for himself," Connie grinned, peeling a banana. "*I* think he's a sweetheart."

"Don't let *him* hear you say that," I warned, despairing of cereal and opting for eggs...*if* I could get to the stove. "He *was* an All-American..."

"That's just *football*," Connie said, finishing her banana. "If I smile and show some *skin off* the field I could have an *eye* in the *middle* of my *forehead*, and ten out of eleven football players wouldn't *notice*."

"I *should* take offense," Melanie said with some conviction. "Al's not *that* shallow..."

"No, he's *not*; not at *all*," Connie agreed, pitching her banana peel into the trash. "*That's* one of the reasons I *like* him."

And the *phone* rang....

***

"*Doctor* Durand," the apparition at my office door said. "Schuyler Colfax, executrix of the estate of Joan Emmerich."

Even though her call had warned me she was coming, she was *still* something of a surprise. Outside a costume party, I'd never seen a grown woman in a cowboy hat and vest—complete with fringe. The rest of Schuyler was business-like, in a khaki-drill dress and reddish hair pulled back and pinned. "Ah, yes, ma'am," I answered, not sure *what* was in front of me. I'd had *enough* surprises that week; here was one *more*. "Executrix? Come on in." I led her into my office.

"Quaint title, *ain't* it? I'm *also* Joanie's attorney, *and* a *friend* of many years, Dr. Durand." I gestured to one of my two side chairs. "You've *met* Constance?"

"Saturday," I nodded. "She was a *surprise*; I *have* to say."

"And *not* my idea," Schuyler declared. "I wanted to explain her situation to you *before* she turned up on your doorstep like a stray cat. But changin' *that* child's mind is like makin' *ice* on a *Texas* river: waste of *effort* on somethin' that won't *last* long." Schuyler's long drawl seemed natural. "Do you understand her *entire* situation?"

"There are some blanks that need filling," I answered. "I'm not *clear* about why an uncle can't take on a teenager for a *year*."

"They barely *know* each other, frankly; he's her *great*-uncle—Joan's *mother's* brother, but was only three years *older* than Joanie. Lieutenant Gerard has his hands *full* at this time. Willis is stationed in El Paso; not a *savory* place right now, in the middle of a *priority* matter for the Attorney General that takes *all* his time."

122

"I see. So, *why did* Connie just come...?" The *way* she answered suggested that I wasn't *going* to get any more information.

"*Her* idea. She wanted to get out of Texas as soon as her mama was in the ground. I couldn't *endorse* her skedaddlin' up *here*, but I could understand her wantin' to get gone before she started to *show*."

"The baby's grandfather...?"

"Amos McCulloch's an RRB: a *rich rotten bastard*. I'd bet a *barrel* of *bucks* to a *bucket* of *beans* that Texas has more of 'em per capita than *any* other state. But, they have the *money* and the *business*, so I *have* to put up with *my* share."

"She's concerned that he might *find* her here. So am I."

"There's *some* danger of that," Schuyler nodded, "but we're *looking into* that matter." Somehow, her looking into *anything* on Connie's behalf felt reassuring. "*On* to business. Connie *should* have given you her bankroll..."

"She *did*. A *tidy* sum, but not a *lot*."

"I have *here*," she pulled a document out of a valise, "a *trust* agreement. *We* will be *co*-trustees until she turns 25. After *that*, the residue is hers to do with what she likes."

"OK." I perused the document carefully, noting that the trust's principal—the seed money—was just over a million. "Do *we* have to *agree* on *how* it's to be spent?"

"Not every detail, no. *I'd* prefer it was spent on her *direct* maintenance, education, and housing for now. Connie's a *hopelessly* practical gal, so I don't *foresee* a spending spree. I'd expect a *reasonable* amount for sundries. No *fancy* cars—a *Chevy, not* a *Corvette*—or extended trips— Spring Break in Daytona, maybe, but *not* a season on Capri. *Here*..." she handed me several shipping receipts. "The Orange Freight warehouse in Granite Ledge should have *these* in a couple of weeks. They'll *call*..."

"These...*what?*"

"They're full of personal items, books, and clothes. All that's *left* of their household."

"Ah. *My* father says that Connie's grandfather's still alive, still incarcerated. *Connie* thinks he's dead."

"Your *father*...?"

"Captain in the Cicero, Illinois PD; the *next* superintendent."

"*I* see. As far as Connie knows, he *is* dead, and I'd be obliged if we could *keep* it that way. Joanie was informed of his *non*-demise and transfer to Brillion Hospital in Tennessee around when she started chemotherapy two years ago. *That* was the first she knew he was still above *ground*. Joanie wasn't interested in stirrin' up *that* bucket of *bull*shit over someone she couldn't pick out of a lineup, so she never *told* Connie."

"I see. Can you help me with the, ah...?"

"*Bill* of *sale* for *Connie*?"

"It's not *that* crude."

"That's what the dying bequest was *meant* to be a *substitute* for, but it's used for all *kinds* of things nowadays, *including* custody of minor children. Since Connie's over fourteen, *she* had to sign it. You were *supposed* to, but since you were unavailable—which in Texas means out of the reach of state courts—you didn't *have* to."

"But in *this* state..." I began.

"Is someone *here* objecting?"

"The school *might*."

"I have *help*," she said, pulling more documents out of her valise. "Affidavits from myself, the witnesses, the doctors, *and* from Joanie herself. Everything attests to what Joan *intended*, *regard*less of the instrument."

"It *might* help. Do you want to meet with her while you're up here? Dinner, maybe?"

"*Plan* to. I'm staying at that Crestview Hotel for a few days. I've never been *in* this part of the world before, thought I'd look around."

"I talked to Fred Templeton last night."

She smiled broadly. "He's a *doozy*, ain't he? His wife's younger; has some physical issues. She can't *carry* a child to term. Fred hired one of his law school classmates, Sam, to investigate Connie and Joan. Sam's a buddy; he called *me* a couple of weeks ago. According to *him*, suitable children for adoption are like hen's teeth in the Templeton's neck of the woods. They put their ad in a *hundred* papers, went through *dozens* of young women before they settled on Connie." She shook her head wistfully. "Sam says this Templeton's just got more *money* than *sense*."

"Is there a *chance*, then, that...?"

"Oh, *no*. Connie's nearly a dead ringer for *Mrs*. Templeton as a teenager."

"The *McCulloch's*..." I started.

She waved her hands dismissively. "*Not* to worry. So *call* the hotel, and we'll get together."

"Sure. You *know* you're named for a vice president."

"Sam Grant's first VP, yep. My name was chosen before I was *born*. Pappy was disappointed I was a *girl*, but I *got* the name anyway."

***

"*How* much," I asked, incredulous. I was on the phone with the real estate agent whose name and number were on the sign outside the ranch house.

"$124,999," the woman named Diane answered. "It's *negotiable*, of course. The seller hasn't listed for long. I've had no other calls on it yet. If you're *interested*..."

"Um, I'm *new* to this, ma'am, and I wasn't sure *how much* to expect..."[1]

"What's your price range?"

"I don't...we've been *in* campus housing."

"You're at *Crest?*"

"Yes..."

"*Assistant* or *full?*"

"Assistant..."

"Tenured?"

"My tenure's in *review*..."

"Does your *wife* work?"

"For the *county*..."

"County employee *and* Crest faculty. Tenure *possible*...you could *probably* go up to $99,000 with *nothing* down; more *with* a down payment. You can get a twenty-year, 7.5% mortgage with payments *close* to what you're paying in rent *now* through the state's credit union. *Less* if you've got *any kind* of down payment. How big a *hurry* are you in?"

Really? "Um, well, we...let's say our family's growing by leaps and bounds and our down payment...we weren't *expecting* to..."

"Well, *that* place would be a *boon* to a growing family. *When* do you want to *see* it?"

"Tonight at five?"

"Fine."

Whew!

***

"How's Connie settling in," Bert asked me at lunch. We were in the faculty lounge, starting to get busy a week before TA orientation.

"She's getting used to us," I sighed, slurping my coffee. "We have a meeting with the Regents Thursday. I need to get her signed up for school tomorrow."

---

1 What I *knew* about home buying then you could stick in your eye and it wouldn't hurt.

"I *heard* about the Regents meeting. If I were you, I wouldn't be *that* concerned about it."

"Why not?"

"The winds of change are blowing. I don't know for *sure*, but I'm inclined to think there won't be *too* much trouble." He bit into his sandwich. "Can you handle two sections *and* a fall seminar?"

"What's the seminar?"

"October's the twenty-fifth anniversary of the Cuban Missile Crisis. I'd *like* to see a three-part *weekend* seminar.[1] I have a lesson plan."

"Let me look." I finished my potato chips. "Connie's taken to calling me '*Dad*,' called Meli '*Mom*' last night."

"Better than '*hey, you*,' or '*fascist pig*' like *some* kids are calling their elders these days."

"It would have been less...odd...if she'd grown *up* doing it."

Bert set his sandwich down. "Ya know, Curtis, I *envy* you."

"*Envy* me? Why?"

"A teenager appears on your doorstep that you'd never clapped eyes on before. She says her mother thought *so* highly of you that she entrusted her care to *you* after she was gone." He shook his head. "Any *idea* how big a *risk* that child was taking, getting here on her own, *hoping* that you wouldn't slam the door in her face, that your wife would make her feel *safe* if not welcome?" He shook his head again. "Any *idea* how much *trust* both mother and daughter *had* to have to allow them do *that*, sight unseen? That this woman remembered your strength of character *that* deeply?"

"Didn't *think* about it like *that*."

"Think about it like *this*: when the first pioneer families set out across the sea to come here, there was no going back, no telephones with salvation on the other end. There wasn't for *Connie*, either. There was just an unknown shore with natives that would either kill or nurture. The only friendly voice for Connie was a *lawyer* and an uncle she didn't know. But *some* pioneers knew there were already colonies that would give them some respite. For Connie, you *are* a colony."

"I don't *think* Connie was concerned about being scalped, Bert," I said, "though I get your point about the unknown."

"But now you're looking to buy a house?" I'd *also* mentioned that we were *casually* house-hunting.

---

1 Weekend seminars are offered for Continuing Education Units (CEU) and were an excellent way to attract out-of-town scholars and show off the school.

"With Meli expecting again and Connie with us, we're outgrowing the two-bedroom, and we can't expect *bigger* on campus in less than a year. Not much choice."

"Never *did* that; never *had* to."

"*You* were a Jenson Scholar, too, yeah?"

"I was the '38 Jenson Scholar; BA. in '42; commissioned in '43. Like you, I got a waiver so I could come *back*.[1] Got back from Manchuria in '46, and Helen met me when I got off the ship in San Francisco. I got de-mobbed, we bought our first car and drove back *here*. I completed in '50 and got on the faculty the same year; Helen, two years later. Been in campus housing ever since. So I never needed either a mortgage *or* a lawnmower."

"Soon, it might be *my* turn to envy *you*."

***

"Well," Diane beamed as we all piled through the front door of the sprawling ranch house. "House was built in 1970; *original* owner's selling after a *messy* divorce. Gas heat and hot water. *Four* bedrooms, *three*-and-a-*half* baths on the main level. A full basement with the beginnings of a mother-in-law apartment. *This* is the living room..."

We'd arrived in two separate cars and met Diane there. I'd picked up Connie at our house; Melanie had collected Maria from school. The house was just a half-mile from Crest's east gate, a mere *two* miles from Melanie's job.

What impressed me *first* wasn't so much the house as it was the broad swath of lawn that had to be *twenty yards* from the front door to the sidewalk—our current front lawn wasn't *six feet*. A side yard on the left side sloped gently down to a chain-link fence *ten yards* away. Another ten-yard swath of grass on the right adjoined an adjacent lot with its twenty-yard setback to a house with an *enormous* mansard roof. With a *thirty-yard*-long backyard bounded by fences on all three sides, the house was larger than every house and room I'd *ever* lived in *combined*.

I listened to Diane drone on, watching Melanie look around at the fireplace, the big picture windows, and the halls that branched off in two directions. Connie followed Maria as she dashed around, in and out of rooms.

---

1 I had to take a year off between my BA in '77 and starting grad school in '78 because I'd contracted mononucleosis that spring. I needed a waiver to resume my grant status if I wasn't *continuously* enrolled.

"We could fit our whole *house* in this living room," I said, somewhat in awe.

"It's 4,500 square feet of living space on a little *less* than a quarter of an acre," Diane said. "The *kitchen* has a *built-in* gas range *and* double-oven *and* refrigerator-freezer..."

We explored the big house from the basement to the attached three-car garage's attic. Maria declared a corner bedroom to be *perfect*. I appreciated a paneled den as big as our current living room. Melanie marveled at the open-plan kitchen with a counter/island and dining space, windows on two sides with French doors to the backyard. Connie looked around a big, bright bedroom with an adjacent bathroom, walk-in closet, and wall-to-wall shelves.

Maria inevitably made her way out to the backyard with Connie in tow. Maria spied a neighbor's swings and made a mad dash through a side gate. Soon, *more* kids poured out of the neighbor's house...and a couple of adults and a teenage girl. Fearing an altercation, I started in that direction until....

Connie started shaking hands, smiling widely as the little kids swarmed the swings. Maria seemed *very* familiar with one of the children. "Classmate," Melanie said, watching with me. "*Charlene*, I think."

"Ah." Connie was in an animated conversation with the teenager, giggling about something.

"Nice neighborhood; close to the schools," Diane joined us.

"Uh-huh," I said, watching Connie and her new friend do some sort of a cheerleading move, followed by some laughter.

I *think* it was the surprise, but the adults just stood around watching the little kids play and the teenagers' animated conversation. No one was *screaming*; no one was *fighting*...

It must have been fifteen minutes before the grownups next door had had enough and called for their children. "Maria, honey, *c'mon*," Melanie called. "*Dinner's* waiting."

Reluctantly, Maria hopped off the swing and stomped in our direction; Connie joined us. "Ally's a junior at Granite Ledge; her *brother's* a senior this year," Connie said. "*She's* a cheerleader; *I* said 'not *this* year' and told her why. Her brother's a cross-country runner; his *friend's* expecting, only it's not *his*. Her little *sister*...yeah, was an *oops*, she thinks."[1]

---

1 It always amazed me how teenage girls could find out *so* much in *so* little time.

"Well, ah," I finally said, checking my watch, "I think *this* would do *quite* well..."

"*Great.*" Diane waited...*patiently.* "*This* is when you're supposed to make an *offer.*"

"*Offer* of...?"

"An *offer* to *buy*," Connie mumbled.

"$99,000 seems a *little* high," I said to Diane, then looking at Melanie (she nodded), then Connie (she shrugged), then Diane again.

"So *give* me a *number* that *isn't*," Diane sighed, staring into space.

"OK...say...$88,000, *just* for the sake of argument."

"Say *$90,000* first," Connie mumbled. "Just *say* it," she prompted. I glanced at her; she winked with a *little* smile.[1]

Huh? "OK; *$90,000.*"

Diane sighed. "I'll *start* with that; they'll probably go to $96,000."

"OK, that's..."

"*Probably* about what they're *expecting*," Connie sighed.

Diane smiled at her, surprised. "I *think* you *just* bought a house."

Sure. And furniture, a lawnmower, a snowblower, and a table saw. I can learn to make furniture...hmm...

***

"*Wow*," Melanie exclaimed, gazing at the linen suit Connie had found. "Light, dressy, *and* casual with the vest but *without* the jacket. You *didn't* find *this* at Chapman's for *this* price."

"No, Bumble Bee Studios, a *new* store a block over," Connie smiled proudly. "*Just* opened, and *everything* was on sale. Shoes and everything *else* at Chapman's."

"*And* lunch with Al," Melanie asked.

"We ate with some friends of his in town. *Seem* nice enough."

"*Which* friends," Melanie asked.

Connie reeled off some names, *none* of whom I was familiar with. "*Carol's* got a sister, Francine, who I *think* is your age," Melanie said.[2]

"Yeah, *senior* this year."

"Well, great," I said. "I talked to your mom's lawyer this morning."

"Did Schuyler bring the paperwork for my *trust fund*," Connie asked.

"She *did.*"

"She *said* she'd be up here to deliver that *and* the shipping papers for all my worldly goods." She hung her purchases in Maria's closet with a

---

1 "*Trust* me," it said.

2 How women keep *those* things in their heads is *another* mystery

sigh, next to her freshly laundered *three* shirts, *two* skirts, *one* sweater, *one* casual cotton dress, and *three* pairs of jeans, joined by her *borrowed* blouse and skirt. "*Not* much to wear *weeks* before school starts."

"*More's* coming," I said.

"Not *that* much more for *this* climate," Connie sighed, sitting on her bed. "And *nothing* for *maternity*." She seemed bleak. "I'd *rather* have Mama."

"I *know*," Melanie said. "*This* is hard."

"*Nothing* like what I've been *preparing for* since Mama said she was terminal." Connie breathed deep. "I spent *weeks* planning to meet you, to either be put up with or *not*." She looked up at me. "Today, you showed me my *own room* in a *new house*." She shook her head gently, wiping away a tear. "*Not* what I expected, Dad."

"*We* didn't expect a teenage *daughter*, either, dear," Melanie sighed, "*certainly* not one calling Curtis *Dad*."

"I'm *sorry*, Mom," Connie began.

"It's OK," Melanie said. "I'll get *used* to it. That, *and* a teenager who's calling *me* Mom."

Maria came in from the bathroom, wiping her damp hands on her skirt. "Are you *sad*, Connie," she asked.

"A *little*, baby," Connie said. "I miss *my* Mama."

"Where *is* she?"

"She's gone to *heaven*, baby," Connie said. "But," she smiled, "*I've* got a *surprise*."

"So does *Mommy*," Melanie added, sitting next to Connie. "Connie and Mommy are having *babies*."

I guess they worked it out. "That's *right*," I said. "You're going to have a little *brother...or sister*."

"You have *babies* in your *tummies*?" Maria's school gave a basic "birds and bees" lesson when a classmate announced the coming of a sibling; we'd signed the permission for it.

"Uh-huh." Connie took Maria's hand and put it on her belly. "Feel *that*? *That's* the baby waking up."

Maria smiled, putting her other hand on Melanie's belly. "Is *your* baby waking up, *too*, Momma?"

"No," Melanie said. "*My* baby's too little. Connie's baby is *bigger*."

Maria, fascinated, looked at both women with awe. "Will the babies like *horses*?"

"I don't *know*," Connie said. "You'll have to *show* your mommy's baby *your* horses. *This* baby is someone *else's*."

I noticed Melanie's face change. *They had not worked THIS out.* "Whose," Maria asked.

"A family in Michigan. I'm growing *their* baby because they *can't* grow their own."

"Why?"

"I don't *know*. They asked *me* to grow *their* baby, so I *am*."

An elegant answer to a complex question Maria would be bound to ask: *where did Connie's baby go?* Connie already *had* the answer.

Connie seemed to have *so* many answers...too many? *I wonder...*

***

"You don't *mind* me calling you 'Dad and Mom'...or should I stick to 'Curtis and Melanie?'" With Maria in bed, we had repaired to the kitchen to talk about...I wasn't *sure* what, but Connie *wanted* to talk about *it*. "Mama's gone; you *feel* like you *could be* my dad. After all, Mama *said...*"

"Just around *family*," Melanie interrupted. "Let's not give the gossips outside any *more* ammunition."

"*When* Maria asks if Connie's her *sister* since Connie calls me '*Dad*,'" I murmured, "*what* will we say?"

"Say...'Connie's mom *knew* Daddy a long time ago,'" Melanie said. "It's accurate, concise...."

"And puts *Dad* in a teen jackpot," Connie grinned, "since *that's* what she'll tell her *friends* and *their* parents. No: say..."

"*I'll* tell her, 'Connie's my *daughter by choice. That* makes her *your* sister.'" *That* just came out, I *swear.*

Connie stared at me and shed a little tear; Meli made her patented 'I *don't* believe I *heard* that' face.

"OK," Connie whispered at length. "*Daughter by choice* I am."

"Daughter by *choice* you *are*," Meli added.

We were quiet for a long time, listening to the refrigerator cycle, the ice cubes drop into the tray, the clock ticking. "Dad: *don't* argue, but if you're serious about that house, I want to stick some money into a down payment."

"We *can't* ask you to *do* that, Connie."

Connie rested her chin in her hand, her elbow on the table. "You're *not* asking; I'm *offering*. I've got a *good* idea of what's in my trust fund. How about $25,000?"

"Connie," I said, a little tartly, "you don't *have* to keep trying so hard. We can *do* this."

"I *want* to do what *Joanie* would have *wanted* me to do. The reason we're moving is *me*; I *want* to..."

"No, it's *not*," Meli snapped. "No, it's because *we*..."

"I *know* a fib when I *hear* it, Mom," Connie said quietly.[1] "It's because of *me*, and I *love* you *and* Dad for it. Let your new daughter *celebrate* and *invest* in her new life."

"OK," I said at length, glancing at Melanie; she shrugged enigmatically.

"Just *one* question, Connie," Meli said. "*How* do you *do* it? How do you keep your eternally-cheery attitude after *everything* that's happened to you? You've *barely* had time to *grieve*."

Connie seemed *relieved* by Meli's question but looked away. "I've grieved for Mama for *months* now; she knew she was dying before the doctors did. The day I was elected cheer captain, she said, 'honey; I ain't *got* another winter in me.' I started to grieve for her *there* and *then*.

"I went to that party knowing my friends would support me, so I *had* to stay positive. I knew Katie Morrison would understand 'cause her pappy passed of cancer last winter, and she *did* comfort me some. Then *Jasper* happened. And afterward, I got strength from Leona and her daddy's garden gun and Katie covering me with that towel.

"I want to say that was *all* I needed, but it *wasn't*. After the police brought me home, a *real* nice police gal stayed the night. The three of us played poker and drank moonshine till that gal and I passed out; Mama put us both to bed.

"Next morning Mama said 'Connie: Jasper's paid his price and you ain't got a mark *on* you. That's *Texas justice*, child. Remember *that*.' There's not a day goes by I don't hear her saying that." She reached for our hands. "I *grieve*, Mom; Dad. I *just* don't let it slow me down. I know Mama wouldn't if she was in *my* shoes. About the last thing she said to me...must have been about my birthday...she said, 'don't let the bad parts of your life ruin the good. Make the *good* parts better; you've got your *whole life* to do it in. My grandchildren will never know me, but I *know* their *mother* won't let *herself or me* down."

No, she won't.

***

"That house," Meli murmured as we lay in bed, "seems perfect."

"Mm," I agreed.

"We can *probably* afford it, even *without* her down payment." I heard a familiar rustle before she tugged the drawstring on my shorts.

---

1 Connie had an uncanny ability to see through *everyone's* bullshit. There wasn't a lie, fib, prevarication, or "spin" that she couldn't detect.

"She's helpful, courteous, got her *own* money."

She rolled, her back to me; I ditched my shorts and spooned behind her. "She's *so* much help. *Table* this discussion."

OK... I obliged her desires.

I was *just* about to drift asleep *after*, when, "what if she *is* as bright and determined as she *seems* to be?"

"She would be the most *remarkable* teenager in the country."

Quiet...until I found Meli on top of me again. "And I *can't* get *enough* right now..." she sighed.

It was *wearing*, but I *managed* to *accommodate*.

"Maybe she *is* the most remarkable teenager in the country," Meli whispered in my ear *later*, "and *you're* the most remarkable *man* in the *world*," stroking...gently...

Again? Really?

Meli lay with her head on my belly, worn-out *finally*, when we heard Connie in the bathroom *not* being sick, then heard her go downstairs. "Shit," Meli sighed, "she *heard* us."

"You *sure?*"

"*Pretty* sure, yeah."

"We don't make enough noise to wake Maria."

"Maria's *used* to it; doesn't know what *it* is. *Connie...*"

Oh, great; she heard us...how many times?

Wednesday, There Was Another Surprise

'Hi," the young female clerk behind the counter said, "how can I *help* you?" I hadn't been *in* a high school since I graduated in '73, so I wasn't *quite* sure what to expect when I took Connie to Granite Ledge High.

"*Transfer* from *Texas*," Connie drawled, putting her last report card and her purse on the counter.

"I have her birth certificate and a custody assignment," I ventured. "She's living *here* now."

The clerk studied our documents for a moment, looking puzzled. "*This* is a *custody* assignment?"

"That's what *Texas* uses," I said, shrugging resignedly.

"One *moment*, please." The clerk left, going into another room behind the counter. A woman and a young man approached the counter moments later; a *different* clerk appeared and took their more *straightforward* transfer. Connie smiled gently at the young man; he smiled back bashfully. *Girl can charm apples off a tree.*

Our clerk came back momentarily, accompanied by an older gentleman. "Never *saw* a custody assignment quite like *this*. But if *Texas* says it's kosher, who are *we* to say it *isn't*? You're Dr. Durand?"

"I *am*," I answered, wondering if *that* was my sole function.

"Very well. Her *birth certificate* lines up. *Vaccination* record?" Connie produced a yellow booklet. "Any identification with an *address*?" She showed him her new driver's license, still warm from the laminator. He scanned it briefly before he leaned over the counter. "*When* are you due?"

"February," she answered.

"There's one *other* expecting young woman that I *know* of this year, a senior like yourself. Get your doctor to fill *this* out." He handed us a form. "It states your fitness to participate in school activities *and* do PE. Do you have a *plan* for *after...?*"

"Adoption."

"*Very* well. *Here's* the *district's* application for admission. The school *needs* it by the first day of class on Wednesday the 9th of September: three *weeks* from *today*. Forms and fees day for seniors was *last* week, so I'll catch you up *today*. You'll *have to* meet with a counselor—I'll get you in to see Mr. *Chambers*—to set up your *classes* so we can figure out your *fees*. You can get your *books...*"

We filled in the application while we waited between meetings, saw the counselor, went to the book store, and then paid our money—the nearly $300 included a lab fee for geology.[1] She only *needed* another five credits to graduate; her school days *were* short. On *my* advice, she signed up for Latin I *instead* of a second study hall. We made a *quick* stop with the school nurse to leave Connie's doctor's name and contact information.

I was mildly surprised that the school accepted Connie's pregnancy more readily than they did her custody assignment. I certainly didn't remember schools doing *that* in the '60s or '70s. Then again, I didn't *know* of any pregnant teenagers in school...except *one*.

And *here* was her *daughter...*

***

"Altogether, I'm not certain of the *relevance* of the Truxton." I stared at Nina as she spoke with a confidence that I found unsettling.

"Huh," Bert nodded. "I've been afraid *someone* might come to *that* conclusion."

"So have *I*," I sighed, surprised I actually *said* it even if it *had* been niggling at me for months.[2] "The material we're looking at, with a few exceptions, are all...um, not *trivial*, exactly, but..."

---

1 I *didn't* remember high school being quite *that* expensive in the '60s or the '70s, nor do I remember having to pay a deposit on my locker.
2 I was beginning to feel the project was going somewhere near nowhere...and in slow motion, at that.

"Of *limited* import," Lew said. "We're making a Herculean effort to establish provenance for documents that no one may ever *care* about. Lists of *lumber* stocks; correspondence about horses, sheep, and corn; grades of cattle and sheep, even the best combinations of donkeys and horses to make *mules*. We spent a *week* working on a *recipe* for *fertilizer*. Most of these documents are anonymous, some use *obvious* pseudonyms, but we don't *know* for *whom*. *Some* we can't make heads or *tails* of." He sighed heavily. "I can *do* the science, but *frankly*, I'm *not* sanguine about the *value* of it—about the *possibly* injudicious use of the time and materials expended in the effort."

"I *have* to agree," Nina added. "There's not *much* in *most* of the documents we've examined that has any *appreciable* value to scholarship."[1]

"A question, if I *may*," Connie drawled. I'd given her a bare-bones outline of the work we were doing on the Truxton.

"Certainly, Connie," Bert replied, "ask away."

"Can someone please define 'appreciable value' for *me* in *this* context?" I thought she should be exposed to the nuts and bolts of the history *job* just to see if it really *was* something she wanted. Being an occasional *buff* was one thing; being a working *scholar* was quite another.

"Well," I said, "'appreciable value' suggests that documents *should* have some import, some *viable* bearing on the record..."

"Archives are for *working scholars*," Nina declared. "They have limited time to look for what they need. What we're finding, for the *most* part, has *very little* scholarly interest."

"Um," Connie made a face. "if I might *add* something?"

"All right," Bert shrugged; we all made similar gestures.

"A couple of years ago, I was rummaging through a *junk* shop's bargain bin in San Antonio. I found an old ledger; hand-sewn, cloth cover torn. It was *full* of ink entries I could barely make out, but I saw *one* pencil entry—*Maddy Fulbright, one baby coffin, $1 on credit*—clear as day. *That* intrigued me, so I bought it, and I studied it with a magnifier and a black light.

"It *had* to have been kept by a carpenter's *second* wife who cared for three *step*-children—she was *about* 22, but even *she* didn't know for *sure*. She kept a record of *everything* her husband's business bought and sold between February of 1853 and September of 1857. There were entries for lumber, hardware, tools, paint, varnish, shellac, brushes, even rags. She recorded sales for tool handles, tent poles and pins, sluice cradles,

---

1 We chose the documents to study at random. There was a *lot* of dross.

tables, chairs, stools, wagon parts, buckets, casks, barrels, crates, her husband's labor on buildings, *and* coffins.

"She used the *back* pages for a diary. Her family moved with the mining camps down the San Antonio River as the gold and silver were worked out. She bore two children in those camps; *both* died before they were a year old. I *think* she died after September 12th, 1857. Her last entry on that date said she was *very* ill. Her entries *ended* abruptly; about 2/3rds of the ledger was used. Since I don't have her *name*, we'll never know for *sure*. But I learned more about the everyday business of the mining camps from that *one ledger* from a junk pile than I did in a *month* of searching the county museum archives.

"For context to *your* discussion, I wrote about her in my *Smithsonian* article: I called her *and* the article 'Maddy Fulbright's Creditor.' Maddy's descendants found *me* after that article ran." She smiled at everyone. "Is *that* what y'all *mean* by 'appreciable value?'"

"She's a *ringer*, Curtis," Nina declared, shaking her head. "*Get* her fingerprints, and we'll find out what institution she's a refugee *from*."

"Young *woman*," Lew nodded, "*this* little band of scholars *thank* you for your *clarity*. 'For want of a *nail*, a *shoe* was lost...'"

"I *started* this project with the assumption that the Truxton *contained* forgeries..." I began.

"*That's* what you said in your *book*, Curtis," Connie interrupted. "*Then* you said, 'these documents tell us of a historical road we have *not* taken—a past we have not *seen*. As Frost did in his poem, we *must* consider *why*.'" She smiled demurely. "Have I over*stepped*?"

"No, Connie," I said. "Not at all. You've reminded us of why we go through all this *pain*."

"Yes, *indeed*," Bert declared. "No archivist can know just *how* their documents will be used. They only hope that *someone* will use them, eventually. All we can *do* is record what we find, archive it in the appropriate context, and leave it to other scholars to see if it fits in *their* current puzzle."

"How much of the Jenson *is* used, Dr. Hubbard," Connie asked.

"Well, admittedly not as much as some *other* archives," Bert answered, somewhat surprised, "but we have a steady stream of queries. Our microform project is *nearly* complete, so we'll be making *those* available to preserve the documents themselves. I *have* thought of compiling a list of recent additions to the archive, including new identifications, and submitting it to the academic publications. Beyond *that*, it's strictly word-of-mouth and reputation."

"Someone should *do* a study on how much of any archive is typically *ever* used," I said. "But I don't think we'll *like* the results."

"Probably not," Nina agreed. "So *many* are never even looked at, though we *know* what they *say...*"

"*Do* we," Connie asked. "We know what the *last cataloger* said, but is *that* the last word? I've found *several* uncatalogued documents stuffed into archive boxes. We probably *all* have."

"I know *I* have," I agreed.

"*I* have, too," Nina said. "Scrambling around looking for material on Terry Allen,[1] I found an original sketch map of a little town in Mexico drawn by *Lieutenant* George Patton in 1917."

"Yes. *I* know it as well as anyone else." Bert agreed. "Once in a while, I find something in the Jenson that *should* have been cataloged. Now, *here*," he took up our latest list. "*Another* five documents *next* week, then we'll take a break when school starts, take up the project again in October. *That's* all for *this* week. *Thank* you, ladies and gentlemen. And, *Connie*," as he reached to shake her hand, "*thank* you for that *gentle* reminder of *why* we're *doing* this."

***

Connie and I walked back to our townhouse from Jenson Hall, slowly pacing in the dank humidity and bright sunshine. "My life is *here* now," Connie declared. "not a *bad* life, I suppose."

"It's what you make of it," I answered. "You *seem* to be able to make *friends* easily enough."

"*One-on-one*, sure," she sighed. "*That's* easy. But my first day at The Rock? *Whole* different story, Dad."

"The *Rock*?"

"It's what the *kids* call Granite Ledge High."

"But didn't that guy say there was another...?"

"The queens and the lionesses will *know* who her friends are and may even know the *father. I'll* be on my own. *New Girl* is one thing; *Pregnant Girl* is another; *New Pregnant Girl, that's* something *else altogether.*" She sighed. "Allies would help, *preferably Cool* Kids."

---

1 "Terrible" Terry de la Mesa Allen was a US Army officer in both world wars. It was odd that a legal history scholar would pursue such a subject, but we all had side projects *not* in our specialized fields. *I* was starting to work on the Industrial Revolution in America at that time.

"Maybe your new neighbor?" *If we should get that place...*

"Yeah." We strolled along for a time, but I could *hear* her thinking. "A *class ring* would *seem* to answer a *lot* of questions before they're asked."

"Rings come from *boys*." I shrugged. "Al?"

We walked some more. "That would *never* work. Our *age* difference is too great, but...he doesn't *have* to be the father, but he *could* be *a boy*." We walked on. "No; nobody *heard* of me around here before Saturday; *his* picture's in the showcase." We walked on. "Jerry Hoffmeier's a *sweet* guy; he *could* be *a boy*...if he'd *do* it. He's *not* attached." We walked further. "I'll *ask* Friday night."

"You after deception?"

"*Misdirection*. What *they* don't *know can't* hurt them."

"If it *works*, what does it *do* to the boy? *They* have reputations, too."

"Yeah. I don't *know* him, and *he* doesn't know *me*, and I *ain't* gonna..." She stopped. "I shouldn't be *thinkin'* about *using* people like that."

"Glad you stopped yourself. You had me thinking something I didn't *want* to think."

"What's *that*?"

"You've struck me as a caring young woman up to now." I glanced at her. "*That* kind of scheming didn't *fit* that profile."

She took my hand and squeezed. "You're *right*, Dad. *Thanks* for the reminder." She sighed. "I'll blame hormones."

"You *might* be *right*, honey." We walked on. "The guy you're *looking* for has to..." *...think as I did.*

"Mom says he would *have* to be *willing* to *love* me."

You've taken this up with her? "*That* would be ideal. In *your* case, at least to *like* you enough to *be* there when the going gets rough."

"Like *you* were *there* for Melanie during *her* pregnancy? That's not mere *like*, Dad: that's *love*."

"*Like* isn't 'mere,' honey. *Like* is the *key* to love. Any *guy should* be there for a *gal* he *likes*; he needs to be a *friend* in *need*. Love comes *because* of like. It's different for guys than it is for gals..."

"Why do *you* think *that* is?"

"Men used to *stake out* their mates, *fight* for them. Our protective instincts are in our DNA, *certainly* in our *social* conditioning. Even if a woman is a *friend* and *not* a mate, it's hard to turn that off."

We walked between the shades of buildings in the afternoon sun. "I'm trying to imagine *that* conversation; your involvement with her *before*; Maria's *father*...."

"It was pretty simple," I interrupted. "We'd been friends for *years*. She was in *trouble*; I could *help*. The father was *nowhere* in the picture."

"I imagine you *volunteered* to..."

"*Sort* of," I sighed. "The way it *ended up*, it *felt* mutual."

"Of *course*, Dad." We walked on. "I can imagine a *lot* of things, but how *you* were feeling then? *That* must have been tough."

"It was more *bizarre* than *tough*," I mumbled at length. "I went through a *lot* of *changes* in a few moments. Meli was a *friend* for whom I felt a great deal of *fondness*. That we *could* love each other...it was... can't *quite* describe that transformation, but I *don't* regret it. Maria's *our* daughter, made in passion and born in love."

"And *my* baby," she said softly as the townhouse came in view, "made in *violence* and *born*...I *want* to have what *you* and *Meli* had *then*, but..." her voice trailed off.

"We still *have* it, honey. You *will*, someday. With *someone*..."

"*Someday* with *someone*." She sighed. "I can't put a *guy* I don't know through *that* now. I'll *first* make a friend who will hold my hand when they *take* the *baby* away, like I *know* I *have* to do." She glanced at me. "Just hope the McCulloch's don't..."

"Me *too*," I said, reaching for the doorknob.

"Gotta *admire* a man who's willing to accept *another* man's child like *you* did."

"I'm taking *you* on."

"*That's* what I *meant*."

***

"Wow, *hi*, you guys," I heard Melanie at the front door just as we were setting the table for dinner when someone knocked.[1]

"Who," I asked from the kitchen just as Mom walked in. "*Whoa*," I exclaimed, "*how* did...and *Darla*? When...*Karen! Geez*, this *is* a surprise."

"Just thought we'd *drop* in," Mom said. "And you *must* be Connie. *I'm* Connie Durand."

Connie ignored the offered hand and went straight for the hug. Mom, surprised, seemed grateful all the same. What surprised *me* was when Connie began to weep. "I was told you were some sort of a sage Superwoman," she choked. "You're *everything* Mama said."

"No *cape*, dear," Mom grinned, stroking Connie's head, "and I *shouldn't* get into tights anymore. But, I can whip up a *mean* dinner at a restaurant. Come on; *I'm* buying."

---

1 Front-door surprises were common that week.

"So, how long are you *here*, Mom," I asked as we all sat in a nearby family eatery.

"Oh, a *few* days," Mom answered. "Long enough to catch up, for Darla to get to know *your* family and to *meet* Connie." She smiled at her namesake. "Your eyes are like your mother's."

"People have *said* that," Connie smiled.

"Did you have contact with your mom when you were in the foster home," Darla asked.

"I saw her every month at least," Connie answered. "My foster parents didn't make an issue of it since Uncle Will was often *with* her when she came." She sipped her water. "Do you *like* the Air Force?"

"Oh, sure," Darla answered. "I have another *year* of obligation, but I'll stay for the twenty. You're a *senior* this year?"

"Yeah. Karen: what do *you* do?"

"I mostly chase the kids around, but I also do legal work for my husband," Karen said. "*I remember* your mom. She...I'll *just* say I couldn't *answer* her question so I took her to see *Mom*."

I stared at Karen; she glanced back with a wink. Mom gave us that enigmatic grin of hers, the one that said, "now *you* know, too." Connie glanced at me, then Karen, then Mom. *Change the subject.* "Mom: how's *Dad* these days? He said he *might* be moving up?"

"Oh, your father needs to be a better politician. Connie, do...?" she started, then stopped when I cleared my throat. "*Curtis*, another semester starting soon? And Maria will be in Pre-K?"

As supper progressed, with its homey back-and-forth banter, I knew that Connie was becoming more and more distracted. Despite her natural ability to get along with *anybody*, the rash of questions was wearing.

I was getting edgy myself. I felt as nervous as I did the night before my final doctoral defense. The stakes were just as high.

***

"You *asleep*?"

"That's *got* to be the *stupidest* question since God asked *Cain* about *Abel*."[1]

"I *know*." She reached for me. "Want *help*?"

"Would that be for *you or me*?"

"*Yes*."

---

1 Genesis 4: 9-10. How would the Almighty *not* know, or was it the first rhetorical question?

We were just *getting there* when we heard Connie stumble into the bathroom, killing the *mood*, as it were, for a *few* minutes, anyway.

But we managed to *rekindle* my *spark*, as it were...*and* get to sleep, nonetheless.

Is she hearing us, or is she just getting sick?

Thursday Was When We Pled Our Case

'**D**octor Durand," Moe nodded as we entered the Regents Interview Room, a room as darkly imposing as the Long Room. Rather than three professors with whom I was familiar talking about a subject I knew well, we faced five millionaires who I knew only barely but who wanted to speak of the morality of a situation few could understand. "*Miss* Emmerich, *please*, be seated, *both* of you. This is *not* an inquisition. *Please* try to be at your ease."

"Yessir," I answered, as breezily as I could. We were directed to side-by-side padded armchairs, which were, surprisingly, *more* than comfortable.

"I'm grateful the Committee would *meet* with me, sir; ma'am," Connie offered as we sat next to each other. She nodded deferentially to the only woman present on the Committee, Angelina Silver Crest.[1]

"We are *more* than *happy* to meet with you," Angelina said, a little *too* cheerily...*said the spider to the fly.*

Our chairs faced a foot-high, curved dais about ten or twelve feet away, on which were perched seven small desks, five of which were occupied.[2] The room was darkly paneled to about chin-height, painted

---

1 The widow of Captain Crest's great-great-grandson, Mordechai Crest. The Committee consisted of the elder descendants of the founders of the school.
2 Not all members lived nearby or attended *all* the meetings.

bright white above. Light poured into the room from windows just below a coffered ceiling. Stenographers occupied three small tables by the door. The room *felt* like it was designed precisely *for* meetings of this kind.

"Doctor," Alan said, "the Committee *greatly* appreciates your contributions to the field of history, especially the work you're doing with the Jenson Collection. This meeting has nothing to do with your reputation as a scholar." As a Jenson scholar, I'd met Alan Jenson—and the rest of the Committee members—at school events. "Met" in this context meant simply shaking hands and exchanging banalities.

"Yessir," I agreed, "it has to do with Connie's *condition*."

"Not as *simple* as that, Doctor," Moe said. "Wish it *were*. We are concerned here with the moral atmosphere of this institution. Miss Emmerich, this is *not* a star chamber. We only want to verify some facts...to hear the *facts* from you directly."

"Yessir," Connie smiled. "I *think* I understand."

"*Do* you, Miss Emmerich," Alan asked. "*What* do you *understand* of Crest University?"

"I've wanted to come here since I was nine," Connie said. "*Altum Spectant*[1] has been my *personal* motto since I first read about the school when I was in 4th Grade."

They looked at each other, confused—she'd put them off balance. "*Where* did you read about us," Alan asked.

"My mother and I followed Curtis's career in the Chicago papers. We read his articles *and* his book," Connie answered. "I've *seen* your course catalogs. Your annual rankings have been steady for twenty years." She inhaled deeply. "I've always been interested in history like Mama was. I learned of the Jenson Grant when Curtis was awarded his Ph.D. I decided *then* that *I* wanted to be a Jenson Scholar."

"I *see*," Alan said. "Is Dr. Durand your *biological* father?"

"No," Connie answered, grabbing my hand. "Mama *said* he *wasn't*."

"Dr. Durand," Alan asked, "is this *correct*? We *heard* differently."

Already? "Joan—Connie's mother; my neighbor in Cicero—told *my* mother that I was *not* Connie's father in '69," I said softly. "*That* said," I went on, "Melanie and I, ah, *may* adopt her." Connie *may* have broken a bone in my hand, but I went on. "Mom's *in town* now if you *want* to...."

Again, they were startled, and again they looked at each other. "*That* won't be necessary," Alan finally sighed. "How did you come to *be* here, Miss Emmerich?"

---

1 *Always aim high*, the school's motto.

"Mama passed two weeks ago," Connie said. "I *came* because Dr. Durand is my guardian."

"And you knew *nothing* of this *or* this young woman, Dr. Durand?" Alan sounded incredulous.

"*Nothing*," I answered; Alan nodded.

"*Miss* Emmerich," Angelina cleared her throat, "I realize that *this* may be a sensitive subject, but, for the sake of this institution, we'd like to hear *your* version of..."

"My *assault*," Connie deadpanned.

"Your ...yes," Moe said quietly. "We've seen what Bexar County had to say about it. We've also seen what the witnesses said and seen *your* statement. Now, we want to hear from *you if* you're up to it."

Connie gripped my hand tighter. "I *was* a cheerleader who was *supposed* to worship *him*. ...." I *tried* to listen dispassionately as she told a *short* version of what she'd told Meli and me, finishing with, "*hindsight* tells me I should *not* have worn a *bikini* to a *swim party*."

It was *deathly* quiet...for a moment, I could *swear* I heard the electricity buzzing through the filaments of the ancient desk lamps.

"We're *so* sorry," Alan said finally. "If you'd *want* to..."

"I'm *fine*, sir," Connie sighed. "Jasper's been taught *his* lesson."

"As it happens, I *know* Amos McCulloch," another member of the Committee, John Davison,[1] declared. "I *spoke* to Amos just yesterday." Silence. "He's *aware* that you are carrying his grandchild but does *not* know *where* you seem to have *gotten* to." Silence again. "Is *this* by *design*?"

"*He* and his boys are the reasons I *left* Texas, sir. The McCulloch's would want custody if only to use the child to get at *me* for...well, they hold *me* responsible for Jasper's injuries."

"Which *were*," Alan asked.

"Jasper will have trouble *sitting* for some months," John said. "His *behind* was *thoroughly* peppered. He *also* suffered some damage to his lower back. His *athletic* career's probably over. I've done business with Amos McCulloch for *twenty years*, young woman. *You* are *impugning* the *honor* of that *family*...."

"*No*, sir," Connie *loudly* and *boldly* interrupted. "Amos McCulloch is a manipulative sonofa*BITCH*—excuse my *French*—who *uses* everyone he *meets*, and his boys are no *different*. The *men* in that family *have* no *honor*. That old man raised three sons who strut around as if their *flop* don't stink. He forced our best quarterback to *quit* the team so *Jasper* could

---

1 A great-great-great-grandson of Captain Crest.

take his slot. And *then*, we barely got into the *regionals* last season, and *everyone knows* it was because Jasper's a *lousy* leader, even if they don't *say* it out loud. His two daughters are lucky they get *any* of their *father's* attention at *all*. The youngest got *in trouble* last winter, and she *had* to get it *taken care of*, even though she didn't *want* to."

Deep silence followed....

"*HAH*," John laughed. "*Exactly* my impression *and* my information."

Then I heard Alan chuckle; then Moe. "Who's been *charged*, Alan," Moe asked.

"Several of the McCulloch boy's *helpers* were arrested and charged as accessories," Alan answered. "*Their* families don't *have* old man Amos's connections. Jasper's facing no charges *yet*, though how the county plans to prosecute the *helpers* without charging the *helpee* is beyond *me*. The young woman who *shot* him, Leona, *hasn't* been charged, and, according to the district attorney, *won't* be."

"Glad to *hear* about Leona; thank *you* very *much*, sir," Connie said. "I *believe* the McCulloch's *were* making noise about civil suits."

"They *were*; they *are*," Alan said. "They'll *go* nowhere. Are you willing to sign a criminal complaint?"

"I already *have*, sir," Connie answered. "I was told, because there were so many witnesses, that I would *not* have to testify in a criminal trial, though I am *willing*. I've been deposed *twice* already."

"Getting back to the present," Angelina said suddenly, "the *issue*, Miss Emmerich, is that an unmarried and *expecting* woman associated with Crest University is an *affront* to our moral code *and* a violation of Dr. Durand's employment contract. You *do* appreciate *that*, do you *not*?"

"I'm not sure I *do*, ma'am," Connie said flatly, staring her *straight* in the eye. "Your moral code and contract clause would hold that Lot's daughters—the mothers of Israel—would *also* be an affront. *They* wanted to preserve humanity, even if they got the old gent so *drunk* he *supposedly* didn't know *what they* were *doing* two nights in a row— *hard* to believe."[1] There were *some* chuckles. "The Almighty had *just* burned Sodom and Gomorrah; his daughters wanted to *make life*." *That* dumbfounded them, but not *near* as much as when she continued. "You *can't* read Genesis in St. Barbara's *and* condemn *a baby* and *me*. It's *not* an outcome I wanted, but it's *not* the child's fault. All the child and I are asking for is a chance to continue *my* life so the *child* can have a decent life of its own."

____

1 Genesis 19: 31-35.

You coulda heard a pin drop; I swear I heard Moe's neck swivel as he shook his head in disbelief, grinning widely.

"Do you see yourself as Lot's *daughters* or as *Lot?*" This was from a member who'd yet to speak: Christian Barnard Jenson-Fiske.[1]

"Some *still* call the daughters rapists, so *I'd* be more like Lot," Connie answered. "*Their* sins have been remitted *or* just ignored. But *God* didn't condemn *Israel* for what they did, nor did he condemn Moab or Ammon, the boys borne of those unions. John Calvin *didn't* think *they* thought the world had ended since they went *out* of Zoar—which presumably still *had* people—into those hills.[2] *Still,*" she smiled slightly, "you'd *think* women such as they *and* their *mother* should at least have had their *names* in the *Bible.*"

Several Committee members smiled; Alan *nearly* laughed. Thinking back on "Connie vs. the Committee," I reflect on how easily this unassuming young woman managed to *stun* five educated adults, as though it was an everyday occurrence.

"Young woman," Moe said softly, "you are *quite* the scholar; *quite* the thinker. Do you plan to *attend* Granite Ledge High?"

"I *am* registered, sir," Connie said. "I *have* to finish well if I want to be considered for a Jenson Grant."

"For what it's worth, we're bidding on a house off-campus," I added. "She won't *have* to come on campus..."

"Dr. Durand," Angelina answered, "*that* won't eliminate the inevitable *gossip.*" She waited. "*That* is what concerns us here. Faculty and staff families *must* be the templates for our society. An unmarried pregnant woman is *not* part of *that* template, *regardless* of what *popular culture* claims. *Already* there appears to be rumors floating around campus as to paternity for both your *child* and for *you,* young lady. How would *you* plan to address *that?*"

"The same way I'd address *any* unfounded claims, ma'am," Connie said, "with *facts.* The *child* may be unintended, but it *is* wanted. I see myself as carrying someone else's *wanted* child. I feel *no* shame for doing so, no *matter* the act that created it."

"As for *me,*" I declared. "Though I *could be* Connie's father, I'm *not.* She is *my daughter by choice* and shall *remain* so. Anyone who wants to throw *her* in *my* face can deal with *that.*"

That just came out, I *swear.* Connie had an *incredibly* strong grip.

---

1 A great-great-great nephew-in-law of Weymouth Jenson
2 Genesis 19: 30.

"Far be it from *us*, Dr. Durand," Alan declared, "to be *that* critical. Saying *that* took a *great* deal more courage than I believe anyone *else* here *has*."

"*A-men*;" "more than *I've* got;" "me, too," were among the murmurs.

"I hope you *realize*, young lady, that this Committee must balance *your* needs and desires against those of the school," Angelina pronounced. "As *compelling* as your account is, we still have the *fact* that you are *not* married, which is..."

"One of *many* factors we have to consider," Moe interrupted. "Miss Emmerich, can you excuse us while we speak to Dr. Durand?" The men, including myself, stood while Connie left; she gave me a brave wink.

I waited in silence as the Committee sat again. I made to sit until Moe asked, "*Possible*, Curtis?"

"*Timing's* wrong, but yeah," I said, *still* making to sit....

"Her *mother* was your *neighbor*, Curtis," Alan asked.

"Girl next door, yeah," I answered, *still* trying to sit....

"*Hot* summer, hey," John said.

"*You* don't know the *half* of it," I said, *still* trying to sit....

"My condolences on your loss—Connie's *and* yours," Moe added.

"Thanks," I said, *giving up* on sitting.

"*Quite* the young woman, Dr. Durand," Angelina declared.

"She *is*," I agreed.

"What shall you do if the child *isn't* taken up," Alan asked.

"Put another potato in the pot, another chair at the table." *If we adopt her...grandfather at 32.*

"*That* may be cause for another hearing," Angelina said. "Providing this Committee *doesn't* ask for your resignation *before* that time."

"I realize that my job is on the line," I said, "but *all* we ask is to consider this *one* case...."

"*Then* what, Doctor?" Christian's voice was strict, angry. "*One* case becomes a *score* in *no* time. Neither this Committee nor the school can *afford* to *police* the student body as we did *ten* years ago; we *need* the enrollments.[1] We *must insist* that the faculty and staff be *ideals* of conduct."

"*Excuse* me, sir," I asked, I *hoped* with sufficient deference, "but how long are you going to be able to *find* faculty and staff—let alone students— who will meet your criteria? Firing existing staff for not *conforming*..."

"We don't *fire* anyone," Angelina snapped. "They *resign*...."

---

1 At around $25,000 a semester all-in for undergrads and *slightly* more for grad students, we *were* about on par with Harvard. Without state *or* federal money (that Harvard *took*), we *had* to be.

"We demand their resignations under threat of lawsuits for breach of contract," Moe declared, "against which they cannot *afford* a defense. A *distinction*, Angelina, *without* a *difference*. We *know* they won't sue us for their jobs by the same token, so we just beat them to the punch. Dr. Durand has a point: how long can we keep *doing* this? How long before no one wants to *teach* here because they are *not* paragons of *our* definitions of virtue? Those definitions *do* shift, Angelina, whether we *like* it or *not*."

Silence.

"We must consider this matter in closed session, Dr. Durand," Alan said. "We *thank* you for your honesty and your attendance. If you will *excuse* us...?"

"Expect to *hear* from us...or *not*...*soon*, Dr. Durand," Moe said.

I met Connie outside, sitting on a concrete bench in the shade, gazing at the quad. We sat quietly for some time, waiting for one of us to speak. "*That* was..." I started.

"One for the books," Connie sighed. "They won't be forgetting *that* meeting for *quite* a spell."

"Sorry it *happened*, Connie."

"I *know*, Dad." She shifted on the bench; it was the first time I *thought* she was showing under her form-fitting top. "I just *wish* it had *never* happened."

"You would never have known *us* if it *hadn't*."

"Yes, I *would*," she sighed. "Mama was dying anyway. Me being pregnant was just...even if she *hadn't been*, you *probably* would have seen my application for the Jenson and called when you saw Mama's name."

"Just curious: have you *had* any counseling...?"

"A rape survivor's support group contacted me after it happened, said I *needed* counseling. I said, 'Leona gave me all the counseling *I* needed.' And it's true: I felt *so* much better because Jasper got shot for what he did. And Momma was so *happy* she'd have a grandchild, *regardless* of circumstances."

"None of my business, honey, but...before *that boy*...?"

She reached for my hand. "I *thought* I was in *love* with a boy that I *made* love with last spring. *He* dumped me *after* Jasper...he's *gonna* play football next year." She squeezed. "Sex *didn't* mean what I *thought* it would, what I suppose every girl *wants* it to mean. It felt *good* because I *cared* for him, but it *wasn't*...."

"It wasn't unicorns and rainbows," I sighed. "It rarely *is*, honey, but it's *better* when you *love* your partner and *know* it's forever. The world seems emptier knowing your mother is *not* in it. Come on; I'll buy you *lunch* in the faculty lounge."

After lunch, Connie asked, "can I borrow your car? I have an appointment for an ultrasound exam at 2."

"I'll *take* you if you *want*," I offered with some trepidation. I'd seen some of those on TV—didn't look *this-worldly.*

"No, thanks, Dad. I...*Mom* offered, too. I *just*...no, thanks."

Some things you just want to do alone.

***

"Hi, Mrs. Durand," I heard a young woman's voice say, "is *Connie* home?" It was eight at night, my family had gone to the hotel already. They were worn out from their visit to the Crest Landing Historic Site, their Sonoco River Tour, their Jenson Stone Quarry tour, and their self-guided tour around the campus.[1]

"She's putting Maria to bed," Melanie said. "*Come* on *in*, kids." Jenny and Jerry stepped into the living room, gazing around quickly. "Can I *get* you anything?"

"*No*, thanks;" "*not* for me, Mrs. Durand," were the answers she got.

"*Evening*," I said warily, "is Connie expecting you?"

"*Sort* of," Jenny said. "We met at the *doctor's* office this afternoon; talked about doing *something* tonight."

"Oh," I ventured, "Dr. Georgeson?"

"I was going *out* as she was coming *in*; she asked if *I'd* stick around for her ultrasound."

"Huh." Melanie glanced at me and shrugged. *Changed her mind.*

"Ah," I said. "How was *that?*"

"I'd never *seen* one before," Jenny said. "You can't *see* much more than grainy shadows, but Dr. G. said everything looked normal for *about* twelve weeks."

Jerry looked vaguely uncomfortable. *I feel for you, boy.*

"Well, I hope they say the same thing about *my* baby," Melanie said. "I get mine *next* week."

"Oh," Jenny said. "I didn't *know*..."

"Just *ten* weeks," Melanie said, "and my *second*, so *this* is old hat."

"*Someday*," Jenny said, elbowing Jerry with a grin, "*me*, too."

Jerry started visibly. *Not his idea of a joke.*

---

1 Granite Ledge had a *lot* of summer tourists. There were also three ski lodges in the area.

"Hi, guys," Connie said softly, descending the stairs. "Not *too* loud; Maria's *listening.*"

"*Hi*," Jerry smiled.

"So, *what* did your ultrasound..." Melanie asked.

"Yeah, *sorry.* I saw Jenny, and I suddenly decided I *didn't* want to be alone. Everything looks *OK*, Dr. G. said."

"It's *OK*," Melanie nodded. "I *get* it."

More like you wanted someone closer to your own age. "You'll tell the family," I asked.

"I'll give *them* another update this weekend."

"Jenny said you wanted to go *out* maybe," Jerry said. "*We* were going to hang with my *team* if you want to *join* us..."

"*Lots* of *guys*," Connie asked; Jenny nodded, grinning. Connie smiled broadly. "I'll *change*..."

***

As the 11 o'clock news was wrapping up the week of floods in Bangladesh and tornadoes on Mars, Connie returned, weary but bright nonetheless. "*Great* bunch of kids," she sighed, sitting in the love seat. "That Academy: good school?"

"I've *heard*," I said. "The students I've *had* from there *seem* OK."

"Met *Jenny's* friends from The Rock there."

"There...*where*," I asked.

"Cool J's; a burger joint on Broad at 12th Street. *Good* French fries. Found I can't *stand* the smell of peppermint right now. I'll *have* to try the peppermint shakes *after*..."

"*I* used to hang out there," Melanie said.

"Yeah? The place has old neon lights; half of 'em are *dead.* Your *parents* might have hung out there, Mom."

"*Maybe*," Melanie said.

Connie sat back and closed her eyes. "My life may not be *perfect*, but it's *pretty good.*" She looked at me. "Can I *talk* to Mom *alone* for a *little* while, Dad?"

It wasn't ten minutes later that Melanie came up to bed; Connie was still downstairs. "What was *that* all about, if I can ask an *indelicate* question?"

"Oh, *not* much," she said, getting undressed quickly. "She wanted to know if her *arousal* was *supposed* to be *high* at twelve weeks. I told her *mine* is at *ten*." She whipped the sheet off of me and laid down *on* me. "I told her *not* to listen; it *might* help."

"Pregnant girl didn't *want* to *talk* about..." *her enhanced sex drive with a man listening.*

"No, she *didn't.*"

Friday Came and We Chose Our Daughter

'**S**o, we *got* it," We'd *just* sat down to breakfast when the phone rang.

"Yep. They *passed* on the $90,000 bait and settled on $94,000," Diane said. "Come down to the office and sign the formal offer. I'll get the credit union the information. Do you *have* an insurance agent...?"[1]

As I hung up, scanning my notes, Connie handed Maria a banana, glanced at me. "I have lunch with Schuyler today. I'd like you and Melanie to come, too."

"*My* family, too," I asked.

"*Ours,* Dad, but *sure.*"

***

"*Pleased* to *meet* y'all," Schuyler drawled. "*Always* a *pleasure* to break bread with *clients* who have be*come* friends."

"*Pleasure's ours,* Miss *Schuyler*," Connie answered, sounding a *bit* like Scarlett O'Hara in *Gone With the Wind*. "How long will you stay?"

"Just 'till Monday," Schuyler said, opening the huge menu. "Got a *taste* for *grouse*, but I don't *see* it on the menu."

"Never *seen* grouse on a restaurant menu," Mom said.

---

1 There was a great deal more to buying a house than I had anticipated: insurance and utility deposits, and taxes and escrow...

"*Neither have I*," Schuyler deadpanned before she split into a wide grin.

We exchanged light conversation while the waiter brought the bread and water; asked about beverages. "*Can't* have a *proper* lunch with*out bourbon* and *branch water*, son," Schuyler drawled.

"Ma'am," the boy said, waiting.

"*White* soda, please;" "I'm *working*; coffee" "*Cola*, please;" "I'll stick with *water*, thanks;" "*Lemonade*, please..." came the other responses.

"S'all *right*, then, son," Schuyler drawled, "Make mine *sweet tea*. Cicero, y'all from?" We talked about hometowns and families until our meals came and went, and Schuyler asked, "so, *Connie*, honey, how are *you* fittin' in up here?"

"I *love* it here," Connie answered. "The Durands have accepted me."

"Get along with Maria and do your own laundry and you get along with *all* of us," Melanie said.

"*That's* terrific." Schuyler reached into her valise, pulling out a blue-backed legal document. "*I'm* here, among *other* things, to execute *this*."

She handed the original of Joan's will to Connie and a copy to me. It was a simple document with all the required flowery language in front. It left a tidy sum to Joanie's Place—her foster care transition charity—but had two unexpected legacies:

> *I leave, will, and bequeath the sum of $500,000 to the Jenson Foundation to preserve and maintain the archive known as the Jenson Collection. I also leave, will, and bequeath my collection of historical documents to the Jenson Foundation for inclusion in their Collection.*

"I spoke with the Foundation this week," Schuyler declared, "and I gave *them* this inventory. I just needed somewhere to *send* 'em."

I perused a list of some 1,000 items dating from 1780 to 1850, many having to do with the national expansion into the Gulf states. "I had no *idea* she was collecting documents," I said.

"She *was*," Schuyler said, "most of her professional life. She told me that she always *wanted* a career in history, just never had *time* for it. She dictated *this* codicil in her last days." Schuyler pulled out *another* document. "I was to find *you*, ma'am," and handed it to Mom.

My mother was a resilient, resourceful woman who could sniff out a story in her sleep. When she read the codicil, it was the only time I'd *ever* seen her *truly* surprised.

> *I leave, will, and bequeath $1,000,000 to the University of Chicago to endow the Constance M. Durand Chair of Journalism.*

"She wanted to acknowledge your *courage*, ma'am," Schuyler said, "and your dogged devotion to reporting on your son."

"Did you *know* about this," I asked Connie.

"Mama *talked* about leaving something so everyone would remember *your* mom."

"Yes, she did," Schuyler said.

She left Connie the residue of her estate[1] with me as her guardian. And...

> In the event that Constance should predecease me, I leave, will, and bequeath the residue of my estate to Curtis Harrison Durand.

I was *never* sure *what* to make of *that*.

"For a restaurant owner, she did *extremely* well for herself," Mom said. "Business *must* have been good."

"She got most of her *properties*—and a good number of those documents—playin' *stud*," Schuyler drawled. "I *swear* that gal could bluff and *bullshit*—and *see through* bluff and *bullshit*—better than *any* lawyer, politician, cattleman, or salesman *anywhere*."

"She taught *me* to see through it," Connie said.

"I lost ten grand to Joanie within *four hours* of meeting her," Schuyler grinned. "She bluffed me outta $500 with a *pair* of *fours*. I knew *then* I *had* to have her as a client *and* as a friend. And lastly, *this*," Schuyler handed a cardboard envelope to Connie, "arrived this morning, by *express*."

Connie pulled a document out, reading quickly. "I *don't* believe it," she sighed. "I *can't* believe it." She passed it to me.

It was a termination of parental rights, signed by Jasper McCulloch.

"It's for *real*. Your Uncle Will sent *this* along with it." Connie read the scrawled note before passing it to me, shaking her head.

> *Connie;*
>
> *Your decision to give up the baby has to be free and clear. I've made sure of it.*
> *Be safe.*
> *Will Gerard*

"The Rangers found that Jasper McCulloch has enough sex assault allegations to lock *his* ass up into the next *century*," Schuyler nodded. "There are at least three *other* children Jasper's fathered over the years. If they sue for *support*, it'll destroy Old Man Amos's business reputation and *bankrupt* him. So," she sighed with satisfaction, "Jasper relinquished his parental rights to *yours* in exchange for, well, *let's* call it *prosecutorial discretion*."

---

1 After everything was liquidated over the next six months, it was somewhere in the neighborhood of $900,000.

"*Uncle Will*," Connie shook her head. "I barely *know* him."

"You don't *have* to," I said, winking at Melanie. "He's just looking out for a damsel in distress."

I never met him either, but my mind's ear could hear a low, husky Texas drawl, saying, "I'd be *proud* to, Missy."

I glanced at Melanie; she did her little shrug. "Connie: *do* you want to be adopted?"

The whole room stopped. "I'd be *honored*," she finally grinned. "Constance Emmerich Durand," she said. "How's *that* sound?"

"More like a *married* name, Connie," Melanie said softly.

"I want to *keep* Emmerich...*Dad?*"

I didn't *want* to explain what made me cry. Connie's mother called herself "Joan Emmerich Durand just after I *thought* we *might* have made Connie" on the hot, wet, passionate summer night the astronauts landed on the Moon, a fond memory recently renewed.

***

"*C'mon*, Connie," Jenny called from her old Mercury convertible, "I saved you a *seat* in front." She'd pulled the crowded car into the alley behind the house.

"*Go* on," Melanie said, waving her out the back door. "*Have* fun."

"I think she'll be OK," I said, watching from the kitchen window.

"I *know* she will," Melanie agreed. "Wish I'd *known* her mother."

"I wish *you* had, too."

And how would my life have been different if THAT road had appeared in the yellow wood?

***

Connie fit into the Granite Ledge/Crest University community well. Her charm won *nearly* everyone over. She was a popular peer tutor for history *and* cheerleading. Jenny was her La Maze coach when John Allan Templeton was born on February 6th, 1988. They took him away three weeks after the birth, as required by state law. Jenny *and* Jerry were there when it happened. Connie gets cards and pictures that she shares with them...*and* us.

My son, Charles Albert Durand, was born on March 20th, 1988, six months after we moved into the ranch house. Maria adores her little brother...*most* of the time.

Connie, Jenny, and some other girls went to Galveston Island on Spring Break in '88; no *boys* were allowed. Jerry took Connie to his homecoming cotillion, her Winter Formal, his Spring Fling, and her Senior Prom. Of course, Jenny was on his *other* arm for all four events. The three of them were practically inseparable.

Connie *didn't* win the Jenson Grant for 1988. She lost out to a girl who was *just* as studious and dedicated. She enrolled at Crest in '88, anyway. When we adopted her later in '88, she kept her *own* name, explaining that it was too complicated to *change* it everywhere. While true, it may not have been the *only* reason. Nonetheless, she uses *Durand* from time to time.

The Jenson Collection was renamed the Jenson *Archive* in 1988. The Emmerich *Collection,* with Andrew Jackson material, has become a stopping point for scholars who also study the *Jenson's* Jackson documents. Together, they chronicle a *significant* part of Old Hickory's pre-presidential law practice. We continue to work on the Truxton *Collection,* partially funded by Joan's legacy. Every once in a while, we *find* diamonds in that coal pile.[1]

We never heard *anything* from the Regents. As Moe said, we'd hear from them...or *not.* The morals clause in our contracts disappeared over the years. Crest University joined the 20th Century just in time for the 21st.

Our ranch house has helped me round out *my* carpentry with plumbing,[2] carpet-laying, and other domestically-required skills. I *got* my table saw, a toilet snake, *and* a snowblower. I make furniture from time to time when I'm not working on a book or an article, grading essays, or doing *other* academic stuff.

As I had heard, a home is a lump on your real estate into which owners pour blood, toil, sweat, tears, and time...*and* tools.

Like parents do their kids.

---

1 A common misconception, but it worked for Superman, so just go with it.
2 The fine print in my marriage vows, it turns out, *forbids* me from touching plumbing with tools. I found *this* out one *very* expensive weekend.

THE PAST AND THE PROLOGUE

On Tuesday, HE Made
An Appearance

It is said by the literary mavens that Shakespeare practically invented the English language as we know it today. I don't know about *that*, but this passage haunted me for quite a while:

Whereof what's past is prologue, what to come in yours and my discharge.[1]

The Bard's Antonio was plotting to kill a couple of guys so *another* guy could become king. He was going to *write history*. The choice was *his* to make.

Or *not. That's* the point Shakespeare was trying to make. Antonio had a *choice.* Everything before *that* moment was a preparation for the opportunities and fortunes—or *misfortunes*—to come. And what he did was his choice to make, based on *that* preparation.

Plays were the *furthest* thing from my mind when I heard over my shoulder, "Dr. Curtis Durand," as I closed my classroom door.

I answered, "that's *me*," as I turned to face....

"My name's Steve Wabrzeznoski,"[2] *HE* said, standing *perfectly* still.

This was the *one guy* in the *whole* world who I did *not* want on my doorstep—Maria's biological father. I knew who *HE* was because

---

1 *The Tempest,* Act 2, Scene I.

2 Pronounced *Zab-zen-sow-ski*. Meli always said it was pronounced the way it was spelled. She was *wrong*.

looking at him *felt* a little like I was looking in a mirror maybe twenty years from now, even if he was only two years older. He was a little taller, had my light-brown hair streaked with grey;[1] my eyes, *sort* of, and about my build. But he had my *face*, and *certainly* the jaw I shaved every day.

And I didn't know *what* I was going to do. "What can I do for you?" I tried *not* to hint at any familiarity.

"You can tell Meli I *need* to see my daughter."

I breathed deep, trying to be nonchalant. "Why?" It *was* a good question.

This kind of confrontation only occurs in movies or on TV...dramatic effect and all. It's *usually* done with lawyers present after many rounds of papers are filed. I *knew* this because I had *some* experience with custody and parental rights matters with some students.

"Because I have a *right*..." Steve started.

"*Don't* start ticking off your 'rights,' *sir*," I said, as calmly as I could manage, foregoing trying to pronounce his name. "You gave up your 'rights' when you told Melanie 'so long' after she said she was expecting."

"My *lawyer* thinks different," Steve said, *just* as calmly.

"Then go through *him*, and *only* through *him*," I answered. I locked my classroom door (which I *never* did), turning my back on him with some trepidation. Like many people by 1991, I had heard horror stories about indignant bio-dads who did violence to those who defied them. Admittedly, *most* of those stories *were* in '*based on actual events*' movies or daytime TV talk shows.

Steve stood behind me, waiting, I believe, to continue with his witty repartee. I started to walk away...and he walked *with* me. "If there's anything specific you need *right now, say* so. Otherwise, I have a *staff* meeting *after* lunch." I *tried* to sound like an arrogant, stuffed-shirt academic far too busy to be bothered by this *interloper* and *not* simply a history teacher with a Ph.D. *And*, my staff meeting was *tomorrow*.

History was being made at that moment in southwest Asia, where a shooting war had started in Iraq. Jenny Rizzo was over there, somewhere.[2] Several of my students—Reservists and National Guards—in several classes, *and* some school staff, had been called up last summer and fall at the same time as Jenny's unit at Holman Field. We knew some had been shipped overseas; we hadn't *heard* from others in weeks or months.

So I had *other* things to think about, rather than this latecomer's claim on the daughter I'd spent the past eight years nurturing.[3]

---

1 That *I* didn't have yet.

2 Jenny was a fuel handler in an Army Reserve helicopter unit.

3 Maria was just short of her eighth birthday.

Steve, perhaps expecting conversation, dogged slightly behind me as I went out of Jenson Hall and headed for the Crest Administration Building in a biting cold wind. Last night's snow had been neatly piled on the grassy patches in the quad and now buried the benches, the yew hedges, and half the birch trees. As I tried to hustle through the wind, there was *Steve*, keeping pace...

He followed me into the Administration Building silently; I suppose still expecting engagement. I stopped at the double doors of the Faculty Lounge across from the side entrance, with its large and imposing sign that read FACULTY AND INVITED GUESTS ONLY. I turned, looked at Steve, and said, "*you* are NOT invited," and went in.

"Can you at *least*..." was the last I heard. Steve *didn't* follow. *At least he's not trying to barge in.*

The Faculty Lounge was part lounge and part cafeteria. It took up nearly half the first floor of the Jenson Admin Building and was the only "professor's country" on campus. There were *also* undergraduate-only and graduate-only lounges in dorms and apartments that, admittedly, were not *nearly* as well-appointed, staffed, or stocked as the Faculty Lounge. Even though students had to pay a hefty fee to attend Crest, the amount spent on on-campus student luxuries *was* modest.

At close to noon, several faculty members were milling around the coffee and donuts. I saw Helen engaged in conversation with another professor by the hot water pots. I nodded to her, then made for the phone cubes and called Melanie.

"*Melanie Durand; how* can *I*..."

"Honey, *Steve's* here."

Silence. "Steve...Wabrzeznoski?"[1]

"Yep. He says he wants to see Maria. Says his *lawyer* says..."

"Yeah, *bullshit*," Melanie said loudly. Meli *rarely* swore like that. "I *knew* something was going wrong today. Where *are* you? I mean, what *happened*?"

"He showed up outside my classroom, followed me to the Faculty Lounge. He *could* be outside *now*."

"*Shit*," she spat. "Can you get *rid* of him?"

"*Good* question." The Crest campus was private property but *not* restricted. It was *open* in that anyone could come in, sit in on classes, go to the bookstore or libraries or eat in the Central Cafeteria. The exceptions were the lounges, the Hermann Field House, the Jenson

---

1 *She* pronounced it *Was-ber-sen-naw-ski*. As long she *didn't* pronounce it *"Throat-Warbler Mangrove"* like Monty Python, I *knew* what *that* name was.

Endowment Executive Building, and the Jenson Archive Building that had *just* been finished. "I can ask security."

"OK."

"Your *mom's* here. Should I...?"

"*Quietly.* Not *everyone* needs to know *our* business."

"Someone already knows *some* of it," I said. "How else would he know to look *me* up?"

"Good point. Talk to Mom. I'll...figure *something* out."

By this time, Helen had got her tea and was idly watching me from an overstuffed divan. I dialed the number for security, rolling my eyes in mock frustration for Helen's benefit. "Security desk," a woman's voice answered.

"Is Chief Mueller there," I asked.

"Mueller," the gruff voice answered after a moment. Ken Mueller was a medically-retired former state trooper who headed the 30-person private security force. I knew Ken vaguely, having had little contact with the organization, but he *audited* some of my classes.

"Chief, this is Curtis Durand. I'm in the Faculty Lounge, and there's a guy outside the door who followed me here. I *don't* want to have to interact with him. Is there anything you can *do...?*"

"We can *ask* him to leave, Dr. Durand," Ken answered, "but unless he's doing something untoward, we'd have a hard time *telling* him, legally."

"There are ways, and there are *ways* of *asking*, Chief," I said.

"There are *indeed*, Dr. Durand. I'll try a more compelling *way*. Give me fifteen minutes."

I hung up, trying to formulate my conversation with Helen. She didn't know *anything* about who Maria's birth-father was other than I *wasn't*. We'd never *openly* talked about our nearly decade-long lie of omission.

I caught her eye and cocked my head towards the dining room door; she nodded slightly. Hungry I was not, but I needed privacy. I got a cup of coffee and an egg salad plate from the buffet and sat at a corner table. Helen followed a few moments later.

"Spill," she said pointedly. I always admired her ability to cut to the chase.

"Maria's *bio*-dad's showed up," I said. "He *was* just outside. Security *may* be removing him."

"Huh," Helen shrugged. "What's he *want?*"

"To see Maria. That's all he's said."

"Uh-huh." Helen looked away. "Bert will *have* to be told."

"Absolutely, but we'd want to keep the circle small." Bert was, by then, the *Emeritus*[1] Jenson Endowment Professor of American History.

"Yes." She glanced at me. "And *Maria?*"

"I don't know that she'd understand," I said heavily...and possibly ignorantly. I didn't *know* what 2nd Graders were learning by then, but I didn't *think* the issue of *biological* versus *de facto* parents was a part of their curriculum.

"Maybe *not*," Helen agreed, "but Connie *might* be able to explain it to her."

"Yeah." Connie could explain anything to anyone with an uncanny ease that *I* didn't understand.

"You *should* get an attorney," Helen added. "Murray?"

"Yes." I *tried* to eat; it was a struggle, but I managed to get some egg salad down. "I have a discussion group this afternoon," I said. "Need to focus on *that*, for a *few* minutes, anyway."

"Curtis, dear," Helen sighed, "this *could* get out, you know."

"*I* know," I said, trying *not* to imagine the ramifications of exposing that old secret. They could easily go *beyond* personal and social, *possibly* extending into the ethical, the legal, and *potentially* into the professional *if* the Regents got involved. "Cross *that* bridge when we get to it."

Layer upon layer...

***

"*OK*," I started, nodding to the student next to me. The discussion rooms were set up with chairs in a circle. "The *first* English and Dutch settlements in America: New Amsterdam, the Carolinas; Jamestown, John Smith and them. And the first *bare* contacts with the natives."

Steve, to my relief, had gone, and I *didn't* see him on my way back to Jenson Hall.

"*Bare* is right." This was from our sole reentrant—a guy about my age. Discussion groups broke the classes into four more-or-less equal parts that met twice a week. Usually, TAs moderated them, but I wanted to stay close to my students and took a group myself.

"Uh-huh. What should we *make* of those early contacts?" Some puzzled looks followed. "*Come* on; this is what discussion group is *for*."

"*What* is," a young man in a cardigan asked.

"Saying what we think of the record," I explained. "We don't *teach* content here. To teach *content* is to *indoctrinate*. Crest history majors

---

1 Retired, in academy-speak.

teach *themselves* the record of the past. The history *faculty's* job is to teach you to *think in historical terms*, to use the concepts we try to impart into your *willing* minds."

"Huh," a young man wearing a Che t-shirt grunted. "So if *I* say that the settlers were cruel and exploitive...?"

"That's a *judgment*, not an *objective fact*," I said. "Making such judgments is *not* our job. What does the *record* say?"

"Isn't *that* teaching content," a young woman across from me asked.

"The *record* is the *content*," I answered. "How *you interpret* the record is how you *create* histories. When you *non-quantitatively* judge the past by saying they were cruel and exploitive you are expressing an *opinion*, not relaying a *fact. Presenting quantitative evidence* of their cruelty and exploitation is what we're supposed to do. *That* comes out of the record."[1]

For teachers, the most satisfying moments in their careers occur when they show students something they *weren't* expecting to see. *That*, for me, was *one* such moment.

"The contemporary records are ambiguous as to the treatment of the Indians," our reentrant said. "Which makes me wonder where that 'cruel and exploitive' version came from."

"That's *another* task for the historian: tracking down the different *versions* of the narratives. If they were *all* the *same*, we wouldn't need so *many* books on the same subject."

The two women in the group stared, gape-mouthed. The cardigan did a puzzled-puppy maneuver. The reentrant nodded. Che blinked rapidly, shook his head as if tasting something bitter, and shifted in his chair uncomfortably before he *loudly* said, "There's only *one correct* version of history."

Really? I grinned rather *too* widely before I spoke:

Man truly achieves his full human condition when he produces without being compelled by the physical necessity of selling himself as a commodity.

"Know what *that's* from," I asked.

"Marx," Che said confidently. "*Das Kapital.*"

"No," I answered gently, knowing that was what many *fashion-reds*[2] believed. "*Man and Socialism in Cuba*, by Che Guevara. Your t-shirt—

---

1 This class, *North America 1600-1770* was a 300-level course reserved for declared history majors. This was the first time they would hear this.
2 Most college students who declared themselves to be *communists* did so because others did, without really knowing what it *meant*. Thus, fashion-reds.

designed by an *Irishman* and selling like hotcakes before Che's body was *cold*—represents everything he *despised*. Che's got a wife and five kids still alive. Think *they* get royalties on that image you're wearing?"

"*BULLSHIT*," Che exploded. "Che was *executed* without trial by capitalist thugs for the 'crime' of trying to liberate Bolivia from capitalism! Herbert Linn has made this *perfectly* clear." This response came with *ever*-helpful air-quotes.

"We're getting far afield, aren't we," the young woman next to me asked. "*This* is nothing to *do* with early North America..."

"It has *everything* to do with North America before their *so-called* revolution," Che declared smugly. "The British colonists *enslaved* the Amerindians;[1] *then* they brought African slaves here to *work* them to *death*..."

"No, they *didn't*," the reentrant said. "The *British* colonists didn't enslave the Indians; the *Spanish* did..."

"Oh, I wish you'd get *that* propaganda out of your head, *sonny*," Che grinned. "Linn has *clearly* said that the British colonists..."

"Linn was *wrong*," I said, rather loudly.

Che stopped and stared at me contemptuously. "Just because Linn tells the *truth*, he's *wrong*?"

"No, because the *evidence shows* that he's wrong," I said gently. Discussion groups met in rooms next to each other. This context is important for what happened next...

"*Very* one-sided is our Herb Linn," Tony Zane declared as he entered our room, followed by another half-dozen people. "Go *on*, Dr. Durand. You've made *this* argument before. Time *we* heard it again."

"*Thank* you, Dr. Zane," I said. "I see you brought some of our acolytes[2]..."

"We *heard* your *discussion* next door," Tony answered. "*Please* proceed." This "invasion" wasn't unusual; Crest prides itself on the freewheeling structure of its discussion groups.

"I'll start with the claim that the British colonists enslaved the Indians. Slavery was technically *legal* in 17th century England, but it hadn't been *practiced* since the Norman Conquest,[3] then serfdom died out under the Tudors.[4] When English colonists arrived in *North* America, all *they* knew of *slavery* was indenture—a labor contract for

---

1 A contraction of *American Indians*, *briefly* popular in American academia.
2 Grad students/TAs, to the professoriate.
3 1066, for those of you who *didn't* know.
4 1485-1603. Ain't these footnotes helpful?

a fixed period. When the *Africans* arrived in Jamestown in 1619, there was neither *system* nor *law* for *keeping* them enslaved. They were *probably* indentured for a standard term of seven years, after which they *might* have been freed as the law required."

"*Were* they," Che asked snidely, "or were they *sold* on another 'contract?'" *Again* with the air-quotes.

"We don't *know*," I said, "the record is silent on that. And there's nothing in the record about the English enslaving Indians, either. There *is* in the *Spanish* record."

Che crossed his arms in defiance. "*Well*, then, *what* did Dr. Linn base *his* case on?"

"*Populist* PR," Tony declared. "He wasn't writing *history*, he was *selling a book*. Herb Linn wrote *A New History of America* to appeal to a *specific* audience—America's counterculture—who obsesses on America's *warts*. Good histories tell the *whole* story. Linn and the other *pseudo-revisionists*[1] only talk about the *evils* in the story. He shaped *a* history that should be called *bovine scatology* with a *pinch* of historical accuracy to ward off the stench. He knew *his* book-buying public would lap it up, swallow it hook, line and sinker...and *look no further.*

"Herbert is an *admitted* anarchist," Tony added. "He's got *no* compunction about that. When we were in grad school together, his primary focus was on publication. *Great*...if you're publishing based on *facts*. But Herb was interested in *sales*, not the actual *truth*. 'I'll let my *readers* decide what's true,' he'd say, and *you*," looking directly at Che, "have proved him correct. Now, admittedly, his interest was in telling *untold* stories, but *untold* stories *are* untold because they're often comprised more of unresearched, undocumented *legend* than *history*, making them *useless* to the *purpose* of history."

"Why's *that*," the young woman near me asked. "What use is history if *not* to tell about the past?"

"History is man's only test for the consequences of ideas," I declared... and everything got quiet like it *always* did when somebody said *that*. "When you *lie* about the past—or make judgments like Linn does— you invalidate that test. Pseudo-revisionists like Linn have an agenda just as that Irishman who designed that logo did. That agenda is to *first* profit from their work and *second* to sell their version so that *their* idea comes up looking better: validation through popularity. Money is their usual drive, but *just* as often, it's to making a living out of honorariums. *Think*

---

1 Revisionists write based on questionable interpretations. *Pseudo*-revisionists write based on rumors, gossip, and *very* selective use of original source material.

now: do you like *writing* your essays, or do you like *having written* them?" I looked around the room at a bunch of blinking eyes; only two pairs were smiling—Tony's and our reentrant's. "We write to be *heard*, *not* for the *joy* of writing. Our writing is our business card and resume, *not just* our shouts from the rooftops.[1]

"When history began to be professionalized in the 19th century," I went on, "when historians started working *not* just to praise princes and churchmen, they needed a *market* for their work—someone to *pay* for it. That *market* became the public schools. History became an important part of civics education—essentially to train future *voters* to think for themselves. This new democracy in America became an example for others to emulate if they *could*. But history for *education* was soon joined by history as a *hobby*—where most of us *started*, surely." There seemed to be general agreement. "Hobbyists look at history as interesting, or amusing, like *we* might view fishing. But *professional* fishermen look at that activity *very* differently, just like many of us look at the *past*, at the *record*, *very* differently. Linn and his kind concentrate on the *popular* audience for sales; *we* can't *afford* to. *They* write scandal for money; *we* write history for posterity."

"Regrettably, Linn wrote a book to be *popular* and ended up being taken *seriously*," Tony said. "Many *scholars* believe it to be serious, but it's *not* why he *wrote* it. In point of fact, he *simply didn't care*."

"There are *others* like Linn," I said. "It's up to *other* historical professionals to parse the difference. Dr. Linn won't acknowledge the difference between the sin and the sinner of the past; we as historians *have* to. *We* need to emphasize that not *all* empires were or *are* evil, despite what some want to declare. 'Imperialism' may have been an overall evil in *some* cases, but was pretty benign in *most*. Even *then*, deciding 'good' or 'evil' isn't *our* job. *We* just tell the story."

"We have to say that even the *reds* practice some form of capitalism," Tony said, "which is simply reinvesting *some* of the profits in the business. Communists or *faux*-communists deny it while watching it happen or encouraging it. Stalin sold seeds for cash to industrialize, resulting in famine all over Russia. A *capitalist* evil, but *done by* a *communist*. Saying *that* is the historian's job; *not* saying it is a polemicist's."

"But racism is *inherent* in capitalistic systems," the *other* young woman—who we'd yet to hear from that afternoon—suddenly said. "We *cannot* deny..."

---

1 Honest writers acknowledge that the writing *process* is painful *drudgery*.

"There's nothing *racist* about capitalism," our reentrant said dismissively. "Green Power and Black Power are joined, or the SLA[1] would never have robbed a bank. Time heals most ideologies, reveals most propaganda and polemical exaggeration for what it is...just that, and *nothing* else." He shook his head. "Facts *always* get in the way of polemics."

Tony and I glanced at each other, thinking the same thought: *this guy's worth watching.* "All right, *my* people," Tony sighed. "Show's *over.* Dr. Durand: *thanks* for the insights."

"OK," I said as Tony's class left. "A *different* kind of discussion. So, the early colonists spent a lot of time doing little other than trying to survive? *Why,* then, would they have *come?*"

"The *usual* reasons start with primogeniture," Che declared, "but isn't *that* wearing thin?"

"How so," I asked.

"Well, a *lot* of the first settlers represented business interests..."

"*Did* they? *What* business?"

We continued *without* much more ideologically-driven arguments for the rest of the hour. I tried to steer the class along an interrogatory path rather than a polemical one, always going back to the record, *not* to other interpretations.

Maybe it *was* the road someone had already taken, but for my *students,* it was one *most* of them hadn't seen before.

And *that* was part of my job.

***

On Tuesdays, I got home about an hour ahead of everyone else. Every *other* Tuesday, Connie got home ahead of me.[2] I found her working on her computer in her study, chin in hand. "*Hey,*" I said as I knocked on her suite door.

She looked up, smiled winningly. "Hey *yourself,* Dad. What's *up?*"

"Maria's biological father's tried to chat me up at school today."

She straightened up, looked concerned. "Uh-*huh.*"

"He wants us to let him see Maria."

"That's the *first* step," she said evenly. "What's *after?*"

"I don't *know.* That's as far as I got before I...I..."

---

1 Symbionese Liberation Army, the outfit that kidnapped Patty Hearst.
2 She was the glee club coach then, *and* she wrote the *Jenson Archive Quarterly,* providing updates to scholars. She was *also* taking three classes that semester.

"Ran and hid," she smiled, running her fingers through her hair. "So would *I*, I think. How can *I* help?"

"We're going to have to come up with *something* to tell Maria just in *case*...."

"*Yes*." She stood up; she'd grown almost as tall as I was. "Then there's the *boys*." In addition to Charlie, my son Jason was born the day before Connie turned 20 in July 1990.[1]

"Uh-huh. Not as concerned about the *boys* as I am about Maria."

"I'll *talk* to her. Oh! I saw a post from Jenny that she made three hours ago: she says she hasn't *slept* in two days. Where she *is*, she wouldn't *say* on a bulletin board system." She glanced at the clock. "*I* need to get the boys."

"OK." *Nearly three; Meli's got another hour and a half before she gets off work.* "I've *got* to work on an article."

"*Back* in a *flash*," Connie said, bussing my cheek on her way out.

I repaired to my professorial garret, my pine-and-paper inner sanctum where small children were *not* allowed unattended *or* uninvited. Since Bert's retirement just over a year before, the primary responsibility for the Jenson Archive had fallen to me. It would *be* my responsibility until *another* Jenson Endowment (*full*) Professor of American History, and Chief Curator of the Jenson Archive was appointed to Bert's position. I'd thrown *my* hat in that ring just for form. So had a dozen academics from inside *and* outside Crest. I'd had three interviews with the Committee, but I didn't *expect* to get the appointment.[2]

What I'd been spending most of my time[3] on for a little over a year had *very little* to do with the study of history but *everything* to do with the nature of the sources. A *big* chunk of my time was spent trying to decide if the pale brown lines on a disintegrating piece of stock were written by its purported author or by someone trying to make a quick buck by passing off a forgery to a *non*-discerning collector.

I fanned through the printout of the latest draft of my article on the evolution of American penmanship and wondered, is there any way I could get more esoteric?

---

1 Jason's conception triggered the completion of the mother-in-law apartment in the basement, soon followed by my vasectomy. It had a full bath, a small kitchen, and a separate basement entrance from the backyard.

2 I'd only been on the faculty for nine years. Most assistant profs wait that long and longer for the tenure that I'd won in five.

3 All I *have* is *free time*: I go to work, I grade essays; I fix stuff around the house; play with the kids; eat; sleep...everything's *free time*.

Mass production of steel dip pen nibs began in 1822, and their users began creating more uniform lines. This made it easier to discern where and how a writer was trained. The differences between the 16th-century italic cursiva—*in use in the Americas until the mid-18th century— the 17th-century* monde—*seen as late as the 19th century—and the 18th-century* roundhand *scripts are even more starkly pronounced.*

Important stuff; vital, even, when evaluating a manuscript letter written, purportedly, by George Washington. Washington's known handwriting in the National Archives was predominantly in the *roundhand* style, which he learned from a John Ayres copybook, found now in his library at Mount Vernon. We'd *just* discovered a document in the Truxton Collection in something approaching *copperplate*, which Washington had used *nowhere* in the National Archives.[1] That *and* the ink wasn't rusty enough,[2] and the stock[3] was too thin.

So this item was *likely* a forgery, placed in Category F, a category we'd just created. There were just another 26,598 more *quite possibly* fake documents in the Truxton Collection for us to evaluate and classify.

But, I'd become a glorified librarian/graphologist.

I'd started asking *cui bono*[4]—not just from the sale of the forgery, but from the implied validity of its content, and who would benefit from having it accepted as authentic? Who *were* these early autograph hounds outside the government and other "official" archives? And *who* had Xerxes been buying *from? That* had started a whole *different* line of inquiry, *another* folder in my bulging cabinet drawer....

"Hello," I heard Melanie call from the kitchen. I glanced at my watch: she was early.

"Hi," I answered just as Maria dashed through the living room just outside my den. "Connie's gone for the boys..."

"Yeah," Melanie said, coming into the den, unzipping her coat at the same time. "I got Maria from dance class; we *traded* today."

"*That's* what happened," suddenly remembering their quick exchange that morning.

"Didn't *think* you'd remember." She flopped her coat in my recliner and sat on it. "*Steve,* eh?"

---

1 Forgers often used the wrong writing style.

2 Indicating a factory-made ink, which Washington never used.

3 Washington often wrote on hemp paper, but frequently parchment. In *this* case, the *paper* was machine-made, unknown in Washington's lifetime.

4 Latin for *who stands to gain*? Hang around academics long enough and you start *thinking* in tongues.

"So he says. Not *quite* like looking into a mirror. He seems older."

"Only two years." She leaned back in the squeaky chair. "Would that he'd *just...*"

"Yeah. Gotta wonder: why *now?*"

"*That's* what's got me stumped. Nine *years* ago I told him...and he said 'so long.'"

"Is that *all* he said?"

"It's the most relevant."

"Maybe it isn't *now*. How much can you reconstruct in your mind?"

"*Nearly* all of it, especially that dismissive hand-wave when he walked away." Maria started her record player. She would practice her dance in front of her mirror for at least as long as the record lasted.

"He asked who the *father* was?"

"Yes. I said, 'you! Who'd ya think?'"

"He didn't say 'are you sure,' or something like that?"

"No."

"Did he ever have *cause* to think you were stepping out on him?"

"Well...there *was* that time...yeah. He asked..." She blinked. "He asked, 'who's *Curtis?*'" She started as if it were a revelation.

"What did *you* say?" *Um...yeah...*

"*I* said, 'a boy at home.' *He* said, 'you said *his* name the other night.'" She shook her head slightly. "Why didn't I remember *that* before?"

"You *said* you flashed on me when you *conceived...Hi*, honey," I grinned at Maria standing at the den door. We'll never know how long she had been listening to us with her *big-eyed* puzzled-puppy look. "*Good* day in school?"

"Yeah." She looked at Meli. "Does *conceived* mean got a baby, Mommy?"

"*Yes*, it *does*, honey," Melanie smiled nervously. "Wh...*where* did you learn *that?*"

> "*Charlene says Ally conceived on Halloween.*" Next-door neighbor Allison got married last August. "*Charlene says Ally's baby will come out in June.*"

Instant 2ⁿᵈ Grade birds-and-bees lesson. "Well, *that's* nice," I said as Melanie tried to recover some semblance of composure. "How was dance class today?"

"We learned how to dance like *this!*" She quickly demonstrated a Russian squat dance, much to Melanie's amusement. We saw Charlie dash by a few minutes later, coat and mittens trailing. Connie came in, carrying a dozing Jason for a quick viewing before taking him to his crib.

"Well," Melanie declared, "let's get dinner started." *That* meant that everyone needed to repair to their dinner stations: Maria to set the table; Connie to the kitchen; Melanie to the pantry; me and the boys to *their* rooms.

Without *that* minor organization, we'd have been in chaos.

I only hoped that Steve wasn't going to cause *more* chaos.

***

"Did *anyone* check the mail today," Melanie asked, wiping Charlie's face after dinner. Charlie was *less* of a struggle to feed than Maria had been at nearly three. Jason was *barely* weaned and had yet to fully *accept* soft food. A good deal of his strained pears was on the floor.[1]

"*I* didn't," I admitted, putting the last silverware in the dishwasher.

"*I'll* check," Connie offered. I forgot all about it, putting the roasting pan in the drainer; wiping down the carving fork and knife; wiping down the sink. Once again, the thought occurred to me: *these laminate countertops are the cheapest part of this house... I should think about tile or...*

"*What*," I heard Melanie say. "What's..."

"Letter from Schuyler," Connie said quietly. She set the rest of the mail on the kitchen counter and opened the envelope, frowning at the contents. "Huh," she sighed, passing one page to Melanie.

Melanie read quickly, starting briefly before she passed it to me.

Connie:

> *I hope this is finding you well.*
>
> *The Illinois Department of Corrections has informed me (letter enclosed) that your grandfather, Jud Emmerich, passed away on December 15th, 1990, in a US Bureau of Prisons nursing home in Tennessee. You were his only living family and needed to be informed. As executrix of your mother's estate, I've taken the liberty of releasing his remains for medical research (copy enclosed). The check enclosed is the residue of his prison account.*
>
> *Let me know if you have any questions.*
>
> *I am yours, & Etc.*
>
> *S. Colfax, JD*
>
> *P.S. I want more from you than a Christmas card, girl!*

---

1 I once suggested placing high chairs in garbage cans and washing the kid down with a hose after meals. Meli was *thinking* about that.

"Well, rest in *peace*, I suppose." The enclosed letters from the Department of Corrections and the Bureau of Prisons were *horribly* brief.

Connie giggled softly and without mirth. "*Thanks*, Grampa-I-Never-Met." She held the check out: just over $300.

"There's a *flimsy* in here," Melanie said, pulling a thin piece of paper out of the envelope. She and Connie scrutinized the form. "Wish I knew more about *this* kind of thing..."

"Don't they get *paid* for working," I asked.

"How would *I* know," Melanie teased.

"*Think* so," Connie said, somewhat more seriously. "Pay Rate...Wages...Deductions...Interest Earned. Gotta wonder what the taxpayers are paying convicts *interest* for."

"Yeah, all of a hundredth of a percent. Maria makes more on her savings account." Melanie shook her head slightly. "Well, it's *money*, honey."

"About *right*," Connie agreed. "Put it in the bank and make it..."

Then the doorbell rang; I went for it absently. "*Hi*, Dr. Durand," Jerry Hoffmeier said at the door. "Is *Connie*...?" He was in the Liberal Arts program at Crest.

"Oh, I *forgot*," Connie said, reaching past me. "*C'mon* in, sweetie." They pecked lips, chatting about *something* as they descended to Connie's suite. It wasn't the *first* time I'd seen them express *that* degree of affection; she obviously cared for him a great deal. But *sweetie* was only since *late summer*, as far as I could recall.

I had to think: *what's next?* Even if they weren't mine *biologically*, *both* my daughters were my *responsibility*. It was hard to turn *that* off. I was *supposed* to 'lose' both of them sooner than later.

But I *didn't* want to lose Maria to a stranger. *That* was certain.

***

For the next few hours, watching TV—even the war news—I *resisted* going downstairs to *check* on Connie and Jerry. If I *did*, I didn't *trust* a 20-year-old. I was a *bad parent* to a young adult if I *didn't*.

I just wasn't sure if I *should* trust *sweetie's* hormones.

Connie came up *with* Jerry *before* the local Late News came on with its recap of the war news. She wore the same clothes she had on when they *went* downstairs and shared—*you* know—as he left. I took her lack of wardrobe change as a good sign.

"How's *he* doing these days," Melanie asked absently.

"Fine. Worried about Jenny like we *all* are." She smiled at me, standing behind the three-cushion couch, winking broadly. *I know what I'm doing.*

I winked back. *I hope so.*

"I have a friend who *might* be able to help with the *Steve* situation," Connie said softly.

"Anyone *we* know," Melanie asked, glancing at me.

"No, we met at the range;[1] he works out at the pool."

"Help us...*how*," I asked.

"Just...*more* information is better than *less*, Dad."

"Probably," I said; Melanie shrugged. "Let's *meet* him." One of those pregnant pauses followed when something more needed to be said. "Connie," I said, "*this* might get messy. No matter *what* happens, I will *always* love Maria because I feel she's *mine*."

Silence as she knelt behind the couch and kissed my cheek. "*We know*, Dad," she whispered, kissing Melanie's cheek. "*We* love you, too. I *have* to tell you something I *should* have mentioned before. After Jason was born, we were all out in the yard, and Maria asked me, 'where's *your daddy*?' I was so surprised I just said, 'I don't *know*.' She pointed at *you*, Dad—playing with Charlie—and said, 'that's *my* Daddy.' Then, she pointed at *you*, Mom—sunning yourself on the patio[2]—and said, 'that's *my* Mommy. I came out of her tummy like Johnny came out of *your* tummy. Your *Mama's* in heaven.' Surprised she remembered me saying *that*."

"So she *knows* you're *not* her *real* sister," I said, watching Melanie's face transform so fast in so many different ways it was hard to figure her out.

"She *knows* you're too *big* to be a sister like *she* is to Charlie and Jason," Melanie sighed. "She knows *roughly* what's meant by *Mommy*, but *Daddy's* still just a name, I *think*."

"She calls me her *choice-sister* to her friends," Connie said.

"*You* can talk to her about *birth-daddy*," I said, glancing at Melanie, who nodded. "She sees you as a *pal*; *we're* just her parents."

"OK," Connie agreed. "I'll take her to school in the morning. I don't *have* a class until 10." She waited for a beat...then another. "I'll ask *him* tomorrow. He's *always* at the range Wednesdays."

"All right," I said as the weather guy predicted snow for the weekend. "We'll figure this out."

---

1 Connie kept her guns—inherited from her mother—in a locked cabinet in her bedroom.

2 Meli managed to keep her shape but she gave up on bikinis after Charlie. I only ever saw Connie in tank suits.

"We *will*," Melanie declared.
One way or another.

***

Meli was awake as we lay in bed; I could *tell*. She was *thinking*, trying *not* to sleep. I could tell *that*, too.

So I waited, listening to the wind outside, the clicking of the flap-number "digital" alarm clock beside our bed. *She* knew *that*, too.

"I have a *plan*," she rolled towards me, taking my hand. "Just hear me out."

So I listened. The plan was *plausible*. It prevented possible embarrassment, questions from family, friends, and especially the Committee of Regents.

"OK," I sighed. "Let's get some *sleep* before..."

And Jason suddenly made his gurgling first cry that said, "I'm either wet, poopy, cold, or hungry. *Service* me."

We had Meli's plan; we had hope.

And it was *my* turn to *service* Jason.

Wednesday, We Got Help

'Good morning," I said into the phone. Morning chaos was just then upon us, that period between the end of breakfast and everyone getting out the door for their day. Morning phone calls were *not* always good news.

"Curtis, good *morning*," my father said. "Is *Connie* there? *This* is official."

Official? "Yeah, sure." I held the phone to my shoulder, shouting downstairs. "Connie! *House* phone for *you!*"[1]

"*OK*," she yelled back. A moment later, she picked up the extension in the basement. "*Got* it, thanks. *Hello?*"

I hung up.

Dad was Superintendent of the Cicero Police by then and had said *official*. Connie was an *adult*. That didn't keep me from wondering what it was *about*. I helped Melanie get the boys into the mini-van in the garage while Maria finished loading the dishwasher, waiting for Connie.

Maybe ten minutes after Dad called, Connie stomped up the stairs, slinging her book bag/purse over her shoulder. She looked...*concerned*. "Anything...?"

"*Later*," Connie murmured, pecking my cheek and taking Maria by the hand. "*C'mon*, buddy," she sighed, "*dusty trail* time."

---

1 She had her own phone line in her suite.

***

"Curtis; Melanie," Murray Elk smiled when we came into his office downtown. Like *some* other Crest faculty (including the quarry engineering professors and the equipment operation and maintenance instructors), Murray had a career *outside* the university.

"Murray, you're looking *hale*," I said, shaking his hand. We knew each other from around the school, *and* he'd handled Connie's adoption. "Something *different* this time."

"You look pretty good yourself," Murray said, gesturing to a couple of armchairs along the wall. We met him in the Carleton Building, the largest Old Town[1] office building. "What can I do for you?"

"*Kind* of a paternity matter," Melanie said, with her *hedging* face she used when something *kinda* needed doing that she knew I was too tired or busy to do. "The *possible* biological father of *our* daughter showed up yesterday. She's been *raised...*"

Murray took notes. The first time anyone heard Melanie was pregnant, they also *heard* that *I* was the father...and Murray just took notes. "*I* see," he nodded, glancing at me. "*Curtis* is on her birth certificate?"

"Yes," Melanie said, "but it's *not* that *simple*." She shot me a look that said *follow the plan*. "There's a *possibility* that *Steve's* her father. *Slim, but...*"

"Ever tested to find out?" Murray glanced up at us. "The test is painless, simple. *Might* be the first step..."

"We're all type B+ blood," I said. "She had hepatitis as an infant and both Meli and I were tested, so we *know*. DNA testing's over $2000 and pretty new. Never saw the *need*."[2]

Murray glared at Melanie. "If you *know* for a *fact* that Curtis *cannot be* the child's father, *don't tell me*. Understand? I *cannot* lie to the court."

"Yes," Melanie and I answered.

"So, you have *not* had testing done?" We both shook our heads. "Tell me about this *possibility*."

"I was at State in April of '82," Melanie said quietly. "*Steve* was my boyfriend. We had a *big* fight at the beginning of Spring Break. *He* took off; I was *lonely* and *hurt*, and I called Curtis."

That I *answered* no phone calls from Meli *at that time* was not *addressed*. That *we* were intimate *shortly after* that call that I did *not* get

---

1 Granite Ledge was roughly divided into Old Town—hugging the Sonoco River south and east of the Interstate—and New Town north and west of the Interstate.
2 A year before I counseled a student caught in a "who's my daddy" trap, so I knew what *they* cost.

was *implied* but not *stated*. We could *NOT* have been *intimate* ten yards apart...but we weren't *saying* that.

Note that we did *not* lie to our attorney.[1]

"She got home in June," I continued, "*that* was when she told me she was pregnant. We got married two weeks later because my family was in town for my graduation."

"I see," Murray said, scratching some notes. "Has Steve ever *seen* the child?"

"I don't *believe* so," Melanie said. "I told him I was pregnant the last time I saw him that June. He asked if it was *his*. I said she *was*. *He* said, 'I don't *think* so, Meli. *So* long.' Turned around and walked away." She shook a little, wiped a tear.

"I see," Murray said, scratching more notes, advancing a box of tissues. "He *knew* about the child, but *you* weren't *sure* of paternity?"

"Not *certain*, no," Melanie agreed, squeezing my hand.

That, as far as I knew for *certain*, was *not* untrue. Meli didn't *tell* me if there were any *other* men in her life then, and I didn't *ask*.

"Without the *science*, we can't *know*," Murray nodded. "Regardless of biology, Curtis has been the child's *de facto* father. Steve *doubted* paternity and walked away? In *this* state, *that's* abandonment, *regardless* of the science." He knitted his brows. "Any inkling *why* he's asking now?"

"None," Melanie said. "Only thing I can *think* of is that he *might* be ill. His father died young, but I don't know of *what*."

Murray pointed to a framed tribal membership certificate on the wall. "Any possibility he's a member of a *tribe*?"

"I don't *know*," Melanie said, gazing at the document. "Would *that* matter?" She glanced at me, surprised. The idea had frankly never occurred to *either* of us...not with *that* name.

"It *could* if he *were* part Native American and wants to claim her for his tribe. *Whole* different ball of wax if *that's* the case."

"Think 'Wabrzeznoski' is a *common* name for Native Americans, Murray," I asked mildly, mangling the name.[2]

"No," Murray said with a chuckle, "but genetically-linked conditions run in *some* tribal families. Even if he's only *part* Indian he *could* be carrying some trait that could be passed on. I've heard of genetic markers carried to people only a *sixteenth*-Indian."

"*No* idea," Melanie said.

"Well," Murray said, "if he comes with papers, or an attorney or tribal representative contacts you, tell them you're represented by counsel, let *me* know, and I'll take it from there."

---

1 Don't ya *love* lawyer tricks?

2 I can't even SPELL it twice the same way.

In the lobby, we tried *not* to think about the ramifications of Maria being a member of a tribe or having some gene that could lead to something dangerous in the future. We also tried *very* hard NOT to think about the possible ramifications of Meli's *plan*. "I have to get to work," Melanie sighed, closing her coat against the cold.

"Me, too," I agreed. "Now, we wait."

How long?

***

How long?

I thought about that as I drove under the Interstate and up the four-mile-long slope to the east entrance of campus. The Interstate ran along the south side of the river for about fifty miles to *South* Granite Ledge, which had a residential population of 2,100. Then it crossed the river *eastbound* on the Ludendorff Bridge[1] into the middle of Granite Ledge (no modifiers) and turned east again. The whole of Granite Ledge was a mile and a half long by perhaps a mile wide. The nearest working *commercial* quarry was near South Granite Ledge.

I include this little travelogue only because I want the reader to understand that this was a small community, where all the permanent residents knew pretty much everyone. The only mysteries were the new Crest students, students and faculty in the new two-year Granite Ledge Technical College[2] and *some* of the kids at Granite Ledge Academy. There's a great deal of money around Granite Ledge *and* several industries supporting the quarries and the remaining farms. There just weren't a lot of people; *perhaps* 45,000 at peak between fall and spring; 25,000 mid-summer.

When I got to Jenson Hall, I was approached by a woman in casual business attire accompanied by a large, black woman in a security guard uniform who I knew only as Tibbs. "Dr. Durand," Tibbs nodded, "this is Detective Morris, Granite Ledge PD. She has some questions." Detective Morris flashed her credentials.

---

1 *Harvey* Ludendorff designed the 405-foot double-swing railway bridge across the Sonoco, finished in 1895, deactivated, and converted to a road bridge when a new rail bridge was completed upriver in 1935. The Fiske Memorial Bridge upstream carried the Interstate's *westbound* traffic.

2 Where some of the more *technical* subjects of quarry science—equipment maintenance and the like—were moving from the University.

"Fire away," I said, leading them into the building. "Let me drop my coat and bag." We passed through my lecture hall[1] to my office. "So, shoot."

"We've had reports of a man asking around town about your family," Detective Morris began. "Someone who fits your description but is *not* you. Do you have a brother who *might* look like you?"

"No," I said. "He's my wife's ex-boyfriend from State. *He* believes *my* daughter Maria to be *his*."

"Ah," Detective Morris said. "Have you *heard* from this person?"

"We met, *briefly,* yesterday," I said, trying for non-committal. "We just consulted our attorney in case he chooses to make an issue of the matter."

Tibbs and Detective Morris exchanged glances. "He *was* on campus," the guard said. "You had him removed yesterday?"

I nodded. "I asked if he *could* be removed, yes."

"He was outside the Hubbard's residence early this morning," Detective Morris said, "demanding to *see* the professor. *They* called security."

"I see. Where is he *now*?"

"Security office," Tibbs said, "waiting for the results of *this* conversation."

"I questioned him as to his business," Detective Morris said. "I told him we'd had reports in town about his inquiries. I told him a stranger asking questions was *legal*, but red flags go up when those questions are about a little girl."

"How long has he been asking around," I asked, curious that *this* was the first we'd heard about *that*.

"First of the year," Detective Morris said, "near as we can *tell*. We filed the first *report* two weeks ago. Filed another on *Monday* that someone was asking about a *Hubbard* child at Fiske Elementary." She looked uncomfortable. "Did your wife pick your daughter up Monday?"

"They had a Martin Luther King program Monday that we *all* attended," I said.

"You, your wife, your daughter, and your...?" Detective Morris asked.

"*Adopted* daughter *and* my two sons." *Explaining* Connie was complicated *despite* her adoption. Her *name* didn't help.

"I see," Detective Morris asked. "Any chance your *adopted* daughter might have had contact with this Steve?"

"You'd have to ask *her*," I said, "but she would have mentioned it if she *had*."

---

1 "Mine" in that it was one of the two I was assigned, so were a professor and three *assistant* professors. My office and another assistant professor's office connected both of them.

"We *did* ask her this morning," Detective Morris said. "I *want* to talk to your wife."

"Sure, no problem," I said, "you *know* where we live, I presume? *She* works for the county."

"We *do* know, Dr. Hubbard," Detective Morris answered. "And we *will* speak with your wife." She waited, glancing at Tibbs. "Two *other* people have been asking about your family."

"Really," I said, mildly surprised. "Any idea as to *who*...?"

"Two people *also* named Wabrzeznoski,"[1] Detective Morris said. "A *younger* man, claiming to be the brother of the *other* one. The other is a woman claiming to be a sister with a *different* last name.[2] Has anyone *else*...?"

"No, not yet." I regarded Detective Morris curiously. "*Tell* me, Detective: *why* has it taken *this long* to...?"

"I *have* no defense for *that*, sir," Detective Morris declared, looking away. "*This* file landed on my desk just *last night*. I..." She looked sheepish. "It's not an *excuse*, but I'm Granite Ledge PD's *only* investigator, and I've *had* the job *just* over three *weeks*...."

"In her *defense*, Professor," Tibbs interrupted, "I *believe* GLPD lost three people to mobilization last summer...."

"*Five*," Detective Morris corrected, "*including* our investigator. That's 20% of our strength now on Active Duty in the Gulf. Since Thanksgiving, I've worked *fifteen* assaults, *twenty* robberies, and an attempted homicide. For *every ten* students who come here every semester, at *least* one grifter comes, looking to take advantage of their youth and inexperience." She looked straight at me. "All excuses *aside*, sir, someone asking questions about a little girl kinda falls *down* our list."

"And we're *as* guilty, sir," Tibbs declared. "But I've only been on *this* job since last September. I came from the State Police, medically retired like our chief, so it *ain't* my first trip to the fair. We've lost *nine officers* since last summer for the same reason: the *war*. We have to fight the *biggest* fires *first*, Professor."

"I *get* it," I said finally.

And I really did.

***

"Dr. Durand," a budding scholar asked, "from an *archival* standpoint, how close are we to complete source saturation in American history?" This was my graduate lecture/discussion course, Sources and Archives.

---

1 I couldn't *begin* to give you *their* version.

2 I dimly wondered if they all pronounced *Wabrzeznoski* the same way.

"*Excellent* question," I answered. *I know where you got THAT from.* "And the *answer* is...not...even...*close*." I went on in academic-speak, describing what *source saturation* meant in the history field—a concept borrowed from electrical engineering. *Saturation* should have been *exhaustion*, but some egghead prizewinner from an Ivy or Oxford called it *saturation* in a journal article, and the term stuck. Without the academic gobbledygook, it described a condition where all *reliable* sources had been used and deemed *adequately* interpreted.

"Not *all* sources, surely," another grad student asked some ten minutes later. "How can we be sure we've found that *last* letter, that *last* diary?"

"Mm, indeed," I said. "The short answer is we *can't*. Look at that *Supplement* to the *OR*."[1]

"*Yes*," another student declared. "I just read an article that suggested that only about *10%* of all the orders and reports from the Civil War were *in* the original *OR*."

"*And* two of those volumes were called *supplements*," I agreed. "What did that article say about how *that* archive was created?" I tuned out because I'd *critiqued* that article.

The process the War Department used was simple. They *asked* the holders of the material—the actual participants in the conflict—to *mail* it in. It was at *least* as methodical as old Xerxes buying old paper by the bushel-basket...which is literally how the Jenson *started*.

"Is there a *good* way to build an archive," a student asked, shaking me out of my reverie.

"*Framework*," I declared. "*Start* with a *framework*. Decide *first* what your archive is *for*, then build *on* that purpose." Not at *all* what Xerxes did, but what did *he* know? As I went on, talking about how library science and document preservation got involved, I found it odd that *later* archivists—with their names enshrined on the Archive's wall—didn't see fit to do more than sort and catalog the documents by date and author's name, disconnecting the acquisition data that was associated with *most* items as though they had no significance to the authenticity of the documents.[2] William Truxton was the first person

---

1 *War of the Rebellion: Official Records of the Union and Confederate Armies*, *OR* for short. The 152 volumes—plus a color atlas—were compiled from 1864 to 1911, published as they were finished. The *Supplement* was a hundred *more* volumes published by a private company nearly a century after the last *OR* volume was published.

2 Acquisition data was recorded in bound books until Bert took over, but was *challenging* to reconnect because it was often wrong.

to do anything *organized* about sorting and classifying the documents within it...*and* reconnecting the acquisition data. I finished with, "the *Jenson* is organized on a more open, less *focused* scheme that, frankly, could *use* some sprucing up."

"The Jenson's a composite of *several*, isn't it," one student asked. "The *Truxton*, the *Emmerich*..."

"The *Truxton's* special," I interrupted. "It's always *been* a work in progress..."

"The *Emmerich*," another asked. "Any relation to your *daughter?*"

"Connie Emmerich *was* our *ward* before we adopted her," I said slowly, knowing that the *professor's real daughter* gossip was common on campus. "Her mother was a dear friend who passed away and entrusted my wife and me with Connie. The *Emmerich* Collection was what Connie's mother amassed over her lifetime." I looked around; *more curious than anything else.* "Sources aren't *always* archival." I went on as planned, talking about how *non*-archival sources get pulled into collections, then libraries, then archives, and eventually to data graveyards called *national archives.* At this early stage in the course, it was high-level.

At the end of the class, the inconvenient questioner stepped up to the podium. "Dr. Durand, I didn't *mean* to be impertinent..."

"You *weren't*," I said. "Just *not* something to *talk* about in class. You're a transfer, yes?"

"I came from OSU for my master's, sir," she said. "I *met* Connie at glee club. Somebody in The Cubes said she *was* your *real* daughter. I just..."

"I *get* it. Just don't perpetuate *that* fraud, OK?"

***

"Bert, you had a visitor?" After class, I called the Hubbard's, eager to find out if Meli and I had some *fast talking* to do.

"Yeah," my father-in-law answered. "Who the Hell *is* he?"

"*Long* story," I hedged.

"I'll *bet.* Says he wants to see *his daughter?* Who's *his* daughter?"

"Maria," I sighed. "The *rest* will have to come from Meli."

There was a long silence. "He's Maria's *biological* father?"

"He..." *NOT going to perpetuate the fib in the family.* "He walked away from them."

"*You* didn't." Another silence; I heard my classroom starting to fill up again. "I keep *track*, Curtis. You never *claimed* to be Maria's *birth*-father; not to *me.*"

Melanie presented the three of us as a unit to her parents. She never actually *said* I was Maria's biological father. *My* name on Maria's birth certificate was, Meli said, symbolic.

"*I'm her father*, Bert. That's an *end* to it."

"Yes, I suppose it *is*, Curtis."

***

"*Mom; Dad—this* is my friend, Paul. He's the guy I *told* you about."

"Dr. Durand," Paul said quietly, extending his hand. He'd knocked on our door just before dinner. "*Pleased* to meet you." Paul was about six inches taller than I, maybe fifty pounds heavier. I wasn't a *good* judge of such things, but Paul looked like he *could* be dangerous...just the way he carried himself.

"Paul...*what*," I asked as he shook Melanie's hand.

"*Shull*, sir," he answered.

"Our daughter says you can provide some, ah, *assistance* to my family? Not sure what she's *told* you..."

"*Enough*, sir," Paul said. "I've gathered from *other* sources enough to know *roughly* what's going on."

"What is it that you *do*, Mr. Shull?" Melanie regarded him suspiciously.

"Private investigator, ma'am. I have references, including Crest University."

"What would the *school* need...?"

"Background checks, sir. Private investigation's *not* like the movies. *Most* of what I do is make phone calls and send letters; collect old phone books and other material. I also put a *lot* of miles on my car."

"You met at the *range*, and *swimming*, she says," I said.

"Yessir. As an alumnus, I *can* use the Hermann Field House."

"*Really*," I said, surprised. "What was your major?" I thought better of asking *when* he graduated. I couldn't tell how old Paul *was*, but I *could* tell he was older than *me*.

"Pre-law, sir. I graduated from State law school in '83."

"Can you find out about Steve Wabrzeznoski, see what he's about," Melanie asked.

"I *can*, ma'am, and I *will*. Just tell me everything *you* know about him and I'll take it from there."

"What's it going to *cost* us, Mr. Shull," I asked.

"*Friends* and *family* discount, sir."

That gave me pause. Connie made friends of nearly everyone she met—her natural charm was hard to resist. *Friends and family discount* suggested *more*. Then I thought briefly about how she looked at Jerry. Connie didn't *touch* Paul, didn't look at him *that way*. *Maybe just trying to impress...or just wanting to do a pal a favor.*

"I *have* his Social Security number on an old tax return," Melanie said, "and I *know* where he *was* living..."

"*That* would be of *enormous* help, ma'am," Paul said.

Melanie had made copies of what she had. It was a little remarkable that she kept it because she was so bitter about his dismissal of her.

But, maybe, *somehow*, she anticipated something like this.

***

"Hi, everyone," Jerry announced, following Connie into the kitchen after dinner.

"Hi, Jerry;" "*Hey*, Jerry;" "*Jerry*;" "*Unka* Jerry;" "*Gaa*;" were the responses he got. The reader can parse *who* said *what*.

"Tell *them* what you heard, sweetie," Connie prompted.

"Yeah, OK. The 123rd's been called up." He left it there, hanging in space. The 123rd Division was the state's National Guard division;[1] several of its *units* had already been called to Active Duty. Jenny was in a *Reserve* unit home-based in town; *more* local people were in the 123rd.

"Where'd you hear *this*," I asked quietly.

"I was down by the Army recruiter today," Jerry said, holding Connie's arm; she bit her lip. "I've been thinking we could use some *help* paying for *my* school.[2] Guards or Reserves pay a fair chunk of change for member's schooling."

"Ah," I said. "It's a *thought*."

Connie glanced back. "It's what *Jenny* did; how she got...but it wouldn't be until this *summer*, though, right?"

"Right," Jerry said, stretching an arm around her. "*Not* for a while." He kissed the side of her head softly, murmuring. "*Not* for a while."

"Well, I wonder if *Greg* has been called," Melanie said, pulling Jason out of his highchair and planting him on her hip.

"That guy you work with?" I pulled Charlie out of *his* chair, setting him on the floor.

"Yeah; he's in the 123rd. Let's go in and see the news." The next few minutes entailed the usual herding of cats,[3] *moving/guiding* two small

---

1 Shared with three other, adjoining states.

2 The school only offered tuition and credits for faculty children. Fees and books could cost *twice* the tuition. There were *many* scholarships, but faculty brats weren't eligible.

3 Or pushing string.

190

children, *carrying* another in diapers, and guiding two young adults *and* two grown-ups from the kitchen to the living room where our *whopping*-great 31-inch TV was mounted in the wall. Two armchairs on each side of the sofa in front of the TV only *partly* filled the room.

We watched the drama unfold on the other side of the world. Because of the time difference, we saw what had happened the night *before*—there was an eight-hour time difference. The ghostly images made through the night vision devices, the tracer bullets up and down, and the comical (to us) loops of artillerymen serving cannons that were banging away at distant targets seemed *other-worldly*.

I glanced at my children on the floor. Maria seemed fascinated, occasionally tracing lights with her fingers as she worked a puzzle. Charlie glanced up from his wind-up car when loud sounds came across. Jason watched Charlie's car and waved his ring toy, sitting up and lying down, resisting sleep. Connie watched from the sofa, I think because she *knew* people in harm's way. She held Jerry's hand, who *watched—I* believe—for the same reason.[1]

"*Same* clip," I said after the 10-second scene of soldiers loading *huge* bullets on helicopters that we'd seen over and over since the shooting started Monday. We strained to see if *Jenny* was in it. She *wasn't*, of course. Fueling *and* arming at the same time and place would be too dangerous. Even *civilians* knew *that*.

The national/international news of the war took up most of the half-hour, focusing on the conflict from the air, adding a story about destroying sea mines in the Persian Gulf. Commentary from congress-persons and from civilians took up about five minutes. "No blood for oil" protests were given short shrift; there was a *war* on, man.

The program transitioned to the local news, with reports about local people involved in the conflict...but *nothing* about the 123rd. *There are rumors in every war.*

We switched to the kid's programs, so Maria could drill her brothers on their numbers and ABCs as she *loved* to do. Her brothers paid *some* attention and *maybe* learned something. Connie and Jerry hung out on the sofa for a few minutes, whispering *something* I couldn't make out.[2] They went downstairs just as we put Jason to bed at 7. Melanie and I moved to the sofa after putting Charlie to bed at 8.

---

1 *More* than just Jenny. Granite Ledge-based units sent a total of 149 Crest students, faculty and staff to the Persian Gulf 1990-91, more per capita than any other municipality in the state.
2 Pretty sure that *was* the point.

We hadn't heard *anything* from Connie and Jerry by Maria's bedtime at 9. "*Should* we," I asked Meli.

"*Not* yet," she answered. "It's only *been* an *hour.*"

"Two," Connie mumbled from the doorway behind us. "He *just* left. *Talk* to you guys?"

"*Sure,*" Melanie said, patting the sofa between us and turning the TV off.

Connie sat and took both our hands. "I talked to a detective earlier." She wore the same *pants* as at dinner *sans* shoes; hair *down*; makeup *removed*; fresh *sweatshirt.*

"I *heard,*" I said.

"So did I," Melanie added.

"I assured her I didn't *know* anything about Steve," Connie said.

"Same *here*; at least, nothing *lately,*" Melanie said.

"What did *my* dad want with *you* this morning," I asked.

She squeezed our hands. "My birth-*father's* been arrested in Baltimore in a sting. The FBI *might* call me for blood tests; I gave Charlie *my* number."

"Dad's a good cop," I said. "Checking all the boxes."

"Yeah," Connie sighed. "I'm beginning to think this *internet* might be a great thing." She fell quiet. "I found out on a bulletin board that I have a *half*-sister with a rare blood type who needs a kidney."

"What *kind* of a bulletin board," Melanie asked.

"Family locator," Connie said. "I put in what I *knew* of my birth parents a few weeks ago—I knew *his* name—and got an answer this afternoon."

"*Your* blood was typed when you had *Johnny,*" Melanie said. "*Yours* is common as *dirt.*"

"Yeah, that's what I said, so we're probably not a match. Charlie said that Mom's *second* foster father—your *neighbor,* Dad—passed away some time ago." She fell quiet again. "I'm worried about what Jerry *might* do if the war lasts as long as it *could.*"

"Why *wouldn't* you be," Melanie smiled.

"But not the *same way* as I'm worried about *Jenny.*"

"You don't *feel* the same about Jenny, honey," I said. "At least, I don't *think* you...."[1]

"No, I *don't,*" Connie giggled. "*Not* the same."

"He's *right,* honey," Melanie said, giving me a look. "Your feelings for Jerry are *supposed* to be different. That's *new,* isn't it?"

"Yeah, just since Jenny left. Fell into each other's arms, I guess. She

---

1 OK, that *was* somewhat crass, but...

knows about *us*. Those two have been neighbors and friends since they were *born*. *Just* so you *know*...Jerry and I...we've *talked* about *it* with *all* our clothes on...like you *and Mama* said, Dad."

"Just be *careful* with your degree of exposure,"[1] Melanie murmured. "*Don't* go beyond *second* unless..."

"Unless I'm *sure*, Mom," Connie sighed.

Unless you're sure, honey.

***

"They *are* close," Melanie said as she climbed into bed.

"*How* close? No *bra* this evening."

"She took it off after dinner; she *was* wearing one this morning."

You check these things? "When she went downstairs with *Jerry?*"[2]

"They're trying *domesticity*."

"Which means *what?*"

"*He* waited in her great room while *she* took her makeup off in her bathroom and changed in her bedroom before she *joined* him.[3] They want to see what living together *might* be like before they go any further."

"Oh. More staid than *our* first night in The Cubes."

She batted my arm. "Got *that* right. She sighed. "She hasn't *had* sex since *then*; says *he's* a *technical* virgin."[4] She cuddled next to me. "*I* think they're sweet."

"*I* think *they're* platypodes[5] among young adults these days; *unbelievable* at first sight. They've been *an item* since September, and they *haven't...*"

"They came *close.*"

"How do *you* know *this?*"

"She was *terrified* about their friendship *after* Jerry got cold feet. I told her to talk it out with *him*." She *gently* pushed my pants down, kissing my chin languorously, followed by a familiar rustle and flapping of covers. "They *did*."

"Huh," I murmured as she reached for me, and I for her. "Sensible kids."

"Yeah," she whispered, wrapping her arms around me. "She's *on the pill*."

"Oh," I said, pulling her to me. "So, she's..."

Careful.

---

1 Melanie's practical invention. First-degree exposure was *swimming* attire or the equivalent; third-degree was *no* attire.

2 Paternal alarm bells *rang,* ambiguously. She *was* a legal adult.

3 The apartment was three *separate* rooms, *with* doors *and* locks.

4 By 1991, defining *virginity* was challenging.

5 The *proper* plural of *platypus*: look it up.

It Was Thursday
When We Got News

It was *way* too early on a Thursday morning to be anyone *but* someone official at the door. Even so, breakfast and getting kids ready for *their* day could *not* wait. Though not *expendable*, I *could* be *spared*.

"Looking for Melanie Durand," the young cab driver declared on the outside of the storm door.

"She's *occupied*," I said, slightly annoyed.

"Just a *moment*, please, Professor Durand," the young man said. "I *only* need to..."

"Serve *papers*," Connie said from behind me. "*Just* a moment."

There's something unnatural about standing in the front doorway of your own house, staring at someone just outside that door to whom you have *nothing* to say, *waiting* for the person they came to see. *What do you do, where do you look? Do you have a staring contest? Do you check your nails as you idly hum a little tune...what?* I knew the cab driver vaguely—he had been a student.

After an *interminable* few minutes, I heard, "*yes*," behind me, "*I'm* Melanie Durand."

"*Yes*, ma'am," the cabbie said, holding out a thick envelope; she came around me and opened the storm door. "You've been *served. Thanks*, Dr. Durand."

"Let's get the kids going," I said, snatching the envelope away from her. "Time enough for that *later.*"

***

We met for an early lunch in a New Town tavern. Since it *was* addressed to *her,* I handed the envelope over. Melanie opened the big manila folder, pulling out a sheaf of paper paperclipped to a letter. "*Oh!*"

"*What?*"

"*This...*"

Dear Ms. Durand

I am Rodgers Breen, Attorney at Law. I have been retained by Stephen A. Wabrzeznoski of your intimate acquaintance during the period October 1981 to June 1982.

During your last conversation with Mr. Wabrzeznoski, you declared that he was the father of a child you were carrying. Mr. Wabrzeznoski questioned paternity and was rudely dismissive of your declaration of the same.

Mr. Wabrzeznoski has become aware of medical issues in his family, from whom he has been estranged until recently. This awareness has compelled him to seek you out. He was gratified to learn that you did not terminate your pregnancy.

Mr. Wabrzeznoski's only concern is for the child's welfare, especially concerning the medical history in his family. He suffered a clinically-isolated case of multiple sclerosis (record enclosed) last year. This event and his recently-discovered family history of cancer compelled him to begin this action. There is also the matter of the child's possible membership in the Tonawanda Seneca Nation. Mr. Wabrzeznoski's mother's father's father may have been an elder in the Seneca Nation.

We need to make arrangements to meet at the earliest possible moment....

"*Holy...*" I said, gasping.

"*Yeah,*" she said sadly. "I *dreaded* that something like this *might* happen."

"How?"

"I knew *nothing* about his family—he never talked about them except to say his dad died young." She scanned the letter again. "I wonder what *happened* that he's *suddenly aware...*"

"Maybe his bout with MS," I ventured.

"Maybe." She finished her coffee. "I gotta get back."

"Me, too," I said, finishing my coffee. "I'll get *this* to Murray."

As the plot thickens...

***

"Let's *suppose*," I started two classes later, "that we wrote a history of America that pivots on the year *1619*." Twenty-five blank faces looked back at me. "*Think* about it. What would *its* thesis be?"

"Year before *Mayflower* landed," one student ventured. "*How...?*"

"How *indeed*," I said. "It would have to elaborate on why *that* year..." This class was Themes and Trends in American History, a 400-level course. I had changed my class format because I was *suddenly* interested in *counterfactual* history.

"When the first *Africans* were landed in the English colonies," another student declared.

"*Yes*; August 20th, 1619, on Point Comfort, Virginia—today's Fort Monroe. The ship was the English privateer *White Lion*, carrying a Letter of Marque and Reprisal issued by the States-General—the Netherlands—then at war with France. The official in whose name that Letter of Marque was issued had been beheaded in May of that year, but *that's* not important here.

"*White Lion's* crew took those *Angolans* off a Portuguese slave ship; Portugal was then an *ally* of France. These *lawful* English pirates *weren't* slavers. They traded their twenty or thirty Angolans—the record is unclear as to how *many*—for *supplies* because they'd been blown way off course in a storm. But suppose we wrote a history that said that those people were *intentionally* brought here for the *sole* purpose of *being* enslaved in 1619. How would *we*, writing such a thing, *continue* such a story?"

"Well, it *is* credible. Slavery *was* practiced here," a young woman, one of two African-American students in the class, said. "It started in North America *before* 1619; in the Caribbean and South America a *century* before. 1619 is the year that *English* colonists took on their *first* slaves..."

"Those people in Jamestown would have been *indentured*," I said, "*not* enslaved. The colony *had* no slavery, no law *for* enslavement, and no infrastructure to *maintain* it. And we don't know anything *about* what happened to the Angolans *after* their indenture expired. Could *we*, having declared *contrary* to evidence, say that the Africans arriving in 1619 was *intentional* and continue with an evidence-based narrative?"

Silence. "Why *not?*" This came from the other African-American, a husky reentrant man with a scarred face.

"Because the evidence for that thesis is to the *contrary*," I answered. "*So, why* would *we* want to make a *bigger* deal out of *1619* since African slavery was already *here* in the Spanish, Dutch, and French colonies?"

"To *emphasize* an *American* slavery narrative," a woman in the back said. "To make a *point* of the damage this *land of the free* has done." *Again* with the air-quotes.

"Uh-huh," I agreed. "*Why?*"

"Isn't *that* just a different point of view," the black reentrant asked.

"*Is* it?" I let that sit for a moment. "Why do we *write* history?"

"To tell stories..." *another* angry young *white* man wearing a Malcomb X t-shirt declared, "to *teach* about the past; to *learn* from it."

"Learn *what?*"

"The consequences of ideas," someone in the back announced.

"*Ah!* Does changing the *emphasis* here do *that?*"

"No; it *proves* a *point* about *race*," the black woman declared.

"Prove *what* point about *what* race?"

"*Slavery* was the *basis* of a *country* founded by *whites*," the black man said.

"Does propagating *that* demonstrable *lie* prove that point?"

"The Declaration of Independence says "all men are created equal," yet Jefferson *kept* slaves," Malcomb X declared.

"Was *that* an 18th-century rhetorical flourish *or* was it a commitment to chattel slavery?" No answers. "What would we *want* to say about slavery in the colonies *in general* in our *new* narrative?"

"We *might* say that there were abolitionist sentiments in Britain that the slaveowners in America were afraid would catch on..." another student ventured.

"We *might*...but we'd have to *ignore* the abolitionists in New England, *wouldn't* we? Wasn't *that* where the war started? If the Revolution was fought to *preserve* slavery, why wouldn't *slavery* have been mentioned in the Declaration of Independence," I asked.

"It *was*," another student declared. "That passage in Jefferson's draft was removed."

"Yes it was in*deed.*" I turned on the slide projector and lowered the screen behind me. "*This* one:"

> *He[1] has waged cruel war against human nature itself, violating its most sacred rights of life and liberty in the persons of a distant people*

---

1 The Declaration of Independence was addressed to George III.

who never offended him, captivating & carrying them into slavery in another hemisphere or to incur miserable death in their transportation thither. This piratical warfare, the opprobrium of infidel powers, is the warfare of the Christian King of Great Britain. Determined to keep open a market where Men should be bought & sold, he has prostituted his negative for suppressing every legislative attempt to prohibit or restrain this execrable commerce. And that this assemblage of horrors might want no fact of distinguished die, he is now exciting those very people to rise in arms among us, and to purchase that liberty of which he has deprived them, by murdering the people on whom he has obtruded them: thus paying off former crimes committed again the Liberties of one people, with crimes which he urges them to commit against the lives of another.

"Pretty clear that Jefferson thought slavery to be evil, *and* that *Britain* wanted to keep slaves in the Americas," I said. "*Why* was this passage removed from the Declaration," I pressed. "Who *removed* it? Better still, who *wanted* it removed?"

"Georgia, the Carolinas..." the black man said. "Some merchants in New England..."

"So it would pass Congress," the black woman said. "*With* it, they'd never get the votes. *Without* it, it might *look* today as if the *real* object of the Revolution was to *keep* slaves..."

"The Founders would have *said* as much *at the time*," I said. "*Not* including his passage on slavery was merely *expedient*. One might claim *that* as proof of the Founders' perpetuation of slavery. But, what *happens* to our new non-fact-based narrative?"

I was always gratified to see young minds *suddenly* see a truth they hadn't seen before. Here it was *again*.

"It doesn't even get off the *ground*," the black man said. "Goes nowhere. Where are you *taking* this, Professor? I appreciate that your job is to teach students to *think*, but..."

"I'm *taking* you to *this*," I held up a document. "Two weeks ago, we researched *this* document cataloged in the Truxton Collection." I changed the slide:

Jan'y 12th, 1777

My Dear Adams;

...This project of ours, independent of Britain, depends upon the support of the French and the Dutch. Since the Hollanders have never delt in Africans, and the French do so only in the New World, we

must take care that they do not realize the true motives for our cause,
which is to defeat the abolitionists in King George's court...
Thos. Jefferson

I turned around. "Everyone can *read* it?" Many nods...but a hand went up. "Question?"

"What *code* is that in?"

"Not a *code*; cursive handwriting," another voice said.

Huh. She can't read cursive. "What do we *make* of it?"

"Well, he's *wrong*," our black woman said. "The Dutch *did* deal in the African slave trade...and the French kept slaves in India *and* the Caribbean."

"And *Adams* was an abolitionist, *and* Jefferson *knew* it," another voice said. "Jefferson *wrote* the deleted passage..."

"Exactly. But wave *this* around," as I then did with the original document, "and someone *might* believe just the *opposite*. Something like *this* can upend *our* narratives...if it *were* authentic. *This* one we *know* is *not* authentic, not *just* because of your contextual reasons, but the *paper's* 19th century and the *ink's* wrong."

I set the document down, turned the projector off, raised the screen. *Now or never.* "Ladies and gentlemen, I *have* an ulterior motive for this foray into the counterfactual...a *personal* one. In the coming days or weeks, you *may* hear some *intensely* personal things about my family that are *not* flattering. Some people may want to rewrite some parts of *my* family's history, *not* for good reasons. If you have *any* questions about what you might *hear*, please come to me directly. *Any* questions about *anything at all* before we go on?"

"Is *Connie* your biological kid?"

"No. She's *our* daughter by *choice*. We adopted her."

"I heard *different*."

"You heard *wrong*."

"Are the *other* children yours?"

"*Yes*."

"Is the trend towards a racist foundation of America a good idea?"

"*Better* question. *That* gets back to the *purpose* of history..."

My answers will be all over campus by dark. Better we deal with it first.

***

"*Hey*, Bert," I said, I *hoped* breezily. We met in the Faculty Lounge, where I picked up dinner rolls from the cafeteria. "Looks like a *passel* of snow coming our way."

"Sure *does*, Curtis," Bert agreed. "Hope you've got enough gas for your snowblower."

Thanks for the reminder. "Sure; always keep a *full* can on hand after *last* year." *Ran out of gas with fourteen inches on half the driveway. Damn near broke my back digging out.* "Anything *new* on the war front today?" I knew he checked in on cable news during the day.

"Nothing extraordinary, no."

"Meli got *served* this morning," I said casually. "It seems Steve wants to *push* the issue; says something runs in his family."

"Ah, mystery *solved*, then."

"*Addressed*, anyway." I sighed. "Got a minute?"

"Sure." He gestured to the same corner where I'd spoken with Helen. "Shoot."

"MS, apparently."

He sucked in his breath. "*Whew.*"

"*Possible* tribal membership; cancer..."

"*Yuck.*"

"Do we know anyone familiar with the eastern Indians?"

"I *do*; so do *you*: Norm Hammond.[1]"

"Thought *he* did Europe?"

"His *hobby's* pre-Revolutionary Indian relations."

"Ah." I looked away. "*When* do you *let go* of your kids?"

"You *don't*; not *entirely*." He regarded me with his hollow-socketed, ever-rheumy x-ray eyes. "Connie?" I nodded. "Her mother was a *big* part of your youth before Connie was *born*, from what you've said. It's *that* connection that *you* hold onto more than anything else." He smiled wistfully. "As an *educator*, I've sent many thousands of young people on their way, including *you*. As a *father*, four. But they *still* vex me from time to time. Someone like *Connie*..."

"You know Jerry Hoffmeier?"

"Of course. *They're* together?"

"Since *Jenny* got called up."

"Connie's got a better head on her shoulders than most of the *faculty*, Curtis. It's your job to be *concerned* but not *obsess*, especially not over *that* one. Besides, she's an adult now."

"She's got a half-sister who needs a kidney..."

"Oh? Thanks for the *timely* reminder, Curtis," Bert reached into his pocket. "I'm *late* for my meds. Dinner at our place Saturday?"

"Three o'clock."

---

1 Professor and head of the Eurasian History Department. His specialty was Early Modern (1500-1700) Europe.

***

"Hello?" I'd answered the phone in the kitchen, having *just* cleaned up after dinner.

"Curtis: Moe Hardin."

"Yessir?" *Oh...shit...* I pulled the receiver into the pantry, stretching our long-suffering cord to its limit. Melanie looked at me quizzically. I motioned for her to get the kids out of the kitchen. Connie picked Jason up and led the parade into the living room.

Moe cleared his throat. "I received a note yesterday—unsigned—that declares that you are *not* the father of that little girl, Maria. Everyone *else* on the Committee got the same note." Silence. "Now, *who* in *Hell* would *say* such a thing?"

"Melanie had a *previous* relationship, sir," I answered quietly. "He just showed up here Tuesday. There's a *possibility*, she thinks..."

"*Damn,* Curtis." Silence. "This *doesn't* look..."

"It's *not* Meli's fault, sir," I offered. "They quarreled and, well, we *saw* each other afterwards. I *knew* about their tiff; *we* just didn't think he would *come back*..."

"*Tell* me about it, Curtis: what you *know* about what happened."

"Well..." I thought quickly; Meli quietly knocked on the door jamb, listening, arms across her chest. "I've known Meli since I first *got* to Crest," I explained. "We've been *friends* since we *met*." Melanie nodded. "Christmastime, '81, *my* girlfriend dumped me on her way out of town. Meli helped me *through* it, not *quite* platonically but *not...you* know." She raised an eyebrow. *My own part of your plan, babe.* "Spring break, '82, she called me, and I went up to State." She winked. "Come June she told Steve the baby was *his*. He said, 'don't *think* so,' then, 'so long.' She came back *here. Then* we..."

"Yes, I *see*." Silence. Sometimes you can tell the difference between an "I see" that means, "I *understand*," and one that says, "yeah, *bullshit*." I didn't know Moe well, so the silence had me on tenterhooks. Meli wrapped her arms around me, laid her head on my shoulder.

"*That* comports with the information *I* have." Silence again. "Curtis, will you submit to DNA testing if the school were to *pay* for it?"

"Yessir," I said boldly, knowing what the results would be *and* satisfied that *our plan* would cover as many bases as it possibly *could. I've bathed her, fed her, played with her, wiped her tears when she fell down and applauded her triumphs when she got up. I'm the only father she's ever known. So what are YOU gonna DO about it when you find out I AIN'T her sperm-donor, Jack?*

At the same time, I wondered what information Moe *could* have. Meli and I had been seen around campus for *years* before we became *official; that* he *could* know. Anything *else...*?

"The Committee *may* want to meet on this, but I cannot imagine what *for.*" Silence again. "May I *speak* with your lovely wife, Curtis? I won't take long."

I handed Meli the receiver. "Yes...*Moe!* How *are* you? *We* haven't spoken in *ages*...And *Florence*...Terrific. And you have a *great*-grandson now; *Eric's* oldest daughter's *first...wonderful!* Congratulations, Moe! And how *is Mandy* these days...yes, *certainly...Oh*, yes, what I *heard* is *quite* accurate...Oh, *call* the big lug my *rebound*, but I've *loved* him since I *met* him, Moe...Yes, of *course*. I'll look *forward* to it. My *best* to the *family*, Moe. *Good*-night."

I suppose my slack-jawed astonishment at her familiarity with the almighty Chairman of the Committee of Regents *was* amusing.

Meli kissed my chin and sighed, "I *kid*-sat for his youngest daughter, Mandy—*Amanda*—my *senior summer*[1] while Florence—his *wife*—was recovering from an appendectomy *and* gall bladder surgery and Eric was in Japan with the Navy. My family's *known* the Hardin's ever since I can *remember.*"

"Might have *helped* if you'd recalled that association when..."

"Neither Moe nor the Committee would *hear* of it. This isn't *like* other schools, babe."

It was *not, indeed.* Crest was a tight-knit community, but signs of favoritism or special treatment were *strictly* frowned upon, and *actively* avoided. "Didn't know you kept in *touch...*"

"*Oh*, no; just the gossip I hear and what I see in the *Rubble*[2] and the *Intelligencer.*[3] I haven't spoken to a Hardin in I don't *know* how long. He wants to get together for *dinner* or something."

We shuttled the kids to bed one by one. Connie called it an early night, though we heard her in her study, rattling away on her computer, talking on her phone.

Meli and I sat up, listening to the rising wind, whispering about the ramifications of a secret only the two of us knew about.

Not caring.

---

1 The summer between the end of junior year and the beginning of senior year. It was said to be the *best* summer for teenagers.

2 The school paper, published bi-weekly September to May by the English/Journalism Department.

3 Granite Ledge's sole daily newspaper.

Friday Was Pandemonium

'**D**addy: who's *that?*" Maria pointed out the living room picture window at someone leaning against a car across the street.

"That's someone *Mommy* knows," I said, gazing at Steve. "Stay *here*, honey."

I ventured out into the cold, biting wind, smelling the storm in the air. This part of the world, like the Great Lakes where I grew up, had identifiable weather patterns, and a storm *was* coming. "What can I do for you, sir? The letter from your attorney said..."

"He wrote it; I *didn't* endorse it," Steve said through the cold. It looked as if he hadn't shaved in a while...at least not since Tuesday. "I *want* to *talk* to *Meli*."

"Gone to work," I lied.

"I've been here since 6 this morning, Dr. Durand. *Don't* lie."

"We're getting the kids ready for school; ourselves ready for work. In *fact*, you're sorta in the way here. The road isn't wide enough to *turn* with you parked across from the driveway..."

"I'll move *after* I've talked to Melanie. That's the *end* of it."

"I'll *call* the *police*."

"*Call* away."

I went back inside, picked up the phone, and called the number we had posted above the kitchen phone. Before I spoke to anyone, Melanie took the receiver away from me and hung up. "*Give* me a minute," she said.

"I'll go *with*..." Connie started.

"Hang back," Melanie said quietly. "Just *give* me a *minute*."

Melanie went out; Connie behind her; I watched from the window, not sure *what* would happen. Melanie crossed the road while Connie waited in the driveway. Meli spoke with him for a few moments before he drove off.

"Something's *off*," Melanie said when she came back. "Something...*I* don't know. Let's get going...."

"*But*..." But...but...what?

"There's no *danger*, babe; trust me. I'll call Murray from work. We'll talk later."

O...K...

***

"So, for this *evening's* gala," the chancellor went on at the first budget meeting of the quarter, "our *goal* is to ensure that we can maintain the Alumni Scholarship Fund near its current *peak* levels." That fund was a *big* chunk of the Jensen Endowment. It was how at least 2/3rds of our students paid for school. It was *also* the reason for that evening's black-tie event in the Xerxes Jenson Ballroom in the new Jenson Archive Building.

"Are you *going* tonight," Tony murmured to me.

"Representing the Archive," I answered. These meetings—this was only *one* of *many*—were among the most painful parts of my job. Why did *I* have to go? Because about five minutes of each hour-long lecture/meeting had to do with the Jenson Archive, *that's* why.

"*Amy's* going," Tony added. "Bringing her new husband."

"Ah," I said in mock surprise. Amy Gilchrest's *first* husband passed away suddenly in the spring of '88. She married a grad student in December of '90.[1] The department's Christmas party was pre-empted by the celebration...*and* the gossip. "Did he complete?"

"He *will* in June," Tony said as the chancellor droned on and on about the importance of the evening's event. "His dissertation is on Grant's economic policies and the westward expansion. The *damn* thing is dull as dust, but he's done the work. Got a twist that's original."

"Huh," I said, listening to the chancellor rattle on about raising money, budgets, raising money, proposed changes in the curriculum, making money with research, allocations, and the prices of the different colors of mid- and high-grade granite by the metric ton.

---

1 The groom was thought to be *half* her age...and *that* was *anyone's* guess.

"And in *closing*," the chancellor said...and the room breathed a collective sigh of relief. "The Committee has accepted the proposal for a Ph.D. in quarry science, and Jenson Stone will provide seed funding..."

"At least it won't come out of *us*," Tony murmured.

"*Our* budget's..." I asked.

"*Next* up," Tony said. The History Department was the *second*-biggest cash cow in the school; the American History Department was the biggest part of *that* Department.

Our dean, a pleasant woman I barely knew, moved up to the podium, papers in hand. "Thank you, Chancellor Dow. The History Department is *pleased* to announce the selection of the *next* Jenson Endowment Professor of American History..."

"*Um*," Tony said loudly; others froze in disbelief. This kind of thing was usually done in department meetings, between semesters.

Yeah, UM. "I didn't *think* they'd," I said....

"...The *youngest* full professor in Crest University history... *Doctor Curtis Harrison Durand.*"

Ah...WHAT? Many hands stood me up; Tony braced my arm. I suppose I *did* stand, the applause in the room quite muted, so I *thought*. I nodded uncertainly at my well-wishers; shook everyone's hand as they were offered.

The dean *didn't* move away from the podium; I was *not* expected to make a speech, thank *God*. Instead, the applause died down and people stopped reaching over each other to congratulate me. And I sat down again, stunned. Whatever was said in the rest of the meeting was a complete mystery to me.

Seventeen and a half years before that morning, I came to Crest University as an undergrad. That day I became the head of the most prestigious American history department in the country, if not the world.

At 35, I'd *just* been given a lifetime *near*-sinecure. I would have to work like a *dog* to promote the Department for the rest of my career at Crest.

So forgive me if I forgot *all about* Steve for a while.

***

"*Hi*, honey," I said into the phone. "Had the quarterly chancellor's meeting this morning..." I'd called her office from mine to pass on the *great* news, sending a TA to hold court with my class.

"Steve *just* left here," Melanie said quietly. "I *think*...there's definitely something *off* there."

"OK. I *just* wanted to..." *Tell the love of my life that I'd reached the peak of my profession...*

"He was at Maria's *school* earlier," she went on. "Didn't get past the front office, of course, because his name isn't on the list. They *didn't* call the police, but...they *said* he was acting strangely. I'd *just* got off the phone with the school when he came *here.*"

"Strangely...*how?*" It was apparent that my news was gonna have to wait—hers was *far* more urgent. I was weary of our lives being disrupted. And I *wasn't* convinced that we weren't in any *real* danger.

"They didn't *say*, but...when I *talked* to him this morning, he talked about the *danger* Maria was in."

"Danger? What *kind* of danger?"[1]

"*That* was the *weird* part. He said the danger from above and below; from *beyond* and *before*." She was quiet. "*Sort* of like...oh, *shit.*"

"*What*, babe?"[2]

"Spring Break, '82, he wanted me to go to Mexico with him. I couldn't afford the *time* because I was finishing my thesis."

"What did he do for a living," I asked. *I don't know why I'd never asked before.*

"He was a stationary engineer, but he went to State part-time. *That's* how we met, in my last elective—art class. Anyway, he was *funny*, but he had *moments*...he was depressed sometimes. I'd *told* him over and over before then I *couldn't* go with him. He'd timed his vacation for Spring Break and everything. He came to pick me up for the airport, and I said '*no*.' He started saying that we *had* to go, that the danger from above and below would *consume* us if we stayed. I just thought he was...he used to say 'and all above and below,' when I know he meant *everything.* Quirkish, but *harmless*, I thought. But he was so *insistent*, said it was important. 'More important than my career,' I asked him. He said 'danger from above and below.' *That* time I said, 'that's *crazy*,' and he went *ballistic.* Stomped off, and I didn't see him again until June."

She'd never *told* me that before. I never *asked*; I didn't think it was important *or* any of my business. *Now*, though... "He was *how old*, babe," I asked.

"He was 29 when we met; 30 when he...yeah." *Late*, but within the age range for the onset of schizophrenia. As an educator, I'd read articles

---

1 DING! DING! DING!

2 Ding?

on recognizing the signs in young adults. As a faculty brat, Meli had probably seen it in the student body.

"Makes *sense*, honey," I said. "*Get* in your car; *let's* go home. I'll get word to *Connie...*"

"*After* lunch, OK," she answered, then... "no, *I'm* OK. I've got stuff I need to *finish* here."

"OK, babe. Is it too late to get a sitter for tonight? I'd *really* like you to..."

"No, dear, I'd just as soon *not* do *another* rubber-chicken fundraiser, if you *don't* mind. Besides, *Connie's* wearing *my* gown."

"OK, honey. See you after work, then."

It'll keep.

***

"*What* time's the event," Melanie asked, wiping up Jason's pureed peaches. He had eaten *some* of them but had deposited the remainder on the floor probably in protest against the *service* more than the *cuisine*.

"Not until eight," I said, wiping gravy off Charlie's face. It was moments like these that I *really* appreciated Connie's help—she and Maria had gone for *our* fried chicken dinner.

We were *just* ending the nightly Siege of The Boy's Dinner when Connie came in *with* our dinner and *said*, "*he's* outside, in his *car*, parked across from the house."

Shit. "OK," I said, "*I'll...*"

"Get the boys into the living room, babe," Melanie said quietly. "*I'll* see what he wants."

"We *know* what *he* wants," I said, not concerned with *what* Maria heard at that moment.

"Then maybe he *should*," Melanie declared. "I'll...*just* handle the boys, OK," she said to me before glancing at Maria. "Connie, *please* stay with Maria?"

"Of *course*, Mom. *C'mon*, buddy," Connie said, taking Maria's hand and leading her downstairs. "*Let's* go down to *my place*."

I sat the boys in front of the living room TV, turning on a kid's show, watching out the picture window. Melanie and Steve were like statues for a few moments before Steve became animated, stomping his feet and waving his arms before—suddenly—he stopped.

Melanie turned towards the house. Steve followed her, then was walking alongside her, silent. I heard Melanie at the front door, saying, "say *hi*; I'll give you a *card*; then you'll *leave*. Under*stand?*"

"OK," Steve said.

They came in the door. "*Hi,* everyone," Melanie called. "Old *friend* dropped by; I have his *Christmas card* that came back." She looked around. "Maria? *Connie?* Come *meet* Steve."

Charlie, the curious three-year-old that *he* was, toddled towards Steve. Jason crawled across the floor towards the door. Connie and Maria came up the stairs just opposite the door. I offered my hand; Steve ignored it because...

I've always thought Maria sensed the tension—increased by Connie holding her pistol behind her back[1]—and decided to defuse it. *Bold* as brass, she walked right up to Steve and said, "Hi."[2]

"Hello, Maria," Steve said, squatting down, bringing his face down to her eye level. "*Pleased* to meet you. *I'm* Steve, your *mom's* friend. You *look* like..." Steve started.

"*Here's* your card, Steve," Melanie interrupted, tapping him on the shoulder with *somebody's* Christmas card with a wrong address.

"*Thanks,* Melanie," Steve said, taking the card before standing and turning to the door. "Well, *pleased* to *meet* you *all.*" And he left, the screen door banging because I hadn't adjusted the gas cylinder for the cold weather...

It might be incongruous, but *that* was all I could think of at *that* moment.

We *all* watched from the picture window as Steve trudged away in the *biting* cold. At the end of the driveway, he turned for a final glance at the house, then shuffled to his car and drove away.

"Was *that* smart," I whispered to Melanie.

"It was *kind,*" she answered. "Sometimes, *that's better* than smart."

She was right, of course.

***

"You look *lovely,* honey," I said, meaning it. The Athletic Department had selected Connie to represent *them* at the shindig. It was her first time at one of these, but she didn't seem phased by the glitter and the glam of the horribly wealthy and pretentious, the mundane and the gregarious...and that was just *three* of the checkbooks-on-legs we were there to *charm.* "You do Melanie's dress *honor.*"

"*Thanks,* Dad." It was a black, off-the-shoulder, floor-length gown. "*Haven't seen* Annie yet. *Hope* she got her gown OK."

---

1 Which Maria no doubt *knew.*

2 Maybe I'm giving an 8-year-old too much credit.

"Neither have *I*," I said, glancing around for Ann Bergdorf, the 1988 Jenson Scholar. Her attendance would have been *mandatory*. She and Connie had been *gown*-shopping before Christmas.[1] "Me, too. Think *that'll* satisfy *Steve* for a while?"

"*Maybe*." She grabbed a passing champagne flute. "His *sudden* interest in...*Paul*," she nodded, surprised. Our private gumshoe beckoned to us from the door discretely; we drifted in his direction.

"Just a quick update," Paul said, taking the champagne from Connie, "*not* going to take up *much* of your evening. Steve was in a mental institution until three months ago, undergoing treatment for schizophrenia. His insurance ran out and they made him an outpatient. He *was* living with his sister's family."

"What about the rest of his family," I asked, smiling at an assistant professor who mumbled congratulations on her way past us.

"His *father's* been in treatment for *years*, nowhere *near* as bad as *Steve*..."

"Meli said his father died young," I said.

"Nope; still going strong," Paul sighed, sipped the champagne. "His family's been looking for him. I took the liberty of telling *them* where he was."

"Well, thanks," I smiled, trying to make it look like more congratulations or good news—Paul's presence in a turtleneck and leather jacket attracted attention and people were starting to notice us. Or was it *Connie*, the youngest staff member and *certainly* the *loveliest?*[2] Or was it the youngest *full* professor east of Kansas City?[3] "I'll tell Melanie..."

"I *called* there," Paul said. "Told *her* what I told you. That's how I knew you were *here*."

"Ah," Connie grinned, making a quick turn as her dress flared. "*you* just wanted to see *me* in *formal*wear." Her hair was twisted into a soft plait that she tossed casually.

"Yeah, *that's* right, doll-face." Paul chuckled lightly. "I thought it was important that you know, too, since he's still *around* someplace."

"Certainly is," I said. "Had a *visit* from him this evening."

---

1 As written in their contract, Jenson Scholars agreed to attend all fundraising events if it was physically possible. Only doctors could get them out of it. Part of the stipend was dedicated to a formal wardrobe.

2 In my *completely unbiased* opinion, of course.

3 *That* would have been *me*.

"Really," Paul declared. "Well, if *I* should see him, I'll just get him to go home."

He left, and we split up to mingle appropriately with the trust-funds-made-flesh that are the lifeblood of private schools. It's cynical, I know, to regard our benefactors that way, but there's really no *better* way to describe them. Connie and I were shills for the Endowment. She knew it instinctively and didn't seem to mind.

"*Congrats*, Curtis," Polly Winfield she whispered from behind me while kissing my ear. "I *knew* you'd be *my* boss someday."[1]

"*Thanks*, Polly," I said, taking her hand off my waist. "Maybe you'd want *my* old job?"

"Naw," she said, stepping alongside me. "Got *my* sights on *higher* ground."

"Ah," I answered, getting a *brief* appreciation for her glittery gown and its *plunging* neckline. "You bring *your* ball and chain?"

"He begged off, the *coward*," she sighed. "I don't *blame* him. Is *Amy* here yet?"

"Yet to make *her* entrance," I said. "Just now looking for a Jenson or a Crest to make my *obsequence* known."

"Over...*there*," she pointed towards the punchbowl. "You brought Connie? *Lovely* girl..."

"She *is*, yes. She's *here* for the *Athletic* Department."

"Oh, *yeah*, that's *right*. Well, *I'm* going to go do *my* duty with the Chin's," as she wandered off, weaving through the crowd in the direction of the alumni who donated the most to the Asian-American Scholarship Fund that helped fund *her* job.

I took *that* cue to weave through the crowd to pass some time with Alan Jenson, John Davison, and *their* wives. I was barely in earshot of them when Amy Gilchrest and her new husband made *their* entrance, arm-in-arm....

The room fell quiet...but *not* because of Amy....

"*Durand*," a loud voice called from behind the happy couple. "DURAND," the voice called again, louder, from inside the room. "*DURAND! I'm here to SAVE my daughter!*"

Oh. Shit.

"*Durand*," Steve called again shrilly; approaching a scream. "*DURAND, you sonofaBITCH! You're MOLESTING my...*"

---

1 The Jenson Endowment professor, traditionally, led the American History Department. I decided there and then to hold an election for a *chairman*.

But *that* was the last he got out. Two burly security guards seized him; another slapped a gag on his mouth. Then, *somehow*, Connie materialized at Steve's elbow.

I stood across the room, gape-mouthed and probably looking like a complete idiot, before I realized what Connie was saying. "It's *OK*, Pops," she soothed. "He *hasn't* mistreated me. *Let's* just go *talk* about this..."[1]

The guards hauled Steve out, struggling, while Connie picked up her skirts and followed them.

"I thought your ward was an *orphan*," Alan said, suddenly at my elbow.

"She...*that* guy..." *How to explain this...ho-boy.* "He..."

"*He's* a previous relationship of *my* daughter's," Helen explained, suddenly appearing at Alan's elbow. "He's *obviously* confused, and he *may* be mentally ill."

"But your *ward* called him..." John cleared his throat.

"Connie *has* that *effect* on people," I managed. "You *know* from personal experience how *charming* she can be." Helen caught my eye; winked discretely. "My *wife* and I *adopted* our *former* ward," I said expansively so that everyone around could hear me.[2]

Helen watched out the door as the guards and Connie managed to get Steve under control...*if* restrained. "*Charming* girl, that one."

She is that.

---

1 Of everyone in our family, Connie kept the most *consistently* level head.
2 Though we'd done *that* deed two summers before, we didn't publicize it; hadn't mentioned on campus until yesterday. Because Connie didn't change her name, *few* noticed.

Come Saturday, We Had Questions

'Gotta give you high marks for quick-thinking, Connie," I said as we drove home after the party ended. We'd done what we were *there* for, keeping the Alumni Scholarship Fund at its current levels. Hard to tell with *some* donors, but...

"So did everyone *else*," she sighed. "Had to get him outta there fast; it was the *quickest* way I could *think* of."

"Almost like you were expecting him," I said, pulling into the driveway.

"I *was*, sort of. Figured he'd be following us somehow." She was quiet as the garage door opened. "Broke up the tedium of that *party*, though."

"That it *did*," I agreed. "Started a whole *new* round of gossip, though."

"Yeah." She reached for my hand as we went into the house. "Now the whole *world* knows."

"Knows what," Melanie asked. In her robe and flannel nightie,[1] she was waiting for us in the dimly-lit kitchen.

"We adopted Connie," I said. "*Steve* showed up at the party..." I explained what had happened. "Now everyone in the county will know our *business* by Monday."

"At least they *won't* know about the *other* business," Meli sighed, shaking her head. "I heard from Amy Gilchrest that you stole her thunder."

"Technically, *Steve* did that," Connie said, hanging her coat in the front closet. "We just...*what?*"

---

1 That she *never* slept in, preferring babydolls or *nothing*. Why call it a "nightie" if you never *sleep* in it?

"Just..." Meli sighed, smiling at Connie in the half-light of the kitchen. "You're *quite* fetching, my dear. Our *daughter*, Curtis: all grown up."

"Well, your *all-grown-up daughter's* tired and going to bed." She pecked our cheeks. "I have a *date* tomorrow...no, *tonight*...and I *may* be out the door before you get up: glee club practice. I *should* be back by mid-afternoon. 'Night."

***

"What *did* you tell Steve," I asked, listening to the night sounds.

"We'd *talk* about visitation with the *lawyers*," she answered. "He started raving about the *danger* she was in, that *we* were in. Then I asked if he wanted to *meet* Maria, and he calmed down."

"Huh." We managed to get to sleep, but at 4:14, Jason lodged his *second* complaint of the evening about the poor service. It being Meli's turn, *she* got the honor of getting up and finding out *which* staff failure he was complaining about.

"Hungry," she sighed, slipping out of her robe twenty minutes later. "Too *tired* to go for a bottle, so I *weakened*."[1]

"Good thing *you* went. *I'd* have trouble honoring *that*..."

"*You'd* just give him a *bottle*," she batted my arm. I heard a familiar rustling before she stretched an arm across my chest. "We've *got* to mark your *glittering* achievement," she whispered.

OK.

***

I said, "yes? May I help you?" to the strangers at the door just before noon. Snow had begun to swirl around the trees, lighting on the driveway and sidewalks like beautiful-yet-malignant messengers.

"*Mr.* Durand, is *Melanie* around," the middle-aged woman asked.

"She *is*," I answered. "*Who* may I say...?"

"David Wabrzeznoski and Anna Wabrzeznoski Favor; Steve Wabrzeznoski's brother and sister."[2]

"Well, we've *just* got kids organized for *lunch*," I said.

"Oh, *we'll* come back," David said apologetically.

"No, *please*," Melanie called from the kitchen. "Have a seat in the living room. Just give me a *minute*."

---

1 She nursed. We were working *hard* to wean him.

2 *Their* pronunciation of their name was *similar* to Steve's but *not* the same. At least they *didn't* pronounce it *Smith* or something *completely* different.

"You'd *better* come in, " I said.

"*Thank* you." David was a man of middling height whose only physical characteristic shared with Anna was the shape of his face. Their eyes, hair, everything else was different. "We don't want to take up *too* much of your time."

"I'll relieve Meli on *kid* duty," I smiled, beating a hasty retreat. "*I* can..." I started quietly. For once, Saturday lunch was relatively quiet, mac and cheese being consumed avidly; even *Jason* decided the cuisine was to his liking.

"Like I'm *dressed* for company," Meli grunted, brushing her hair back with her hands and straightening her jeans. "Passable?"

"*Lovely*, dear," I smiled brightly. But the look I got on her way to the living room said, *yeah; right.*

I listened as they exchanged pleasantries. I imagined Meli taking a seat on the stone step under the TV as our guests perched on the sofa. Their conversation was quiet, but I could make out phrases, including "Steve's *usually* pretty good about his meds," and "he *hasn't* been violent."

"He's *here*; there was an altercation at a fundraising event," I heard Meli distinctly say. "Not *violent*, but disruptive. He's somehow got the idea that Curtis is molesting Maria."

"*Oh*," David exclaimed, followed by some more back-and-forth that I couldn't make out.

After several more minutes, the kids were done with lunch; Jason was ready for a nap, and Charlie wanted to play with his trucks. Maria watched me, absent Mommy, looking for clues as to what Big Sister should *do*. "Maria: can you *take* Charlie to *his* room, please?"

She unloaded Charlie from his chair and asked, "potty, Charlie?"

"*Potty*," Charlie answered. Maria led him to the half-bath off the pantry. Charlie was in the *process* of potty training, which was taking hold with Big Sisters, *not* so much with Mommy and Daddy.

I had to carry Jason *through* the living room to get to *his* room. Of course, my youngest son took the opportunity to *bring up* a portion of his lunch on my shoulder just as I was trying to pass *discretely.*

As I was cleaning Jason and myself up, Maria passed through the living room with Charlie, where she had a *brief* exchange with our guests. I *distinctly* heard, "her eyes are *just* like our father's," and, "she has *Mom's* hair," coming from the living room as she planted Charlie on the floor with his trucks.

She just turned eight for the love of God. You people could upend her world.... I put Jason in his crib and went to Charlie's room, watching

Maria idly pushing a truck around as her brother pulled a wheel off *another* truck.

I felt I should have *said* something, *asked* her something.

For the *life* of me, I couldn't figure out *what*.

I'm not sure how long I watched my children sitting Indian-style on the floor. Charlie nodded off after a while, and Maria shuffled his trucks to the shelf like she'd seen me and Meli and Connie do *countless* times. She sat again, looked at Charlie, and declared, "I'm *his* sister." Then she looked up at me. "Connie's my *sister* and *your* daughter, too."

"We *made* her our daughter *and* your sister," I said softly.

"You mean '*dopted?*"

"Adopted, *yes*. Don't you remember?"

"Yeah. A boy in my class is *adopted*." She was still for a moment. "My *birth*-daddy," she mumbled, looking at me sideways. "Steve?"

"Yes." *What ELSE was I supposed to say?*

"Am *I* adopted?"

"No. Mommy's *your*...no." *How in HELL am I supposed to explain THIS to an eight-year-old?* "That's not...we don't *have* to...."

"Don't you *want* to choose *me* like you did *Connie*?" There was a slight quiver to her voice.

Minefield ahead... "Sure; I'd choose *you* any time, sweetheart. We'll talk to Mommy *after*...."

"After Steve's brother and sister leave?"

"Yes; *then*." *HOW, in the name of everything that's holy, did she get so smart so fast?* "I'll adopt *you*, too."

She stood up, wrapped her arms around my neck. "I *love* you, Daddy."

Me, too, sweetheart.

***

"Well," I asked Melanie, sitting in the living room maybe half an hour later. Maria was playing in her room. Jason and Charlie were still napping. "What was *that* about?"

"*Well*..." she stopped, hearing Connie come in the garage. "Let's get *her*, too."

I called to her as she entered the house; she wandered to the couch.

"It's like Paul said," Melanie said as Connie sat between us, "Steve's schizophrenic and *may be* bipolar. He got it in his head to find me a couple of weeks ago. He left his *sister's* place last week, *must* have run *out* of meds. *Then* he found out about Maria. Can't say *how*..."

"Easy," Connie said, "if you know *how* and *where* to look."

"He's *not* dumb," Melanie said.

"Does he still *work*," I asked.

"Yeah," Melanie sighed. "*Still* employed at a water treatment plant. Because it's a *union* and *city* job, he's got great benefits, is nearly *impossible* to fire, and has about a *gazillion* hour's leave saved up."

"What does he *want* from Maria," Connie asked.

"Just what that lawyer said in that letter. The lawyer said he was lucid then."

"Where *is* he *now*," I asked.

"Campus security turned him over to the police again last night. They took him to the hospital. They *sedated* him, but they couldn't *hold* him. Since he got into the Jenson Archive Building without permission, the school *could* charge him with trespassing."

"They *won't*," I said authoritatively—*without* authority, of course. "The school's *not* going to..."

"No, probably not. His sister just wants to take him home."

"Did they *say* anything about tribal membership," I asked.

"Family lore has it that there's *Seneca* in the family, but no one's *confirmed* it. Steve's smart enough to throw *that* into the mix."

"Maria wants to know why *she* hasn't been adopted like *we* adopted Connie," I said softly.

"That's...oh, *shit*," Melanie breathed.

"*I'll* think of *some*thing," Connie closed her eyes slowly.

I told her, "Connie: think, 'yes, honey: Mommy and Daddy *want* to choose *you* as they did *me*.' *That's* the *direction* our conversation took. She also knows *what* Steve is, and *who* just left here." Both women stared at me, surprised. "She heard and understood it *all*. Maybe not the *mechanics*, but the *gist* of it. I *said* I'd adopt her."

"We should *all*..." Meli started.

"*No*," I declared. "Just *Connie*. Don't want to *look* like we're ganging up on her."[1]

"Taxonomy, *not* biology, OK," Connie said softly. "Biology comes... *hi*, buddy."

Maria, of course, stood in the hall, puzzled-puppy look and all, listening and watching.

"C'mon, buddy," Connie prompted. "Need to *talk* about..."

"Adopted," Maria said, walking slowly towards the couch.

"Well, yes," I said. "We just want to answer *your* questions..."

---

1 I remembered *that* much of my primary education training.

"I came out of Mommy's tummy," Maria said, stopping in front of us, "but Daddy didn't put me in there. *Steve* did, like Ally's husband did." She looked at Melanie, then Connie. "Right?"

"Yes...*that's*...right," Connie said calmly.

"*Steve's* my *birth*-daddy," Maria continued. "*Daddy's* my..." she looked confused.

"*Real* daddy," Connie answered, glancing at me. "*Just* like *he* is *mine*. He's Charlie's and Jason's *birth*-daddy *and* their *real* daddy."

Maria was quiet, thinking, looking at the three of us. "Why?"

Oh, NO; the dreaded pre-teen WHY. She wasn't on *that* track for very long at five and six, but *now...why this minute?*

"When Mommy had *you* in her tummy," I threw caution to the winds, "Steve wasn't *feeling* well, so I took over for *him*."

Simple; accurate; truthful. Not a counterfactual or single *degree* of spin to be seen...then...

"*Why?*"

"Because I *asked* him to," Melanie said. "I *knew* you'd *need* a *real* daddy, so he said he *would,* and he *has been* ever since."

"*Why?*"

"Because I've loved you ever since I heard your heartbeat in Mommy's tummy," I answered.

"Remember when you felt Johnny moving in *my* tummy," Connie asked. Maria nodded. "And Charlie and Jason? Wasn't *that* cool?" Nods. "Well, Dad thought *you* were pretty cool, too." She glanced at me. "And *my* mama knew Dad before *I* was born. She got *sick* and asked Dad to take care of me. So, he made *me his* daughter, too."

As an educator, elegant explanations of complex issues to targeted audiences are gratifying to see and hear. As a father, our three-part collaboration—dreamed up on the fly explaining *why Daddy and not Steve*—bordered on the miraculous.

"Do you *want* to be adopted, Maria," I asked.

Maria looked at me for a very long time before she looked at Melanie, then Connie...before she shrugged. "*OK.* Can *I* watch Rugrats now?"

The three of us heaved a collective sigh of relief. "*Sure,* honey," Meli grabbed the remote and slid the tuner box before she asked Connie. "How was glee club, Connie?"

"Oh, the *usual,*" Connie answered, lolling her head back on the sofa. "We practiced while the basketball team tried to see if they could keep going and not *suspend* their season."

"Why would they do *that?*"

"They lost *three players* since the season started: one for eligibility and *two* were called up."

"Called...oh, for the *Army?*"

"One *Army*; one *Air Force*. The Army guy wrote his girlfriend in glee club, said his helicopters have been attached to the Puking Buzzards." Connie smiled at our puzzlement; Maria got up and went to the kitchen during a commercial. "*Slang* for the 101st Airborne Division, according to *the guy* in the club."

The guy was the *only* male in the glee club who I knew to be a veteran. "*His* helicopters..." I repeated.

"Yeah," Connie mumbled. "*Jenny's* helicopters, too. The Army guy said they're practicing for some *secret* mission."

Suddenly...perspective...for everyone.

***

"How've you *been*, Bert," I asked at dinner. We'd brought Maria and Charlie but left Jason with a teenage sitter.

"*Rested*," Bert said. "No *classes*, no *meetings* unless I *want* to go. *Emeritus* is being *good* to me."

"And he's still doing his research," Helen sighed. "*I* might pull the plug at the end of this year." Helen still taught freshman and sophomore English composition and literature...the reason they were still in faculty housing, though they *had* moved to a smaller place.

"*And* annoying the librarians," Al intoned. "*Frieda* bent my ear the other day."[1]

"Still working on Roger Sherman,"[2] I asked.

"Him and James Wilson,"[3] Bert answered. "Neither one of them *ever* had a major biography. I might venture on a series on The Six."[4]

"A *worthy* effort," I said in my *most* scholarly tone. "Just keep at it."

"I *intend* to...as much as the doctors let me," Bert sighed.

---

1 Frieda was Al's off-campus *housemate—both* said they were *entirely* platonic. My, how the culture had changed.

2 Sherman had the unique distinction of having signed *all four* of America's founding documents: the Continental Association, the Declaration of Independence, the Articles of Confederation, *and* the Constitution. Bet you never *heard* of him.

3 Wilson was one of the first Associate Justices of the Supreme Court.

4 *The Six—including* Sherman and Wilson—signed both the Declaration of Independence *and* the Constitution.

"Are you *still* sick, Grampa," Maria asked innocently. She remembered seeing Grampa Bert in the hospital after his pacemaker installation, more curious than frightened.

"A *little*, honey," Bert said. "I'm better than I *was*."

"So, what's this guy *want*," Helen asked as we did the dishes while Al and Bert entertained Charlie and Maria.

"A *relationship* with Maria," Melanie answered. "He had a bout with MS not long ago. It *can* be genetic; Maria may be at risk of that...*and* his mental illness."

"And he may have *Seneca* in his family," I added.

"Oh, *jeez*," Helen shook her head. "A *whole* other ballgame." Several years before, a staff member went through a legal tussle with the Onondagas when her child's father demanded visitation based on his membership with that nation. When that legal hassle became public, the campus saw picket signs and chanting for the first time since Vietnam. "Did you have *any* inkling at all, Meli?"

"None," she answered. "As far as *I* knew, he *had* no family."

"Well, let's *hope* he doesn't ask for...*hi*, honey," Helen stopped, staring at Maria in the doorway.

Maria affected her curious cant to her head. "Are *you* talking about my *birth*-daddy, *Steve*?"

"*Yes*, baby," Melanie said.

"Uh-*huh*," Maria said, climbing up on a kitchen stool and looking at Melanie. "Is *Steve* sick, too?"

"*Yes*," Melanie smiled.

"I *swear* to *God*, she *just* went to the bathroom," Al quietly sighed from the doorway. "Then I heard her in *here*." He stared at his sister. "We'll talk *later*." He shifted his gaze to me. "*Won't* we?"

***

"This is *most* curious," Bert handed me the summary of Truxton Collection's Document T-9543, reimaged under black light:

54 bottles of Madeira
60 demi-bottles of claret
8 jugs of corn whiskey
22 bottles of porter
8 bottles of hard cider
12 buckets of choc beer

7 bowls of rum punch[1]
Paid on receipt £4, 9s, 8p[2]

"A bar bill," I said. "*That's* a new one." We were in his den, a larger room than the one in his old house.

"Yeah," Bert agreed. "Seems like a *lot* of booze for fifty-odd people." This 1783 meeting was well known, the headcount and attendees documented. We'd *been* working on this document for some time, written on common hemp paper.

"It's a *total* bill, Bert," I said, "not just for the *guests* that we know were there. The beer and porter *probably* went outside to escorts, grooms, and horse-holders. Even the tavern *staff* probably got a jug or two of whiskey and a few buckets of choc."

"Yep," Bert said, "*not* so alarming, but *expensive*. December 4th, 1783; Fraunces Tavern, New York.[3] This is the *owner's* accounting. Lacking any *other* of Samuel Fraunces' writing, we're not sure *who* wrote this."

"Maybe the museum knows," I mused. "They might be *interested* in this piece."[4]

"*Could* be." He leaned forward with his elbows on his knees, chin in his hands. "The *time* has *come* to write the story of my time in China." He pointed to one of many stacks of paper on a table. "*That's* where I'm starting. We can find a military historian to *help...*"

"*I* can do it," I said. "I'll figure it out."[5]

"OK." He sat up again. "Something *else* on your mind?"

"How much I have to tell *my* family about..."

"Yeah." He waited. "*Charlie's* a reasonable man; I think *he'd* understand. Your *mother*...I don't see a problem."

"Meli has an *alternate* scenario." I ran our *I called Curtis after our fight* version for my *possible* paternity past him. I *also* added the *Connie's not mine* story to justify his faith in Mom's response.

"Huh," Bert said, sitting back in his chair, briefly scanning a bookshelf. "My *boy*—my *friend*—I've known you since you were *eighteen*. When you said you wanted to marry Meli that afternoon, my *first*

---

1 These units of measure were smaller than any contemporary equivalents.

2 America used the pounds sterling that were in circulation until 1792.

3 The day and location where Washington announced that he was leaving the Army.

4 Archives traded with and donated documents to *other* archives from time to time.

5 As specialized as history *is*, I was venturing into a century and a discipline I knew little about. I'd have a *lot* to learn.

thought was, 'they've finally *admitted* it.' Then, *Meli* said, 'we want to raise *our* baby together.' *That* gave me pause. *Not* because I thought you were *virgins*, but because you seemed so *distant*—even that Christmas when you were together every day—as if by *calculation*. Friends, yes, but *lovers*? I didn't *think* so; not *then*. Helen explained that Spring Break story to *me* as Meli explained it to *her*. *She* didn't quite believe Meli; *I* didn't, *either*. But we *also* knew what you and Meli had felt about each other, even if you wouldn't admit it."

"It *was* by calculation. You were my *advisor...*"

"If *either* of you had *said something*, I'd have made Tony Zane your advisor without a *thought*, even at *that* late date in your program." He templed his hands; placed his chin on them. "Maria's *not* yours—biologically."

"*No.*"

"The *first* time you and Meli were *together* was her first night in The Cubes."

"*Yes.*"

"But you *are* Maria's *father* as far as the *world* is concerned."

Yes.

***

"So, *what's* going on," Al asked after we put the kids in the mini-van. The snow, swirling lightly when we arrived at the Hubbard's, was heavier as we were leaving. "What's this about *birth-daddy*?"

Melanie gave him a quick rundown, chattering in the wind, huddling in front of our running engine. "So, Curtis might *not* be Maria's..." she finished.

"I *saw* you, buddy," Al said, his face inches from mine. "I was working in the publication center that Spring Break. You were *there* nearly *every* day; so was *I*." He turned to his sister. "Of course, the center *was* closed on weekends *and* Good Friday."

"You...um..." I stammered. *But I WAS at State for a day, and we saw each other,* [1] *albeit from across the street, for ten seconds.*

"You've stayed *quiet* all this time," Melanie said rather loudly against the wind.

"*Don't* lie," I said against the wind. "If anyone asks, just say what you *know.*"

"I'll *say* what I *saw*," Al said, shaking snow off his hood as he turned to me. "Tell me the *truth: Are* you Maria's...?"

"What would you *do* with the *truth* if you *knew* it?"

---

1 Time flies like an arrow; fruit flies like bananas. Isn't linguistic ambiguity a fascinating study?

"The *less* I know for *certain*," Al grinned, "the *less* I can *attest* to." He turned to his sister. "*Don't tell* me, either, Meli." He kissed her cheek. "It don't *matter* to me."

Maybe not.

***

"He *won't* say anything unless someone asks," Melanie said after the kids were in bed and I'd walked the babysitter home two houses down.

"Probably not," I agreed. "Her *light's* still on." Connie left the basement stairway light on when she was out at night.

"Not *that* late yet," Melanie said, plopping down on the sofa and turning on the TV; it was barely 9. "Want to *talk* to *her* yet tonight."

I watched out the big picture window at the driving snow accumulating. In the three years we'd been there, the snow had reached the living room's big picture window only once, the time we ran out of gas. *That* night, it was already six inches above the sill. "What does the *weather* say?"

"Let's look at that weather channel," Melanie said, changing stations on the slider. "Never...*here* it is."

We watched the newscaster point to the maps, the satellite photos, *then* there were ads, *more* maps, *more* photos, *more* ads, the weather in *Iraq* and the *Persian Gulf...*

Finally came the *local* forecast, which was *snow, gusting wind, low of 10. Tomorrow: snow early morning then clear, high of 15.*

"I *thought* cable news was going to be more comprehensive," I mumbled.

"Maybe it *will* be one day," Melanie declared, throwing a blanket over both of us. "We can wait for the news...or Connie."

"Whichever comes first."

Which, of *course...*

I woke up just before midnight, and Connie's light was off; the TV had some rerun on.

The snowdrift was *nearly* a third up the window.

Sunday Came

oly...Wow. I haven't seen THAT much snow here...ever. "Hey," I nudged Meli after looking out our bedroom window, seeing nothing but snow on trees—LOTS of snow. "I hear small children in the kitchen." It was nearly 8...*late* for us.

"Mm," she groaned. "If Maria's got them *that* far, Jason will stand changing, and *maybe* Charlie."

"*I'll* see to it." I pulled on a sweatsuit and made my way to the other end of the house. I looked out the living room window, and snow had drifted halfway up. *It has to be more than a foot on the driveway...*

I heard voices from the kitchen...including one I *hadn't* expected. After being as quiet as I could, I was surprised to be greeted with *several* voices, including... "Don't *freak*, Dad."

"Huh," I said, as authoritative a *huh* as I could muster at 7:51 on a Sunday. "You didn't *think* to...?" ...*tell us you had a gentleman guest for the night?*

"Didn't want to risk waking the *kids*," Connie said, putting a sippy cup in front of Charlie. "We didn't get in until *after* 12. Jerry was *stuck* here."

"It took *three hours* to get *here* from the movie, Dr. Durand," Jerry said, putting a bowl of cereal in front of Jason. He was wearing a sweatsuit I *knew* to be Connie's. *Domesticity, huh?*

"OK," I said softly. "Just...Maria, did you *help* with Jason?"

"*I* did Jason, sir," Jerry declared. "*Two* younger brothers. Maria got *Charlie* on the potty, *didn't* you?"

"I *did*, Daddy," Maria chimed in proudly.

"Well, OK, then," I sighed. "Do *your* parents know where you are, Jerry?"

"Un*likely*, sir," he said. "I've been in an apartment since August."

Did I already know that? "Ah. Well...let me let *Meli* know..." He glanced past me and blushed as I heard a *gasp* and a *swish* behind me.

"Let me know *what*," Melanie said. "*Don't* turn."

"That we have a *guest* for *breakfast*, dear," I said mildly.

"I can see *that, dear*. Now, if you'll *excuse* me..."

"*Sorry*, Mrs. Durand," Jerry called.

"*Melanie*, Jerry," she answered. "We're *beyond* formality now."[1]

"Call me *Curtis*, Jerry," I said, bussing each of my children on the head. "You're *old* enough *and* sleeping with my daughter..."

"*Later*, Dad," Connie said, putting cereal in front of Charlie.

"I wouldn't *abuse* your hospitality, Dr...Curtis," Jerry added, pouring cereal into Maria's bowl. "I want to be *welcome*."

"You *are*, Jerry," I said, giving Jason more apple sauce. "Was *Quigley Down Under* any good? Didn't think you *liked* westerns, Connie."

"It was Jerry's turn to pick, and it was *great*," Connie said softly. "I *don't abuse* your trust, Dad."

I know, sweetie. But this BOY in YOUR sweatsuit...

***

There is a four-foot drift in the front doorway and a foot and a half on the driveway....

"Ever *see* the *like*, Jerry?" We had *just* opened the garage door, gaping at the brilliant white wonder outside. The snow had stopped and the sun blazed by mid-morning. The relentless, *cutting* wind that had pushed snow against the house and the garage door has subsided. Jerry's car, parked behind mine, was buried to the door sills and covered with at *least* a foot of snow.

"Not *lately*," he agreed. "The weatherman said we got 21 inches; the most since 1966." Clad in his snowsuit and boots that he had wisely brought in the night before, he sprayed oil on a snow shovel. "I'm *really* sorry about..."

"Jerry, it's OK. I'd just want some *notice* in the future." I paused, listening to the light wind in the garage. "Connie's a grown woman, can make her own decisions about *that*." *Did I just say that?*

He approached the door opening. "We haven't *gone that far*." He turned back towards me. "I'm twenty and...I *want to* with Connie. We

---

1 Meli was *just* a bit *too* casual that morning.

were *cold* last night. We *were third-degree exposed* once before, but I *still* couldn't." He looked slightly miserable, regarding me as if I were...not *sure*, exactly, but maybe an elder brother or a bartender.

Could *any* father expect a situation like this? The object of *Jerry's* affection was my *daughter...*

It suddenly dawned on me that I may *have to* have this kind of talk with my *sons* someday. *That* was a revelation.

I was an educator, a history teacher, and a *guide* for young adults. *What* could *I* teach a young man about the difference between *sex* and *making love?*

"*Been* there, Jerry," I lied. My first *third-degree exposure* was with Joan, and *neither* of us had *any* trepidation whatsoever getting *close-but-no...* "Try just being *comfortable* in bed together *first.* Nothing *else,* just *that.* Naked, underwear, *fully* clothed, what*ever.* Just *comfortable.*" *Then just let nature take its course...maybe.* "She *knows* what to expect. Let *her* lead. One *caution:* not *all* her experience has been..."

"*Pleasant.* I know. She *says* she's *ready;* says she'll *wait* for *me* to be ready." We stared at the snowdrift-that-was-the driveway again.

"Patient woman like *her,* Jerry: hang on for dear life." He stared at me; I nodded. "OK. Here goes nothin'." I started the snowblower, adjusted the choke for the cold, pointed the chute forward, and pushed into the drift...*slowly.*

Connie started on the front walk when the snowblower reached the end of the driveway. Meli relieved Connie after an hour, while supervising Maria and Charlie playing in the snow. Jerry and I finished the driveway and pulled down the roof drifts. Then, all *we* had to do was wait for the county to come by and put *their* drift in our driveway.

I tried a new tactic when I saw the front loader[1] come by on its first pass. I stood at the end of my *clean* driveway and held a shovel across my chest as if it were a rifle, glowering as menacingly as I could imagine a history professor could. The machine angled its plow blade before it reached my driveway and took great pains *not* to push snow *my* way that time. My neighbors also benefitted from my weary bluff.

It was two that afternoon before we were done. The hot chocolate was ready by the time we'd had our showers. The chili was ready, and the cornbread was coming out of the oven just when Harold and Betty Hoffmeier knocked on our door with their two youngest sons.

---

1 I knew it was a piece of construction equipment; Connie *told* me what it was, specifically.

Sunday meant overtime for homeowners, parents, teachers, AND snowplow drivers.

***

"Pass that *cornbread*, please, Melanie," Betty asked. "Never *had* cornbread like this."

"Old family recipe," Connie said, winking conspiratorially. "Add a *slug* of *bourbon* to the *batter* and..."[1]

"It's *terrific*," Harold said, breaking more into his chili. "*Have* to remember that, Betty."

"Indeed, yes." Betty gazed at her son, who, like any young man whose parents were breaking bread with his lady-friend's parents for the first time, was as nervous as a cat in a doghouse. "How's *work*, Jerry? We haven't *seen* you since Christmas."

"*Great*, Mom," Jerry answered. "*Just* great. *School's* fine, too. How about *you* guys?"

"Pretty much the *usual*, Jerry," Harold said. "Connie, I have to *thank* you for calling..."

"It's time *my* parents broke bread with my *boyfriend's* parents," Connie mumbled.

"So you're *official* now, Jerome," Betty asked with a grin.

"*Yeah*, Mom," Jerry said at length, glancing at me. "If *Curtis* and *Melanie* don't mind." Declarations of affection to parents were important, even in the freewheeling '90s.

I shared a glance with Melanie, trying *not* to break out into a wide grin. "Of *course* not, Jerry," Meli replied, keeping a straight face. "You two have been friends for *years*."

"Our relationship has become more...*more*, Mom," Connie said softly, glancing at Jerry *like that*. "We *love* each other."

"*Yes*, we *do*," Jerry agreed, returning *her* glance.

"Well," Harold said with a smile. "She's a fine young woman, Jerry. *Good luck* to you *both*."

"We're *not* going to..." Connie started.

"Make any *other* changes until we graduate," Jerry interrupted.

"*Wise* decision, Jerry," I said. "Once you go any *farther*, stuff *changes*."

"It *does*, yes," Harold declared. "And I *really* like this chili, Connie. *Bourbon*, you say?"

---

1 We didn't *keep* liquor, so I had to wonder what she *did* use.

"In the *cornbread*, Harold," Connie said. "*Mom* made the chili..." We went on with idle chitchat for the rest of the meal.

The Hoffmeir's left soon after dinner. The kids were tired, and we had to get them to bed.

I relieved Jerry at the sink after a few minutes cleaning up. Meli relieved Connie on the counters. "Don't *you* have *homework* to do... downstairs," Meli mumbled. I nodded towards the stairs.

So they *went*.

And we were left to finish the cleanup...which *wasn't* much. "Good kids," I said, watching the weather channel's endless secession of commercials.

"*Great* kids."

"I *still* hear the TV down there."

"Me, too; a *little* louder than she usually has it."

"Huh." I reached for her polyester-encased thigh. "*We* should turn *our* TV up."

She reached for mine, wrapped in denim. "When was the last time we *did it* on a sofa?"

"If you *have* to *ask*, it's been *too* long."

She glanced at the clock. "*Ten* minutes." We killed the lights and indulged in some *preliminaries* before Jason registered *another* complaint *exactly* ten minutes later. We made the *best* of our *special time* on the sofa, with the TV turned up *just* a notch so Jerry couldn't *hear us* when *he* departed out the front door just after 11:30.

Which was a *good* thing.

Monday Came, and The Past Was Prologue

'Who's...?" I asked after the knock on the front door.

"Police," Connie frowned.

"I'll see."

I opened the door to a somber-faced, uniformed sergeant and another officer. "Is *this* the residence of Melanie Durand?" The sergeant sounded officious.

"Yes," I answered, "please, come in. We're *just* getting ready for..."

"We won't take long," the other officer announced. "If Ms. Durand is available?"

I seated the officers in the living room and relieved Melanie in the kitchen. Thinking the worst—an accident involving her parents—I sent Connie with her. The kids were quiet as they finished their breakfast; I strained to listen to what was being said in the living room.

They were right: it *didn't* take long. Melanie and Connie came back into the kitchen in about five minutes, distressed but not *parent-accident* distressed. "Steve," Meli whispered to me before our have-a-nice-day kiss. "*Later.*"

"He's *dead*," Connie whispered during the same ritual. "*Later.*"

I had a mid-morning class where I went through the motions, followed by a department curriculum development meeting, where the remaining staff who *hadn't* congratulated me did so. I proposed an *election* for a *department* chair; no one objected and set a schedule for candidates to announce themselves. Regardless, the Jenson Grant chair was supposed to bring in the *best* talent. Any *two* of my fellow professors had more publications than *I* did at that stage.

But Steve kept coming back to haunt my thoughts. *Why* I don't know.

***

"He didn't *have* money for a room," David said. That evening, Steve's siblings, David and Anna, came by the house about an hour before dinner.

"His credit cards were all maxed out," Anna sighed. "He parked behind a store; everything was closed on Sunday."

"He left the engine running to stay warm," David continued. "They *think* the snow just slid off the store roof and buried his car. They don't *think* it was suicide."

"*Terribly* sorry," Meli said solicitously. "If there's *anything...*"

"He left *these*," Anna said, handing over a couple of envelopes. "*You* were his emergency contact: he never changed that."

One envelope was marked *Melanie*; the other *Maria on her eighteenth birthday*. Meli handed me hers after she read it:

January 26th, 1991
Meli,

This is hard to write through the meds, but I owe you an explanation. I was losing control that winter we were together, and I struggled not to show it. I was hoping I could find a cure I read about in Mexico. I didn't; there isn't one.

I know you were better off without what I was becoming. I knew she was mine, but the part of me that held onto my sanity said, 'walk away and save them.'

Our Maria is a beautiful little girl. She shouldn't know about me until later.

I'll be leaving Monday, spent my last cash on gas to get back to my sister's place.

I won't bother you anymore. My family will leave you alone.
Steve

"He left another one for us: it *wasn't* a suicide note," David said. "Our father's *mildly* schizophrenic," he went on, "but well controlled. We've always known he was a *little* off. Mom covered for him until *she* passed..."

"Of ovarian cancer two years ago," Anna said. "*I'm* at risk; one of my daughters *already* had a scare at *twelve*. So you need to be vigilant of both Maria's physical *and* her mental health. There's no history of MS in our family; Steve's *may* have been an isolated case."

"What was the *rift* over," Melanie asked. "When I knew Steve, he insisted his father died young and that he had no living family."

"He was *ashamed* of Dad," David said. "Of the four kids, he was the youngest and the *least* able to understand Dad's eccentricities. No matter what anyone said, Steve always felt that Dad did what he did just to spite *him*."

"It was paranoia that manifested itself first in Steve," Anna said. "Everything was calculated against *him*. It started in high school, but only in spurts. It got worse as time went on."

"But Steve went into Dad's profession after high school...*and* pursued art as Dad did," David said. "Steve wouldn't *talk* to him but wanted to *be* him."

"Wanted to *be* his missing father," I suggested. "That's what teacher's college would say."

"That's what the family counselor said," David agreed.

"We should stay in touch," Melanie said finally.

"Well," Anna said, glancing at David. "Maybe..."

"How would you explain *them* to Maria," Connie asked.

"She *knows*, more or less," I said.

"We'll think on it," David said. "Now, we'll let you get on with your evening."

The rest of the evening was unremarkable, watching the air campaign and the *Scud Stud* on the news, the threats and the bombast and the tracers and the rockets and the bombs...*still* looking for Jenny or any other familiar faces in the news clips.

As we turned the TV off in the living room, Connie came up, smiling. "Got a minute?"

"Sure." We sat on the sofa; she took both our hands. "My half-sister found a kidney."

"Great," I said, meaning it. *But that's not the only thing you want to talk about.*

"My birth-*father's* going to jail for a *long* time," she added.

"OK," Melanie said softly, waiting for the reason for the big grin.

"Jerry and I want to thank you for the opportunity to meet with his parents."

"What was the *problem*," I asked. "And *don't* hand me that *bilge* about..." Something was going on between the Hoffmeir's, and it *wasn't* parental jealousy.

"Somebody said *something* at Christmas," Connie answered, "about the living arrangements in his townhouse. A girl was paying rent to stay in his spare room. I *know* her; she's in *glee club* and *has* a boyfriend in the dorms. She was waiting on a vacancy in an apartment building. She moved *out* first of the year."

"So words were said that *couldn't* be taken back," Melanie said, glancing at me.

"*Pretty* much," Connie sighed. "But we *fixed* it."

"Fixed more than *that*," I asked...*instantly* regretting it.

Connie cocked her head at me, a grin on her face. "*Dr. Durand: how forward* of you." She bussed my cheek, then Melanie's, getting up. "*Thanks*, Mom; Dad. *Love* you."

We know, honey.

***

Maria didn't ask about Steve again. Around Easter, we got a check for his bank account balance, which we put into Maria's. Shortly after, his life insurance from work paid off—Melanie was the beneficiary. Maria got that, too.

The Crest basketball team continued the season with only nine players, finishing just two games out of first place in the regional playoffs...better than any Crest University basketball team had *ever* done. The glee club was at every game.

Jenny and her unit came back to a hero's welcome in late spring. They'd been part of the 101st Airborne's Forward Operating Base deep inside Iraq that February, a crucial part of the attack into Kuwait. Jennifer Rizzo was awarded the Bronze Star and a promotion for her unstinting efforts.

Jerry *did* join the Air Force, training as a cargo specialist with the local Air Guard air refueling wing. It did help to pay for his schooling, and after the Soviets collapsed, it seemed safe to Connie.

My official investiture as a full professor, as expected, didn't come until just before the beginning of the 1991-92 academic year. There are some traditions you just don't violate.

Connie bought a condo near Jerry's complex that fall. On weekends and holidays, she returned to her basement—with Jerry sometimes— giving *us* a reprieve with the kids.

Bert's memoir, *Three Camps: A B-29 Crewman's Memoir of Imprisonment*, was picked up by a book club and did reasonably well. One critic wrote: "Curtis Durand, stepping out of his Early American roots, manages the text well." Eh, not bad for someone who barely knew the period or the specialization.

I've often imagined young Steve Wabrzeznoski waving pregnant and crying Melanie away. He *knew* he was the father of her child but also knew that his incipient madness would drive them apart, possibly scarring Maria *and* Melanie for life.

I knew what he gave up when he did that. It's a privilege to be called 'Dad.' Even if it's by *another* man's child.

Take my word for it; there's *nothing* else like it.

EPILOGUE

We write our own histories: of our collective past, our lives, and our families. But neither Frost nor Shakespeare had *any* idea *how right* they were when they talked about the past *works*.

In his "Road Not Taken," Frost was talking about the road he *did not* take, *not* the one he *did*. He thought he might take *that* road someday but knew that he could not.

Shakespeare's Antonio, poised to commit murder in *The Tempest*, said that everything that has come before was preparation for the *now*, for the next few *moments*, for the next *actions*.

We can never know, in our lifetime, how *right* he was.

Our history is *ours* to *live*, but it's *not* ours to write. History is the tracks we leave as we live our lives: the roads we choose, the people we choose to love and care for, the versions of our past we use to explain our present and guide our future.

We *live* what people *in the future* will call *history*.

Future history fans and those who become professionals in our lofty discipline will, as we do today, speculate about the paths we took and those we did not. Perhaps—with the benefit of infallible 20/20 hindsight—they will even go so far as to vilify our choices or, at the very least, wag an admonishing finger. So be it. They weren't *there*; they didn't *have* to decide *now, this instant*.

As Meli would say, they didn't have to make *that* choice.

As Connie would say, the life you *don't want* or the one you *do*.

As Jenny would say, they weren't *in* that desert.

And *I* say, in the future it will be easy to talk about the Past Not Taken when the ever-powerful *present* demands we chose what to do *now*. People in the future will make up things that *didn't* happen to justify what they do *now*, what they feel *now*, how they act *now*.

Or *not*.